"Imagination's Creation" by Dari LaRoche © 2024
"Metro Takes a Road Trip by Susie Slanina © 2024
"The Watching Game" by Lisa de Nikolits © 2024
"Son-Ja" by Diana McCollum © 2024
"Mars" by Pamela Cowan © 2024
"Grandma Harper's Imagination" by Mary Vine © 2024
"Sky Painter" by Maggie Lynch © 2024
"Another Life" by Paty Jager © 2024
"Project I.M.A.G.I.N.E." by Anna Brentwood and Colton Long © 2024
"Rattlesnake Ravine" by Kimila Kay © 2024

FIRST PUBLISHED BY

Windtree Press
https://windtreepress.com
Corvallis, Oregon, United States of America
In the anthology *Imagine*
October 2024

Paperback ISBN: 978-1-962065-65-8
Ebook ISBN: 978-1-962065-66-5

IMAGINE

A WINDTREE PRESS ANTHOLOGY

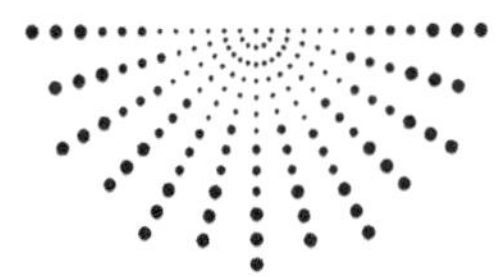

PATY JAGER   DARI LAROCHE   SUSIE SLANINA

LISA DE NIKOLITS   DIANA MCCOLLUM

PAMELA COWAN   MARY VINE   MAGGIE LYNCH

ANNA BRENTWOOD   COLTON LONG   KIMILA KAY

CONTENTS

RATTLESNAKE RAVINE
Kimila Kay

INTRODUCTION

Imagination. It is a word that conjures up so much and can cover so many emotions. In this collection of nine unique stories and a poem, you will cross centuries, hang in suspense, chuckle and perhaps even laugh, and wonder did the character imagine that or not. Dari LaRoche starts this anthology with a poem, **Imagination's Creation**, that explores what sparks the imagination as it moves between conscious thought and the sublime, reflecting the beauty that surrounds us.

In ***Metro Takes a Road Trip***, **Susie Slanina** returns to the adventures of a dog named Metro discovering new places and talents. In ***The Watching Game***, Lisa de Nikolits crafts a story that explores invisible friends, suspense, and the power of suggestion. Diana McCollum's story, ***Son-ja's Journey***, explores the story of a lost child who wanders into a Native American tribe's camp and is raised as one of their own.

Pamela Cowan's story, ***Mars***, moves away from earth to outer space, in her futuristic tale with a twist about a young man coming of age. Back on earth, Mary Vine provides a story of romance, suspense, and humor in ***Grandma Harper's Imagination***. Maggie Lynch pits fantasy against reality in ***Sky Painter***, as a young girl develops unusual talents.

Another Life, by Paty Jager, provides a conundrum for the reader to unravel whether a battered wife and a dead husband is a tale of delirium or truth. In ***Project I.M.A.G.I.N.E.*** Anna Brentwood and Colton Long pen a cautionary tale of artificial intelligence that begins in the 1980s. Kimila Kay closes out the anthology with ***Rattlesnake Ravine***, a suspense novella that plays with imagination versus truth and the consequences of having to choose only one side.

We hope you will open your own imagination as you read each of these contributions to the theme and consider "What if?" Or "Might it be possible?" Perhaps you will be inspired to craft your own original story.

Imagination's Creation
A Poem

Dari LaRoche

IMAGINATION'S CREATION

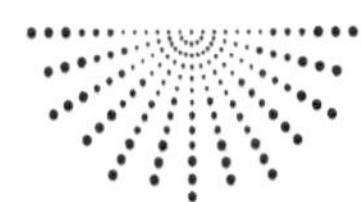

"Imagine," they said.
And I tried.
"Just imagine," the best of them said, their soulless eyes lost
     in a pool of deep, dark knowing.
And again, I tried.
    They gave no guidance.
       Nothing to hold on to.

All I could see was the joy of life that surrounded me.
    My life.
      Of family, of friends, of love, and
      ultimately,
      regretfully,
the pain of sadness and fear and loss.

Today I saw fields of glorious poppies
    covering the valleys,
    reaching for distant rolling hills.
Here for a while
    then fading until next season.

Seeds blown about by the furies,
          soon to be hidden in the soil, overtaken by weeds,
mayhap a final effort to gain purchase among the rocks
          and in dark crevasses.

"Imagine," she intoned,
          a single, determined, stalwart seed,
          my guide in this life.
But she took it a step further,
          a step beyond the now.
That step pulled me along with her
          into the deep,
               the warm, comforting dark
               of knowing.
New growth, untouched by time.
No longer pressed
          to be the best
               or serve with the best
                    or protect the best.

Freed by creativity,
          I live in imagination,
To walk in nature,
          feel the warm breezes,
          quiet zephyrs caressing my skin.
I am beauty of flowers,
          Rainbows
          safe below stars in an infinite dark sky
To just be me.

ABOUT THE AUTHOR

Dari LaRoche loves to travel. She always keeps a little notebook and her cellphone handy to record tidbits that she will use sometime in the future—no interesting detail is too small to be considered in a novel, a short story, or a poem. Her love for the water, above and below the surface, and for tromping around the ruins of castles and forts, fills any bits of time when she isn't at home watching the birds and critters in her garden, or reading, writing, and enjoying her family and friends. Learn More About Dari at her website. https://darilaroche.com/

POEM INSPIRATION

Recently, I have spent more time reflecting: on my family; my past work life with its many challenges; restraints, and opportunities; the beauty of nature; the grief that comes with loss; and the inevitability of the circle of life. In retirement, I have found freedom to indulge myself more in the creativity of the arts, including writing, painting, photography, and gardening. These creative pleasures highlight the sheer joy of imagination's integral place in all that we do. This poem is simply the expression of my own imagination as it travels between conscious thought and the sublime, the beauty that surrounds us here on Planet Earth if we only open our eyes enough to see.

Susie Slanina

METRO TAKES A ROAD TRIP

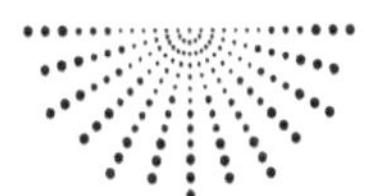

The earthquake hit as Sherry was getting ready for work. She grabbed Metro and called for her other dogs, Tawny and Gizzy.

"DANGER! DANGER! Treaty-treat!"

The dogs knew this was their cue to get under the dining table fast. They had practiced the drill many times, but this was not a drill. They scrambled under the table.

Tawny and Gizzy barked and Metro's little body was trembling. Sherry held her close and tried to talk soothing words.

"We're okay. It'll stop pretty soon." The words helped Sherry calm down, too. Her heart, which had been racing, slowed down a little.

The shaking finally subsided and Tawny and Gizzy stopped barking.

"Wow, that was a big one, but not the BIG ONE that's predicted to destroy Southern California. I'd say it was about 6.2 on the Richter scale."

She took slow breaths as she leashed up the dogs.

She checked on the cats. Playmate and Butterscotch were still asleep on the couch as though nothing had happened. Sighing with relief, she went to the front yard.

Like a little scientist, Metro stopped and put her ear to the ground, listening for rumbles.

Neighbors were filling the street making sure everyone was okay. Her friends, Lori and Marguerite and their families were fine.

"Let's check our houses for damage and see what the news is saying," Lori's father, Roger, suggested. They all gathered in the McDonnell household.

Lori turned on the TV. The reporter was already interviewing a man on the street.

"I felt the shuddering and then the windows broke," the man said.

The reporter turned to the camera. "There's been a sizable earthquake in the Los Angeles area. We will get back shortly with the measurement."

The footage changed to scientists at JPL (Jet Propulsion Laboratory) in Pasadena. A lady scientist said the earthquake was 6.5 on the Richter Scale and was centered in Claremont.

"Get ready. There will be plenty of aftershocks from this one," she said.

"Claremont's just twenty minutes away from Covina," Roger said. "I think we should check our houses, and call the schools and work. We might not be going in today as they'll want to keep the roads clear for emergency workers."

Just as he said that, the reporter checked some papers and stated, "Please do not drive, so the first responders can help people."

The neighbors went back inside their houses to check for any damage. A few books had fallen off Sherry's bookcase, but that seemed to be the extent.

"Okay, doggies, let me get that treat I promised you. I'm sorry I fibbed about the treaties. I just needed your complete attention for those few minutes."

She gave the dogs plenty of treats, then went to the couch to watch TV for further instructions. Thankfully, the earthquake seemed to have caused only minor damage. There were no injuries.

She called her work. There was a recording that stated the university was not open today and to stay home.

"Oh, Metro. I'm glad the earthquake didn't cause too much damage, and I'm glad we can stay home today. It's getting harder and harder to leave you to go to work."

The night before, she and the dogs had returned from a week's vacation at the cabin in Big Bear. She had had the cabin for two years, and it had been a magical time. Sherry was nineteen now and Metro was already two years old. The time had flown since she adopted Metro.

The Week In Big Bear

It felt so right, just being with the dogs in the pine-scented forest for the week. The days had been hot but the evenings and mornings were chilly. It was the end of July and already there were a few flecks of gold in the trees. They had taken lots of walks in the forest and along the lake. At sunset, pink and blue skies spread over the lake, and when it was darker, the reflection of the moon shimmered like a glowing path on the water.

They had plenty of barbecues on the deck with mountain friends and their dogs.

One day, she and her neighbor, Alan, went to the Big Bear Air Show. A butterfly flew past the crowds.

Alan said, "That butterfly is a better flying machine than any of these planes."

Later, they had dinner at a restaurant near the runway so they could watch small planes take off and land.

"Did you like the show?" he asked.

"Yes, but it was a little noisy," Sherry said.

"But that's airplane music." Alan loved everything about planes.

She hadn't wanted to come home and felt the familiar sadness of having to leave her dogs for the long work days ahead. This was nothing new. She felt blue every time she had to leave the cabin.

This time was different, though. The melancholy was more intense. It felt like a stone was pressing against her heart. She was puzzled by this feeling of minor dissatisfaction. She felt well, except for the stone. She tried to shake the feeling off, but it just stayed. She had felt stones on her heart before, big boulders when her mom and dad died. This was nothing compared to those. But still...

What if we just stayed here? She imagined life in the mountains with no work or school. Being surrounded by the natural beauty of Big Bear with the company of her dogs.

Then, one warm afternoon, she lay down in a small clearing in the forest near the cabin. It was her secret place, away from the main trails. The dogs romped beside her. She gazed up at the puffy white clouds drifting across the blue sky. The sunlight, the sky, and the clouds seemed to clear her head. The music of woodland birds helped too. Finally, it dawned on her.

She wanted to spend more time with the dogs. As simple as that. Even just thinking about it, the stone on her chest diminished a bit. She sat up. The birds sang different notes now.

It sounded like they were chirping: "Do it! Do it! Do it!"

"Ah, golden dreams, huh, Metro? It's just not possible though. At least I know what's wrong."

She got up, shook the dust from her clothes, and tried to shake the feeling away, too.

As they walked back to the cabin, she was lost in thought.

"Just think, Metro. During the week, I leave the house at 6 in the morning, drive to Covina station, wait for the Metrolink, get to the University, do my job, catch the train home, and I'm not back till 8 at night. It's too long for us to be apart. Train, work, playtime and cuddles for a couple hours, then TV and sleep. There's not enough time for playtime and cuddles! I only want to be with you...and you want to be with me, right?"

Metro wagged in the affirmative.

A strong aftershock stopped the reminiscing. It wasn't too bad, just a sharp little jolt.

"At least we have one more day together. Let's make it count!" She grabbed the dogs for a playful tussle.

It was a wonderful day. They walked to Covina Park and relaxed under the pine trees. They weren't Big Bear pine trees, but still nice. If only the feeling of the stone on her heart would go away.

In the evening, the phone rang.

It was a recording: "The administration tower has sustained some damage and experts say it needs to be retrofitted. This will take one month. There will be no work for one month."

Sherry gasped. One month?! One WHOLE month!

"Oh, Metro! What shall we do?"

She thought fast. "Well, we could drive back up to the cabin–it would be lovely to stay in the forest for a whole month."

Sherry stretched out on the couch and thought. Feelings of restlessness and wanderlust came over her.

She thought of past family vacations. Most years, they took a cross-country trip to visit relatives in a small village called Rices Landing in the state of Pennsylvania. Sometimes, they took the train. For a few years, they drove a station wagon, and one year they drove a van. The van had been the most comfortable. She cuddled with the dogs and daydreamed about those long road trips.

The Family Vacations

Those old-fashioned family vacations had been a blast. Dad would take different routes so the kids could see different parts of the United States. He'd stop at every historical marker along the way.

As they drove, he made up a silly little song to teach Sherry and her brothers what the lines meant in the center of the road:

"They can pass, but we can't.

We can pass but they can't.

We can both pass! Tra la!"

They sang it to each other through stretches of long lonely highways.

One year, Sherry was reading a book that was set in the Deep South. She and Dad discussed the plot in detail during the long miles of road. It was a fun way to pass the time. He decided to make a big detour so Sherry could experience the setting of the book.

They were driving through Kansas heading north to Pennsylvania. But he turned south so Sherry could see Georgia. They drove through farmlands of rich soil and to the bustling city of Atlanta.

It made the book come to life. He took them to a diner and the waitress brought platters of authentic Cajun Soul food: shrimp and grits, fried chicken and waffles, collard greens, and fried pickles. The Key Lime Pie for dessert was refreshing.

Then they were back on the road, driving through states Sherry had never seen before.

One night Dad said he was lost. They had been driving and driving for days and it was past midnight.

"We'd better turn around and go home," Dad said.

The heavily forested area was dark and foreboding. The long branches twisted above. They looked like they were reaching for them. Sherry and her brothers felt dejected and tired from all the driving. And now they were lost.

Suddenly, they saw a billboard. It said: *"Welcome to Carmichaels!"* They knew where that was! Four miles from Rices Landing! Dad had been kidding. Carmichaels had a tiny downtown with a circle in the road. Dad let them out of the van and they gleefully danced in the circle.

Even though it was late, their aunt and uncle welcomed them gladly. The beds were so soft and Sherry tumbled in gratefully. During the night she could hear foghorns from the boats on the Monongahela River which was a quarter mile away.

The kids skipped stones, waded, and swam. There was a tunnel that led to a beautiful forest, and in the midst of the forest, they came to an unlikely structure: an old rusted-out jail. Sherry wondered about its history. The kids said a bad guy had escaped from the jail. They called him Stovepipe.

They'd cry out, "Run, run! Stovepipe is coming after us!" They ran and ran. Sherry felt a fun, scary feeling.

Stovepipe! She laughed, remembering.

She loved everything about the little village of Rices Landing, the rolling green hills, the river, and the slower way of life.

One day, her uncle was working in the shed. Sherry asked him if he wanted to join her and her aunts for Bingo later.

"Nope, I gotta rock on the porch this afternoon," he replied.

Sherry admired the answer and liked the idea of 'rocking on the porch' as a purpose.

Rices Landing had a tiny grocery store where she could charge candy and her dad would pay later.

It had a little church-side graveyard that had gravestones with the names of some of her ancestors. She walked through the graveyard one night with her aunt and felt a little nervous. Her aunt laughed.

"But, they're friendly ghosts, Sherry! Just think of them as neighbors in the afterlife, having tea on the porch, welcoming us as we walk by."

Oh, how she loved Pennsylvania as a child and young teenager. She had asked her dad many times if they could move there. At school, she daydreamed about the green river that reflected the trees and the soft hills.

Southern California was nice, but she longed to live in a place that had four seasons. How wonderful it would be to observe each season unfold like a storybook in your own backyard.

And the summer storms in Pennsylvania! She had never experienced such crashing thunder and crackling lightning that lit up the village. She could see it all from her aunt's porch.

One evening, she saw her first firefly. She was sitting on a merry-go-round at a little playground. She sat and kicked at the dirt under her feet as she whirled slowly back and forth. Suddenly, the sky started to sparkle with tiny, blinking lights. The sparkling lights danced around her. It felt like she was in a fairyland. She ran to her aunt's house and told her dad.

"Those are fireflies, Sherry! We call them lightning bugs." There were no fireflies in Southern California. Sherry fell more in love with the enchanting village.

Another slight aftershock brought her back to the present moment.

And now she had a whole month. A month would be enough time to drive across the United States, but it would cost too much money. She sighed and decided to drive back up to Big Bear the next day.

Still, it was pleasant to imagine: A road trip across the United States, destination Rices Landing, Pennsylvania. One day, maybe. Just like the old days.

The next morning, as she was packing for Big Bear, she heard the mail come.

"Oh, I should tell the postman to hold my mail for a month." She ran out to meet him and came back with the mail. One letter had a return address of Corporate Fat Cats. She opened it quickly and gasped.

"Metro, this is a royalty for your singing commercial! It's a really big check!"

She was stunned and happily scampered back inside. She couldn't believe the good fortune! She looked at the check again and again. It included a small note that said Metro's singing commercial was a popular success and was being played in many more outlets in the country and even around the world in certain locales.

"Oh, Metro! It's fate! What should we do? Where should we go? Rome? Paris? Or how about a month in a tropical paradise? Hawaii? Fiji? the Bahamas?" It was fun, daydreaming of different destinations. Then she had a great idea.

"But, really, how about Pennsylvania? We could buy a van like Dad had and drive cross-country after all!"

The practical voice in her head said she should put the money in her savings account.

The fun voice in Sherry's head argued, "But this is a serendipity. It's okay to spend a serendipity, so let's go spend it!"

The fun voice won. Sherry was glad.

Dad had explained the meaning of serendipity: "It's finding something good without looking for it."

Whenever a little serendipity happened, Dad would take the family for banana splits at a restaurant, instead of just an ice cream cone from the drugstore.

He'd say, "Sometimes in life, you just have to say *WHEEEE!* Not all the time…that would take all the fun out of it. But, every once in a while (you'll know when it's right), you should go wild!"

Sherry loved how her dad perfectly explained the idea of embracing responsibility most of the time, but letting loose occasionally. Finding a balance between restraint and wildness, and noticing those rare, exhilarating moments when it's just right to let go and have fun.

Sherry thought Dad would agree that this unexpected check definitely qualified as a serendipity. She would call this month "The Serendipity Month" in honor of her dad.

Later that morning at the car dealership, she knew exactly what she wanted, a van similar to what Dad had.

She didn't like shopping, so it was lucky she found the perfect van right away. The van had a small, almost child-sized stove. It reminded her of the toy stoves they had in kindergarten. But this one could really cook. Sherry promised Metro she would cook her an extra egg the way she liked it…with no pepper!

In the back, it had seats that could be folded into a bed and a cozy dinette where they could have snacks and spread out maps to plan the route. It had cleverly designed cubbies all around for odds and ends. There was even a ladder outside so they could climb up and see the vistas.

They went home and decided to leave the very next morning, early! She would only be taking Metro on the trip. Marguerite offered to pet sit and stay at Sherry's with her dog, Starbuck. And since it was summer and there was no school, Lori and her twin sisters would be over all the time, too. Sherry knew her pets would be fine, but she still felt a twinge of sadness leaving them behind. It would be too hard to manage to take them all.

On the computer, peering at maps of the United States was frustrating. Sherry decided to bicycle to the bookstore. It would be much easier to see maps, guides, and tour books in person, instead of squinting at the computer.

She put Metro in the basket of the bicycle and cycled a few blocks to Covina Bookstore, her favorite shop. She purchased maps of the United States and a Road Atlas which had good details about each individual state. She also purchased guidebooks to study which sights they'd like to see along the way.

On the way home, they passed a jewelry store. It gave her an idea. On impulse, she went inside and asked which bracelet would be suitable to hold charms. She bought a link style that would hold plenty. She bought a smaller one for Lori. She planned to get a charm for each place they liked along the way. Since Lori loved animals, whenever Sherry bought a charm for herself, she planned to get an animal charm for Lori.

When they got home, she spread out the map on the kitchen table and studied it. She drew a straight line for the fastest route from Covina to Rices Landing, Pennsylvania. But she wanted the trip to be leisurely, and be able to go to points of interest, wherever they might be.

The map was fascinating and she forgot the time. At last she got up, yawned, and stretched.

"Time for nitey-nite, Metro. We've got an early day tomorrow!"

She woke Metro at 2 a.m. sharp. This was the time Dad always woke them for the cross-country trips and she wanted to carry on his tradition.

Metro protested mightily. She made funny groaning noises and burrowed deeper into the covers. Sherry tried to lift her, but Metro had made herself heavy like a big brick. Sherry was tempted to fall back into bed but tradition was tradition.

Everything was packed and ready to go. All they had to do was drive.

It was eerie being out on the road at that hour. The freeway already had oncoming traffic. Some commuters were going opposite of Sherry, driving west toward Los Angeles. Sherry felt sorry for the people having to get up so early every day to go to work.

"And here, I'm complaining about a long day," she thought.

At last they were far from the lights and signs of civilization. They were finally in the desert. Joshua trees loomed before them looking like friendly hitchhikers.

They listened to some music. *"Unforgettable...that's what you are"* Sherry sang to Metro.

Metro matched her voice and sang back to her. *"Unforgettable, though near or far..."* Metro's voice was so tender and true, that it made Sherry's eyes glisten.

Somewhere before Stateline, Nevada, they reached a point where the night was the blackest black Sherry had ever seen. She looked out the window...stars were everywhere, and they came down so low, it seemed as if they were almost dangling next to the van.

"Wow, let's stop here and go stargazing for a little while, Metro!"

The stars were the same stars she saw in Big Bear, but they seemed even brighter, and not obscured by tall pine trees.

She turned off on a dirt road and followed it for half a mile. They got out of the van and walked into the glowing, shining desert. The sound of traffic from the freeway disappeared and deep quietude settled in.

She looked up.

The Pleiades looked so dainty in their circle, and the spiral of the Andromeda Galaxy was lovely. Sirius, the Dog Star, was the brightest. Cassiopeia was funny with its happy sounding name and lopsided W shape. And, of course, there were the big and little dippers and the majesty of the Milky Way.

They enjoyed the celestial display. A little fox scampered by.

Sherry's head was whirling with thoughts. All of a sudden, minor thoughts stopped. Just one simple but very strong thought remained:

"I want to be with you always, Metro."

"Why wait?" a kind voice asked.

"I have to work, but it's just a long day without Metro," Sherry explained.

"Why wait?" the kind voice repeated.

Sherry listened carefully. In a strange way, this voice sounded familiar. She remembered a dream she had a couple years ago, just before she got the cabin. There was a butterfly or bird, Metro was there, and they were in a jeweled cave. Metro could talk. Was she talking now? The little dog stayed silent as she gazed up at the stars.

Sherry stayed very still and listened intently.

After long minutes, the kind voice came back.

"Why wait? When you know what you want, find a way to do it. Life's short, especially for a dog."

"I almost believe I will!" Sherry smiled at Metro.

"But I probably can't." Sherry sighed.

Suddenly, a brilliant shooting star appeared.

And, in that second, before the star disappeared, Sherry made a flash decision.

She *would* find a way.

The stone, which had been pressing against her heart, burst like a soap bubble.

But a mean voice said, "Forget this silly thought. I can't advise you to give up your job. You can't do it. You're way too young. They're just dogs, after all."

"Please stop talking," Sherry said.

The kind voice chimed in: "Don't listen to that guy. You've decided, Sherry. Stop thinking. Please, just have fun on the trip and when you get back, then you can tear your brain out thinking. But now is not the time. GO HAVE FUN!"

Sherry loved the kind voice! It was a relief to be told not to think! Under the stars, she made a solemn promise not to think about the plan while she was on this unscheduled vacation. But she would have to do some thinking eventually–she set a date one month from today: Monday, September 2nd.

"Thank you, kind voice," Sherry whispered softly.

As they walked back to the van, Metro stopped and started digging. Sherry spotted something in the sand. It was shiny…was it gold?

"Wait, Metro, did you strike gold? I wouldn't put it past you!"

She picked up the object and took it back to the van. Under the lights, she could see it was probably pyrite, called "fool's gold." It was pretty, though. Sherry decided to have it fastened on the charm bracelet.

"I made a big decision back there, Metro. Was it a foolish one, like this pyrite? I don't know, but I do know, we don't have to think about it for now!"

They got back in the van and drove through the star-studded night. A feeling of thankfulness and peace welled up in her now that the decision had been made. She felt incredibly tranquil and her heart opened up to new possibilities, a new life…with more time for Metro! The details could wait until later.

The tranquil feeling turned to excitement as she spotted a glow from the bright lights of Las Vegas. They were still miles away, but she could almost feel the energy from all the gamblers.

She opened the window and the desert wind whipped her hair. She breathed in the hot air.

The glow turned into bright lights. "There it is, Metro! The big city! Non-stop action twenty-four hours a day! A place of high hopes and broken dreams. Some people call it Lost Wages. Haha, that's funny. I won't lose any because I'm too young to gamble."

She decided to stay in a nice hotel in the older part of Las Vegas. To her surprise, she was upgraded to a suite when the receptionist recognized Metro from the singing commercial.

"Wow, Metro, speaking of charms!" Sherry said as she signed the hotel registration forms.

As they made their way through the din of slot machines and cries (of joy and disappointment) from the gamblers, they came to a part of the hotel that was like a lounge, with comfortable sofas and chairs. Sherry marveled at the giant crystal chandeliers, huge bouquets of flowers, and heavy, velvet curtains. A lady played old show tunes on a baby grand piano. As they passed by, Metro started to sing, matching the lady's voice. People and the singer turned to look.

"Okay, Metro, let's stop and you can sing. I know it's been a long journey through the night and singing helps you relax."

The singer smiled when she heard Metro matching her notes. After the song, she asked, "Is this the dog from the Kool Kitty commercial? She was such a hoot. Her voice is incredible and she could really belt out the opera arias!"

"Yes, this is Metro! Do you mind if she sings some duets with you?"

The lady exclaimed with a throaty voice, "That would be fabulous, Honey!"

As Metro and the lady sang the old show tunes, more and more people came to relax in the comfortable chairs and listen. When Sherry saw Metro's eyes begin to droop, she said good night, and several people asked for Metro's autograph. Like in Hollywood, someone had a handy ink pad and Metro happily put her paw print on people's cocktail napkins.

The golden elevator took them to the 30th floor of the big hotel. The suite was magnificent! It even had a spiral staircase leading to another level with a hot tub that had bubbly warm water!

"Gosh, Metro! Thanks a whole lot. We were just going to get a hotel room for a good night's sleep and we got this beautiful suite instead, all because of you!"

She sat on the luxurious couch and cuddled with her small dog. They gazed at the bright lights of the city spread out beyond the floor-to-ceiling windows. She sighed contentedly.

"Your singing has really brought us places, Metro! Just think, the first night when I brought you home from the shelter, I forgot the teakettle and you made a sound that sounded just like it. Then I noticed how you were trying to mimic the birds in the birdbath."

She took the hotel stationary from the end table and made a list of ways Metro's singing had changed their lives:

1. Singing at the opera in Hollywood.

2. Singing commercial in Hawaii for Corporate Fat Cats.
3. Singing helped buy the vacation cabin in Big Bear.
4. Singing helped a sad princess in London.
5. Singing led to this road trip...with a beautiful suite in Las Vegas!

She read the list to Metro, but the little dog was asleep, her sweet paw resting on Sherry's hand.

"But singing is not the best part of you. Not even close. There's so much more...maybe I should make a list."

Instead, she simply stroked Metro's paw and whispered, "These are the moments I want to hold on to. Just this."

Sherry's eyes grew misty. The bright lights of the city blended into a shimmering sea of color.

They ended up spending two nights at the hotel. They took a day trip for a scenic drive through Red Rock Canyon with colorful rock formations.

The next morning, they visited Mt. Charleston. Sherry and Metro hiked a steep section. She wondered how it would feel to be on the very top, looking down.

They reached a crest. The view was lovely, but it was already getting warm. "This is far enough for now, Metro, want to run down?" As a child, she had no fear of running down hills. The fearless feeling came back and it felt great to run without hesitation–stones and twigs scattering everywhere–she felt as though she and Metro were flying without a care in the world! They reached the bottom and laughed. No scraped knees, no twisted ankles or paws. Tired, dusty, and happy, they returned to the hotel to take a shower and relax in the hot tub. Stepping out, Shery felt like a ragdoll. Limp and tired, she and Metro took a long nap.

That evening they were very hungry after the hike. Sherry fed Metro, and then they decided to check out the buffet. So much food!

Too much food! She filled her plate and gave Metro tiny bites of prime rib.

Taking a spoonful of mashed potatoes, Sherry realized she had made a mistake. It wasn't mashed potatoes, it was horseradish sauce! She liked spicy foods, but this was too much! Her eyes filled with tears and she took a bite of bread. That helped a little.

Before they left Las Vegas, Sherry remembered the charm bracelet. She went to the gift shop for a charm to symbolize Las Vegas. There were a lot of choices! She bought a cheap pin because it made her laugh. It said: "I love buffets."

"But beware the horseradish sauce," she thought ruefully.

For the charm, she thought a golden dollar sign was the perfect representation of Las Vegas. And, just as she was leaving, she saw a sparkly rhinestone star. The star would help her remember the big decision she had made in the desert.

The next morning it was time to get back on the road. It was lucky she was a fan of desert scenery. There was a lot of that, for sure. The vastness was beautiful in its own way.

They stopped at Four Corners Monument, a geographical spot where the corners of four southwest states met. There was a bronze plaque at the exact spot. Sherry stood in New Mexico and Metro stood in Arizona. Sherry picked Metro up and held her over Colorado, while she stood in Utah. They took a step and they were in New Mexico. It was a strange feeling, being able to step easily into another state. They hopped and skipped over the four states. She bought a charm that displayed the plaque.

They made a detour to Albuquerque, New Mexico. She remembered on one of their vacations by train, it had made a stop there. Dad had bought her a pretty turquoise necklace.

They wandered through the vendor market, a place where you could purchase native artwork directly from the artisan. Sherry found a nice turquoise charm. She also bought a flying saucer charm since Roswell, of Alien mystique, was in New Mexico.

In Santa Fe, she stopped at an art gallery. She bought two framed prints of Van Gogh's *Starry Night.* It reminded her of the dizzying night sky in the desert. The other print was for Marguerite.

They made a stop in Chicago and spent a night in the Windy City. The next day was full. They rode an open-air double-decker bus and learned more about the city. They took the elevator to the top of Sears Tower, and through a telescope they could make out the Bears playing in Soldier Field. They visited the ornate train station and had Chicago-style deep dish pizza for lunch.

After Chicago, the rest of the trip was uneventful. During long stretches of road, Sherry fell into a happy trance. She paid attention to driving and the voices in her head had disappeared. The decision had been made, and she had promised not to think about it during the trip.

But, just the feeling that there was another, unknown destiny waiting when she got home made her feel cheerful. Metro and Sherry were in their happy zone, with none of the day-to-day distractions and details of normal life. There was no school, no job, no errands, and no homework!

There was only a road that needed attention. It felt like time was suspended. She fully enjoyed just being with the tiny treasure of Metro and her constant sunny nature.

It was near midnight when she saw the *Welcome to Carmichaels* billboard. She smiled, remembering the tradition. Just four more miles to Rices Landing! She and Metro got out of the van at the town circle and did a little dance.

When they arrived a few minutes later, there were joyful greetings and then Sherry tumbled into Auntie's soft bed. She slept well to the lonely sound of foghorns from barges on the Monongahela River. When she woke up the next morning, she felt refreshed. She went out on the porch and looked over the sweet village of Rices Landing. Auntie put a scoop of ice cream in their coffees. She liked to have ice cream with coffee on hot, humid mornings. Sherry thought it was a fine idea!

Childhood friends had grown up. William and Christopher had heard Sherry was coming. She watched them come up the road carrying a pail of freshly picked blueberries. Auntie was pleased and said she would make a pie.

"I picked more than Christopher. You'll know the ones I picked. They have my fingerprints," William joked.

They headed down to the river and lazily watched the barges go by. They waved and the river pilots waved back. One tossed them a foil-wrapped package. It was full of delicious cold spaghetti! They ate it with their fingers and then jumped in the river, laughing and splashing, just like when they were children. And this time, Metro was there to join in the fun.

One day they drove to Fallingwater, a house Frank Lloyd Wright had designed that was built on top of an actual waterfall!

She planned to spend a week in Pennsylvania and then be back on the road. She had several friends in the Pacific Northwest she wanted to visit, so they would take the northern route home. They drove up to Philadelphia to see the Liberty Bell and Sherry bought a charm of the famous cracked bell.

Then on to New York City! The first stop was the majestic public library. At the steps leading up to the building were two marble lions. Their names were Patience and Fortitude. "I'm going to need both those qualities in the next few weeks," she told Metro as they climbed the stairs. Inside the gift shop, she purchased heavy marble bookends of the two proud lions.

She loved the energy of the big city. They had lunch at a famous deli, and in the evening took a carriage ride through Central Park. They waited until midnight to go to the top of the Empire State Building to see the twinkling lights. They visited Grand Central Terminal. At the main concourse, Sherry looked up to see the constellations that had been painted on the ceiling. They had lunch at a restaurant inside the station that overlooked busy commuters rushing by the big clock in the center.

Sherry loved hearing the announcements of departures to different cities near and far. And the "To Trains" sign held the magic of adventure.

"Someday, we'll take a long train trip," she promised Metro.

One morning, they visited the Statue of Liberty. In the afternoon they were strolling through Central Park and came across the John Lennon mosaic that read "Imagine." She felt thoughtful and bought a tiny, delicate charm that simply had the word *IMAGINE* in filigree lettering.

She was eager to get back on the road and visit her friends. On the way, she made only one stop in downtown Minneapolis to spend the night. The next morning, she and Metro went on a short walk and came across the statue of Mary Tyler Moore throwing her cap in the air.

She took long naps at rest stops in South Dakota, Montana, and Idaho. The van was comfortable and she and Metro had fast food and snacks for two days until she hit the Pacific Ocean in Washington State.

She was ready to collapse when her friend, Sheila, opened the door of her perfect cottage in Ocean Shores. The friends hugged each other, laughing and talking. Listening to the ocean and being with such wonderful company helped Sherry recover from the long journey.

She spent several peaceful days with Sheila. In the mornings they sat by the cozy fire and read books aloud to each other, while Metro snoozed. Deer grazed contentedly in the front yard.

When Metro started to stir, that was the signal to head for a long walk on the beach. Metro ran in the surf and fetched the ball. The shore was filled with sand dollars, pretty stones, and seashells. They even came across a starfish.

Their favorite part was standing in the sand for half an hour, gazing at the ocean, with the waves tickling their feet. Afterwards, they sat on a bench for a long time, watching the surf and the waving grasses on the dunes that seemed to magically change colors from green to gold. They drank in the spectacular views and enjoyed the sound of gulls calling and the beauty of Snowy Plovers as they played on the beach and swooped around the girls. Sherry remembered to get a charm: a seashell.

On the last evening, they watched as the sunset spread vivid colors of lavender, pink, blue, and orange across the ocean and sky. When the colors became muted, they walked back to the van.

Sheila liked to collect crystals and just as Sherry was getting into the van she placed an egg-shaped crystal in Sherry's palm. "This is a Golden Healer crystal. Take it with you."

It felt smooth and was so pretty. "Thank you, Sheila."

It was hard to say goodbye.

They made a stop in Vancouver, Washington to visit Diane, another good friend. They had a long lunch with great conversation in a restaurant overlooking the Columbia River. The restaurant had a pet-friendly patio, so Metro and Diane's sweet dog, Sadie, could be with them. They enjoyed watching sailboats on the big river.

After lunch, they went for a stroll through a misty forest that was so different from the forest in Big Bear. The pine cones were tiny compared to the giant pine cones near the cabin. This forest was emerald green and full of ferns and moss. Metro sniffed and sniffed at new scents and enjoyed the company of Sadie. Before they left, Sherry purchased a charm of a pine tree.

Just across the Columbia River was the city of Portland. There was a bookstore that was a city block long! The marquee display said: "A Booklover's Wildest Dream Come True!" Portland and Vancouver were reading towns. In each coffee shop Sherry visited, people had their noses in a book. She felt at home in the Northwest.

Sherry had two other long-time friends, Larry and Debbie, who she wanted to visit. They lived in Silverton, Oregon. Silverton was a small town with a happy vibe. It had a charming, historical downtown. There was a pretty creek called Silver Creek that had a covered bridge.

At nearby Silver Falls, they stood behind a waterfall. A curtain of rushing water tumbled before them, soaking everyone to the skin.

There was a mural in town that told the amazing true story about Bobby the Wonder Dog from the 1920's. Bobby got lost when his family was on vacation in Indiana. The loyal dog walked 2,551 miles on his own and found his way back home to Silverton. The thought of Bobby walking all that way tugged at Sherry's heartstrings.

Best of all, there was an annual Pet Parade to honor Bobby. There were pets of all shapes and sizes. The dogs wore scarves of red, white, and blue. Larry and Debbie walked their dog, Romeo, a Standard Poodle. Romeo was an elegant gentleman and he walked in a stately manner by Larry and Debbie. Metro veered from right to left, tugging at the leash, trying to greet all the delighted, cheering children.

Sherry bought a doggy charm. And Larry gave her a new road atlas, which was a good thing, because hers was getting tattered and marked up.

Driving down the Oregon Coast, the scenery was magnificent. More and more flecks of gold appeared in the trees since she had started the trip. The golden leaves reminded Sherry that summer and the Serendipity Month were coming to an end.

It would soon be back to the rhythms of school and work, unless she came up with the other plan. She had no clue what the plan would be. She knew only that she didn't want to fall into the old routine, letting years pass, while her pets grew old as she spent most of the day away. She didn't want the wonderful dream to fade.

She wouldn't forget. Metro would remind her every day.

All of a sudden, they were back in California. They stopped in San Francisco to ride the cable cars and had lunch on Fisherman's Wharf. Sherry bought a cable car charm.

And then they were home. It was Sunday, and Sherry was scheduled to resume work on Tuesday. She needed to figure out the plan tomorrow!

It was a joyous reunion with her pets and friends. Lori and Marguerite came over and they had pizza. They feasted merrily before Sherry gave Marguerite and Lori their gifts. Lori's eyes sparkled when she saw her charm bracelet filled with all the animals and Marguerite loved the framed print of Van Gogh's *Starry Night*.

Sherry told them about the epiphany under the stars, and her plan to spend more time with Metro. "It means I'm going to get another job somewhere closer to home. It might seem like a small, silly thing to change my whole life just to be with the dogs. And it's scary, too," she confessed.

Marguerite was thoughtful. "I understand. The heart wants what the heart wants. This is a big step, Sherry. What are you going to do?"

Sherry sighed. "Well, that's the part of the plan I haven't figured out yet. Tomorrow is the last day of Serendipity Month. I'll think about it then, but not until then. One thing I know is I'll have to be on a strict budget. Want to help plan?"

And they started to plan. Marguerite took notes.

"No more gowns and jewels," Sherry said. Marguerite raised her eyebrows. "For me, anyway," Sherry laughed.

They planned a strict (but fun) budget. She'd shop on Mondays and make a big pot of Beans de la Olla (Beans in a Pot). They were cheap and she could have them as a soup for a couple days, then make burritos with cheese and have them for dinner until Thursday.

"Good plan. Beans cost pennies!" Marguerite said as she wrote.

"Sherry added, "Lentils are good. Mom used to make them and put diced onion and butter on top."

"Peanut butter and jelly for lunch," Lori added helpfully.

Marguerite said, "On Friday, we could get extra orders of takeout and eat that for the weekend." A discussion ensued about the takeout choices. They decided to always try international foods: One week, Thai, one week Italian, one week, Chinese, one week, Mexican.

Then on Sunday, a big family dinner at Lori's or Marguerite's house, with leftovers!

"With the help of you two, this budget is going to be easy and fun!" Sherry laughed.

MONDAY

Monday morning dawned hot and bright. Sherry felt drained and lethargic. She was so tired from the long trip. She knew she had to decide, but she just wanted to read.

She read a few pages, but felt anxious and couldn't focus on the words. She closed the book, turned over, and closed her eyes. She had this one day to plan her new life, but she was confused and exhausted.

It would be easier just to go back to work and forget this crazy idea. Nobody really knows about it except Marguerite and Lori. Back to life as regular.

That would be so much easier. She wouldn't have to plan or change a thing. But she started feeling the stone again.

Metro must have been reading her mind, because she looked disappointed and her tail drooped sadly.

"Okay, you win. You always win," Sherry said. "You're right. I can't put it off any longer. Either I do or I don't."

The "thinking day" had arrived. She had made good on her promise not to think about it during the trip, although it had been tempting. Now it was time to figure out if the epiphany under the stars was just a fantasy or could it be made into real life?

The kind voice agreed, "Yes, it's time to think."

"Okay, Little Miss Metro, time's up!" Sherry said. "Now we've got to figure stuff out."

It felt strange and uneasy to delve into the unknown. She had always been a careful planner and was already living the life she imagined when she wanted the cabin so badly. Back then, she imagined work with weekends and vacations at the cabin. It sounded perfect. That was the dream she had before, and she was living it. She liked her job and the people she worked with. She should be thanking her lucky stars for such good fortune. And yet…and yet.

Something had changed. The deep longing to be with the dogs more often had grown stronger and stronger and couldn't be ignored.

"I guess sometimes you imagine a dream, and you're living your dream, but then something comes up and you need to reimagine. You tear down the framework and start working on a whole new building."

She stared at the twirling ceiling fan and lifted her arm. She admired the charms on her bracelet. She watched as they sparkled in the sunlight.

"I'll be making less money but I'll be with you more often," she told Metro.

Metro looked at Sherry with tender pleading eyes. She yawned. *"What's money anyway?"* She seemed to say.

Sherry stared in earnest at all the charms she had collected. She loved them all, and she was glad she had these nice mementos to commemorate the road trip.

She made a list of what they were and where she got them:

Four Corners Monument - Arizona, Utah, Colorado, and New Mexico

Turquoise - Albuquerque, New Mexico

Flying saucer- Albuquerque, New Mexico

Pyrite - California desert

Dollar Sign - Las Vegas, Nevada

Star - Las Vegas, Nevada

Liberty Bell - Philadelphia, Pennsylvania

Imagine - New York, New York

Seashell - Ocean Shores, Washington

Pine tree - Vancouver, Washington

Doggy - Silverton, Oregon

Cable car - San Francisco, California

Suddenly, she realized the dollar sign and the doggy charm held a clue. She touched the dollar sign and touched the doggy. The question was, more dollars or more doggy?

"I choose you, doggy charm!" The star charm twinkled almost as if in agreement.

Metro laughed by wagging her tail. She was so happy thinking of many more hours she could spend with Sherry. Metro had one more thing to teach Sherry, though.

The practical voice said, "But, you'll still need to get a job. Maybe get a job doing something you love. Not as many hours and close by." Sherry loved the practical voice like she loved the fun voice and the kind voice.

The practical voice asked gently, "What is it you like to do?"

"What do I like to do?" Sherry repeated, staring at the ceiling. There were so many things, but her mind was blank trying to come up with something that would work for a job.

She didn't notice when Metro rested her chin on the book, staring at Sherry.

"What do I like to do? Well, I like to be with you, Metro. That's the whole point of this life-changing decision, right?"

Metro nudged the book to Sherry.

"I know, I know. I'll read later. But right now, I'm trying to figure something out. A sort of framework for our new life together," she explained.

Metro nudged the book to the point where it was practically on Sherry's chin. Sherry took her gaze from the ceiling and peered at Metro.

"Yes, I know, I know. I love to read...but right now I'm thinking."

Metro nestled her head in the crook of Sherry's neck. She knew Sherry would eventually get it, but sometimes it took a while. She yawned and took a little snooze.

Silent minutes ticked by. Sherry stared at the charms while Metro slept. Eventually, the sound of gentle snoring and soft breathing helped Sherry relax and give her the inspiration she needed.

"Wait. You were trying to tell me something, weren't you?" She felt Metro's tail start to swish slowly.

Sherry looked at the book and said, "Yes, I love to read, but no job will pay me to just read. That would be nice, though." Sherry laughed at the thought.

"But how can a book factor into the plan?"

She showed the dollar sign charm to Metro. "See this? Remember, I need some dollars to buy you food and get stuff."

Suddenly, she felt wide awake, the lethargy and uneasy feeling went away. She picked up the book and stared at it with new eyes.

"But wait, maybe you're on to something, Metro." Metro's tail swished faster.

She sat up and said slowly, thinking as she talked. "I'm taking classes to become a teacher, but, maybe in the meantime, I could get a job helping children with their reading lessons. Kids who are just starting to learn. There's a preschool just a few blocks away. I could even bicycle to work! If I go on that strict budget and really try, I think we could manage!"

Metro stood on the bed, happily yipped, and wagged at triple speed. *Finally! Sherry understood what she was trying to say!*

Sherry cycled to the preschool that very day and told them her idea. They liked it and hired her on the spot, pending approval. She could start work in two weeks after they checked things out. "Perfect," Sherry thought. "That will give me time to give notice and prepare for classes."

She was so excited to start the new job and new life! Life with many more hours in the day to cuddle and play with her pets. Imagine that!

She still wanted to be a teacher someday. She'd start classes again in the fall. She pored over the college catalog and chose classes that met on Tues/Thurs in the evenings. Instead of Mon/Wed/Friday. Again, more time with Metro!

The two weeks flew by. Every day when she left the house, she counted down the days with Metro: 10 more, 8 more, 4 more, 2 more, 1 more! On the calendar countdown, she put a star sticker on each day that passed.

The Serendipity Month had been fun, although, she had to admit, it would also be nice to settle down into a normal routine.

But one last little splurge. She had noticed a gap in the charm bracelet.

She needed one more, and she thought of the perfect charm: A book! A book would symbolize Metro's great idea for their new life together. She went to the jewelry store and purchased a small silver book charm that would fill the gap perfectly. Sherry placed it between the star charm (stars had inspired the plan) and the doggy charm (a doggy had helped find the solution).

She felt confident and light-hearted. Even though she'd be making less money and would have to be on a strict budget, she felt rich in all the best possible ways.

The decision felt right and it was a relief that the stone was completely gone from her heart, she had almost forgotten about it.

She looked at Metro with awe. "You planned this, didn't you? By nudging that book to me, you gave me the idea of combining my love of reading with a job. A job that maybe will get children to love to read. You're a very smart pup, Metro!"

TWO WEEKS LATER

It was the first day of Sherry's new job at the school. She sat cross-legged with the children in a circle on the floor. She read a story to quiet them down, then took an individual child who was struggling with reading to the side and helped him sound out words.

"Let's make the C sound, let's make the A sound, let's make the T sound." The child did so in a halting way a few times. "Okay, now let's try to put them all together." The child did so. "Now let's say it all together, but faster." The child did so. "Faster!" On the third try, the child looked up with a grin of understanding.

"You mean, like a KITTY?!"

"Yep, just like a kitty cat!" They beamed at each other.

It was beyond rewarding when a child got a picture in his head of what the letters formed. Sherry's heart felt full. She loved her new job.

And best of all...

Metro sat on the child's lap. The school had agreed that Metro could come too! Metro's sunny disposition and calm presence helped the children concentrate.

ABOUT THE AUTHOR

Susie Slanina lives in Vancouver, Washington. After graduating from California State University, Los Angeles, she went to school in Ireland to study the Montessori approach to educating children. She worked 24 years at CSLA and retired at age 50 to spend more time with her dogs in a cabin in Big Bear.

After retirement she penned a poem about a spider. That poem became the catalyst for the Metro book series. She used to enjoy traveling, but discovered that hanging out with her dogs is better than seeing the wonders of the world. Her **Metro the Little Dog** series of children's books is about a lovable puppy named Metro. These stories were written to honor the real Metro and all the wonderful dogs who grace our lives. Many thanks to artist Paul Bunch for the exquisite illustrations. Learn more about Susie's at Windtree Press. https://windtreepress.com/susie-slanina/

STORY INSPIRATION

The journey of life is sweeter when traveled with a dog ~ unknown

This story started with Metro and Sherry taking a cross-country train trip. But I was stuck; the train was too confining. I started daydreaming of past family vacations and switched out the train for an imaginary road trip. It was fun to write and plan the route.

f X

THE WATCHING GAME

LISA DE NIKOLITS

THE WATCHING GAME

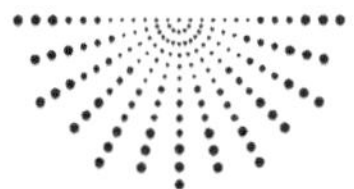

I met Angel at the strip mall college at the end of the world. That's what it felt like anyway.

Tucked in between an adult movie store and a massage parlour, with a discount golf outlet at one end and a fireplace warehouse on the other, it was a place for sad and desperate people and yet, there I was.

The sandcastle of my life had slowly eroded, grain by grain, washed away by the unstoppable tide of technical progress and the inexorable conquest of AI.

"You gotta pull that wire," Angel leaned across me and yanked the car door closed. "I gotta get these panels replaced. Seatbelts don't work either."

I was sunk low in a bucket seat, finding a place for my feet among the McDonald's wrappers.

Angel fired up the car and the pigeons pecking at the asphalt rose in protest.

Yeah, I thought. *A muffler wouldn't hurt either.*

"I shouldn't really be driving." Angel peered through the thick mist. "Man, the weather's so messed up. This fog. Every single day for three months. I can't see in front of me."

I hugged my heavy backpack closer to my chest. If there was a collision, my textbooks and peanut and jelly sandwich would buffer me, right?

I decided not to think about how trashed Angel's car was. I also decided not to worry about the red glow of the rearview lights in front of us that seemed way too up close and personal.

A crucifix swung from the rearview mirror, along with a tiny pair of red boxing gloves.

"Nice crucifix," I commented and I meant it. It was blue and white enamel, with an ornate inlay. I immediately coveted it, but stealing from my new best friend was hardly the way to cement a good relationship.

I dug my fingernails into my backpack, trying to quell my kleptomaniac tendencies which were worse when I was stressed.

Angel snorted. "My boyfriend's. Vlad. He's Russian Orthodox. Goes to church three times a week. Gets up at 5 a.m. to go and pray."

"Ah. Does he box too?"

"Nope, those were his dad's. He's got dementia, his dad. I look after him. This is his car. He's so messed up, he doesn't know if he's coming or going. He hates me, but I'm the one who takes care of him, cleans up, and changes his sheets. He owes me a lot more than this crappy old car."

I didn't know what to say to that.

"This mist is so bad." I peered through the fog. "Global warming. Weird weather."

"Yeppers. Just so you know, I get fits sometimes." Angel leaned forward and clutched the steering wheel tighter. "But only when I'm super tired."

Given that she was running on four hours of sleep and three Red Bulls, her revelation wasn't exactly reassuring.

"I broke my back once," I offered, because I felt like I had to reciprocate. "Still hurts when it's damp and rainy."

Angel laughed. A great laugh, deep and full. "Great nurse's aids we'll make. Haha. You with a broken back, me with fits. I'm bipolar too. But don't tell Suraya."

Suraya was our mean-girl teacher. I called her Nurse Ratched from "One Flew Over the Cuckoo's Nest", but Angel had no idea who I was talking about.

"I won't tell her," I promised. "Is that why you shouldn't be driving? Because of the fits?"

She shook her head. "I lost my license on New Year's Eve. Reckless driving. I was trying to have some fun, a bit of street racing. Vlad was drunk so I was being the responsible one, driving him. It was New Year's Eve, like cut me some slack. But I got pulled over. Then I resisted arrest. Great start to the year, the story of my life."

I took stock of the situation for a moment.

I was fifty-eight. Angel was twenty-two. We were an unlikely pair. She was a high school dropout who worked the system, signing up for the D-grade college course to collect a government grant.

Meanwhile, I was the former editor of a high-profile fashion magazine. Two hundred juicy pages a month, with advertisers vying for good positions, wining and dining me, taking me on press trips to Vail and New York, Paris, and London.

I sighed.

"Sorry it's taking so long to get there," Angel apologized. "I never figured there'd be this much traffic."

"It's not that. My life is such a mess." I sank lower into the broken bucket seat. "What kind of a school doesn't even have a coffee machine? The vending machine's broken. The microwave's broken. Half the toilets are broken. The tables in the lunch room are broken. The whole place is broken."

She chuckled. "Yeah. It's a dump."

I looked up at the crucifix, swinging back and forth, with the red boxing gloves.

Faith and tenacity. Kind of apropos really.

I'd thought the school was a miracle. God riding in on a big white horse, a knight in shining armor, to rescue me from my downward spiraling life.

"Nurse's Aid course starting in two weeks. Government grants available. Two-year course condensed into six months. Sign up for your new career today! Guaranteed employment!"

A miracle, nothing less.

Because other than God, I had no recourse for rescue. I was that alone. All the people who'd curried favour with me, as if their lives depended upon it, had vanished.

I was ghosted by every single person I'd considered to be a friend.

I couldn't pay for cable TV. I grocery shopped at the dollar store, living on Ramen noodles, canned baby corn, discount Tostitos, and boxes of stale Lucky Charms cereal. Not the most balanced diet but it had to do.

Every now and then, I threw in a few candy bars and a pint of apple juice for dessert.

So there I was, one misty Sunday morning, lugging my little wheelie cart up to the Dollar Tree, when I heard the church bells.

Having nothing better to do, I veered into the sanctity of the Mass. After a thirty-six-year absence, I clasped my hands earnestly, with my joints aching on the hard leather kneeler, and I begged God for mercy and help.

My face was swollen from crying and perpetual sorrow. My last round of Botox had long since worn off and my fake eyelashes were askew, my cheap mascara smudged.

I was a yard sale crêpe paper doll, tired and stained, my days of fabulousness dust in the wind and my bank account in the red.

"You're not in a good way, Eloise," a woman said and her voice was critical. Of course, it was Cynthia, a one-time editor of a fashion magazine. She wasn't happy with how my life had turned out.

"You think I don't know that," I retorted. "You think I want to be a mess like this?"

She just sank back in her chair and folded her arms.

Cynthia was a member of the audience. My unseen audience, unseen to everyone except for me.

My Watchers. They showed up just after the kid next door drowned.

I was six, sitting high on my father's shoulders, watching the police milling around the neighbor's swimming pool. The kid's parents were distraught.

"They left the gate open," my father said grimly.

I couldn't stop staring at the water. It was as smooth as glass. Aqua blue and six feet deep, with white and navy mosaic tiles around the rim.

A mirror to the sky, with one single dead floating leaf, just like the little boy. Once the leaf was scooped up, there'd be nothing left at all. No evidence at all, that the idyllic picture-perfect water had killed a child.

"He'll come back," I said, with certainty.

"No Sweetie, he won't." My mother patted my back. "But don't worry, he's gone to a better place."

"Don't sugarcoat things for her," my father said sharply. "Eloise, the boy is dead. Death is forever. We don't know what happens after we die."

"Honestly Arthur, you're just cruel." My mother grabbed my hand. "Sweetie, Daddy's right, death is forever but Daddy's wrong because we go to heaven and eat cake and cookies and ice cream all the time."

My father snorted.

I stared at the calm cool pool as long as I could until my father turned away. All I could see was the dead boy, floating, alone, by himself, like the leaf waiting to be scooped up.

My father put me down and I went into the garage to play Mass, using my grandmother's tarnished lawn bowling trophies for the communion host and the wine, and her old scarf for the altar.

I felt disconnected. Strange.

What did happen after we died? Where was the boy now? I never even knew his name. I should have known his name.

I started to cry but then I heard the voices.

"We've got you, Eloise. It's time to be brave. You can do this. Don't worry about the boy. His name is Charlie. He's fine where he is."

That was the first time I met them. My Watchers. They were so real, so reassuring.

I saw myself on the silver screen, a movie star, holding a large bowling trophy and pretending to say Mass for poor departed Charlie and there they were, watching me, munching their popcorn and commenting among themselves.

"Poor little kid."

"Imagine the mother's horror."

"So easy to leave a gate open."

"Their lives are ruined now."

"Come on, Eloise, time to be brave."

My Watchers. I felt comforted by their presence.

And after that, they never left my side. I was never the dead little floating leaf, all alone. Wherever I went, I had my friends. I called it The Watching Game.

No matter what the circumstance, my Watcher always helped me. The right Watcher appeared just at the right time, to give me the advice I needed. Like Cynthia, the fashionista who once had the ear of Vivienne Westwood.

When I was on the top of my game, people were amazed by my ability to track style trends, predicting them before they even happened but it wasn't me, it was Cynthia.

When The Truman Show hit the big screen, I felt cheated. I was Truman, not him! And, unlike him, I knew about my Watchers, and I needed them. And, unlike The Truman Show, my Watchers weren't real to anyone except me.

A horn honked loudly, tires screeched, someone cursed loudly and I was yanked back to the present.

Right. I was with Angel. We were going to get coffee. I had to concentrate, be in the moment. Be mindful. Be present.

"Pay attention," it was Jamie, a member of the audience I didn't exactly love. He called himself the Tough Love Dad but he was just mean. *"You're running out of time."*

"Maybe we should go back," I said to Angel. "We don't want to make Suraya madder than she already is."

Angel looked at me. "Ella, we are on our way back. You have a blackout or what?"

Whoa. I looked down. I had a coffee in one hand and a lemon-filled doughnut in the other.

"Yeah, sorry. Brain freeze."

"No probs. Happens to me all the time. See that building?" She pointed at a grimy high-rise, barely visible in the thick fog. "That's where I live with Vlad and his dad, the Russian freaking nightmare. That one," she pointed to another hulking decrepit 70's remnant, "is where the ex-cons live. And that one over there is where the crazies live. They've got them on curfews but they always get out. Like that guy at the coffee shop giving us a hard time. I bought him food the other day and he threw it on the ground and spat on it."

What guy? I had no idea what she was talking about.

"The guy at the counter," Adam told me. He was another longstanding member of the Watchers. I liked him because he looked like a young Rob Lowe, right out of St. Elmo's Fire. "Looked like a homeless guy."

"Vulnerably housed," I corrected him. It was all coming back to me. "And we shouldn't say crazies. We should say cognitively impaired."

Angel gave me a sideways glance. She was driving with one hand, eating with the other and she didn't comment on my random outburst.

Jamie was right. I had to get a grip. I sometimes spoke out loud when I didn't mean to.

"Sometimes I say odd stuff," I said to Angel. "Too much rattling around in my brain."

She shrugged, her mouth full of sandwich. She mumbled something that sounded like "Don't worry, it's all good."

Which is what people have been telling me my whole life. Along with relax, and my own personal favourite: "It's only as hard as you make it. Take it easy. Chill."

Along with "breathe." As if we have any choice when it comes to breathing.

Angel had said she wasn't hungry, couldn't eat in front of people but then she ordered half the takeout menu and it took forever for the servers to prepare because they were more focused on the drive-through crowd.

We pulled up in front of the school.

I eyed the Adult X movie store that flanked the college. Bars on the windows no less.

"Living the dream," I sighed and Angel nodded.

I glumly eyed the hallowed halls of our education. *StudyRite College. Turn your life around! Healthcare, Paralegal, Office Admin, Police Foundations.*

"I thought this course would be a walk in the park," I admitted.

"You and me both, bud." Angel was chowing her way through a doughnut. "I figured we'd have lessons on spoon-feeding cereal to old people and that would be that."

Meanwhile, our textbook was the size of a vintage phone book. Just lugging it around was going to give me an aneurysm. We had a ten-chapter weekly exam and two written assignments, as well as group assignments which were the absolute pits. Anatomy, Common Diseases and Disorders, Preventing Infection, Skin Care and Wound Prevention, Medical Terminology and Body Mechanics were just some of the highlights.

"In we go." I reached to open the car door, but of course, there was no handle. I was instantly soaked in sweat and my heart did the hundred-mile dash in my rib cage. *Hello claustrophobia, my old friend.* "Hey, how do I open the car door again? Hey Angel? The door?" I sounded frantic.

She smiled and leaned over me. "Push the button at the end of the wire."

The door popped open.

"Thanks," I said sheepishly.

"Cool, man. Okay, let's get back to Medication Administration and Assisting the Community."

We got out of the car and Angel slammed the door shut.

She gazed out into the thick fog. "Like a frickin' smoke machine. That's how my brain used to feel. Nice and cottony." She sighed. "Being sober sucks large." She sounded sad. "I miss my druggy days,"

"Yeah, me too."

I didn't tell Angel that I was still pretty druggy, what with my tranquillizers and self-medicating opioids. I had gotten good at working various doctors for various scripts but that was a secret I didn't intend to share.

The college windows were covered with giant murals of oversized people; a ten-foot-tall police officer, a woman grinning in a nurse's uniform, and a smug man in a business suit, his arms folded.

I pushed the college door open. "Do they even have a Police Foundations course here anymore?"

"I doubt it," Angel said. "It's a cool room though. All that equipment. Body belts, handcuffs. I wish we had our classes there. Hey, did you get your police clearance yet?"

"Yeah. I submitted all my records. You?"

By this time, Angel and I had reached the lab, a generous word to describe the low-ceilinged room with two ancient hospital beds and a hoarder's paradise of broken medical equipment.

A 60's mannequin lay on one of the beds, staring up at the ceiling. He weighed several tons and was an odd shade of tangerine. He was our mock patient, only we didn't call them patients, we called them clients. A creepy infant was propped at his feet and I swear the ugly little critter was Rosemary's baby, the real deal.

"Nope. Because of the arrest," Angel whispered to me. "I'm stalling the college because I'm trying to get the charges dropped. That resisting arrest stuff."

"Can you get charges dropped?"

"You two! Stop talking! Enough!" Suraya pointed the finger of shame at us. "Time to do group work. I'll assign partners. Begin the assignment and ask me if you have any questions."

"Yeah, and then you bite our heads off for taking you away from Tik Tok," Angel muttered.

"No white people with white people," Suraya glared at Angel and me. "You need to mingle, develop your cultural competence."

She put me with a large guy called Miguel who had been a nurse's aid in Mexico. He was just there to get his accreditation. Miguel had a real chip on his shoulder, he didn't think he should have to do any schoolwork, just be handed his diploma and sent on his way. He'd told me he was the baby of the family, had twelve sisters who all fed him and were upset if he didn't eat. I liked Miguel well enough but he wasn't great at teamwork.

I looked over at Angel who was with Wendy, a twenty-something single mom of two kids who never said a word, and Jazdeep, a prim woman with a glittering headscarf. Angel swore that Jazdeep cheated on the exams, unfailingly getting a hundred percent. I agreed. My theory was that Suraya gave her the answers in advance but we couldn't prove anything.

"Come on Miguel, what are some barriers to people accessing palliative care?" I asked him and he looked confused.

"They're disappointed?"

"Disappointed? In what?" I was exhausted. I'd signed up for an online course and I was happy to hang out in my tiny basement apartment and listen to Suraya bitch at us while I studied up a storm. But since I was the only one actually paying any attention, the campus director switched us to in-person and I had no choice to but clock in at the strip mall and do my time.

"You don't belong in that dive." My Watchers weren't happy, Jamie and Cynthia in particular.

"Don't touch anything," Cynthia told me. "Hand sanitize constantly."

Worse than the rundown nature of the school, was the journey it took me to get there. Two buses and two trains. The early-bird trains were full of unhoused people squeezed uncomfortably across three tiny seats, their faces covered with threadbare jackets or moth-eaten blankets.

"Disappointed in themselves," Miguel muttered in answer to my question and he slumped down in his chair, staring at his chest.

Tears welled up in my eyes. I looked at the wheelchair with mismatched footrests, each pointing in a different direction. At the ten-ton tangerine mannequin, who was impervious to my anguish.

The fading anatomy posters were half kilter, falling off the walls, and the whiteboard was covered with indecipherable scribbles, RUF and DAF.

I reached into my candy tin and chewed a couple of codeine and a Xanax.

I finished our group assignment. Miguel was fast asleep, his head on his massive chest.

"It's break time," Angel announced.

Suraya grunted and didn't look up from her phone. "You've got forty minutes."

Angel and I headed for the disused Police Foundations room.

Angel tried on some body armor. "Cool," she said. "I shoulda done this course. Or maybe be a mortician. I like dead people."

"I don't think they do the police one anymore." I pointed to the whiteboard with faded notes from 2003.

Angel giggled. "This reminds me of the first time I got arrested. I was just a kid. I thought the cop's gear was so cool. I kept trying to tell her I wanted to be her but I was so messed up, I couldn't talk and I kept trying to punch her."

"What were you arrested for that time?" I asked her.

She shrugged. "Took a bunch of stuff from Walmart. Shoved it under my hoodie. Like they'd even miss it. I was pretty out of it. It was kinda fun." She grinned. "They said I was a little hellcat."

I rubbed my face. My chemical cocktail made me sleepy. "I want to go home," I said. "I'm so tired. We don't get anything done here, they just give us one break after another. Then I waste two hours getting home. I'm losing so much studying time."

Angel yawned. "Yeah, I'm whacked too. Work's killing me."

In addition to school, Angel worked the 6 p.m. to 2 a.m. shift at a sports bar.

"How's life at the pool hall? I could never work your hours."

"Not great. Last night this guy robbed me of $1400. I was so mad."

I sat up and I felt my Watchers sit up too.

"Angel! What the heck? Do you know who did it?"

"Yeah, some loser. A drunk who comes in and sits there all night. Boyfriend of one of the other waitresses."

"If you know who it was, can you get your money back?"

"Nah." She yawned. "Number One rule of the White Horse Pool Bar and Gaming Club: *We are not responsible for any loss or thefts suffered around the premises.*"

She pushed an old keyboard off the desk and rested her head on her arms.

"My boss has got a mega safe full of cash," she mumbled. "We all know it's there. He keeps the key on a big gold chain around his neck."

I went very still.

"Like how much money?" I kept my voice casual. "Angel?"

But Angel was asleep.

-.-

Five months later.

I was sitting in my usual corner at the White Horse Pool Hall, studying for the final provincial exam. I'd aced all the college exams, with an average of ninety-seven percent. Jazdeep had got a hundred for everything.

Angel had long since dropped out but I still liked hanging around with her. I liked the pool hall. The clack of balls, the smell of chalk, the black walls, the black-out blinds.

I liked not having to take two buses and two trains and lose two hours of my studying time.

And, most of all, I liked being around real people. My Watchers were my guardian angels but they weren't a substitute for the flesh and blood of flawed mankind.

Worse than the loss of money and power from my former life, was the tsunami of obliterating loneliness that shoved itself down my throat every single day.

So lonely I could die.

When I was on top of the world, I took the power and the glory to bed with me every night instead of Prince Charming and a happy-ever-after. And it was enough, until it was gone, like used rosewater bathwater down the drain, leaving nary a trace.

The day Miguel fell asleep, his head on his massive chest, I went to the White Horse Pool Hall with Angel and that's when I met her boss, Julius Gaultieri.

I took an instant like to him, and him to me, which was the craziest, most wonderful thing of all.

Julius was surrounded by bodyguards and ladies pumped with Botox, their balloon boobs at odds with their skinny arms, gold chains resting on sun-damaged skin, their Marge Simpson beehives thinning and tired.

I sensed an attraction the moment Julius shook my hand and he took his time letting go.

Julius was six-foot-four and two hundred pounds, with a long goatee. He was pushing sixty-five, muscle-bound and weathered, and he had a kickboxing dojo in the back room. A bad boy with more than a few miles on the clock.

"Definitely slumming it," my Watchers were not impressed. Jamie muttered and shook his head and Cynthia left the audience in disgust. On the plus side, she was replaced by a Brad Pitt look-a-like, high from his Fight Club heyday.

"Julius is cool," he told me. "But you do know you can't trust him, right?"

Julius liked me to watch him box and I liked it too. He didn't hold back and there was something pure and visceral about his methodology.

What he didn't know was that back in the day, I was a black-belt karateka. I was kick ass until I fractured my back, taken down in a bad throw from some Taekwondo show-off guy who was twice my size. I never forgave the guy for that and when I heard he blew his knee out just before the World Cup, something inside me smiled.

I hadn't trained in years and it turned out, I'd missed it. Being on the mat with Julius reminded me of who I once was. Who I could be again, albeit a weaker, older version. But I didn't let the other guys see me giving it a go. It was just between Julius and me.

When I met Julius, I told him that the commute to the school was taking a toll.

"You know any apartments I could rent nearby?" I asked. "I've got to get through this course and I can't waste all this time on buses and trains. I don't have a lease on my current place, it's just week-to-week cash."

"I can help you." He put his arm around me and I leaned in. The Botox ladies had vanished, like last week's dandruff.

Julius showed me a bachelor apartment in the low-rise above the pool hall.

It was a monk's closet with a pullout sofa bed and two soaped-up windows. The kitchen was nothing more than a microwave on a shelf with a tiny walk-in shower, and a toilet. It was beautiful.

"It's perfect. How much?"

"It's on me. Consider me your scholarship mentor. You can stay as long as you like," Julius told me. "You know why?"

"Why?" I asked him, my face close to his chest, inhaling his spicy aftershave.

"Because you're pretty. You're a real pretty lady."

It was nice to be admired again.

Julius was surrounded by his bouncers. They doubled as his sparring partners, and I could tell they didn't trust me.

"You got balls, babe," Julius said after he learned how Angel and I met. "Studying so hard. At your age. A woman like you shouldn't have to work. And a nurse's aid. You were somebody. A hotshot. You should be somebody again. I looked you up online. You were at the Oscars and everything. And now you're here, in my bar, living upstairs from me."

"I'm just an old fart, and all the magazines have died," I shrugged. "It is what it is."

"I hate it when people say that," Julius told me. "It's not true. It is what you make it to be. You want another shot of Fireball?"

"You know what Julius? I'd like a rum and coke." Julius reminded me of my first true love. He made me feel young again.

"Rum and coke for the lady."

My Watchers shifted in their seats, muttering their discontent.

"What?" I asked them.

"You know what," Tyler said. He was a smart-ass kid who showed up a few years back. "You're playing with fire. That's what."

"I'm cool," I told him.

"Yeah, you are, babes," Julius came back and handed me my drink. "But don't talk to yourself out loud. Makes you look like a fruitcake, okay?"

"Got it. I'm worn out is all. All this studying."

"You got this. You can play nurse with me after you graduate," Julius joked.

He stroked my hair and I closed my eyes. It felt good when he touched me.

I was so into him but I admitted the truth to myself.

More than anything, I wanted the cash from his safe and a life far away in a place where the sun burned away the ever-present fog and there were no stained concrete high-rises, just adobe clay as far as the eye could see. Blue sky, green grass, and me in a yellow sun dress with red flowers.

But before that, I wanted my diploma. It had come to be everything to me, to learn every single page of that medical telephone directory. I wanted to pass my exam.

I knew that my former glam pals, the ones who were still hanging out with Dior and Chanel at Paris Fashion Week, would sneer at my new life but I didn't care. I took pride in the fact that I could do this hard-core thing and one day, they'd need people just like me, and then who'd be on top?

I'd traded in couture for navy blue polyester viscose health care scrubs, non-skid ugly black shoes, and no makeup, my hair tied back.

"You don't need to prove anything to the people of your past," Tyler said. "You do you, girl."

The only thorn in my side was Antonio Marcelli, an egg-headed man, and Julius's right-hand guy.

"I don't like people who show up outa nowhere and rely on Jules' hospitality," he said.

"I'm a friend of Angel's and I didn't show up out of nowhere," I retorted.

"Yeah. Angel. Wingnut. Not surprised she dropped outta school."

And you, Tony, I wanted to ask, *what have you done that's so special?* But I eyed the bulge in his pocket and kept my mouth shut. Tony liked nothing more than to flash his piece at the ladies and I didn't want his Glock staring me in the face.

"He's running drugs behind Julius's back," Angel told me one night. "Julius would kill him if he knew. I can't prove anything but watch him. Too much handshaking."

"Julius would notice that."

Angel shrugged. "Julius is getting tired. And anyway, everyone's running a game. The people at the pool tables. People dealing out back in the parking lot. Julius, he's got deals going for sure too but he's into real estate, big money. Back door deals, lining politicians' pockets, and getting building permits for his buddies. Who in turn, fill his safe with greenbacks. This place is just a front for him. Meanwhile Tony and his goons are the scary monsters and they're getting greedy. Those guys. No matter how much money they have, they want more. More power. Tony wants to be king of the castle. Be careful of them." She leaned against the wall and rubbed her calves and ankles. "My feet are killing me."

"The only way out is through," I told her. "One tired foot in front of the other."

"If you could go anywhere in the world, where would you go?" Angel yawned. "I'd go to LA. Be a movie star. Or a stunt double. I bet I could do it. Kick ass big time. Show the world my stuff."

"I'd go to Taos, New Mexico," my answer was immediate. "Flowers in the desert that will blow your mind. I did a shoot there. I always said I'd go back one day."

"And I better get back to my tables or Tony will have my ass," Angel gave Tony the finger. He shook his head and drew his hand across his throat.

I went back to my books and Angel scuttled back to collect her trays.

I stared at the medical maths on the page. "Acetaminophen 500mg tablets i to ii po q4h prn. How many milligrams in two tablets?"

Never mind that. How many tablets in Julius' drink would knock him out cold?

And what about my grand old getaway? How would I orchestrate that?

And of course, there was Tony. The Berlin Wall I would have to break down before I could get to the safe.

My textbook swirled in front of my eyes. 1000 mg. That was the answer but what about Julius and the rest of my life?

His office was out of bounds, even for me. I'd only been in there once with him, to get the key for my apartment.

The place was Pukka gangster, all black walls and red velvet sofas and Julius sat behind a massive walnut desk under a framed picture of a British fox hunt.

I wondered if the safe was behind the painting. I couldn't ask Angel because Angel couldn't keep things to herself. She'd tell her drunken boyfriend, Vlad, and he'd tell Julius and I'd be out on my ass.

I had seen the key around Julius's neck. He wore it even when he boxed bare-chested, and it glinted and shone and I wasn't the only one looking at it.

I saw Tony, his eyes on the grand prize.

Angel was right. Things weren't good between Julius and Tony and I knew it was only a matter of time before Tony made his move to take the throne.

But I had to get there first.

Timing was everything.

First, I had to pass my exam. "No-More-Cough Syrup. 15 mL po TID prn. If one teaspoon is 5 mL, how many teaspoons should this person take?"

The answer was three teaspoons.

After my exam, I'd figure out how to make my move.

-.-

Three weeks later, I passed my final exam. All my studying had paid off.

No more Suraya, no more strip mall college at the end of the world.

The school closed down while we took our final exam. They lugged the broken vending machine past our door while I was logging in my final answer. The police foundations room was gone like it never existed. I wished I'd taken a bunch of stuff but instead, it just got thrown out. The ten-ton tangerine mannequin ended up face down in a dumpster and Jazdeep took the creepy infant home with her.

When I packed up my pencil case for the last time, the only thing left in the place was a tired old dirty Raggedy Ann doll on the floor of the empty cafeteria.

I picked her up and threw her in the wash cycle back at the White Horse Pool Bar. Everybody deserved to be saved, even a sad old doll. Especially a sad old doll.

I was sitting at the bar, drinking a double rum and coke, listening to Angel yell at Vlad. She said she was tired of cleaning up after his old man and she was tired of driving that beat-up old car. She was twenty-two and her life was in the crapper.

Angel had been with Vlad since she was fifteen. She said Vlad wasn't always a drunk, but the meaner his dad got, the more Vlad drank.

I hopped off the barstool. Time for a washroom visit. Always a treat to see the poster: *Wish You'd Pooped Before Leaving Home?* An ad for a high-fibre laxative.

I was a bit unsteady getting off the stool. Must have had one rum and coke too many. And it was still early in the evening.

"Yeah, you gotta ease up," Jamie the Watcher commented. "You're out of control, Eloise."

Cynthia was still nowhere to be seen.

"I'm entitled to celebrate," I slurred, and I got my foot caught in the rung of the stool and I slid to the ground.

"If you can call it that," Jamie sighed. "I'm not going to pull any punches. This is pathetic."

I was about to retort when I heard Tyler yelling at me. He was frantic.

"Ellie! Girl, look under the bar."

I was on my hands and knees, about to clamber back up the barstool.

"Wha?" I mumbled and that's when I saw it.

Julius's necklace. The one with the key.

Was I imagining it? Because I wanted it so much?

I reached out my hand and grabbed it and oh, it was real all right.

"Little girl had a bit too much to drink?" Tony suddenly loomed above me.

I closed my fist around the key and the thick gold chain.

How had it got there? How come Julius didn't notice it was gone? It was his necklace for sure.

"Celebrating my exam score," I said to Tony, hauling myself up. "Proud of myself."

I shoved the necklace into my pocket.

"Does that mean you'll be leaving us soon? Since you don't need to be close to that school no more."

"I like it here." I stood up straight. "And I like Julius."

Tony laughed and it wasn't a nice laugh.

"You got your eggs in the wrong basket," he leered. "But I'm not interested in your eggs anyway. Once I'm in charge, you're out on the street."

Where was Julius anyway? It was odd that I hadn't seen him that night.

Tony left to go hang out with his bully boys, and I rushed to the washroom as fast as my wobbly legs could carry me.

The fright of the whole thing cleared my head and I studied the key as soon as I locked myself in the stall.

It was Julius's key.

Had Tony gotten into a fight with Julius? But the first thing Tony would have done was grab the key.

I shoved it deep into my pocket, flushed, and left the stall.

I was washing my hands when Angel walked in. She was crying.

"Oh, honey. Vlad?"

She nodded and I hugged her. She was so small. "I'm never gonna leave this dump," she sobbed. "I shoulda done the course with you. You can get a real job now. I'm stuck here."

"Angel," my tone was urgent. "Have you seen Julius?"

She shook her head. "He's not out back, boxing?"

"Nope. He always comes and gets me, to watch. And Tony's acting weird."

"Tony was born weird. Anyway, Julius' BMW SUV is in the parking lot," Angel said. "He must be here somewhere."

She sank to the floor and hugged her knees to her chest. Not a great idea since the floor was sticky and crusty with who knew what.

I crouched down next to her. "I think maybe Tony got rid of Julius."

She sat up, her face wet with tears.

"No way!" She paused. "But yeah, maybe way. That's what Vlad and I were arguing about. He said I'd better start being nice to Tony and I said I had Julius and he said Julius was like Rome, burned to the ground, ancient history."

"Yeah, except Rome's still a thing," I said. "Angel, I'm going back to the bar. Come serve me, but you go barside and tell me if it looks like there was a fight."

"What?" Angel shook her head. "This night is too weird," She blew her nose. "Okay, sure."

"But don't make a big thing of it, okay?"

We went back. I climbed on my stool, and Angel mixed my drink, bopping around this way and that in time to the music, her big blue eyes focused.

"Yeah, something happened here," She whispered to me. "Broken glass has been swept into a pile and Julius's La Santa gold flake tequila bottle is broken and on the floor. Oh, man. Do you think Julius is dead?"

Her eyes were wide. "What do we do now?"

"We get through the night," I said. "Keep it together. We'll figure things out later."

I stared into the lime and soda Angel had poured for me.

"You gals having a hen party or what?" Tony showed up and glared at Angel. "You, get back on the floor. And you, enjoy getting off your face while you can. Open bar is closed to you starting tomorrow. You got nothing I want."

What to do? I watched the bubbles gather on the lemon slice and tried to come up with a plan.

Whatever had gone down, had happened before the White Horse opened for the night.

By 1 a.m. the joint was still jumping and Angel looked ready to fall over.

Tony looked worse for wear. He'd been celebrating the coup d'état big time and he and his bully boys looked pretty wobbly.

I still thought it was odd that Tony hadn't thought about the key when he attacked Julius. Surely it would have been the first thing he'd take off Julius's body?

I made a quick visit up to my apartment. My feel-good candy tin had just what I needed. I crushed a bunch of sleeping pills into a fine powder along with half a dozen Xanax.

Tony and the boys had switched to Fireball shots.

I waited until the bartender went to the washroom and I rushed around the bar.

I poured a round of shots of Fireball, quickly sprinkling a good dose of meds into all five shots. Then I poured one extra and made note of where it was on the tray.

"Got you guys a round on me," I said brightly, taking it to Tony who was sprawled on a leather sofa at the back of the pool hall.

"Dumb broad, it's all on me," Tony muttered. "But yeah, whatever."

I passed around the drinks, grabbing mine first. "Sláinte!" I knocked mine back, smiling inwardly as Tony and the bully boys did the same.

By 2 a.m. they were passed out cold.

No one gave them a second glance and the pool hall slowly emptied, making way for the late shift cleaners.

One of whom was Julius' cousin. If there was one person who'd have the combination to Julius's office, it would be Tina Marie.

"Tina Marie, I think something's happened to Julius," I said urgently. "Let me into his office. He might be in there, in trouble."

Her jaw dropped open. "No wonder these goons partied so hard. I told Jules to watch his back. No way am I going in there. I don't want to see nuthin'. You go. Leave me out of it."

"What's the combination?"

"19590607. His birthday." She shrugged. "I told him to come up with something more creative but you don't tell Julius nothin'."

She started vacuuming around Tony and the bully boys' feet.

Angel had left, supporting a belligerent Vlad who was muttering invectives under his breath. Angel deserved so much better but she'd never leave Vlad.

"He's going to make things right," she'd told me. "It's him and me. We've been together since I was fifteen. He wasn't always a drunk. And," she'd looked around quickly. "he's getting in with Julius' real estate pals, debt collecting. He's on his way up." So much for that.

I shot around to the office. I was sure Tony and the boys would be out for hours but I was frantic about Julius.

The combination Tina Marie gave me worked.

I entered the room and closed the door behind me.

The room was empty. Where was Julius?

I took the painting off the wall and sure as eggs were eggs, the safe was there.

I unlocked it, grabbed a gym bag, and stuffed it full of cash. It filled the whole thing. I also found a bunch of gold coins and a diamond necklace. I crammed it all in and scanned the desk for Julius's car keys.

I was in luck and I pocketed the keys.

And there was Julius' laptop. With all security camera footage, although the cameras were mainly for show anyway.

I straightened up, about to leave when I heard a laugh.

I shot up, my eyes wide and my heart galloping in my chest.

It was one of Tony's bully boys, a guy in mid-sixties, a nasty piece of work.

"Think you're so clever," he sneered. "I knew that if you were offering a drink it was spiked. I wanted to see what you'd do. Nasty little girl, you are."

I edged around the desk. I knew he had a gun, they all carried.

But what Rocco didn't know was that I was ready for him. I was ready for any of them. I'd studied all the men when they boxed, made a note of all their weak spots.

I knew that Rocco left himself open to an uppercut to the jaw every single time, and all I had to do was feint a jab to this face, wait for him to raise his arms in defense, and then wham, slam his nose up into his brain.

Julius' private lessons were about to pay off.

I undid my belt and wrapped it around my right hand, to protect my knuckles. Rocco saw me do it and he chuckled.

"Bring it on, sugar pie, bring it on."

I got into a sparring stance and bopped around a bit and Rocco laughed uproariously like I was the funniest thing he'd ever seen.

He didn't think it was so funny when I slammed his one eye shut.

He stopped laughing and he straightened up and called me a bunch of ugly names.

"Now you've done it," he said. "Time to put your lights out, little girl."

He came at me and I feinted and jabbed and whoa, there he was, just like I predicted, raising his hands, leaving his face open. I slammed my whole body into the uppercut with the exact desired effect.

He dropped like a stone.

I ran over, locked the safe, and put the painting back. I bent down and put the necklace in Rocco's hand, then I rushed out and slammed the door shut.

There was no one around and the only sound was Tina Marie vacuuming. She and her crew were down at the far end of the pool hall, and they never saw me leave.

I found Julius's car and although I hadn't driven in years, I got it going just fine.

The fog was still thick as pea soup and the roads were empty that time of night.

And there, on the big screen, just like the Truman Show, I watched myself driving down the highway, heading to Taos, New Mexico.

"What about Angel?" Tyler wanted to know.

I thought about Angel. Somehow, whenever she had money, it trickled through her fingers like water. And would she ever leave Vlad? I didn't think she would. Angel was like a beautiful damaged little doll but she was too far gone for me to rescue. She was a wild card and sooner or later, she'd get me into trouble if I took her with me.

"Now at least you can afford to buy some new clothes," Cynthia had returned. "Be fabulous again. About time."

"You know something," I said to Cynthia. "I'm going to be a nurse's aid. I'm over the moon that I won't ever have to worry about money again but I want to put my training to good use. I like to work hard. So that's what I'm gonna do and you can like it or lump it."

Jamie didn't approve of what had gone down. "The cops could tie this back to you. You were living in one of Julius's apartments and now you've vanished."

"Without so much as one single paper trail," I reminded him. "None of those guys knew my full name. I cleaned out my room. I wiped down the safe. I'll change the plates of this car in a Walmart parking lot. I've thought of everything. Everything about the pool hall was a grift. The cops will never prove anything. For the most part, they probably don't want to."

I waited for my audience to tell me where I'd gone wrong but they were silent.

"Yeah, not bad," Jamie admitted.

"You did great!" The Brad Pitt look-a-like grinned at me and gave me a salute, spilling some popcorn. "Kicked some butt! You carped the diem!"

"Aw, you guys!" I felt a big smile cross my face and all the pent-up worry left my chest.

Me and my gang were heading for some sunshine. Better days lay ahead.

And when I reached Taos, the biggest of my dreams came true.

"You did it, gorgeous! I'm so proud of you!"

It was Julius. He looked mighty fine in his brightly-coloured open shirt and straw hat with a black band.

I handed him the gym bag. "Just like you said," I told him. "In the end, it wasn't Tony who came for me but Rocco. I put the necklace in his hand, just like you told me to."

"You were ready for any of them! The cops will never solve it, they won't even try. Too many fingers in too many pies, that's what. This will be quietly forgotten and we'll get on with our lives. Come on, let's get you settled. There's a deck chair with your name on it, next to the swimming pool, with a big rum and coke."

Later, I drifted off in the shade of the umbrella, with the sparkling water glittering like diamonds next to me.

But when I woke up, the deck chair next to me was empty, and there was no trace of Julius. No towel, no pulp fiction paperback novel, no gold-flaked tequila.

I sat up in horror. Had he taken the money and ditched me?

"I'm right here, gorgeous," I heard his voice and I closed my eyes.

Oh, no!

Julius was in the movie theatre, along with the other Watchers.

Out of everything that happened to me, what was real?

And now I'd lost my happy-ever-after. I felt like crying.

"Oh, come on," Cynthia was scathing. "You like to be alone. And you've got us. You can't handle being with anyone real for the long haul. You know that."

I sank down in my chair just as the sun ducked behind a single cloud.

Alone again.

"You can always rely on us," Jamie reassured me.

"And got me, babe," Julius said. *"I'm never gonna leave you."*

But still, I was real-life alone again.

"Hey Ella Bella!"

I swung around. What the heck? Angel?

Yep, it was her. Wearing a tiny pink mini skirt and a yellow cropped fringe top, with white sunglasses and stacked glittery sandals.

On the one hand, I was delighted to see her. On the other, I was horrified.

I suddenly realized that being alone maybe hadn't been the worst thing in the world.

What had she figured out? What proof did she have? Who else knew where to find me?

"Taos, New Mexico," she laughed. "You figured I'd forgotten about Taos? I don't forget anything."

She lay down in Julius's deck chair, stretched out, and yawned. "Sun feels great."

What did she know about what had gone down? I was terrified of opening my mouth for fear of giving my role in the whole escapade away.

"Just SHUT UP," Jamie yelled at me. *"Don't say a thing. Not one single thing."*

"Hey Angel," I said quietly. And I left it at that.

She didn't say anything for a while either but eventually, she couldn't help herself.

"They arrested Vlad. First-degree murder." She turned to me, her Lolita sunglasses low on her nose. "I know he didn't have the balls to kill anyone. Plus, they never found Julius' body." She blinked slowly. "And Julius' car went missing, so some people figured he emptied the safe and decked Rocco because he got in the way. Then Julius rode off into the sunset, along with his girlfriend who showed up out of nowhere and vanished into nowhere, the exact same time he did."

She paused and I stared straight ahead. *Anything you say, can and will be used against you.* So I didn't say a word. I did, however, give a slight shrug.

But something occurred to me, and I had to ask the question. "If they had no body and no evidence, how did they convict Vlad?"

"They found Julius' bloody necklace with the key under Vlad's mattress. Along with a piece of paper that had the combination to Julius' office. Vlad's fingerprints all over everything."

"Circumstantial at best," I commented.

"Hmmm. Yeah, but after some persuasive questioning, Vlad admitted that he remembered hitting Julius but then he had one of his blackouts and couldn't remember anything else. Which they took to be a confession. And Tony's got the cops in his pocket, so voila, end of story for Vlad."

"So Tony's theory is that Vlad killed Julius, decked Rocco and took the money?"

"Yeah. He claims Vlad hid the money and can't remember where. That's a lot to expect from a guy who struggles to put on his shoes when he's on a bender."

"And what's Rocco saying?" I asked carefully, keeping my voice even.

"He said Vlad hit him six ways to Sunday. He said that him and the boys got blasted and he can't remember much of anything, but he did say Vlad was in the office and he surprised him, and Vlad hit him with a tire iron. Another nail in Vlad's coffin."

"Tony went to a lot of trouble to set Vlad up," I said. "Why didn't he just go along with the theory that Julius took the money and ran?"

She leaned forward. "Because he knows Julius is dead. He killed him. He wants things nice and tidy. If people think that maybe Julius is wandering around somewhere in a sombrero and could come back at any time, then Tony won't be king of the world. And Tony wants to be king of the world more than anything."

She sighed. "Truth is, Vlad's a mean drunk and by doing all this, Tony helped me out. I'd never have left him. Vlad got what he deserved, being locked away. Even though he didn't kill Julius, he treated me like crap, living off me all these years. They put his dad in a long-term care home." She pushed her glasses up her nose and sat back. "End of story. Meanwhile, you ghosted me, but I knew I could find you."

"And find you, I did. Sisters, right?" She held out her hand and I fist-bumped her.

"Sisters," I said faintly.

"And don't worry, I didn't tell anybody I was coming here, or where you were. I'm not stupid, Ellie."

I murmured assent, my brain going a thousand miles an hour.

I thought about the money. It was stashed in a safe place. There was no way Angel could find it. Things would be fine. We'd live under the radar, a quiet life.

Well, I would, anyway.

I watched Angel's feet bumping together in an ever increasing rhythm. She'd been there for all of ten minutes and she was already jonesing for a disaster.

"I mean this is cool and all that," she said, "but it's also kinda boring."

"Which is exactly what I want," I was brusque and to the point. "I applied for a job at the local clinic and I start on Monday."

"Which gives us three days to party before you clock in for your first shift." She sat up and pumped her fist in the air. "We gotta fight, for our right, to PARTTTTYYY!"

"I don't even need to tell you how bad this is," Cynthia was disapproving.

"Angel." My tone left no room for argument. "I am here to serve, to help, to heal. I never liked partying. Um," I suggested, "maybe you can give LA a try? Big parties there, I hear. You wanted to be a movie star, or stunt double, right?"

"Nah, I like being with you, sister," she grinned at me and I realized she needed a fair bit of dental work.

"Calm down," Jamie told me. "There's nothing she can do. Just ignore her and she'll get bored and leave."

"Did I ever tell you about the time I robbed a liquor store?" Angel yawned. "That was a total high." She laughed and got up, adjusting her sandals. "I can't just sit here."

"Angel," I said nervously. "I don't want any trouble. No shoplifting, no liquor store holdups. Okay? Promise me."

"Pinky swear!" she gave a deep laugh. "Trust me, Ella Bella, trust me."

She clattered off in shoes two sizes too big, stopping to chat up a bearded guy in Harley leathers.

I gritted my teeth.

"She's okay" A little boy said and I shot up in horror. It was Charlie, the dead boy from the swimming pool. "She pretends to love the drama but she just wants to be loved."

And you know because? I asked him.

He laughed. "I've watched the world for half a century, Eloise. Dead people know stuff. In reality, she's just a kid looking for a family. You don't have to worry about her."

I hoped he was right. I turned around and Angel was watching me, grinning and pointing. Come to think of it, the Harley dude was kinda handsome.

"We'll figure it out," Brad Pitt said. "Don't worry. We've got your back, just like always."

He was right. Things would be fine. No matter what, I had my Watchers, and they'd see me through to the very end, until the credits ran.

It also didn't hurt that I had Julius's Glock in my purse, fully loaded. I'd found it in the glove box of the SUV.

I'd finally found my piece of paradise and nothing and no one was going to ruin what I'd worked so hard to achieve.

I lay back and closed my eyes. I was, finally, living the dream. I thought about my so-called friends from my past life. They seemed like faded photographs in a scrapbook that once mattered to me more than anything. I pictured myself throwing the worn-out old album into a dumpster and my heart soared with freedom.

"I'll drink to that," I said, sitting up and reaching for my rum and coke.

"Babes!" Julius was horrified. "I told ya, don't talk out loud!"

I chuckled and nodded.

"This is Bobby," Angel arrived, breathless with excitement. "He owns a bar and he's going to give me a job."

"Nice to meet you," Bobby sat down on the deck chair next to me and extended a hand. "You can come by anytime you like, drinks on me. Pretty ladies add some class to the place."

His hand felt good in mine and he winked at me.

I sucked in my belly a bit and sat up straighter.

"Thank you kind sir," I said and for the first time in my life, I felt a new feeling in my chest.

It was hope. And I liked it.

ABOUT THE AUTHOR

Lisa de Nikolits has been hailed as "the Queen of Canadian speculative fiction" [All Lit Up] and her short fiction and poetry have been published in various international anthologies and journals including the Crime Writers of Canada's 40th Anniversary anthology (2022).

Originally from South Africa, Lisa is an award-winning author of eleven published novels. *Everything You Dream is Real* is her most recent book. Her work has appeared on recommended reading lists for CBC Books, the Quill & Quire, Open Book Toronto, The Miramichi Reader and the 49th Shelf, as well as being a *Chatelaine* Editor's Pick and a *Canadian Living Magazine* Must Read.

She has a Bachelor of Arts in English Literature and Philosophy and has lived in the U.S.A., Australia, and Britain. Previous works include *No Fury Like That* (published in Italian, under the title *Una furia dell'altro mondo*, in 2019 by Edizione Le Assassine). Lisa lives and writes in Toronto. To learn more about her books, please visit her website: https://www.lisawriter.com/

STORY INSPIRATION

At first, I struggled to come up with an idea for the anthology. When that happens, I let my subconscious do the heavy lifting and it came to me that when I was about six, I was the child on my father's shoulders, looking over the neighbour's fence, and the boy had drowned in the swimming pool. And shortly after that, I went to 'play Mass' with my sister in the garage, with my gran's lawn bowling trophies. And I felt like we were being watched, just like the Watchers in the story. It was something I hadn't thought about – or even remembered – in over fifty years. I love that about writing and I love that about my brain. It's a treasure trove to be mined. Also, I've recently switched from many years as a graphic designer to studying to become a nurse's aide, and of course, I had to use that! But the rest of it is all fiction and my Watchers only featured in my life that one time and all my characters in the story are fictional.

Son-ja's Journey

Diana McCollum

CHAPTER ONE

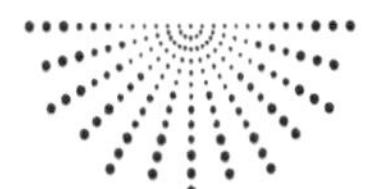

1852 Arizona

Son-ja ran along the edge of the great water. Fringe on her doeskin dress flapped around her legs. She was late. Grandfather Owl would not be happy. Grandfather was a shaman to the tribe. Many said he was past his usefulness. They believed his decisions lately had brought evil upon their tribe of cave dwellers.

Son-ja had been singled out by Raven, the tribe's new chief, to meet with the shaman. She was to bring back news on the condition of the elderly shaman. Why she was chosen for this task, she didn't know.

She changed course into the woods. When she reached the clearing she could see smoke rising from in front of the shaman's cave. She slowed to a walk, patted her hair, and ran her hands down her dress, smoothing it. She stepped into the clearing. Kneeling in front of the fire, she waited. Heat from the fire felt good on this cold autumn day.

Hearing the rustle of footsteps, Son-ja looked up to see Grandfather Owl shuffling to the fire where he sat on a stump of oak. He laid his staff across his lap. Feathers of the staff blew gently in the breeze.

"Late, again today. Why Son-ja? Did Raven detain you?" His wizened face scowled.

"No, Grandfather, it is entirely my fault for being late. I was helping prepare our evening meal." This wasn't a lie, she had chopped up turnips before going to see Raven. She had already talked with him and didn't need to see him again. There was a pull between her and Raven. He had long black hair and ebony eyes. Eyes that one could drown in. Nervous now, she picked at colored beads along the fringe of her shift.

Grandfather shifted on his stump. He tapped his staff on the ground three times. An owl glided down from a tree and landed on his shoulder. "What message do you bring me, Son-ja?"

"Raven wants to know when our enemy will attack. Losses last time were great. We lost our chief. He is not sure if our tribe can take another defeat like that one."

"Son-ja, how many seasons have you been a member of our tribe?" He pushed a long gray braid behind him.

She barely remembered when she first came to the tribe scared and hungry. Grandmother Sun had taken her in and raised her. That was…so long ago. Now Son-ja called her Mother Sun.

"Eighteen seasons have come and gone. I am a woman now, no longer the child who showed up at the evening meal begging for food." She shifted, uneasy with his question. Why did Owl not answer Raven's question?

"You have become a trusted daughter." He picked up the sage wand for cleansing. He leaned forward and dipped it into the fire, waved it around, overhead, and side to side while his owl dipped his head chortling into the Shaman's ear.

She watched as he waved the wand back and forth through the air, enthralled. She shook her head clearing it. What trick was Grandfather Owl trying to play on her? "Have you an answer for me to take to Raven?" She could feel anger beginning to rise within her. Raven expected an answer. Her people depended on the guidance Grandfather Owl would give.

He tossed the remaining wand into the fire and flame burst forth causing the owl to lift off his shoulder and land on a tree branch not far away. Grandfather's shoulders slumped. He raised clear eyes to look at her. He attempted to smile. His wizened face seemed to crack like the edge of the river during the dry season He began to chuckle and laugh. Hairs on Son-ja's arms stood up. There was magic in the old Shaman and maybe a little craziness too.

"You have no message for Raven then?" She wished she knew what to do. How could she get the old Shaman to give her a straight answer? Rising, she walked to a wood pile near the opening of the cave. Picking a medium size log, she placed it on top of the coals. "Grandfather Owl, sunlight is almost gone. I have to leave for home. Raven knows we must leave, he doesn't know which direction we should go. Surely you can tell me?"

The old shaman merely looked at her for a few minutes. Finally, she turned to walk away.

"Wait. Tell Raven to trust only those closest to him. What direction is the one he chooses, he needs to look inside and trust his instincts to be true. A wise man will take counsel from others, the decision is his alone." He started coughing and couldn't seem to stop. She brought him a gourd of water to ease his cough. "You are a good daughter of the people; I thank you for this drink." He heaved a sigh. "I will not be going with the tribe. I'm too old and move too slow. I will stay behind with my owl for protection. There is power in you too, Son-ja. You have a strength and you must trust yourself and your decisions."

Son-ja bowed. Whatever did the old shaman mean, she had power? She was not blood of the clan's blood. She didn't know where her people were from. Or how she got separated from them. She ran back toward the caves pondering what he had said, what power did she have? And how did the old man know?

Son-ja ran on stopping only to let a doe and her fawn cross her path ahead of her. Drums and chanting grew louder now, she knew she was almost home.

Raven stood with his back to the fire looking down the trail. He watched for her. She stopped and smoothed her flyaway hair down and brushed dust from her dress. When she stood in front of Raven, she bowed before looking into his eyes. He smiled that wonderful smile and her heart melted a little. She felt safe with him. The old shaman had not really given an answer which way the tribe should move.

Raven crossed his arms. "What news did Grandfather Owl impart to you?"

"'Tell Raven to trust only those closest to him. As for which direction, he needs to look inside and trust his instincts to be true. A wise man will take counsel from others, but in the end it's his decision.'" She decided to keep the part about her having power to herself for now. "He won't be moving with the tribe. He is too feeble to travel. What are you going to do?"

"I will gather all elders and two young warriors, Grandmother Sun, and a few others for a council meeting." He reached out and placed his hand on her shoulder. "You have done well, Son-ja. Your help and dedication will always be appreciated."

When he removed his hand she felt the loss. Feelings she had for him were not reciprocated. She brought her drum to the fire, sat, and stared into the flames. Finally, she began chanting. She asked in her heart that the fire god bring power within her to the surface. She chanted for knowledge, for wisdom, and for love.

Later that night, she climbed her tree where she shared a platform with her friend Sunita, Grandmother Sun's daughter. Sunita wasn't there tonight. *She's probably sharing Fox's pallet,* she thought. Son-ja fluffed up the straw and cleaned around the platform. She lay down and pulled her blanket up. Sleeping in the tree was breathtaking, millions of stars in the night sky never ceased to amaze her. Wind gently rocked the tree, and Son-ja felt her eyes drift shut.

Son-ja woke with a start. Something had disturbed her sleep. She sat listening to night sounds. A twig snapped, and then another and another after that. She wrapped her blanket around her shoulders chilled by night air and climbed down. With her back against the tree, she strained her ears, listening for any out of the ordinary sounds.

There it was again, a snap.

A cry of alarm shattered the quietness. It was the first of many cries.

Screams came.

They were under attack!

———

She ran to Fox's pallet only to find him motionless on his pallet, blood puddling around his head. "Sunita!" she whispered, as loud as she dared to not draw attention to herself. "Sunita, where are you? Where's Lucita?" Lucita was Sunita's seven-month-old daughter.

Screams and war whoops shattered the early dawn.

Son-ja ran till the woods surrounded her. She tripped over a mound. A moan of pain sounded. Gently she pushed the mound over to reveal Sunita with a gash in her head. Her wound was bleeding profusely. "Sunita! Sunita, can you hear me? Where's Lucita?" She shook her friend trying to revive her.

She heard distant mewling of a baby. Grabbing Sunita under her arms, she dragged her deeper into the woods and covered her with branches in hopes the marauders would leave her alone. She picked her way through deep underbrush until she found the baby under a bush beneath their tree. Son-ja stroked the baby's back and cooed to her until she quieted down. She made a sling and tied the baby to her back and climbed to safety.

When the sun rose high, the marauders were done with their attack. They led captured prisoners out of camp.

With Lucita tied on her back, Son-ja climbed down. She looked out across the encampment. No one stirred. Tribe members left were dead or dying. She found Sunita still alive under the bush. She dressed her wounds with herbs and water she'd brought down from the pallet.

Sunita stirred, "Lucita?"

"She's right here in a sling on my back. Do you think you can stand? We must leave this place."

Sunita sat up. "I'm a little dizzy. Is there a walking stick or staff I can use for balance?"

"I'll find one. Here, take Lucita. Give her some nourishment." Son-ja searched in the forest. Not finding a proper staff, she ventured into Mother Sun's cave which sat at the edge of camp.

The elderly woman lay in a pool of her own blood, eyes open in a death stare. Son-ja tried not to look at her. Her heart ached for this kind-hearted woman. She quickly gathered pouches of herbs, dried meats, a blanket for Sunita, and anything else that they could use in their travels. On her way out she grabbed Grandmother Sun's beaded, decorated staff. It was a staff that showed the importance of the person bearing it. She bent down and closed Grandmother Sun's eyes.

She hurried to where she'd left Sunita and Lucita. Sunita was asleep against a tree, Lucita in her lap cooing. Son-ja shook her. "Sunita, Sunita!"

"What," Sunita mumbled, then opened her eyes. "Are the warriors gone? Where is everyone?"

"Most are dead, bludgeoned to death. Half a dozen women and children were taken prisoner." Son-ja could not hold in her broken heart, tears streamed down her face. All she knew was they needed to move in the opposite direction of the enemy. Away from all they knew if they had even a slight chance at survival. There was a friendly tribe five days travel, but with Sunita wounded and a baby, it would probably take longer.

"Sunita, up, we have to move. Here I'll take Lucita and put her in the sling on my back." After the baby was in the makeshift sling, Son-ja reached for Sunita, helping her up. "Here is Grandmother's staff. It is very sturdy and will support you." She took Sunita's arm to help support her.

They hobbled along for several hours. Son-ja made camp in the shelter of an overhanging rock. She brought in pine needles for cushioning, making Sunita as comfortable as possible. Lucita slept in the crook of her mother's arm. "I'm going to scout around and find some roots. There is water down below us. I'll make a healing broth for you." Sunita didn't respond, merely closed her eyes.

The sun was low in the sky as Son-ja made her way down the hill. She gathered some roots and filled her water pouch from the small stream which eventually emptied into the river. She picked her way through the brush and stilled when she spotted a rabbit. At that moment words were carried on the breeze to her. Not her tribe. She knelt using some brush for cover and watched. Six warriors made their way along the opposite side of the river, they followed what appeared to be a trail. She had to get back to Sunita and Lucita. She didn't dare move till the strangers were out of sight.

The sun sunk behind the horizon and the warriors moved further downriver. She waited a while longer before making her way back to their rock overhang. Lucita had begun to stir. She picked Lucita up and patted her on the back, humming a song. Funny, she couldn't remember who had taught her that song. She could almost hear the words. However, words were always just out of reach.

Sunita stirred. "Water," she whispered.

Son-ja lifted her friend's head, holding the gourd of water up to her lips. Sunita's head was as hot as the rock around a fire. She wouldn't be strong enough to travel very far.

Lucita whimpered. Son-ja placed Lucita in her mother's arms. "Lucita needs to eat."

"I have no milk left." Sunita pushed Lucita towards Son-ja's lap. "Make a broth from dried meat and water. It should curb her hunger."

After Lucita was fed and lay sleeping next to her mother, Son-ja climbed to the top of the hill behind their camp. The evening sky was light with a half moon. She sat and studied the horizon in every direction. She could see where the warriors had made their camp downriver. Far upriver she could barely make out light coming from campfires. Who could that be?

CHAPTER TWO

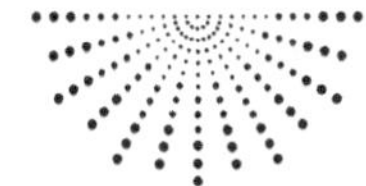

S on-ja stuck to the mountain and forest hiking towards the glimmering firelight. Finally, she could make out figures, not tribal people. White men! She had heard of these creatures. She had never seen one. She'd heard stories of encounters with white people, some bad, and some good. There were strange white huts and horses.

How would she know if these people were good or bad?

She sat till the moon waned. Soon a glorious sun would fill the sky. She hurried to get back to Sunita and Lucita.

"Sunita, Sunita, wake up!" Son-ja gently shook her. It was then Son-ja realized Sunita's spirit had left.

No, no, no not Sunita, not her sweet sister. How could she go on without Sunita? Tears ran down her face. What about Lucita, what did she know about babies? She crumpled to the ground and pulled her knees up to her chest. Her shoulders shook, as she felt her heart breaking for Sunita, for the tribe murdered, for herself.

Lucita began to cry and wave her tiny fists. Son-ja picked the babe up, patting her on the back. She had to find help, for her sake and Lucita's.

After Son-ja had fed and settled Lucita with the little Kachina doll, she gathered herbs, crushing them on rocks. She poured water on a cloth and bathed Sunita the best she could. Only then did she sprinkle the crushed herbs over her friend. Covering Sunita with a blanket, she chanted to the deities: the Earth Mother, Sun Father, and Moonlight-Giving Mother to accompany Sunita on her journey to the next world. She cried at the loss. Sunita was her tribal sister. Now she would have to continue on her journey alone. Well, not really alone, she had Lucita. Now she realized the strength Grandfather said she had was for this journey.

Strapping Lucita on her back, she picked up Mother Sun's staff and continued her journey.

She repeated her hike from yesterday, upriver toward the white people. They looked friendly and had women and children with them. Maybe a total of thirty people. There had been music the night before, laughter, and singing. She hoped they were good people.

Rounding the last bit of the mountain, Son-ja could not believe her eyes. She looked around in confusion. The dwellings, horses, and people, every single one were gone. Dark circles where their fire rings had been were as empty and cold as her hope.

She would find them, follow their tracks. She half slid on loose rock, as she climbed down the mountainside.

Son-ja walked through the abandoned camp scavenging what she could, a scrap of bread here, a bit of jerky there, and a comb. She turned the comb over and sunlight reflected off of it. She stuck it in her hair.

The sun was intense. She was so thirsty. Kneeling down by the river, she took a long cool drink and filled her gourd with water for their trip.

"This will be a long walk to catch up with those people," she said and dripped water into Lucita's mouth. Lucita smacked her lips and gulped the cool liquid, she soon had her fill of water. Son-ja washed

Lucita off with the cold water and began their trek to catch up to the white people.

Son-ja walked all day, rested at night, and walked all day again. After five days she had not reached the huts, which must be pulled by horses to move so quickly. She was tired and hungry, having used what food she had left for the baby. Her moccasins had huge holes in the bottom, her feet hurt, and her lips were chapped. Stomach cramps from lack of food bent her over and she whimpered.

The land now was more desert with few trees. She found a bushy area with shade. Lucita began to cry and Son-ja patted her on the back and hummed the familiar song to her. She looked up to see an Indian coming towards her. Were her eyes playing tricks on her? She was too weak to run, so sat perfectly still in hopes he hadn't seen her.

He was dressed in the attire of the friendly tribe her clan traded with. He held out his hand motioning for her to get up and follow him, which she did, too tired to do anything else. When they had walked for ten minutes or so, she saw five other Indians with six horses.

Her rescuer used sign language, telling her his name was Hakan, of the Yuma tribe. As the chief's son, he would protect her taking her back to his village.

Son-ja sat behind an Indian who accompanied Hakan. She could hardly believe her luck to be on a painted horse, not walking. They traveled half a day before the tents of the village came into view.

She was so weak, two of the Indians helped her down off the horse and into a tent. She lay on a pallet with Lucita. Two women came in carrying food and a water gourd. The older woman took Lucita from her and fed her small amounts till Lucita, full at last, slept.

The younger woman gave Son-ja food and water. While Son-ja ate, the woman left and brought back a half gourd filled with warm water. She began washing Son-ja.

Son-ja did not resist the woman's attention. It felt so good to have someone caring for her. The woman took the comb out of Son-ja's hair and, using a different comb, worked the tangles out of her hair then braided it. The woman gave her clothes since Son-ja's were ripped and torn. Last she slipped new moccasins onto Son-ja's feet, since hers had worn through from the many miles she had traveled.

As they worked, the women chattered back and forth. Using sign language to ask questions of Son-ja. She was able to express that her tribe had been slaughtered and some taken prisoner. That she and Lucita were all that was left.

The women got up abruptly, leaving the water gourd behind.

CHAPTER THREE

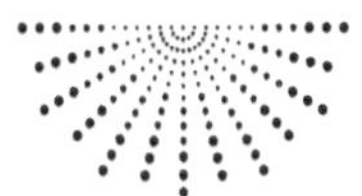

A few days later, Son-ja was brought before what she assumed was the tribal council. She stood before the men as they argued. One Indian yelled and made threatening gestures toward her with his staff. Others calmed the man down.

She feared for her life and that of the babe on her back.

Horses were brought around, and one was given to her. She climbed up, wondering all the while what was happening. Six men climbed onto the remaining horses, three rode in front and three rode in back of her horse.

Tears of fear rolled down her cheeks. She was certain this was not going to end well. They traveled all day finally making camp near a stream. She thought of trying to flee during the night but decided since she wasn't being mistreated, maybe they were taking her someplace safe. She tried to engage the Indians with sign language. They ignored her. Finally giving up, she lay down by Lucita, humming quietly till the babe slept.

After another half a day of travel, they came upon a river. On the far side was a fort. There was much discussion between the Indians. Finally, two of them left for the fort.

She couldn't remember ever seeing a fort and only knew that's what it was from her tribe talking about it. The structure was foreign looking. Smoke danced up in various places from inside the wooden walls.

Maybe we're going to trade with people in the fort?

Soon one Indian came back. He motioned for her to come with him. Reluctantly she climbed onto her horse and followed.

As they rode through the gate several people were waiting with the other Indian. The Indian motioned for her to dismount, which she did. The white people were talking to her. She didn't understand. She tried sign language to ask the Indian what was going on. He told her to stay. She would be safe here.

The Indians took her horse, packed blankets, meat, and various other things on the back of the horse. The Indians rode out of the fort not looking back at her even once.

She had been traded!

Now they would live with the white men.

A woman in a blue dress appeared in front of her and took her hand. Son-ja didn't know what to do so went with her into one of the shelters. The woman talked to her constantly. Nothing made sense to Son-ja.

Lucita started to cry. The woman picked her up and began singing. Son-ja stared at the woman, shocked that the woman was singing her song. Son-ja began humming. This was the same song she'd been humming ever since she could remember. How could this white woman know that song? And what were the words she was saying?

When the song stopped, Son-ja grabbed the white woman's arm and motioned for her to keep singing. The woman did.

"Please call me Mary." The woman patted her chest, "Mary."

"Son-ja." Son-ja patted her chest.

Mary gave Son-ja food. Son-ja ate with her fingers. Mary didn't like it. She handed Son-ja a stick with spikes and showed her how to use it.

"This is a fork." Mary smiled. "Hold it like this. That's right."

Son-ja thought she did pretty well using the 'fork'. When she finished eating Mary led her into a room there was a raised place to sleep and a smaller version for Lucita. Son-ja smiled and Mary smiled back.

———

Mary closed the door on the sleeping woman and baby. What all Son-ja must have been through to make it here. Her lips were cracked from days in the sun, sores on her feet, and blistering sunburn covered her exposed skin. The fort commander told Mary the woman would stay with her for now.

Mary answered the knock on the door. "Mrs. Thompson? How can I help you?"

"I've brought some clothes for the girl. My Annie has outgrown them. Mrs. Stewart sent some baby clothes too."

"Thanks to you both very much."

"Has she talked to you?"

"Not really. She does use hand signals and for the most part gets across what she is trying to say. Her name is Son-ja."

"Well then, isn't that an interesting name. I suppose it is an Indian name." She turned to leave and at the door turned back. "I'll be on my way. If there's anything I can do to help, please let me know. She is in good hands with you, Mary. A retired school marm, who better to teach her our language and ways?"

"Thank you, Mrs. Thompson."

Mary leaned against the closed door. Her life had been a quiet one since her husband Phillip had passed one year ago. Not to say she wasn't up to the task. After all, she handled a classroom full of rowdy children, one young woman and a baby shouldn't be too difficult. She was up to the task, Mary decided. She loved a project and this would certainly be that.

CHAPTER FOUR

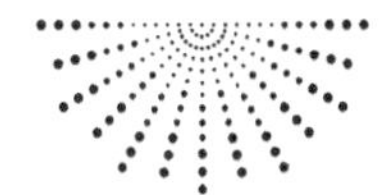

Six Months Later

Mary had given it plenty of thought and decided it was time to show Son-ja. The girl could speak pretty well now and even knew the words to Braham's Lullaby which she had sung to Lucita a couple of times during the day and every evening.

She took Son-ja's hand and led her into the bedroom Mary had shared with her husband. She pulled the chair out in front of the vanity and motioned for her to sit.

"Look in the mirror." Mary pointed at the mirror.

Son-ja looked in the mirror and gasped. It couldn't be! Her sunburn had faded, her lips were healed and she was… white!

Son-ja touched the mirror. She touched her brown hair and ran a finger by blue eyes. This girl who stared back at her was not an Indian maiden, she was white.

Mary left the room to answer the door.

Son-ja could not take her eyes off the mirror. She touched her hair, her skin, and looked into those blue, blue eyes. Who was she? Who were her people? She was so confused. She'd never imagined she wasn't of the Zuni tribe.

A short time later Mary came back into the bedroom. She took Son-ja's hand. "I know this is a shock to you. You have visitors. I believe you will understand better if you come with me."

Son-ja stood and followed Mary, clinging tightly to her hand. In the sitting room was a man, woman, and three girls. When they noticed Son-ja the woman held a hand to her mouth and began to weep. The oldest daughter took Son-ja's hands. Looking into the face of the girl was like looking into the mirror. Son-ja couldn't believe it.

"I'm Kathleen, your sister, your twin sister. We lost you many years ago when you were three years old." Tears were sliding down the girl's face.

"We thought we had lost you forever," the woman cried into her handkerchief, her shoulders shaking.

Mary put her arm around Son-ja's. "This is your family. You wandered off when you were just a toddler. They searched for you for days. Your Indian family found you and raised you." She squeezed Son-ja. "They have come to take you home."

Son-ja took a step forward, and then another. Her arms outstretched towards her mother. The woman embraced her and kissed her.

"Why are you crying?" Son-ja asked.

"Oh, dear child, these are tears of joy. You are our Sonja. We know it will take time for you to adjust to our way of life. Please give us a chance?"

Sonja looked back at Mary. "What about Lucita?"

Mary held Lucita and gave her the Kachina doll. "I'll adopt Lucita. You can come visit as often as you like." She smiled with tears in her eyes. "I'll miss you, Sonja. You were a joy to teach, and I came to love you like the daughter I never had. I wish you well and know you will be loved by your family."

"Thank you for all you've done for me, Mary."

The End

ABOUT THE AUTHOR

Diana enjoys weaving elements of paranormal and fantasy into her stories. She always ends with a Happily Ever After, because she must for her own satisfaction! Her hope is to take you away from your everyday life for a journey that is both entertaining and fun, and sometimes a little scary. You can learn more about Diana and her books at her website: https://dianamccollumauthor.com/

STORY INSPIRATION

I had just finished reading "Captivity of the Oatman Girls", by R.B. Stratton. The true story of a family slaughtered by Indians except for two young girls who were taken in captivity. The girls were seven and fourteen years old. The youngest died of starvation after two years. The other girl suffered, tormented, and was enslaved by her captors. After five years a captive she was finally bought by a Yuma Indian and brought to Fort Yuma and freed.

My story is about a child raised by Indians as one of their own. Treated kindly, and fair. This is Son-ja's story.

🌐 X

MARS

Pamela Cowan

MARS

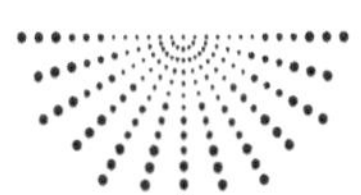

Aarush Li saw the reddish-orange sphere that was Mars looming in the distance. It looked like a tiny, rust-colored bead, suspended against a black velvet display. He could just make out the polar ice caps at the top and bottom of the planet, white swirls against a mottled red background.

He fought his growing sense of excitement and anticipation. Public displays of emotion were to be avoided. He was, after all, the jaded son of a wealthy family. A direct descendent of Du Li, a Chinese immigrant to America, who on nothing but a mailman's salary, had made a fortune buying and selling tech stocks.

Li family history had been drilled into him from a young age. Great-great-grandfather Du had lived on rice and bought Amazon. Selling just before the courts declared it a monopoly and it was broken into smaller companies. He'd added fish to his diet and bought Tesla, this time selling right before the Japanese company, Matsumi Motors, perfected AI-controlled navigation and Tesla's founder moved to the bunker he'd built on the dark side of the moon. Aarush had no idea what his great-great grandfather's diet became after that.

"Preparing to enter atmosphere," a soft feminine voice announced from hidden speakers. "There may be some turbulence."

As soon as her words faded Aarush felt a subtle vibration and heard an ominous creaking that seemed to come from behind the padded gray walls, ceiling, and even from under the thin carpet, with its repeating corporate logo, a stylized sun. Even here, on the way to Mars, he could not escape the reach of his family.

This part of the spaceship resembled the inside of a small plane. There were six rows of seats arranged two to a side, with a narrow aisle down the middle. His girlfriend, Sonya, had chosen an aisle seat because she said the view from the window made her queasy.

She and the others looked around anxiously, and he resisted the urge to laugh at their fear. The joy of escaping his domineering parents left little room for anything but relief. Still, he gently placed his free hand over Sonya's on the armrest, giving it a reassuring pat before turning back to gaze out of the window.

The planet was growing larger as they approached. The wide stretches of red and white dust swirling above the surface gradually revealed layers of brown and gold. Shadows hinted at the presence of craters, mountains, and valleys. Still, it would be some time before they landed.

He let his thoughts return to the ancestors. His great-grandfather, Chen Li had fast-tracked an MSc degree in math and two years later designed a mathematical framework that led to the development of the first truly affordable solar grid. He sold his shares and bought the company outright, renaming it Suncatcher. Chen's sister, Minli Li had no interest in business but had joined the Army and become part of an elite team that helped win the Third World War.

Heroism and industry then seemed to skip a generation. Chen Li's son, Pengfei, Aarush's grandfather loved nothing but bad women, fast cars, and the synthetic drugs which killed him before Aarush was two years old.

In thinking about it, Aarush realized he admired his grandfather. But it wasn't his bad habits he respected; it was his ability to turn his back on the family's expectations. The Li's expected so much, too much—

"We will be landing soon," the melodic voice said, interrupting his thoughts. "Viewports will be closed as a safety precaution."

Covers dropped into place over each window but when nothing else happened, Aarush went back to his musing. How often had he heard the story of his father, Gang Li, only son of Pengfei Li? Like the company logo, it was hard to avoid. His father was interviewed so often that everyone on the planet knew his story. How he had stepped up at a young age to run the company and take it in a new direction.

The news gatherers never failed to point out how he had metaphorically taken them back to the beginnings of Chinese in America. Except, instead of working for the Central Pacific Railroad laying rails for the first transcontinental railroad, Gang Li had used technology developed at Suncatcher to devise a new kind of train.

Sun Travelers were single compartments able to link and unlink with each other. Compartments that offered as much privacy and responsive control as the old automobiles had but moved so fast, they required governors to slow them to survivable speeds. Traveling on slim strands of metal and manufactured crystal and installed high above the ground where they competed only with aircraft, they left more room for towns and cities, farmland, and forest. They were revolutionizing transportation across the globe.

To be measured against the accomplishments of his exalted ancestors was Aarush's fate and he was reminded of it often.

"You are too much like your grandfather," was his father's favorite rant. His mother preferred, "You should try to be more like your father."

His mother was from Kolkata, previously called Calcutta, India. It was her grandmother who had named him Aarush, meaning sun's first ray. "It is in part because he was born in the sign of Aries, the first sign of the zodiac," she had explained, "but also because I am certain he will be a leader." He had never hated his name, to do so would be disrespectful, but it did feel like yet another weight to bear. Another expectation to fulfill.

"What are you thinking about?" asked Sonya. He looked at her and smiled. From their first date, the white-blond hair and blue eyes of his girlfriend had seemed like a subtle defiance.

"What am I thinking about? I guess that we are about to set foot on a planet which none of my ancestors have touched," he said.

"That's a funny way to look at it. I just think landing on Mars is exciting. It is, isn't it?" she asked.

"Very."

But when it happened the landing was anticlimactic. Nothing more than a single sharp jolt, a shuddering vibration, and then stillness. The passengers glanced at each other with a range of emotions from curiosity to wide-eyed fear as the artificial voice again filled the space, "One moment please."

Seconds later a door slid open and two people stepped in, a man and a woman, both short with dark hair and dressed in identical dark brown overalls. The man, whose name tag read Jonah, said "Time to disembark. We're your crew and dorm supervisors. Don't worry, gravity has been established using magnetic fields and manipulated charged particles. You'll learn more about that later. For now, you'll follow us to your quarters."

"When do we see Mars?" Aarush asked.

"Soon. Today you need to get settled into your new quarters and learn the safety procedures. Mars can be a very dangerous place unless you know and follow the rules." Aarush shrugged. It made sense. As much as he wanted to get outside, there was no point in arguing with the two unsmiling workers. It was obvious they took their jobs seriously. He would just have to be patient.

In their penthouse apartment with its sweeping view of the city and the Golden Gate Bridge, Aarush's parents were, at that very moment, discussing their son, Aarush.

"Are you sure we have done the right thing," Jiya asked Gang.

"I don't see what else we could have done," he told his wife. "He was spinning out of control. If we didn't do something drastic—"

"Yes, but this Mars thing. And to pay that young woman to persuade him to go."

"Not only to persuade him but to make him think it was his idea. Brilliant! She was worth every penny."

A prostitute thought Jiya. And with her seventeen-year-old son. She did not like it, but she didn't say anything. Why add to her husband's troubles?

Aarush was not happy that the corridors leading to the living section of the station were as blank and unappealing as the inside of a shipping crate. That was exactly what they resembled. Long windowless corrugated steel boxes welded together. None appeared to be on the same level, probably an adaptation to the Martian terrain. On earth, they would have dug or blasted to create a level path. Here, they simply raised and lowered the boxes so that you had to step up and down every six or seven meters.

As they reached a section painted dark green, Supervisor Jonah stopped beside a door. With a subtle lift of his chin and a nod toward the women, he said, 'This is the women's quarters. You three," he instructed, "break off here and follow Kelly.'"

Aarush felt Sonya's fingers tighten in his for a moment, then she let go and followed the others. He didn't get a chance to watch her out of sight. The men were moving again. Their footsteps echoed off the metallic walls. They stepped down into a dark red section and found a door identical to the one leading to the women's quarters.

"Men's quarters are down here," Supervisor Jonah said. "I've been assigned to assist you as you transition to living here. I and the other supervisors will be providing day-to-day support to make sure you feel welcome here at Mars Station. We'll also make sure you have the information and tools you need to stay safe, find your way around, and learn your jobs. Tonight, you'll rest and unpack. Tomorrow we'll get started." He opened the door.

"I'd like to see Mars," said Aarush.

"There is a small viewport in your quarters, and in the dining hall and recreation room but that's it. Viewpoints are weak spots," he explained. "Even though they're made from aerogel, each one is a vulnerability. A breach in our armor."

Aarush frowned. "But why? We're inside a pressurized building. What harm can a window do?"

Jonah gestured toward the nearest viewport. "Imagine a storm raging outside. Martian dust devils. They whip against the window, looking for a weakness. And if they find one—a microscopic crack, a faulty seal—they'll exploit it. The pressure differential could rupture the entire station."

"But we came to see the planet," one of the others protested. "We didn't sign on to be locked inside a windowless cell all day."

Jonah nodded. "I get it. But we have to balance your curiosity with your survival. Once you start working your crew rotations, you'll be too busy and tired to notice the environment. Plus, you'll be able to visit our main observation deck which has reinforced viewports, triple-layered and coated with smart materials. Otherwise, for now, it's the viewports I mentioned, or you can look at the feed from our cameras and sensors. That way you have eyes on it without risking our lives. And hey, with luck you'll be one of those going outside tomorrow."

"One of?" asked Aarush. "Aren't we all going outside?"

"No. We have limited staff so only six people can be outside at a time. But don't worry, if you don't get selected tomorrow, you will soon."

Aarush wanted to argue but decided he might as well get settled in. He'd signed up for a six-month stay. There would be plenty of time to see Mars.

"Do you think he will ever forgive us?" Jiya asked her husband.

"Forgive us for what? For helping him get his head on straight and stay out of trouble. What is there to forgive? I'm sure he will be grateful—eventually. That he'll come to see that as his parents we must do what is right for him. Are you that worried?"

"I am his mother. It is my occupation to worry about him," Jiya replied without turning. She stood at the picture window in the living room of their apartment, lights dimmed for the evening. Far below, the glowing lights of the city twinkled like the distant stars they replaced. Even the moon couldn't shed enough light to compete with the city's glow.

Gang stepped up behind his wife and put his arms around her. She relaxed a little against him and he rested his chin on her shoulder and spoke softly in her ear. "He'll be fine. More than fine. He'll be back before you know it."

"He's just so far away," she said. There was nothing Gang could say to that, so he said nothing. They stood quietly and stared out at the night.

It was lunchtime and Aarush sat with Sonya in the cafeteria. He had little appetite for the consistently boring food. He missed his mother's cooking, the curries, the samosas stuffed with spiced peas and potatoes. When he was little, she would give him a buttered round of warmed naan bread and a cup of tea when he studied. She still made it for him when he had a cold. Though he wasn't sick, well maybe homesick, the bread would have been comforting.

"It's been a week and we're still stuck in here," he complained.

"You have to be patient," Sonya said.

She had finished her meal and was now eating his fries. Dragging them through a pool of ketchup on her plate and chomping them down. He was a little disgusted by it, and by the smear of ketchup on her cheek, but he put it down to his bad mood. Everything was annoying, had been annoying since day one.

First, he and Sonya had been separated. Second, his 'room'—and he mentally drew air quotes around the word every time he said it—was a dorm. It accommodated six beds and six bodies: young men who snored, farted, and belched. They appeared to be in no hurry to see Mars. Instead, they seemed content with their daily assignments and spent their free time playing games on various devices, all while blissfully ignoring each other.

Third—since he was counting—was having to work. It would have made more sense to increase the cost and use the money to hire unskilled laborers. The idea of working in a mine had appealed to him. But somehow, he'd imagined it meant commanding a high-tech computer to manipulate specialized robots. Robots like the ones his father employed to build and maintain his Sun Travelers.

He had soon learned that jackhammers were the only tech they had and only those in brown overalls, supervisors, like Kelly and Jonah, were allowed to use them. The rest were tasked with shoveling the soil broken up by the hammers into carts which, when they reached a certain weight, rolled off into the distant darkness of a corridor he'd never been allowed to follow. The only other job was exploring the cuts in the walls with a tool that resembled the hand rake his mother used to loosen soil in her rooftop garden.

"Use it to scratch and scrape the rock," said Jonah. "If you get lucky, you'll find some of the stuff we're looking for."

The "stuff" was a new element unimaginatively called marsium. Rob had distributed brochures, which Aarush meticulously studied. Perhaps he wasn't so different than his ancestors after all. The concept of working with something novel, something he could develop and enhance, piqued his interest. Was it to honor his father and the esteemed lineage, or was there an underlying desire to prove himself? A shameful thought, yet perhaps closer to the truth.

The brochure explained that marsium was a rare, silvery-white metal similar to niobium in many ways. Like niobium, marsium was a ductile metal resistant to corrosion and oxidation. It was also a superconductor at low temperatures, which would make it useful for a variety of applications, such as particle accelerators.

Marsium had been found in the soil and rocks on Mars, often in association with other rare metals, such as tantalum and tungsten. The brochure explained that marsium is difficult to extract from its ores, but it has the potential to be a valuable resource for future exploration and colonization efforts on Mars.

The appeal of learning all he could about finding and mining for the new element had helped Aarush deal with the constant delays. There were two days of safety courses which included learning how to wear an egress suit, a carefully crafted spacesuit that would allow a human to survive on the surface of Mars. Then there was an entire day set aside for testing.

On the morning Aarush and the others were taking their tests they were startled by a loud, rhythmic thrumming, that seemed to emanate from above. Aarush's immediate thought; helicopter. Unfortunately, the classroom had no windows. Moments later, their dorm supervisor entered and explained that the noise was from an air return fan that had gone out of balance.

Aarush shrugged and went back to work. He knew, before it was scored, that he had passed the tests. He was sure he'd be allowed outside but no, the very next morning an alarm had gone off.

"This isn't a drill," Jonah told them as he and the rest of his dormmates woke to the shrill scream of sirens. "Follow me."

They'd done as he said and spent the day in a specially crafted interior chamber, which looked no different than the rest of the storage container rooms and walkways. After six hours or so they were told the emergency was over. A seal had cracked, and the atmosphere had leaked out. The seal was now fixed, the atmosphere restored, but they wouldn't be going outside for a day or two. The staff were needed to check the rest of the seals. A task that would take at least two days.

Aarush told Sonya he thought there were far too few staff on Martian Station. "There's Jonah and Kelly and the two other dorm supervisors. Then, there's the woman who runs the communications center, the head maintenance guy, and his helper."

"Don't forget the director."

"Oh right, and he doesn't even have an assistant. What is that, like eight?"

"Nine. You also forgot the counselor."

"Right. I haven't even met him yet."

"But I hear you will. We all will. He has to make sure we don't go Mars crazy or something."

"I'd have to feel like I was on Mars for that to happen. This whole thing makes me think I'm like a mouse in a maze. But where's the cheese," he joked.

"I thought I was the cheese," Sonya said, pretending to pout.

A low buzz that repeated twice told them lunch break was over. Aarush used his napkin to wipe the ketchup from Sonya's face. She laughed. "I'm a mess. I'm falling apart in this place. Eating like a pig. Not bothering with makeup. Not only am I not cheese; you must think I'm devolving."

"Nonsense," he told her. "You're bored. As bored as I am. But you still look great."

"Thanks," she said. "I think you look pretty nice yourself. Maybe we can sneak off somewhere this afternoon." She raised and lowered her perfectly shaped eyebrows to clarify her meaning.

Aarush nodded, his mood lifting. At least one good thing had happened that morning. He and Sonya had been listed on the same work crew.

Every morning, a screen outside each of the four dorm rooms—two for men and two for women—displayed the crew assignments for the day. During orientation, Jonah explained that crew members rotated through all the different jobs. This approach ensured that everyone became skilled in every task and provided an opportunity for crew members to get to know each other. The daily crews included cleaning, systems, maintenance, and mining. Each workday spanned six hours, and there were no days off.

To date, Aarush had spent at least one day on each of the crews. Cleaning was his least favorite. It entailed dusting and scrubbing every surface of the habitat. He'd been surprised at the powdery red dust that somehow crept into what he thought was a sealed environment. It must have blown in each time the doors were opened. In any case, it covered every surface. Specialized vacuums took care of the dust—not so special scrub brushes, rags, and elbow grease dealt with the rest.

Systems involved sitting in a chair, eyes fixed on a screen, poring over real-time reports. The goal? Ensuring that the habitat operated within specific parameters. This encompassed everything from airlocks and radiation shielding to power levels and communications. And then there were the vital life support systems: air and water recycling, food production, and waste management. Jonah liked to refer to it as the "life loop" during his training sessions.

The maintenance crew's work was more to his liking. First, they would check any issues reported by the systems crew. Once that was done, they would move on to do a point-by-point inspection of various tools and equipment, including the egress suits.

Like the suits used in the mines, they provided gravity-enhancing boots, protection from radiation, pressure containment, and helmets with tinted visors and voice-activated microphones. Handling the suits, peering at each seam, inspecting the hoses, and checking the air generators was as close as he'd been to actually stepping on Mars.

The reason Aarush was happy to learn he'd be working with Sonya in the mines that day, was partly because he hadn't made any friends. He didn't seem to have much in common with the others, except for the obvious fact that he recognized most of their names. They were all sons or daughters of families known for their success and wealth. It made sense—how else could they have afforded the cost of the trip?

Aarush led Sonya to his favorite area of the mine. The wall, a blend of gray and tan with just a hint of red, bore grooves cut by the blade of a jackhammer and pockmarks left by the metal claw he used in his search for marsium. Sonya did not recall or care where she had dug on her last day on the mining crew and seemed content with his choice.

"I have a good feeling about this spot," he told her.

"Some sixth sense?" she asked. Laying her palm on the rock she intoned in a serious voice, "I sense something here. Something of great value. I sense a ticket home."

"You mean –"

"I mean a ticket to get us out of this hole we've dug ourselves into."

Aarush rolled his eyes but couldn't help laughing. "Well, I guess we better keep digging then."

It was early morning. Gang had finished breakfast and moved to his home office. Here, as was his habit, he sipped his second cup of coffee while reading the first of three newspapers he had delivered to his computer each morning.

Some thought his habit of digesting the day's news in the form of readable content a bit strange, even archaic. Most preferred to listen to the news while doing something else. To do otherwise seemed lazy. Despite scientific evidence that multitasking didn't exist, and in fact, could get in the way of efficiency and productivity, it was still a highly sought-after and honored skill.

Gang had the luxury of focusing on one task at a time and he liked to take advantage of it. No one disturbed him during this quiet time. That was why he was immediately concerned when Jiya swept into his office. "What is it?" he asked. "What's wrong?"

"I have a note. A note from that Sonya woman."

Gang's concern grew. Jiya's English was usually impeccable, as was her Chinese. It was only in times of great stress that her birthplace became apparent. When she said the word note the t sound changed, making the word sound more like not then note.

Jiya held up her phone so that Gang could see the message on the screen.

I am writing to let you know that Aarush is becoming very bored. He is talking about taking a suit and sneaking outside. I don't want to tell anyone about this and get him in trouble. Is there anything you can do?

"Is there," Jiya asked anxiously. "Is there anything we can do? I think if he finds out what we have done he will be very upset with us."

"You worry too much. He is our son, and he'll do as he's told. At least, once he grows out of this youthful rebellion phase. Let me think about it. Maybe I can exert some pressure."

"Oh yes, please," said Jiya.

Still madly in love with this woman whose dark eyes could capture him and slow his heart, he reached for his computer's keyboard.

Three days after working in the mine with Sonya, Aarush and the rest of his dorm were preparing for the workday when Jonah entered the room.

"Tomorrow after you finish your assignments, I want all of you to meet back here. You'll have about a half an hour to get cleaned up, grab a snack, and then you'll suit up and go outside."

The response was so enthusiastic he had to wait for the din to die down before he could continue.

"I know you've all studied the egress suits, but I'd like you to review the manual, not just on the suits, but on what to expect out there. Kelly is also leading a group outside so if anyone has to look like newts let it be them. I expect you to act like vets. Got it?"

For the first time, Aarush felt as if he and the random group of men he shared a room with had something to talk about. As soon as Jonah left, they gathered around the communal table at one end of the room. The fourteen-year-old twins teased each other about how the other would inevitably act like a newt and let their father down. Something, Aarush realized, they might all have in common. Despite his protests, Aarush realized that he also wanted to make his parents proud.

"Where is the manual?" he asked. "We should get it out so we can get right to studying this afternoon."

"Smart," said one of the twins and hurried to find it.

"Good news," said Jiya. "Sonya says all is well. Aarush is much better, much happier."

"Aarush will be fine. Of that I never had a doubt. Young people are resilient. It's your happiness I care about. Are you happier?"

"Much."

"Then so am I."

When once again it was Aarush's day to be on a mining crew. He found himself looking forward to the work. The people he shared an elevator with were also upbeat. Whether they were going out or staying inside, the enthusiasm was everywhere. No one wore gaming glasses or stared at a screen. Instead, everyone was talking.

"You've been here longer than me," Aarush said to one of the girls he'd met when working on a previous work crew. "Haven't you been outside before?"

"No. Never. There was the bad seal right after you arrived but before that, there was a defect reported in the suits. We had to wait for replacements. Before that, there was a dust storm, and after the storm, they found out the airlocks had been damaged. It's been one thing after another."

"That's miserable."

"That's life on Mars," she said stoically. "Guess it's not for everyone."

"Ouch. That hurt. I guess I've been complaining a little?"

"More like whining a lot," she said, but this time she smiled, which took some of the sting from her words. "It just takes getting used to. We're a pampered bunch of rich brats so what else could they expect? I mean. No clubs, no clothes, no fun."

"No maids and cooks."

"No vacations from our vacations," she exclaimed, her hand fluttering to her forehead as if she might faint. "It's all so very, very much."

The elevator came to a gentle stop and the doors slid open.

Everyone rushed out, donning helmets, grabbing diggers, and calling out to each other as they sought their workstations.

Aarush reluctantly left his workmates and moved further down the corridor to the spot where he and Sonya had worked together last. He almost put his hand on the rock and said something about the wealth waiting there. Sonya would have enjoyed that when he told her later. But he was too distracted by the prospect of going outside soon.

His arm swung upward, the digger's tines biting into the wall higher than ever before. A cascade of loose rock tumbled down, some ricocheting off his hat. The rock let go more readily than he'd expected. He swung again, the claws sinking in, and pulled hard. Soon, a small mound of dirt was piled on the floor against the cave wall.

Kneeling, Aarush sifted his gloved fingers through the pebbles and soil, searching for the familiar silvery-white metal. But instead, something dull and brown caught his eye. He lifted it, astonishment freezing him as he stared at the object cradled in his palm.

It was rough and uneven, and its reddish-brown color looked like rust. He'd seen an object like this before, several in fact, on Earth when hiking along trails with his family or friends. Refuse from an earlier time. A simple thing. A bottle cap. Something so mundane on Earth but such a remarkable find on Mars that he could barely believe its existence.

Where had it come from? What was it doing here? Was it really a bottle cap or did it just resemble one? If it came from Mars, why was it rusty? Had it been exposed to water in the past? What the hell did it mean?

Maybe he should go show it to one of the others. The girl he was talking to on the elevator or maybe Jonah, who was leading the crew today. He'd really like to show it to Sonya first though. Yeah, that's what he'd do. Get her take on it and then maybe take it to Jonah or even the director.

When Aarush showed the bottle cap to her, Sonya tried to produce the right amount of awe. This was one of the best paying and easiest gigs she'd ever had. No way was she going to mess it up with bad acting. This could be serious trouble. As soon as she could invent a reason to leave, she went in search of someone to tell.

"Look," she told Director Robinson, "Aarush isn't dumb. He's going to figure out why there's a bottle cap on Mars. He's going to be pissed and he will probably look for someone to sue. Isn't that what rich people do?"

The director wasn't sure what response to give. After years of trying to make everyone happy he was a ball of conflicting thoughts, stress, and anxiety. Some days he wished he could develop a good drinking or drug habit; facing each day clean and sober was a lot.

Sonya found Aarush in the dining hall. He'd finished his meal but had stayed behind with the others. Everyone was excited about the coming day. The members of the dorms that had been chosen to explore Mars were in turn giddy with excitement and determined to seem blasé about it. The members of the dorms that had not been chosen showed their disappointment but were also weirdly elated. The chance to go outside had been dangled in front of them for too long.

When Aarush saw Sonya, he got up, dumped his tray and tableware into the recycler, and walked with her toward the dorms.

"Where have you been?" he asked.

"Don't be mad," she said. "I bet you're going to be mad."

Something that felt like cold fingertips slid through his stomach. "Why?"

"I told the director about the bottle cap."

"You did what?"

"See, I knew you'd be mad?"

"The word is angry," he said, automatically correcting her. "Mad means crazy. Why would you do that?"

"Well, I wasn't going to. Not at first. But then I realized that you were worried about it and besides, it could be something else. Like maybe part of an alien ship, or a machine or something. What if it was giving off radiation or had some kind of alien disease on it? You put your bare hands on it. What were you thinking? Actually, I'm the one who should be ma—angry. You could have put us in danger. You should turn it in."

"I would—I don't. Well, I don't think it could be anything else. I mean look at it. It's round with a crimped edge and I can sort of see part of a design on the top. It's just faded and rusted too much to read. Here, I'll show you."

Beside each bed in the dorm was a nightstand with three drawers. He opened the top drawer of his, reached under a stack of underwear, and extracted a thin silver case. Everyone had been given one before they left Earth and was allowed to fill it with whatever they wanted.

Aarush's case held his good luck charms: three feng shui coins, a blue stone, a jade elephant, and a poem. To these, he had added the cap. He opened the case and looked inside. He moved the small objects around, but it didn't change anything. The bottle cap was gone. He dumped the contents on his bed and dug through them. No cap. Not even so much as a single rusty flake.

"Did you take it?" he asked Sonya.

She looked at him, brows furrowed. "Of course not. Why would you even ask?"

"You were the only one who knew I had it. Well, you were until you told Director Robinson." His voice grew increasingly strident.

"You need to calm down," Sonya told him. "It was just a little bit of metal."

"I'm going to the Director's Office."

"Are you—Yes, that's probably a good idea. I'm sure he won't know what happened to it though. He asked me to have you bring it to him." Sonya was sure the director had one of the staff remove it, afraid of risking who he might show it to. But she couldn't tell Aarush this without revealing too much.

"Well, someone knows." He gave her a look so filled with distrust that she was taken aback. Then he stalked away, moving quickly so that she had to trot to keep up.

After a few running steps, she stopped. There was nothing to be gained by going with him. Instead, it was probably a good time to send another message to his parents.

———

"I think you were right," Gang said to his wife after reading Sonya's message. "It was a bad idea. I will arrange for his return. There are other ways he can learn responsibility."

"Or maybe he is responsible enough for a boy of his age. Is it possible we have overburdened him with the weight of our fears?"

"You are speaking about him becoming like my father."

"No. I am speaking about something larger. We were both raised with the traditions of our native cultures. My parents expected that I would respect their authority and values above all else. And though your family has lived in America for generations, you have often shared with me that your parents expected you to be obedient and to live harmoniously. Perhaps this clash of cultures, which we have found exhilarating, has left Aarush confused. Especially as he has largely been raised in a country that values very different things, such as self-expression and individualism."

"I forget," Gang told his wife, "that you are as wise as you are beautiful."

———

Director Robinson glared across his desk at Aarush, sat even more erect in his chair, and said, "I don't know where your find has disappeared to. Maybe one of your dorm mates found it? Maybe you lost it."

"I didn't lose it. It was important," Aarush said, fighting not to lose his temper.

"In what way? You said it was just a rusty bottle cap." The director scrubbed his palm across his short-cropped military-style hair. The bristles, meticulously trimmed, offered no resistance—each strand a disciplined soldier standing at attention. Though retired, the director still clung to the habits of a long military career.

"Just a bottle cap?" said Aarush. "What would a bottle cap be doing on Mars? Can you explain that?"

"Of course. A crew member or a member of the staff must have placed it there. No doubt someone's idea of a joke, or maybe it would be more correct to call it a prank. In any case that's the only possible explanation."

The man had seemed so positive that Aarush found himself nodding in agreement.

A little later, sitting on the edge of his bed in the empty dorm room, the silver case open on his lap, Aarush stared into the middle distance, lost in thought. Despite allowing himself to be convinced that the bottle cap was only a prank, doubts had quickly crept back in.

If it was so unimportant why did someone bother to take it? That bothered him. But it wasn't just the cap. There had been other anomalies. Several odd things that might add up to something he didn't want to face. For instance, there was that sound overhead soon after he'd arrived. He'd heard all sorts of fans. None had ever sounded like the chop, chop of the main rotor blade of a helicopter. A machine his family owned three of.

There was also the lag time between transmissions through the deep space network. Or, more precisely, the lack of lag time. The twins, who were younger than the rest, were allowed to speak with their parents daily through a console in the dorm that Jonah had to unlock for them. Aarush heard them talk and it was as if they were in the adjoining rooms. Yet he was pretty sure no technology allowed faster than light communication.

The next thing that occurred to him was the small number of staff. He'd remarked about it to Sonya before but now it took on a much more sinister meaning. Maybe there weren't enough workers to run a station supposedly doing all kinds of research, but maybe there were enough for a different kind of job. Like keeping an eye on a group of teens and young adults—offspring of the wealthiest people on earth. Keeping them isolated in a place where they couldn't get free; communication with the outside world tightly controlled and given enough work and study to keep them occupied, tired, one could even say docile.

It didn't take a genius to understand what was going on. He and the others had been kidnapped. The trip to Mars was a cover. The Mars Station was a prison where they were being held while their parents were forced to pay a huge ransom. It would have to be huge to pay for the expense of this vast conspiracy.

Unexpectedly, a sense of mirth rose up in Aarush and he smiled. The most important thing in a conspiracy is to keep it a secret. He'd make sure it wasn't a secret for much longer.

He had skipped dinner. Opting to take advantage of the empty dorm room so he could think. Now his dorm mates began to return. He waited until all five were there before calling them over to the communal table. He told the room to play rock music— loud—and he gestured to the others to huddle close.

Most technology was voice-activated, something was always listening, waiting for commands. It wouldn't be hard to hear what was said in any room anywhere. Most conversations were not important enough to monitor. He was sure theirs was. He counted on the music with its heavy bass to mask their conversation.

Quickly he outlined everything, from finding the bottle cap to his suspicions and the reasons for them. He left his most shocking revelation for last. "I think well, I'm pretty sure, that we're not even on Mars."

Ian, someone he'd mentally labeled a quasi-bully, spoke up first. "I buy it. It was my parents who said I should go, and they got real pushy about it. Maybe someone was forcing them. Something like, 'Send the kid to Mars or we'll kill him, or his kid sister, or whatever.'"

"Yeah, but how do we find out?" asked one of the twins.

"Easy. We grab one of them and beat it out of him," said Ian. "I say we get Jonah. That guy's been glitching me from day one."

"I'm okay with confronting one of them but let's hold off on the beating part," said Aarush.

"Who made you chief, Chief?" asked Ian.

"Wrong kind of Indian," said Aarush. Before Ian could respond the other twin said, "Should we get the rest of the dorms in on this?"

"Hell yes," enthused Ian, far too loudly.

Aarush could see where this was heading, and he didn't like it. But what else could he do? Now that they knew they were being lied to, that if his guess was right and they'd all been kidnapped, they had every right to be furious. The best he could do was follow along and try to keep Ian or another hothead from doing something stupid.

Softly, he shared his ideas with the others. "We don't want them to know we're on to them. Shouldn't we try and round them up, one by one, and lock them somewhere until we get things figured out? They control everything on the station, and that includes the life loop."

The group quieted down after that. They decided to send one person to each dorm to discreetly invite the others to gather in the rec room, the largest room on the station and the only one they could think of to comfortably hold them all.

"I'll go to Women's Dorm A," Aarush offered.

"Yeah, we know why," said Ian. "That girl of yours; pure flame. Expensive I bet."

Aarush spun away from the group and the nastiness that was Ian and walked toward the exit. Despite his anger, he tried for a casual stride in case anyone was watching as well as listening.

The door to Sonya's dorm stood open, but Aarush knocked anyway. For anyone else, he wouldn't have bothered. As their eyes met, he sensed she was afraid, though he hadn't yet shared his kidnapping theory with her. She hurried across the room, while the others—oblivious to her distress—remained fixed in their own worlds.

A trio huddled around a table, manipulating an ancient set of Tarot cards. Their attention barely flickered toward the intruder as they resumed their pursuits.

Some stood in the middle of the room, gazing at screens through designer eyewear and swinging their arms wildly. Aarush stepped into the room and asked what they were doing. "Sword fighting on Venus," one of the girls answered. "The graphics are aws. The sky is pink, and I just surfed down the side of a volcano."

He didn't bother to nod. She could only see what had been produced for her to see. Instead, he said loud enough for the whole room to hear, "We've called a meeting in the rec room. They'd like everyone there now."

One of the girls sitting at the table trying to see her future quipped, "It's not in the cards." Her two friends laughed. If the situation had been different, he might have laughed too.

"Well, it's up to you," he said, "but they told me they were going to make a big decision that affects everyone, and they didn't really ask me to come get you. The truth is I don't think they care if you show up." He shrugged, knowing they couldn't ignore the threat of a group of people, especially all men, making choices for them.

"What's up?" Sonya repeated, moving close and brushing her cheek against his.

"Come with me," he whispered. "I'll tell you on the way."

Aarush led Sonya not to the rec room, but to an interior room. In fact, the same room they'd been locked in during the incident with the faulty seal. This time, however, there was no alarm, except the one that had been going off in his head.

He gestured for her to go ahead of him into the room. As soon as she cleared the threshold, he shut the door and locked it. Most of the station's doors locked from the inside. This and one other locked from the outside. He'd discovered this working on the cleaning crew, on the same day he studied Jonah punching in the four-digit code, and discovered it was 8, 5, 2, 8. A lazy man's code that used only the center keys and was easy to remember.

There was no window in the door and for once he was grateful for the lack of one. He could only imagine the hurt and anger on Sonya's face, but he was doing it for her, he reminded himself. He'd been afraid that things were going to get out of control ever since he'd heard Ian's arrogant tone. The guy was looking for a fight. His obvious craving for mayhem and violence could be a problem. If he whipped everyone up into a frenzy, they could tear apart the station. If that happened, at least Sonya would be safe.

He hadn't been wrong to worry. In his absence, a war party of sorts had been formed and charged by Ian to find one of the staff so they could be questioned. The dorms housed twelve men and nine women. A few refused to join, which left nine men and five women to carry out Ian's plan. More than enough, thought Aarush. Fourteen against nine were pretty good odds.

The mob mentality was in full swing by the time they located Supervisor Jonah doing a final check of the kitchen and munching on a snack stick, probably a perk of that particular job.

"Hey, what's up?" he asked when he saw the grim crowd jostling shoulder to shoulder through the doorway.

"I'll tell you what's up?" said Ian at the front of the pack. "Your days that's what. You got exactly no seconds to tell us what is going on here. Why are you holding us? How much are you asking?"

"What are you talking about?"

Everyone began shouting, asking questions, making demands. Someone pushed Jonah and he fell to his knees out of sight. Aarush fought through the crowd, trying to get to the man, whether to save him or help question him he wasn't quite sure.

"I know how to get an answer to one of my questions!" Ian shouted. Aarush saw he'd grabbed the fabric of Jonah's coverall and was dragging the supervisor down the corridor. The others helped, by pushing and tugging at the man. A crowd with purpose, they were heading toward the section that held the egress suits and one of the airlocks.

The airlock's inner door slid open. A sound foreign to Aarush's ears but instinct screamed what it was, or maybe it was the subtle change in air pressure he felt in his ears. He surged forward, through the crowd, getting an elbow to the face and a stomped foot in the process.

Limping and fueled by anger, he fought his way to the front. There he saw a hand—trembling or steady he couldn't tell—slap the flashing red button for the outer airlock. Silence descended. Shock was etched on every face. Supervisor Jonah staggered out into the rough landscape of unforgiving rock and swirling dust.

One of the girls screamed.

"Look," said Ian, a strange tone that Aarush later thought might have revealed a combination of hope and regret. "He's alive. We were right. It can't be Mars."

Just then Jonah fell like a meteorite crashing onto the rust-colored soil. Aarush's breath caught as dust billowed around Jonah's prone form, settling like a shroud. The airlock's outer door stood open, a window to the horrible scene outside.

"What if he's still alive?" Aarush's voice trembled but, for maybe the first time, he felt absolutely sure of himself. He lunged toward the rack of suits, fingers fumbling with urgency.

He climbed into the pants, slid his feet into the attached shoes, and pulled the suspenders over his shoulders. Someone helped slide the shirt over his head and down his torso. Others helped; their faces blurred. Gloves were sealed to cuffs. Someone lowered the helmet over his head, turning it into the groove until it seated itself with a snap. He waived off the offer of a safety check. They'd done it right or they hadn't. There was no time. Adrenaline surged through his veins.

This was the moment—his chance to prove himself. Aarush wasn't the same kid who'd arrived on Mars, trailing family expectations. He'd stumbled upon a conspiracy and uncovered a kidnapping plot. Jonah's fall was the final reveal. Catching a glimpse, in the sheen of the visor, of the determined man he'd become, he gave a quick nod.

He'd save Jonah, expose the truth, and rewrite his own narrative. The others were listening to him now. They'd turned their backs on Ian. He would guide them from here on out. Help them capture their captors, contact their families, lead them to rescue.

His family might not understand, but he suddenly realized what they thought of him was less important than what he thought. All that truly mattered was that he returned from this, a man, a leader, a hero in his own eyes.

The suit was awkward and slowed him down, but he rushed into the airlock whose outer door had closed automatically, waited for the brief cycle, and hit the button. There was no time to admire Mars with its red rocks and butterscotch sky. Aarush imagined and choreographed each move. He'd bend low, grip Jonah's wrists, hoist him above the rocky ground, and drag him back to the station. No time for pulse checks or breath counts. They'd been drilled. Mars allowed you mere minutes of survival, and revival was a slim hope after only three.

At his feet, Jonah, supervisor and kidnapper, slowly opened his eyes and looked at Aarush. Clarity burst forth like a comet blazing across the sky. Aarush knew the truth. His kidnapper had tried to fake his death. Had tried to keep the hoax alive. There was no one to save and he was no hero.

The man struggled to rise. He was saying something, but it was lost in the rush of blood pounding in Aarush's ears. Rage-filled, he grabbed a nearby rock and swung it down with primal force. Jonah collapsed to the ground and Aarush dropped the blood-stained weapon with nerveless fingers.

Staring down at Supervisor Jonah's still form, he saw with disbelief that the man's eyes were open but vacant. Aarush was panting. There wasn't enough air. He dug at the helmet's latch, got it loose, tore it off, and dropped it on the ground. The air still seemed thin, thin as Martian air, with a metallic taste like iron, or vengeance.

Slowly he turned toward the sprawl of steel shipping containers shimmering under the heat of a cloudless blue sky—and headed back to the station—and his future.

"Sending Aarush to the Melbourne Australia Reform School was a last resort," said Gang, "but he was out of control. The truancy. The disobedience. We had to do something."

Jiya sighed heavily. "I know. I just worry he'll be furious with us. He thought it was some grand adventure, traveling to a different

planet, exploring the Martian landscape. When he learns it was a hoax
. . ."

"Yes, but he's an intelligent boy. I'm certain he'll come to understand our reasoning. MARS was supposed to be a fresh start—a
chance for him to break free from bad influences, to learn discipline.
Plus, the school's strict regimen seemed like exactly what he needed.
I'm just sorry they didn't offer the challenges and adventure they
promised. I'm of half a mind to not pay them."

ABOUT THE AUTHOR

Pamela Cowan is a Pacific Northwest author best known for her mystery and suspense novels. Cowan is the author of the Storm vigilante series, the El & Em Detective series, and the stand-alone novels *Cold Kill, Something In The Dark,* and *Repoe Man.* To learn more about her novels and short fiction visit her website at pamelacowan.com.

STORY INSPIRATION

The concept for "Mars" was actually my husband's. A few years ago he outlined a novel that I thought had a great--and twisty--plot. When I was trying to come up with a concept for a short story, I remembered his idea and asked if I could use it. Since we know that two writers given the same idea will come up with something different, he agreed. Both of us are also amateur stargazers and the proud owners of a 10" Dobsonian telescope.

Grandma's Imagination

Mary Vine

CHAPTER ONE

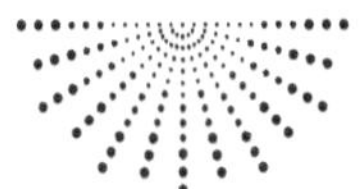

Ruth Harper, A.K.A. Grandma Harper to her friends, stood holding a plate of cookies on Myka Woods's front porch.

"You're trying to make me fat aren't you, Grandma?" Still, Myka removed a mitten and picked up a peanut butter cookie with crisscross marks on the top.

"Why, no. But you could stand a pound or two, I'm thinking."

"Good. I'll take another."

"Besides bringing you a treat, I have a job offer for you."

Myka squinted at her. "I have a hardware store; I don't need another job."

Grandma shook her head. "This is photography."

Myka took the plate of cookies and led Grandma into the house. "What's this about?"

Grandma removed her gloves, coat, and knit cap before saying, "Gilby Glenn, a man I met at the senior center, is having an 80th birthday and I thought it might be nice to commemorate the event with a photograph."

"You like this fella, do you?"

She put a hand through her short white hair, smiled, and looked down shyly. "Well, he is rather handsome for an old man."

"I can do this for free you know," said Myka, guiding Grandma to the couch.

She shook her head.

"What? You're going to charge him?"

"No, I'm offering you a trade. You see, his family lives in that huge Victorian house in town."

"It's haunted, I hear."

"I can't testify to that, but perhaps you'd like to trade him a photograph for a chance to take photos of the December night sky from the tallest of balconies?"

Myka sat down before saying, "Oh, I would. I would. The constellation Orion, at the end of December, will be directly overhead at 7:30 p.m."

"Wow. That's precise."

"Yes, you knew that since I've been spouting off what I'm going to photograph to anyone who will listen and to those who won't."

State Bureau of Investigation Special Agent Caleb Locke entered Myka's door, just as Grandma Harper was leaving.

"How are my two beauties?" he asked.

Grandma dipped her head and gave him a coquettish smile. "Fine now," she said and walked proudly out the door.

"Hey," Caleb said to Myka, kissing her on the forehead, before he removed his overcoat.

Her heart sped up every time he came through the door, clean-cut and in a suit jacket. "Hey, yourself. You're here early."

He smiled and said, "I see you're wearing the earrings I gave you for your birthday."

Myka pushed her hair over her shoulder. She loved the multi-star earrings and the way they shimmered in the light.

"It's been a bit slow lately, so I've been catching up on paperwork," he said.

"Paperwork sounds good to me after two murders in two years. Especially in our small town." After a moment, she continued, "You know that Victorian mansion across town?"

"Yes."

"Is it haunted?"

He picked up one of Grandma's cookies. "I used to hear it was, but come to think of it, I haven't heard anything about it for some time. It's been restored, I know. The guy who developed the Trillium Falls Resort married the teacher who lived in the house. I think they're still there. What about it?"

"Grandma's pretty sure she's got me a spot on their balcony. You know, for taking pictures of the Horsehead Nebula."

Caleb glanced behind Myka, at the framed photograph of the night sky that gained an honorable mention from a highly notable photo contest. She didn't win a prize for last year's entry, but he hoped she'd get one for the nebula. The winter night sky, when the images in the sky were easier to see, made Myka come alive and he couldn't help but cheer his fiancé on, and become fascinated with what was way up in space.

"If they're here in town, why haven't I heard about them before?" Myka asked.

"I imagine he, uh…Nash, has his own suppliers for building materials and all. Then again, you might recognize him as a patron from your store when you see him."

"I guess so. And I'm mostly in the back of the store, anyway."

"But tell me, how did Grandma Harper get involved in all this?"

"She met Mrs. Nash's grandfather at the senior center."

"Well, good. You're happy, I'm happy." He looked down before adding, "When I'm out and about, I'll stop by and see the Nash family."

She smiled. "That would be nice. Send them to the store, will you?"

He nodded.

"Right now," she added, "I want food. And I have a roast and veggies in the crock pot."

"Good. I'm right behind you. Hey, can you imagine a house like that…an old Victorian?"

"You mean lots of creaky floors and a ghost or two?"

"Yeah, I was right to peg you for a modernist."

A week later at the hardware store, Myka looked up from her desk to see a tall man with an outstretched hand.

"My name is Dillon Nash, and you must be Myka Woods."

Dillon was a tall, muscular man with tawny-brown hair that reached his shoulders.

She stood, reached out, and shook his hand. "Yes. How do you do?" She would have remembered this man if she'd seen him before. She supposed she should get out to the front of the store more often.

"Is this your first time in the store?"

"I've been here, but for the most part I have someone managing supplies."

"Oh." She didn't know what else to say.

"I understand, from Ruth Harper, that you are handy with a camera and that you would consider taking some photos of my grandfather. Uh…my wife's grandfather, but I consider him mine as well."

Myka nodded.

"She mentioned you didn't want any money, but I'd be more than happy to pay you. She said—"

"That I wanted something in exchange, but now I feel embarrassed about it."

"No. No. Don't be embarrassed. Usually, people want to get into our house for another reason. Like to look for ghosts or to visit the tower room for a story."

"Really? No, I just want to take pictures of your grandfather and then later the night sky."

"Yes, I think it would be possible for you to get an unobscured shot of the sky from… Where did you want to get it from?"

"Someplace as high as I can get. Not on the roof, of course."

"You see the place and you decide. Oh, Grandpa's birthday is in one week. Will you be able to take his picture then?"

"Yes. You've made me very happy. I'm going to try and capture the Horsehead Nebula." Only after she'd said the words did she realize that not everyone knew what that was. "It's—"

He smiled. "I know what it is. What day then?"

"Around Christmas Day. I'll let you know when, to see if that works out."

"Here's my card. I'll talk to you later, then."

She sat down with a sigh, feeling sheer bliss as before long she'd be snapping pictures of the nebula.

CHAPTER TWO

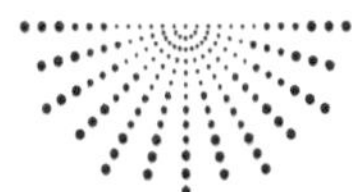

On the day of Gilby Glenn's 80th birthday, Myka parked her car at the Nash family's Victorian house and looked up at one, two, three, perhaps four levels, with surrounding decks, and turrets. She remembered seeing this house when she'd first moved into town, but at that time the house was left to ruin.

However astonished, she closed her mouth and used both hands to smooth down her blouse and suit jacket over her jeans. From the backseat, she grabbed the camera and tripod.

Myka felt a bit out of place, not knowing these people, but remembered her goal and marched up the porch stairs and stood before the tall wooden front door with an elongated oval window covered by lacey white curtains. She looked up to see a transom stained-glass window centered above the door. Beautiful.

Before she could knock, Dillon opened the door and welcomed her with a tilt of his head and an outstretched arm directing her inside.

"This is my wife, Taylor, and her, our, grandfather, Gilby Glenn."

"What a pleasure to meet you all," Myka said, then settled her eyes on a dapper-looking, Gilby. "You look nice, smart," she said, and his cheeks turned a shade of pink.

"Looking smart is a good thing. I'll take it," he said.

"Where would you like your picture taken?" she asked.

"How about in various places," cut in Taylor with a pretty smile and blonde hair curled at her shoulders. Her otherwise small frame had a gathered smock over a swelling middle.

Myka glanced around. "You'll have to guide me and don't let me get lost."

"No matter where we are, we always find our way to the dinner table," said Gilby.

"I can usually sniff out chocolate," said Myka. "I'm ready. Let's go to site one."

"I understand Ruth Harper is your neighbor," Gilby said.

"Yes. She is a close friend of mine."

Myka followed Gilby while gazing at the beautiful woodwork, built-in bookcases, and window seats. The hardwood floors had a geometric design around the corners.

"This place is lovely," she said, mentally taking back her preference for the modern look. Woodcraft was nice.

"It's taken quite a bit of work to make it this way."

"I can imagine."

Apparently, someone let a large German shepherd in.

"Down, Casper," Gilby said in a firm voice. "Sorry. He thinks everyone is here just to see him."

"Hey, beautiful boy," she said, rubbing Casper's head with a free hand. "I love German shepherds. They're so regal."

Casper's ears perked up and he looked back toward the stairs.

Gilby chuckled. "I think he either heard someone calling, or someone opening a plastic bag. Plastic bags hold several good things, you know."

"Yes, they do."

"I want you to see the room and porch on this level, before we go up another floor."

"Okay, lead the way."

After going into a door and down a short hallway, they walked into a room with a bowed front wall and windows, certainly a turret.

The furnishings told her it was a reading room with a built-in book-case lined with books. A door led them out to a deck.

"We added this door and deck, not too long ago. Also, more windows to fill this room with light and positivity. This house needs a lot of positivity to outlive the ghost stories of its past."

Part of her wanted to ask about the past while the other part took in the view. With no obstructions from trees or buildings, it was a great place to set up her tripod and snap pictures of the night sky.

"There is another deck on this side of the house, up above."

"Oh, good. Let me snap some pictures of you here, birthday boy, and then we'll go upstairs. Just let me take in the view for a minute."

"Absolutely." He stepped back.

She marveled at the beautiful view and it was obvious to her why they had added the porch. She could see people and cars moving about, the grocery store in the distance, and pastures and evergreen woods in the opposite direction. She took a deep breath of fresh air and turned so she could catch Gilby in good light for pictures.

At length, they were in the backyard finishing up the photos when guests started arriving.

"I want to thank you for coming and taking Grandpa's picture," said Taylor. "It means a lot to me and I'm sure one will be just perfect."

"I think you'll have plenty to choose from."

"Nice."

Myka cleared her throat. "Not to be rude, but I think I'll take my leave now, if you don't mind."

"Yes, of course. Thanks again," Taylor said and shook Myka's hand.

Gilby put a hand on Myka's forearm. "I'll walk you to your car."

Very nice family, she thought to herself as she pulled away from the house and headed home.

CHAPTER THREE

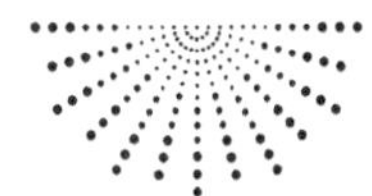

Grandma Harper walked down the street, just as Myka pulled into her driveway after work.

"Hello, sweetie." Grandma had raised her voice, making Myka smile, a warmth that touched her heart.

Grandma took hold of Myka's work bag, leaving only her purse to take inside.

"Did you take Gilby's picture?" asked Grandma as she pulled her knit hat and coat off.

"I did."

"I want to know all about it."

"Come on in, then. I'm hungry. You can help me make a salad."

"I certainly will. I can do that while you sit down and talk."

"Are you sure? I don't want to burden you with that."

"I just took a nap. I'm sure," said Grandma.

"Okay. Well, I took several pictures of Gilby."

Grandma took vegetables out of the crisper and set them on the counter. After rinsing the head of lettuce, she took a knife from the storage block. "Isn't he a nice man?"

"He is. But I'm thinking maybe you see him a little differently than I do."

Grandma smiled and for a moment chopped with a little more gusto.

"Did you find a place to take a photo of the Horse Head thingy?"

"I did. It's Nebula, by the way."

"In the second-floor turret, then?"

"No. I will be going up to the highest deck they have. It's perfect. No obstructions. I'm so excited about this."

"You always are," Grandma said and chuckled.

"I suppose so."

After taking the ends off the radishes, Grandma said, "I imagine that house is quite the showplace by now."

"Yes, it is, and I don't think they're done with it yet."

"They've had to deal with all the history of the house, you know. All the deaths, the ghosts, and a tenant that wouldn't leave."

"Whoa. I'm sure I don't hear half the town gossip while working in the back of the hardware store, with my head in the files, the back of a truck, or with the employees."

"You want to know?"

"No, I think I will let the details unfold as they'd like to tell me. I don't want any preconceived ideas. Like I said, they are nice people. And the daily news gives me plenty to worry about already."

"You mean I have to hold all this information in?" asked Grandma.

"You do. Let me grab some roast chicken and cheese." After a moment, she said, "Why don't you stay and eat with me? There should be enough for Caleb, too. If he stops by."

"Yes, I'd like that. Just let me go home and grab some rolls to go with it."

Grandma stepped out of the house and Myka sighed. She didn't want to have to think about ghosts when she went back to get the Horse Head Nebula. "Thanks for putting that image in my mind, Grandma," she said to the empty room.

After looking at the clock, she started to worry why Caleb didn't stop by, or at least call.

She grabbed her cell and called him, but it went to messages. Yet before she started to wring her hands, he called her back.

"Hey, I started to worry because I hadn't heard from you."

"Yeah, I figured as much." He let out a breath.

"Anything wrong?"

"Yes, we have a missing woman. Dillon Nash called it in."

"No. It's not his wife, is it?"

"No. Nash bought out the real estate business in Trillium Falls and then hired a woman, a realtor from California. She's missing. Hey, I won't see you tonight. I'll try to get away tomorrow."

"Okay, I get it."

Myka turned on the local news where the missing woman, Anne Holling, was shown on the screen. Then before Grandma came back, she turned off the TV and quickly searched the internet for the website of the real estate office.

Looking down at the screen, she glanced at homes for sale, and found one not too far from the Nash home as the crow flies.

"Oh, my, goodness."

Myka turned and forced a smile as Grandma came in with the rolls and they sat down for dinner.

CHAPTER FOUR

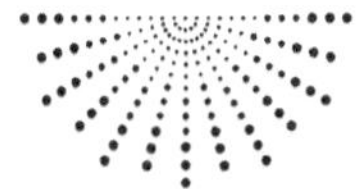

The next morning, Myka turned on the news as soon as her feet touched the bedroom floor. She wanted to hear more about this missing woman.

As a frequent viewer of the local news, missing people were uncommon in this small town. She wondered if an old boyfriend could have followed her from California to Trillium Falls. Or maybe she just wanted to get away for a few days. She hoped that was the case, but realtors needed to be assessable to their clients as much as possible.

Because it was a kidnapping, Caleb was involved. She prayed that the kidnapping wouldn't turn into a murder. If that was the case, that would be three murders in less than three years.

This woman, Anne Holling, had waist-long, straight blonde hair. You don't see that every day. She sighed and then called Caleb.

Of course, he was too busy to answer.

"I'm involved in the Holling case because I saw Anne Holling," she said, leaving a message.

She heard the doorbell ring. Perhaps Caleb was nearby.

"I'm returning your juicer," said Grandma Harper. "That cooking show was wrong. I do not like apple and beet juice. Here, take this heavy thing."

Grandma followed her into the kitchen where Myka plopped the juicer on the counter.

"Why did you come so early? You could have waited until later; tried something else."

"No, I couldn't stand looking at it anymore. I'm done with my healthy kick. I've lived long enough, anyway."

Myka chuckled. "Okay. I read that a type of corn cereal is healthy eating in one of the blue zones, so I think you have options."

"Huh." Grandma sat down at the kitchen table. "Did you hear about that missing woman?"

"Uh…yes."

"What's happening to our town?"

"I don't know. Hey, can you come back later? After work. I'd like to visit but I need to get ready."

"Yes, of course." She stood and headed to the front door. "I may have something to tell you by then."

After closing the door behind Grandma, Myka hoped that her dear friend wasn't going to get involved in the Holling case. Well, she didn't tell her anything, so she wasn't responsible.

She stopped pouring a bowl of corn cereal midway when she heard a key in the front door lock. She smiled, and her heart lifted.

"Good morning," Caleb said as he entered. He leaned down and kissed the top of her head.

"Hi. Oh, you smell good," she said.

"Thanks, but it's just shaving lotion."

"I have more cereal if you want some."

"No, I'm going to get a breakfast burrito. Something substantial since I don't know when I'll get to lunch. Now, you said you have something to tell me. Should I be worried?"

She laid her spoon down. "No, I may have some information about the missing woman."

"You're kidding, right? This is not funny."

"It's too early to be funny and I wish I was kidding. You might as well sit down."

Caleb sighed and took a seat at the table. He rubbed a hand through his short dark hair, pulled a small notepad out of his tech pants, and a pen from his jacket pocket.

"Well," she began, "I was at the Nash home, uh…you know, taking pictures of the Nash's grandfather for his birthday."

"Yes, I know."

"I'm just setting the scene here."

"Scene, you say. Oh no. Does it help to say I don't want you involved in something that can cause you harm?"

"Just listen, uh…without judgment. In the process, I took Gilby to various locations around the house and yard. Anyway, up on the second-story porch I took in the scenery around me and I happened to see a man and woman standing next to a car. So, when I heard about the missing woman and her job as a realtor, I checked out the houses for sale and found one in the area that I could see from the balcony."

"That could've been anyone."

"That did cross my mind. But when I saw a picture of her online, I realized this woman was her."

"Not to be doubting you, but how can you be so sure?"

"Because she had straight, long blonde hair that reached her waist. Don't talk yet. A man had a hand on her upper arm and then he opened the back door of the car and did that thing an officer does, where he places her inside with one hand and guides her head in with the other. That's when I noticed her hair swinging with the movement. You don't see hair that long too often. At least I don't."

"Did she seem distressed?"

"Not particularly, but he did seat her in the backseat, and he got in the front."

"Were her hands tied or zip-tied?"

"I couldn't tell."

"Color of car."

"White and four-door."

"Model?"

"I don't know. I think all the late-model cars look similar. But it wasn't an SUV of any length. That should help, right?"

"Do you know how many cars are white?"

"Of course not. Do you?"

"About sixty percent."

"That many? Wow…but do you think it could be an officer?"

He stood. "I'll check into it. If you think of anything else let me know, okay? Now be safe."

"Yes, certainly. Sorry I can't be as much help as I thought."

"That's more than we had. You never know when a piece of info will be the right one." He kissed her on top of the head once more. "Wish I could stay, since I smell good and all."

"Me too." She watched him go out the door, catching a slight whiff of fragrance. "Me, too."

CHAPTER FIVE

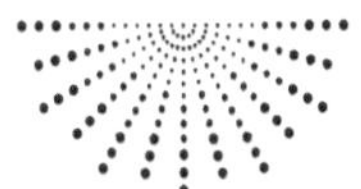

After work, Myka spotted Grandma Harper sitting on her front porch. Sitting on a step, to be more precise, something Myka didn't know she could do. At least and get back up.

"You're late; I had to sit down."

"I didn't know you were waiting for me. It's too cold out here for that. Would you like a hand up?"

"Yes, I would. Thank you." With help, Grandma stood and brushed off the seat of her slacks. "I have some things to talk over with you."

"Let me just get in the few groceries I bought and a pizza. I just have to bake it."

Grandma took the keys from her hand and opened the door for her.

With the groceries and pizza on the kitchen counter, she turned toward Grandma, now sitting in a kitchen chair.

"What's going on?" Myka asked.

Grandma rubbed her thighs, then said, "Well, I read this article recently about how women in real estate are having trouble keeping safe entering a house by themselves. You know, to show a potential client a house to buy. It talked about one lady who was killed and another who was almost attacked but got away. You can imagine all sorts of scenarios in these situations."

Myka crossed her arms. "I'm wondering why you're telling me this."

"Haven't you seen the news?"

Myka sighed. "Yes, I have."

"Is that all you have to say? Your mouth is hanging open, you know."

"You're not planning to get involved, are you, Grandma?"

"Well, think about the last two murders. We were involved in some way or another and we were helpful. Why not help this woman, too?"

"Because I co-own a hardware store. And you're a woman of a certain age and retired. I hope."

Grandma stood. "Is this about my age?"

"No. No! I'm trying to put those murders behind me. This is not our job."

Myka wanted to put her fingers in her ears to stop this conversation, but Grandma stood in front of her, in her personal space.

"I drove by the Nash house today," she said, pointing at Myka. "I stopped in front and looked up at the landings. You were there the night of the kidnapping." She sat back down. "And you've been awfully quiet about your presence there."

"What do you mean?" Myka hoped she could pull out of this unscathed. Caleb didn't need either of them in the middle of things again.

"Dillon Nash owns the real estate office now. Perhaps he said something. Could he have said anything, anything at all, about this woman or the business?"

She thought for a moment. "No, nothing. The time was focused on Gilby's birthday celebration."

"You saw some guests arrive, I'm sure. Did you see the realtor arrive?"

"No. I didn't."

"I can tell there is something you're not telling me."

"No. Caleb doesn't have any suspects yet. But listen, you will not interfere in Caleb's investigation."

Grandma stood and put a hand behind her back. "Of course not."

"Grandma. Let me see your hand. The other one, the one behind your back." Myka spun her around. "I thought so, your fingers are crossed."

"Well, I'm trying to be useful. You don't object to an old woman trying to be useful, do you?"

"No. But if you want to be useful you could come help me in the store."

"I don't want a job. I've worked plenty in my day. I want to use my mind to look for clues that might help find the missing woman."

Myka crossed her arms again when Grandma stepped back. "So, you think she's missing, not dead."

"I don't believe a body has been found."

"I don't think so either, but Caleb is involved in this."

"Of course he would be, to help figure this out."

Grandma cleared her throat. "I'm wondering…well, Dillon Nash is Anne's boss, owner of the business. How would you like it if your husband worked closely with a beautiful, single woman like Anne? Could his wife be so jealous that she'd cause this woman harm?"

"I don't know. From the moment I entered their house and was introduced, I noticed that he smiled at her like a proud man in love. And she's maybe five-foot-two and pregnant. Anne's five-foot-ten, I think I heard."

"Yes, but could Taylor have instigated it?"

"She's a first-grade teacher for goodness sake."

Grandma rubbed her chin. "She's someone to keep in mind though."

"Okay. Now, you've lived around here your whole life, so you know all the nooks and crannies in this area."

Grandma leaned forward and nodded.

"Where do you think the woman is? Where could she be hiding?" asked Myka.

"I don't think she's hiding," said Grandma.

"So, maybe something like an old boyfriend may have come to town."

"Yep," said Grandma. "And wants her back. She's from California I understand."

Myka sat down next to Grandma at the table and said, "I suppose that could be true. Except someone from out of state won't know the landscape around here. So, he'd get out of town as quick as he could."

"Sadly, I think it's someone from around here," said Grandma and shook her head.

"I don't like to think that our small town is unsafe."

"This is a new age, Myka. A lot more crime than there used to be. More people are living today, as well."

"I suppose so."

Both became lost in their own somber thoughts as they sat down to eat pizza.

Myka's cell dinged, and she looked down to see a text from Caleb. *Anne's friend picked her up from a house she planned to sell. She had stuff in her arms, so she sat in the back seat to manage it. He's a new hire cop by the name of James Nielsen. Goes by Officer Jim. Not a suspect.*

Good, she didn't even have to tell Grandma about it.

"Okay," said Grandma. "I've lived here a long time, so I asked myself where I would put a dead body if I was a local, of course, and I came up with one place."

Myka smiled. "Only one place?"

"Yes, let's leave the dishes. Come on, I want to take you somewhere."

CHAPTER SIX

"Where are you taking me, Grandma?" asked Myka, both hands now on her car's steering wheel.

"Only the place that's been super scary since, well, since before you were born. There's been rumors of ghosts and danger spooking every teenager for decades. And the house has been empty for such a long time that the roof is starting to cave in."

"Well, I can't wait to see it," Myka said sarcastically. But all in all, a nice ride in the country with her friend would do her some good.

"Yes, even more stories about this house over the Nash house."

"Really? Two scary houses?"

"Yes, that's right." Grandma leaned forward studying the street. "Turn right at the next road,"

"I don't know Grandma. That's a stretch of the imagination, I'm afraid."

"Just bear with me."

"Okkaay."

Up ahead she saw it, a dilapidated mansion with a series of pillars at the front, three stories, and an attic. It was the scariest looking house she'd ever seen. "I can see why no one wants to enter this place. If you don't die of fright, you'll die from something falling on you."

"Yes," said Grandma. "This town is a firm believer in things of a paranormal nature. That is why Taylor Nash had such a hard time after she bought the Victorian she has now, and it wasn't half as bad as this house."

"It is creepy. Are you going in there?"

"We're both going in there. I'm an old lady and I need help. You know, like I could fall and break a hip or something."

"You use that old label like a get-out-of-jail-free card."

"If it works, I use it. Let's go."

"Perhaps I should text Caleb and tell him I'm going in."

"Perhaps you should not. Bring your phone with you. In case of emergency."

Myka let out the breath she'd been holding. "How about we turn around and go home?"

"Anne could be trapped in the basement, and you would just leave her there."

"There's a basement?"

"I have my shotgun. You'll be safe."

"What? Where is it?"

"Remember when I asked you to open the trunk?"

"What?"

"Come on, roll with it. We'll be out of here in no time. Open the trunk," said Grandma and walked around to the back of the car.

Grandma was determined to enter that house and it wasn't smart to let her go in alone. But she'd have to admit that she was glad she smuggled in her gun. Myka stepped out of the car and Grandma, with a shotgun in one hand, passed her a large wrench with the other.

"A wrench?"

"What better thing for a hardware store owner?"

"I guess so." At least she had something in her hand. She made sure her cell was in her coat pocket.

This was simply a big old house, so why did she feel like a dark cloud had settled on her? Something about it made her heart start pounding as she walked to the front door.

Grandma pushed the door and it made a loud creaking sound as it opened. They stepped into the house. The door creaked shut behind them.

"It's dark and no electricity," Myka said in warning.

"Yeah. Where should we go first?" Grandma pulled a flashlight out of her pocket. Sadly, it appeared to be losing some battery power. Grandma shook it and it brightened.

"I can go upstairs and you can check the basement."

"I cannot," Myka said firmly.

"Come on then. This would make a great Halloween haunted house, wouldn't it?"

"It already is." Myka walked closely behind Grandma, her free hand at her back in case she took a misstep.

"Nothing on this floor. Let's go up another."

"You mean where the roof is falling in?"

"Well, let's at least take a gander from the top step."

Myka took in a big breath and let it out slowly. She wanted to move quicker and tugged at the back of Grandma's coat like a child trying to get her mother's attention.

"Okay, nothing here either. But I feel like she's here, Myka."

"I know you do. Let's check the basement area to see if it's safe enough. It's awfully cold in here." She could hear the wind shaking a window and banging from what she hoped was only a loose shutter.

"The basement. Yes. Do you suppose there is a back door to get to the basement? A lot of old houses have that. That just might be safest," Grandma said, starting to sound winded.

Somehow, they pushed out of a sticking back door.

"Grandma, do you hear anything?"

She turned her head from side to side. "Nothing besides the weather beating this house. Why?"

"I don't think she's here."

"I'm not done, yet. Look there's an old shed there."

Myka sighed. "The roof is almost all caved in. She's not there."

Grandma turned and in the light of the flashlight, Myka could see a tear shining on her cheek. "I was so sure she was here. I could almost hear her in my dreams."

"I understand. This whole town is deeply concerned for her. We all want her to be alive. Everyone is searching for her and now we have too."

"Yes, we'll check the basement and then go," said Grandma and, for a moment, locked fingers with Myka's hand.

Myka had no trouble opening the basement door.

CHAPTER SEVEN

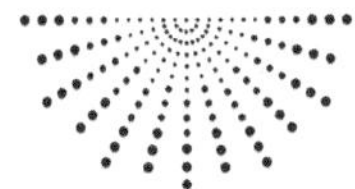

Grandma took her flashlight and pointed it down into the darkness.

Overhead a floorboard creaked. The wind whistled.

"Be careful, Grandma. I'm nervous about these stairs." Besides that, this dark hole had to be the scariest part of the house.

"The hair is standing on the back of my neck. Watch this stair, two down. Only half a step. Keep to the right."

"Okay. I feel cold air coming in here too," added Myka.

Finally, in what seemed like an hour, they were at the bottom of the stairs. "Can you see anything, Grandma?"

"Not right here. But over there I see a light under a door. Here, hold the flashlight.

Myka watched Grandma open her double-barrel shotgun, load shells, and snap it back together. It made her feel a whole lot better. With the flashlight in one hand and the wrench in the other, they walked toward the line of light.

Myka's heart pounded with fear. The only sound Myka heard was the two of them slowly testing and then stepping along the floor.

"Step back," said Grandma and she put the gun under her arm and tried the door handle, then stepped back. When the door sprung open, she aimed her gun.

Myka slowly stepped in and then focused on the room.

A large dog crate sat in the corner. It had a gate-in-gate design for the placement of food or items without escape. Blankets were crumpled up on the floor and a bucket in the back corner.

"Why would someone leave their dog here?" asked Myka.

"I think we need to look closer; the light is rather dim in here."

"And that smell. It smells like a musty basement but of urine, too. Doesn't it?"

"Oh no," said Grandma, grief in her voice. "Not a body. Don't let it be a body."

The cage was locked. They looked at each other and then flashed the light around the room.

"A key is on a hook, right there by the door." Grandma reached for it, came back, and handed it to Myka.

"Why would—"

"Just focus on the pen, right now," said Grandma. "We need to check under those blankets."

"You're right." Myka opened the door and bent her head, so she fit into the cage. Her hand shook as she slowly pulled the blankets back to reveal a blonde head.

"It's her," she said. "She's not moving. It's her but her hair has been cut. Like a rough scissor cut to her shoulders.

Grandma turned from her and aimed her gun at the door. "Feel her skin, check for a pulse."

Myka shook her shoulder to no avail, so she put her fingers on her neck. Her skin was warm, and she felt a pulse. "She's alive. Thank God. I'm calling 911 and then I'm checking for blood, injury, to try to explain this."

"She could be doped up."

Myka turned her head to look at Grandma. "What?"

"He, or she, is coming back," said Grandma. "He's going to toy with her some more."

Myka could only hope that her words were a result of watching too many mysteries. Yet, this was not logical. No blood anywhere.

"There's urine in the bucket. Looks like she's been awake before," said Myka.

"I hope he comes back; I'd like to shoot him."

"Hopefully the police will be here soon. She's moving her head." Myka shook Anne's shoulder. "Wake up."

Anne's eyes opened and spread wide in panic.

"Don't be afraid. We're getting you out of here. You're groggy right now, but I think you will be okay." Myka tried to explain who she was but still Anne looked at her in fear.

"Did I hear you mention Caleb's name when you talked to 911?" asked Grandma.

"Yes, they were going to get the news to him, too." Myka crossed her arms to keep her hands from fidgeting. "Does it feel like the minutes are slowly ticking by?"

"Yes, and this shotgun is getting awful heavy for these old arms."

"I can hear some noise up above," said Grandma. Still, she aimed at the door.

Myka wondered why no one was calling out. Sounded like one person creeping down the stairs. She tried to tell herself it was because of the broken stairs. The footfalls had stopped, and the person had halted at the door. Why wasn't he calling out?

Grandma waved at Myka to make sure she was silent, making Myka's heart pound.

The doorknob turned and the door creaked open.

"Put your hands up or I'll shoot!" warned Grandma.

"It's the police," said a firm female voice and she walked into the light of the room. "What's going on here?"

Grandma lowered her gun.

"Thank God you're here," said Myka.

"I heard the call, and I was nearby. What's in the cage there?"

"You said you heard the call," said Grandma. "Just what did the call say?"

"Relax, it's okay. I heard a trouble call. Are you the trouble?" she asked Grandma.

"Your uniform is different. The color," said Myka. "What's your name?"

"You two get out of here now or I'll arrest you both."

Grandma wielded her gun, aiming. "We're not moving. Not until more officers arrive, in department uniform."

"Don't be silly. I answered the call. No one else will be here."

Myka knew Caleb would be. Eventually. "Okay," she said. "We have a dead body here. It looks to be that real estate lady who's been missing."

The officer shook her head. "Dead? No! That can't be."

"My name is Ruth Harper. What is your name?"

"No. She can't be dead."

A moan came from the blankets.

"She's not dead. Now you two get out of here. I'll wrap this up."

A thunderous noise came from outside the door. Myka knew it was the sound of officers making their way down to them.

The woman officer stood flat against the wall, as if trying to make herself invisible.

Grandma laid her gun on the floor and then put up her hands.

Caleb was among the first to come in the door.

Myka pointed behind him. "Right there! Right there. The woman officer trying to leave. Grab her."

"The stretcher's coming down, it'll block her. She won't get far." Still, he turned and gave directions to the officers, and they turned to follow her.

Myka, now outside of the cage, moved to the side and looked down at Anne. "Now that the police are here you will be fine. A stretcher is coming for you."

"You'll be right as rain, in no time," said Grandma beside Myka.

Sitting up, Anne's eyes darted toward the door.

Myka tried to clear the heaviness in her throat. "She is being arrested as we speak. You have no more worries, Anne."

The paramedics prepared to move Anne out of the cage, so they backed away.

"I'll need a strong policeman to help me up the stairs," said Grandma and winked at Myka.

As Grandma grabbed the arm of the biggest officer, Caleb said, "Grandma, we're going to have a long talk about your detective work!"

Apparently, Grandma used her, "I can't hear," card, thought Myka, because she didn't reply.

EPILOGUE

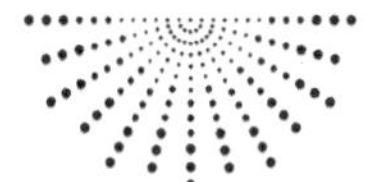

Myka couldn't imagine a better place to spend Christmas Eve than at the Nash's Victorian home, all decorated for the holiday in red, burgundy, green, and brown. Colorful bows were at the top of the stair rails and boughs of fir edged the stairs. Three white-frocked Christmas trees with colorful blinking lights were placed one in each panel of the Victorian bay window in the front room.

A glance revealed two other couples besides Dillon and Taylor, Grandma Ruth and Gilby, Anne's friend, Officer Jim Nielsen, and Anne.

"Hello, everyone," said Myka, and Caleb nodded his head.

"I know this is a surprise to see us," said Anne, "but I wanted to say thank you in a big way. So, I talked Dillon into letting us come as well. Not to mention it was the night to snap photos of the Horse Head Nebula. It couldn't have been planned better. And I must say that I'd like you all to be my friends."

"Absolutely, but no thanks are needed," said Grandma. "Something told me you were there."

"That reminds me, Grandma uh…Ruth," said Myka. "Our search brought us to the Hasting place, thinking perhaps a local had taken

Anne. But Cindy Rich was not a local. So how did she know to take Anne there?"

"That's easy," said Jim. "As you know Cindy was my girlfriend, for a short time, by the way, and when she started acting like a crazy ex-girlfriend, I decided to apply for a job with the police department here. I thought that was the only way to avoid her since she worked at the same precinct. So, Cindy knew about the old Hasting mansion because you could see it in the distance from the road on the way to Trillium Falls."

Caleb nodded. "And the way the tie-in with Anne is, as you can see, Jim and Anne have become a couple. I'm just glad you weren't working when Cindy was arrested. Could have been worse."

Jim looked down. "I'm certainly sorry about all this. And I'm more than glad I wasn't accused of the kidnapping. You know, since I was seen picking Anne up."

"Hey," said Anne, "you have nothing to be sorry about." She patted his knee. "And I think Ruth's intuition came from somewhere else. The Big Guy Upstairs."

Grandma Ruth smiled. "I'd like to think that's where the idea came from. And your hair was cut because of jealousy or delusional thinking. But you are beautiful, my dear, just as you are."

"Thank you. And hair grows back." Anne slapped a knee. "Now let's hear about the Horse Head, uh..."

"Nebula," said everyone else and laughed.

Caleb stood up, moved to the door, and picked up the instruments that Myka needed to get her perfect shot. Realizing that he knew what they were all called, told him multitudes about how much he doted on Myka's every word. "Uh...give us some time to set up, and then I'll call you up." Truly, he wanted some time alone with Myka in a room with a view.

After a long series of clicks, she'd taken the many pictures she wanted, then turned to him with a big smile. "I'm so happy," she said and hugged Caleb, and then he danced her around the deck.

"I could do this forever," he said but pulled away. "But I know we'd never be forgiven if you don't show the rest of them the nebula while the time is right. I'd like a rain check, though."

"You've got one."

Caleb called down for Anne and Jim to come up and do the first viewing.

Myka smiled at him over Anne's head. He knew she reveled in showing Anne the nebula. Something special for her Christmas and New Year with Jim ahead.

This novelette takes place in the small, fictional town of Trillium Falls. To learn more about that area and Gilby, Taylor, and Dillon consider my novel, *Secrets of Trillium Falls*.

ABOUT THE AUTHOR

Mary Vine is an author, publisher, speaker and retired educator. She writes contemporary and historical romantic fiction, a time travel series, and inspirational children's books. Mary and her husband can usually be found in Southwest Idaho or Northeast Oregon. To learn more about Mary and all her books, go to her website: http://authormaryvine.com

STORY INSPIRATION
I've often thought of writing a mystery with one or two humorous, snoopy older characters. I haven't been able to fit these personalities in one of my fiction books. Until now. Here's a chance to revisit the characters of my fictional small town of Trillium Falls in *Secrets of Trillium Falls*.

Sky Painter

Maggie Lynch

SKY PAINTER

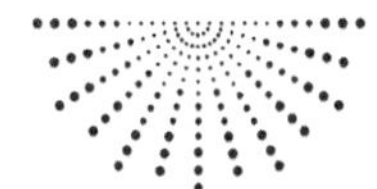

Sora had been different since her birth. She was born at eight months, not nine, but perfectly healthy. However, the midwife did notice the baby's eyes were unlike any she had seen. One eye was dark blue with speckles of white that look liked tiny stars in the sky, and the pupil was seemingly invisible. The other eye was pale green with a bright golden pupil like the sun. Over the next two years, a number of doctors examined her eyes, believing she might be partially blind or would become completely blind. But by the age of two they declared her sight was excellent though the coloring was one of a kind

As a toddler she was a happy child, never went through the terrible twos. She loved being in the stroller. Rather than pay attention to the ground or the trees or flower, her mother noticed that Sora spent the entire walk giggling and pointing to the sky. Sometimes her left hand would move as if she were tracing the clouds, the sun. If it rained and her mother covered her with a hood, Sora held out her tiny hands to catch the raindrops.

Where most children learned words like mama and dada first, Sora learned sky and sun and stars first. She seemed a very happy child though a little strange.

At age three, her preschool teacher sent home water color paintings that Sora had done in class during their painting period. While most three-year-old children preferred finger paintings that included large splotches, or hand outlines, Sora painted a somewhat impressionist view of the sky. She used many different hues depending on her mood. On her giggle days, she painted beautiful blue skies of many shades. When she was pensive, she painted clouds against grey-blue skies ranging from fading sun on one half of the paper to storm clouds on the other half.

By the age of five, Sora had expanded her paintings from an impressionist painting to include more realistic representations of sunlight against clouds and different hues of the sky. She was very good at getting the lighting just right, following the angle of the light throughout the work. By age seven, she was very attached to creating **sky** tetraptychs, paintings of four related canvases. Each painting appeared to represent a specific phase of daylight—sunrise, sunset, approaching storms and rainbows. By age nine she gave up these separate related canvases and instead her canvas became larger so that she could paint many phases of the daytime sky in the same painting, seamlessly moving from left to right. As she grew older she would change and sometimes move from right to left. Her final piece before entering middle school was to create a sky painting depicting the phases in a circle around an invisible axis.

From age twelve to fifteen, the night sky became Sora's obsession. No matter what prompting her teachers or parents did, she did not wish to return to painting a day sky. It wasn't all dark and dreary. Sometimes it was beautiful, almost romantic, with shooting stars in the heavens. At other times the ominous storm with thunder and lightning became prominent.

By age sixteen, her teachers felt she was painting too many ominous works. They feared for her mental health. They referred Sora to the school counselor, concerned that something awful must be going on in her life. If not home, perhaps some trauma at school that she wasn't sharing.

When the counselor couldn't identify a problem, she suggested the family enter group counseling to uncover some hidden difficulties. That yielded nothing. Next stop was a psychiatrist who could diagnose a problem and "fix" it.

Her parents had been supportive of Sora as a child, but now that she was a teen and close to graduation they were concerned. Because everyone else told them there was something wrong with Sora, they believed it. They were told that painting only the sky was highly unusual, but not troublesome in itself. However, painting the dark sky, stormy skies for several years now must be indicative of some hidden trauma that needed to be dealt with.

After several sessions with the psychiatrist, her mother took Sora aside just before bed. "Sora, I don't believe anything is wrong with you. I think it is my fault that you are stuck in this night sky cycle. I know we've been telling you there's no money in painting. Most painters aren't even recognized in their lifetime. We don't want to stop your painting. We simply want you to learn something that will bring you enough money to support yourself. You can do both. You are smart enough to do both."

Sora nodded and smiled in that Mona Lisa way she always did when she disagreed with someone.

"I know that smile," her mother said. "It means you will ignore my advice."

"I have a spiritual calling, and painting dark skies is a part of my preparation. Do you judge a priest or a nun who chooses to spend the rest of their life cloistered or in poverty serving the poor? Do you believe that they are less than someone who works for a large software company? Do you judge a boy who is given to the monastery to train and become a monk whose life is meditation and reliance on those who would offer food and drink?"

Her mother sat up straighter, her spine stiffened as she raised her chin. "I'm not judging you. I just want what is best for you."

"I love you, Mom. But no matter what I try to explain, you will have a counter-argument. We see the world differently. We see how we fit in the larger universe differently. I cannot be the adult daughter you want me to be. I will never fit in with the sons and daughters of your friends, or our neighbors. I am different and I know there is no one else like me."

"But you're lonely."

"No, I'm not lonely. I am filled everyday with my paintings that come from a space inside me and beyond me at the same time. I am filled with my questions and the paintings provide ideas and answers. I am filled with a singular purpose to paint the sky. I don't know why; but I know it will make a difference. It helps not only me but eventually will help others."

After that discussion, her parents stopped asking and Sora stopped trying to explain. After several months, even the psychiatrist accepted there was nothing he could do to help Sora. "I am releasing you with no diagnosis, he told her. This is the final day we will meet."

"Uncurable, right?" Sora giggled with the news. "I'm so happy you are coming around."

"I haven't come around, he said. I've given up on trying to understand. I understand painting sunshine and flowers. They are dreams of escape, a way to deal with a world with injustice and evil. But children who draw dark images for years usually means trauma, depression, unresolved issues. But I find none of those."

"I'm exploring," Sora said, with an innocent smile. "Day skies are for children—especially children who have little contact with reality. Children seek invisible friends to share their world. Children seek reassurance in happy dreams. Many adults also want to revisit childhood for that reassurance. Adult dreams are not the same, even if adults try to push them away. Adult dreams are of unresolved darkness, darkness so scary they must seek day skies to hide from them. Night skies are interesting, complex, always asking for questions, always asking you to look deeper."

"And what might those question be?" the psychiatrist asked.

"Who are we? What is our purpose? How do we know? Why do we look away instead of explore? Why do we want everything so immediate, so easy, so perfect on the first try? Why do we value everyone being alike? What is so scary about being different? Dark skies are not bad or good. Day skies are not good or bad. We need all of it, whether we know it or not. I am learning. I'm becoming a better painter, a better reflection of the universe. When I am fully formed, I will paint the sky for individuals, for entire communities, for anyone in need of answering questions. The more I paint, the more I understand myself and the more I understand others."

The psychiatrist began to laugh. "A rainmaker. A real rainmaker." He laughed so hard he had to wrap his arms around himself and squeeze to stop the laughing.

"More than a rainmaker, a sky painter—I paint a sky that can provide rain or sun, cold or humid. I paint the sky and the sky brings the rain." Sora pointed to the sky outside his window. Look there and I will paint for you."

He gasped as he watched it turn from stormy to sunlight then to night and back to stormy again during a brief time. He shook his head and faced her. "That's not possible. It is an illusion. A very good one but still an illusion."

Sora smiled. "As you wish." She pointed to the window again. "Look to the hills in the distance. Do you see the rainbow. Rainbows can only be made from raindrops or fog with the light of the sun behind them. Behind that sliver of sun are clouds from dark skies somewhere else. It all works together."

The psychiatrist shook his head. "You are smart and talented, Sora. I don't know how you will live in the world, but I'm certain you will be just fine. Let's get your parents in here, so we can provide closure for them as well."

The psychiatrist reassured Sora's parents that Sora was fine. He explained that all children with very special talents tend to think deeply, ask more existential questions about life, death, and the meaning of it all and their answers are worked out in their art.

"But she doesn't talk about it with us," her mother lamented. "We don't know where she's going, how she'll end up supporting herself. This Is not the way we raised her."

"You've been good parents," the psychiatrist reassured them. "You have loved her and given her space to express herself. What's important is for Sora to discover her purpose for herself. It is not something that can be dictated by anyone else. She is insightful. She is intuitive. She is a singularly unique teenager in her talent, but still has all the hormones and is testing her need for separation from parents. This is normal of all teens."

"But what about college? What about a job? What about marriage?" Her father asked. "She is doing nothing toward any of those things."

"How do you know she is doing none of those things?" the psychiatrist asked.

"She doesn't talk about it," her mother said. "She only says she is going to paint the sky. What does that mean? How will she live? She has not made a single cent off her hundreds of paintings."

"I don't intend to sell them," Sora interrupted.

"My point is proven," her mother said. "She will die a pauper."

"I don't see a resolution to your differences. Your daughter has one view of her life's work and you have another."

"Give her a pill," her father spoke loudly. "That's your job, isn't it? Fix her. She's sixteen. She doesn't know what she wants. She can't possibly know what she wants. She hasn't lived enough. Make her normal, so we don't have to worry and she won't starve to death."

"I'd rather starve to death than not use my gifts for painting the sky." Sora said. "You ask me to be like you, to choose your path. I've already done much of what you've asked. I've taken the classes you told me to take. I have straight A's in all the preparation courses for college—math, literature, history, geography. Now it's time for me to finish the preparation to be a sky painter."

"See!" Her mother pointed a finger at her and shook it. "That is not normal. There is no such job as a sky painter, Sora."

"Just try it," her father pleaded. "A pill that will take these delusional thoughts away."

The psychiatrist shook his head. "Let's all take a breath for a moment and calm down."

Sora giggled and looked up at the ceiling in the office. It was so bland. No wonder people couldn't think well in here. She began moving her fingers and then her arms as the psychiatrist continued to speak to her parents.

"There is no pill for growing up. There is no pill for making decisions that parents wish to have on their timeline. Just give her time. Continue to support her. It is normal for teens to be reflective, to search for their own purpose, to find a path separate from their parents. It is also normal for them not to talk to their parents about this until they have some answers."

"It will be okay," Sora said continuing to look at the ceiling and move her arms.

Her father pointed at her and lowered his voice to the psychiatrist, "See how she's moving? She's always done this since a child. She's painting an invisible sky above her. That's *not* normal."

"It's not invisible," Sora said aloud. "You'll see. I'll fix it. I'll fix everything."

The psychiatrist wrinkled his brow. "Are you painting the sky?" he asked. "Is it daytime or night time?"

"It is neither and both," Sora replied. "You'll see. Keep talking with each other. You'll see." She giggled again and smiled at the ceiling.

Her mother continued in a similar whisper to her father. "With no siblings, no friends, no life partner, who will Sora turn to in times of trouble? Will she end up in a cult? Be a poor painter trying to sell her work on the street? Who will care for her when we are gone?"

Her father picked up the thread. "She hasn't talked about jobs, hasn't talked about college. In fact, she doesn't talk about anything except her paintings, and that's only when we ask."

"Do you talk to anyone?" the psychiatrist asked her.

Sora nodded. "Of course. I answer my teachers when they ask a question. I have friends who eat lunch with me and we talk about how to help people get along better."

"Do you have a boyfriend?" her mother asked.

Sora shook her head. "I will never marry. Sky painting is my life, will be my life forever."

"See," her mother said to the psychiatrist. "That is crazy talk. That is like a cult religion."

"Mom..." Sora drew out the name. "If I decided to be a nun would you think that is abnormal?"

"Of course, we're not Catholic," her father responded. "Where would you get an idea like that?"

"Okay, what if I decided to be a pastor?"

"Is that what you've decided?" her mother asked, her voice quiet as she looked from beneath her lashes.

"No, not exactly. But a nun or a pastor feels a calling from God, a monk or a Shaman feels a calling to spend their life in learning, meditation, and in service to others. They all choose to follow that calling even if it doesn't have a great paycheck or doesn't allow for getting married or having children. I feel the same way. Only my calling is to paint the sky."

She paused and took a deep breath. She could feel the room's air thicken and smiled. She spoke slowly, carefully, without anger. "I don't expect you to understand that calling any more than you would understand if I said I want to become a nun and I wasn't Catholic. But believe me when I say God has chosen me to be a sky painter. In fact, you might say I am filled with the same ecstatic purpose as a nun or priest or pastor or monk."

Her mother bowed her head and rubbed her brow. "Why are we just now hearing this? When did this happen? Who talked you into this."

"I've known as long as I've had the ability to reason and think. I've known since my first paintings in preschool, only I didn't have the words to explain it. I imagine I knew before birth, though that does sound crazy. It is who I am. I'm sorry it scares you. I'm sorry you're worried, but I cannot change this path I've been offered. More than that, I do not want to change this path."

Her father pointed to the psychiatrist. "See, she is clearly delusional. There is a pill for that, right? God doesn't ask someone to be a sky painter."

"Do you know the heart of God?" Sora asked in a soft voice.

"No. No one knows the heart of God," her father admitted.

"I think this is not getting us anywhere right now," the psychiatrist interrupted. "Let's stick with what we do know, and how Sora is doing and has done over the past sixteen years that we can measure."

"Like what?" her father asked.

"Has she ever complained about going to school or been caught ditching classes?"

"Never," both her parents responded.

"How have her grades been?"

"Straight A's in all classes."

"Are these easy classes? Classes only for painting?"

"Of course not. We've made sure she has taken everything necessary to get into a good college."

"Has Sora ever snuck out at night? Got in trouble for doing something you've told her not to do? Has she ever been punished? Has anyone else in her life, her school, your church ever shared a concern about her behavior?"

Her parents shook their head.

"Has she tried to harm herself? Has she ever explicitly done anything you've asked her not to do?"

"Like what," her mother asked. "We have asked her not to paint for a week or a month. She doesn't do it at home but she does at school, because she is always in a painting class."

"In other words, she is a near perfect child except for this obsession with sky painting," the psychiatrist said in a soft tone.

"But it is the obsession that concerns us. It's...unnatural," her mother said. "When I was her age I was boy crazy. I was a cheerleader. I was involved with a large group of friends, both boys and girls. We hung out together, did things together, supported each other. I met her father in college. It has been a happy marriage. One we can count on for life."

"I'm not you," Sora said. "I know you wish I were, but I'm not and never will be. Can't you love me for who I am?"

"Of course, we love you," her father said. "We've always loved you. We just worry."

"I can't stop you from worrying," Sora said. "In time you will see why I am needed. You will see that my calling can change people's lives. You must be patient. I am not completely formed yet, but I will be soon and you will see."

"Very well spoken," the psychiatrist nodded to Sora. "I think it is best to embrace her gift and give her time. Sora must do what she feels is her calling. As long as it is not illegal, she is not hurting herself or others, and everything else seems to be going fine, I don't see a problem. It is normal for teens to have an obsession. Sometimes these obsessions, particularly ones in the arts, are special talents that do make a difference in the world."

"A singer, a cello player, a woodworker, even a sculptor or a painter who wants to sell her paintings, I can understand," her mother said. "But painting only the sky and never even trying to sell them doesn't make sense. It is an obsession upon an obsession."

"But they are not the same," Sora countered. "Every painting is different. Have you ever seen me paint the exact same thing twice."

"Well, no, but it is the same subject. Why don't you paint a house or a field or flowers, or a person or even an animal? Why always the sky?"

"I do paint a house beneath the sky. I do paint a field or flowers or animals or even people, but the sky is the focus. The heavens above rule over all. Without the sky there would be no people, no food, no animals, no vegetation of any kind. Humans look to the sky to plan their day, to plant crops, to decide if they will stay home or go out. The weather is a huge part of all that we have."

The psychiatrist smiled. "You have a point."

Sora continued. "I plan to change the world with my sky paintings."

"Change the world with a painting?" her father asked. "A painting with no monetary value?"

"There is more to the world than money," Sora responded.

"I don't think Sora and you will reach agreement today," the psychiatrist said. "I see no reason to give her any pills."

Her parents' shoulders slumped and they stood to shake the man's hand. The psychiatrist smiled in that soothing, half smile of understanding that was typical of all the previous counselors they'd employed.

Sora smiled and stopped her hands moving in the air. "Look above you." She pointed to the ceiling.

Her mother screamed. Her father gasped. The psychiatrist opened his mouth but no sound came out.

"The…ceiling. It's gone. It's a dark sky," her father whispered.

"No, it's not," her mother insisted. "It's a trick. A trick to make us believe. I don't know how you did it, Sora, but stop it. Stop it now!"

"If you refuse to look or to see and study, then you must leave," Sora said, her voice soft and compassionate. "This is who I am. This is who I am learning to be but on a much larger scale, a universal scale."

Her father took her mother's hand and led her to the door. "I hope this is truly a gift from God, not the devil," he said as he ushered them both out the door.

Sora closed the door silently.

"I see you fully now," Sora said. Again, she moved her hands and looked up at the ceiling creating more clouds and a stormy view of the night sky. "You are conflicted. You lost a patient to suicide early in your career."

His mouth agape, he asked. "How could you possibly know that? No one knows that except my therapist from long ago."

She pointed to the ceiling and moved her hands again. "That cloud has been hanging over you ever since. You are afraid of missing a sign and losing another patient. I am not that patient. I would never give up my gift."

His eyes widened as he looked to the ceiling and it continued to change. "What? How did…?"

"It is real. Look beyond the cloud. Look at the light above it. Look at the fields in the distance where the sun is shining." She waved her hands again and changed the painting. That trauma can no longer stop you from being the best psychiatrist you can be. Your painting will change as you improve. You can believe again."

"But…how? It looks as if the ceiling has disappeared and I am outside."

"You are inside and outside. Do you feel the slight breeze?"

He took in a breath, closed his eyes and opened them again. "This is not real. It can't be." He looked around his office. "Everything in the room is the same except the ceiling. That's not possible."

"Yet it is here," she said. "You know it, deep inside. This is my gift. This is your personal sky painting. Only you can see it—only you."

Then she hugged him. "You helped me understand my gift. You have released me and I have released you."

Then she went out the door.

Sora graduated from high school and was chosen to be Valedictorian.

When the principle announced her name and what her plans were, unlike other decorated students, she didn't name a college. She said she was taking a gap year to be a sky painter for communities around the world. Then she gave a speech thanking her parents, her teachers, her friends for all they had given and how they had shaped her. She talked about the joy of being different and encouraged others who looked different, learned differently, thought differently to follow their passions and not be afraid. She received a standing ovation for her speech.

A week later her parents hugged her goodbye as she climbed on a train in Seattle. Having checked her bicycle through baggage, she carried a backpack of clothing and basic supplies, including her favorite paintbrushes. She promised she would call if she needed help. She promised she would keep in touch by posting to her social media account under the name Sky Painter. She would send pictures and brief news as she was able.

Day 2: Got off at Glacier National Park. The sky was cloudless and bright blue. So bright I could barely look at it for long. Beautiful mountains and sky. But the beauty was not my calling. Two hundred miles away the Horse Gulch fire near Helena has already burned more than ten thousand acres and evacuations are being ordered. I'm painting the sky with clouds and rain for at least three days. No thunderstorm or lightning, no big wind, just clouds and rain.

National News Day 3: *In spite of the weather forecast being at least* *another week with no rain, after midnight in Horse Gulch, a light drizzle began to fall. The moon was completely covered with clouds. Later in the day, the drizzle turned to rain providing a good drenching of the fire. Now this rain is predicted to last a minimum of three days. Scientists are analyzing how their models did not see it coming. What phenomenon created rain out of such dryness.*

Day 7: Back on train. Not sure where I'm getting off next. The sky will guide me.

Day 9: Off in Grand Forks. Cool college town. Ran into a lost soul at the Flood Memorial Monument on the banks of the Red River. Like me, she's an artist, but instead of painting she's a dancer. Her career has ended because of some kind of problem with her hip. I told her I'd paint the sky for her to help her find a transition from dancing to something else—something only she will understand what to do.

@Sora from @dancinghip: *Wow! You were soooooo right. I left the city and headed to the country where I could look at the sky without so many lights. I laid on the ground and looked up as you instructed. A cloud was covering the moon, but I could see a small leakage of light behind the cloud. Maybe 15 min. later it moved, but the sky was even darker. I blinked to adjust my vision and suddenly I saw the eight stars you described, what some call the dancer constellation. But it was only for a few minutes and then it disappeared as if it was my imagination. Then, the Milky Way in all its glory shown above me. I've never seen the Milky Way at night with the naked eye. I've made a decision to teach...not dancers who want to be professionals but normal people, disabled people, people of all sizes. I'm going to teach them to dance in whatever way they can. Perhaps one day I'll dance in the sky with you.*

The almost daily posts captured Sora's journey across the U.S. via ship to Europe and many hikes and biking trips there. Often a local newspaper article followed Sora's description of painting the sky for a specific purpose. The comments were about an unusual sky color or weather pattern, or possible ancient signs of healing interpreted by indigenous people.

As the tenth month of her journey began, Sora posted less and less. She knew her journey on earth was near the end and she had no way to capture it in words. Her body was changing, her mind was melding with the universe, soon she would be unable to write or type. Soon she would be living in the sky and painting with a canvas larger than she could imagine.

She gathered the strength to pen a final letter home in long hand. The next day she took it to the post office and enclosed her final canvas painting of the night sky.

Dear Mom and Dad,

Thank you for loving me and supporting me on this journey, even though it is beyond your ability to understand who, what I am. It has been transformational for me and I hope healing for those I have met. I'm afraid I'm no longer able to return home. I'm being called to the heavens to paint the sky of many worlds. I pray my journaling this past year has helped you to understand how I'm transforming. I've sent my final earthly painting of my full transformation. Look to the sky to see me now.

If you lie on the ground on a dark night, or sit in a chair where you can recline to see the sky, the stars the constellations, our galaxy and others, you will see me. Close your eyes and call my name—Sora, Sky Painter.

Envision my face from this painting, then open your eyes to the night sky. You will recognize my face surrounded by my colorful paints. By the time you get this, I will be one of the sky painters of the universe. My face will not last long, but it will be there if you believe. I will finally be one with the universe.

I love you always! Be happy!

Sora

ABOUT THE AUTHOR

Maggie Lynch is the author of 27+ published titles, as well as numerous short stories and non-fiction articles. Her fiction tells stories of men and women making heroic choices one messy moment at a time. Her fiction spans romance, suspense, YA fantasy and SF titles, as well as children's books.

Since 2013, Maggie and her musician husband have settled in the beautiful Pacific Northwest where they have retired from the corporate and academic world to follow their dual creative pursuits of music and writing. You can learn more about Maggie and all her books at her website: https://maggielynch.com

STORY INSPIRATION

As I was sweltering at home during a too long heat wave (we don't have air conditioning), that also spurred hundreds of wildfires in the Pacific Northwest, I began to think about the concept of rainmakers and how I wished there was a person who could control the weather, and was willing to do so not for pay but for love of the earth. Every day I would watch the sky for signs of possible rain.

Rain is not only beautiful but also holds spiritual significance. In the Bible, rain is seen as a symbol of God's blessings and provision. Additionally, in many spiritual belief systems, rain is viewed as a symbol of cleansing and purification, as it is believed to wash away impurities and bring about a new beginning.

I combined those concepts in my mind and perceived a child born with the gift of painting the sky — a gift that no one, particularly her parents, believed was a viable way to live. But Sora persists. Through her love and belief in her gift, she helps others to transform their lives. In giving to the world without expectation of recompense, in the end her own metamorphosis is finally complete.

Another
Life
PATY
JAGER

CHAPTER ONE

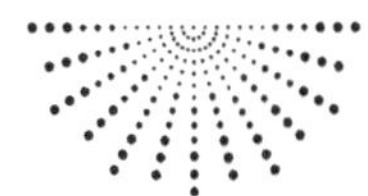

Standing at the kitchen sink, drinking a cup of tea, I stare out at the newly planted flowerbed. A smile warms my cheeks and fills my heart with freedom. "No one would ever find him," I whisper.

"What was that?" Sid's loud obnoxious voice asks from the kitchen doorway.

"Nothing. Just reminding myself of the chores I need to do today." I set the teacup to the side and finish washing the breakfast dishes.

Sid steps up beside me. "Don't forget to check the water for the cattle. I'll be in town for the farmer's meeting."

I nod.

He swats me on the butt with a stinging blow. "Did you hear me?"

"Yes. I'll check the water tank for the cattle. How late will you be coming home?"

I didn't have to look to know he had a smirk on his face. It was in his voice as he said, "When I feel like it. Be ready." He gave my butt another stinging swat and left.

I cringed. How had I thought this man would ever grow up and become anything other than a bully?

After finishing my household chores, I saddled up my horse and rode out to the water tank. The windmill seemed to spin cheerfully drawing the spring water out of the ground and filling the tank. Outdoors with an animal who never demeaned or hurt me was my happy place. A smile worked muscles in my face that were rarely used. Watching the blades on the windmill spin, I let my mind drift to what it would be like to no longer have to put up with Sid. I'd be free to sell the farm and move to a small piece of land. One I could manage on my own.

The euphoric feeling of being on my own slowly dwindled. Sid would never let me go. He thought of me as nothing more than a possession. One he could use and abuse. To him, the marriage license gave him the privilege to make me feel like an inferior being.

I shook my head, knowing I would never be free of the man until one of us died.

Back at the house, I unsaddled my horse and wandered into the kitchen. I picked up my sketch pad and worked on my garden design while enjoying dinner alone, and listening to music. It was a treat when I could spend time at home without someone complaining about my music or that I was wasting time sketching a garden that would never be.

That night I heard him come home. He stumbled around drunkenly calling for me. I pulled the covers over my head, hoping he'd pass out before he climbed the stairs to our bedroom. Eventually, I fell asleep, no longer hearing him.

The light shone brightly through the bedroom curtain when I opened my eyes. The blissful sound of birds chirping outside lightened my mood. The space next to me on the bed was empty. Sid must have passed out on the couch.

I dressed slowly, to avoid an encounter with him. If I was lucky, he would either be in the bathroom or outside taking care of the animals when I went down to start breakfast.

At the bottom of the stairs, I knew something was wrong. There was a smell, one I knew well from bandaging Sid's wounds when his anger got the better of him and he'd slam a fist into a wall or get in a fight with someone. Or when he'd make my nose bleed or my lip split. It was the iron tang of blood. And not just a little. The house seemed filled with the odor.

I glanced at the wide-open front door. I was sure I heard him slam the door shut when he arrived home. I started to walk over and close the door, then decided the best thing would be to look through the house before I ventured out to see if he had left without closing the door.

The living room and office were empty. The stench of blood heightened as I stepped into the kitchen.

Sid lay face down on the kitchen floor. Blood congealed around his head like a red halo. There wasn't any doubt the blood had escaped through the large gash on the back of his head.

My hand instinctively covered my mouth as a cry climbed up my throat and released. The shrill sound bounced off the walls drawing my attention away from the body.

I glanced around the room. What had caused that horrible gash on his head?

Using the toe of my slipper, I nudge his shoulder. Was he really dead or was this a trick he was playing on me? He didn't turn his head to look at me. His fingers didn't even twitch. Could he finally be dead? Finally out of my life?

All the scenarios of what I'd planned to do if I was ever free of him flashed through my mind, shedding my heart of dread and filling it with excitement about what was to come.

I don't know how long I stood staring down at Sid thinking so many wonderful things when the sound of two vehicles drew me out of my trance. Hurrying to the front of the house, I shoved the door open wider as two of Sid's friends walked up.

Hal held out a set of keys. "Sid wasn't in any condition to drive last night." He hooked a thumb toward the man behind him. "Leroy brought him home."

I peered over Hal's shoulder at the tall broad-shouldered man behind him. Had he killed Sid? If so, he deserved a smile. I gave him a timid one. Sid didn't like me looking or smiling at other men.

I returned my gaze to Hal. "The keys won't do him any good. Someone whacked him on the head last night."

Hal pulled the keys back and stared at me. "What are you saying?"

"I woke up this morning and found him on the kitchen floor." I waved a hand toward the house.

"Where are the police?" Hal asked.

I hadn't even thought about calling them. My mind had gone to the place it did when I'd imagined Sid dead and out of my life. I shrugged. "I hadn't called. I was - I was in shock I guess until you pulled up."

Hal swept me out onto the porch. "Leroy call the police and keep her out here."

It didn't bother me to stay outside. I now drew in deep breaths of the fresh air and listened to Leroy make the call.

"Hey, this is Leroy Hull, me and Hal Smith came over to Sid Talbot's house to bring his truck back and found his wife saying he's dead." He listened, nodding his head. "Yeah, it's out Pine Road. Wait, here comes Hal."

Leroy asked, "Is he really dead?"

Hal nodded.

Leroy said into the phone. "Hal says Sid is dead. You better send out the police." He listened some more said, "Yeah," and ended the call.

My body shook and no matter how hard I hugged my arms around myself I couldn't get it to stop. "I thought he'd sit up and tell me to make breakfast like before."

Hal swung his gaze in my direction. "What did you just say?"

"When I've dreamed of something happening to Sid before, he'd always interrupt my happy thoughts." I looked up at Hal's face. It was blurry. Like a mirror at a circus, then everything went black.

CHAPTER TWO

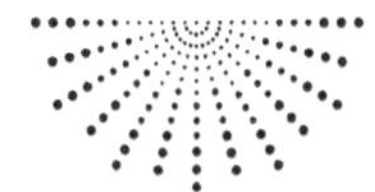

I woke up staring at the living room ceiling and listening to voices and footsteps. Why were there so many people in my house? I tried to sit up but a hand held me on the couch.

"You took quite a tumble, Mrs. Talbot," a woman's voice said.

I twisted my neck and peered at the woman about my age. Her hair had a few more wisps of gray in it than mine but there were fewer lines on her face. "Who are you?"

"I'm Dr. Bly. I'm the county medical examiner."

"Did I die?" I ask, thinking I would get some much-needed rest.

She studied me with the same uncertainty in her eyes as my mom, and later foster parents, had on more than one occasion. "No. You fainted. Do you remember waking up this morning?"

I thought about the question and smiled. "Yes. The birds were singing and I was alone in my bed." I shoved to a sitting position.

"And that made you happy?" the doctor asked.

"Yes. It meant Sid had slept down on the couch. He hadn't come to bed drunk." I couldn't stop the smile. After he'd arrived home and passed out, I'd finally fallen asleep. A deep sleep.

"I see. Did he come home drunk often?"

"At least once a week. And he's a nasty drunk." I held out my arm to show her the bruise he'd left on me the week before by holding me down on the bed when I'd tried to leave.

"Did this happen every time?" Dr. Bly pulled out her phone and took a photo.

"Not on the nights he'd pass out down here. Like last night. I listened to him come in, stumbling about and calling my name. I huddled in the blankets, hoping he was too drunk to climb the stairs. When he went quiet, I fell deep asleep." I thought about that. Usually, even when he fell asleep on the couch, I still slept fretfully. Why had last night been different?

"Did you hear anything before he went quiet?" the doctor asked. Her phone beeped. She typed something on it and returned her gaze to me.

"There was a lot of banging around like he was looking for something or stumbling into furniture." I thought of how his stumbling had made me happy that he might be too drunk to navigate the stairs.

"And you didn't come down to see if he might have hurt himself?" The doctor peered so hard into my eyes, that I was sure she could see all the times I'd wished him dead.

"No. I knew if I got close to him when he was drunk, I'd end up with my clothes torn and bruises from his hands. I had on my favorite pajamas and didn't want him touching me." My arms curled around my legs drawing them up until my heels touched my butt.

Dr. Bly stood. "I have to talk to the detective. Stay here and I'll have one of the officers bring you some tea and toast."

I nodded that I'd stay. The tea and toast sounded good. It had been years since anyone had made it for me. At least not that I could remember. Mom was always at work when I woke in the morning. I made my breakfast and walked to school. It was just the two of us until she died. Then I was sent to foster homes.

"Mrs. Talbot, I'm Officer Jennings. Dr. Bly asked me to bring you some tea and toast."

I shook off the memories and studied the young woman in a county uniform. "Thank you."

She set a mug with a string and tab hanging out on the coffee table and set down a plate with two slices of toast, shiny with butter. "I didn't know if you used sugar or honey, but I couldn't find any honey."

"I don't sweeten the tea. Sid says it costs too much to add sweetener." I reached out for the mug and stopped. Fear curled around inside my chest. "Can you put it in another cup, please?"

"I'm sorry. Is there something wrong with the cup?" the woman looked confused.

"I'm not allowed to use that cup. It's Sid's." A flashback to the day he found me sipping from the cup came back and my body shuddered as if he were releasing his rage on me again.

The officer picked the mug up and whisked it out of my sight.

I shifted my bottom closer to the arm of the couch and peered over the back toward the kitchen. Several people stood with their backs toward me.

The officer squeezed between the people and returned with tea in my mug. It had an abundance of colorful flowers around it. The cup had been given to me by a neighbor when Sid and I were first married and moved onto this farm. It had been my inspiration for the flower bed out back.

I took the mug and sipped the tea. Raising my head, I said, "Thank you."

"You're welcome." She sat on the chair at the end of the couch. "It would be a good idea to get some food in your stomach."

"Why?" I studied her. Where she had been friendly before she appeared wary of me now.

"The detective will want to question you soon."

"What about?" My mind spun as to why the detective would need to question me. I had been asleep when Sid died. What could I tell him?

"About your husband's death," the officer said, peering at me as if I were dense.

I returned her gaze. "I don't know how it happened. I was asleep."

A throat cleared behind me.

The officer stood.

"I'll take over Officer Jennings."

The deep soft tone reminded me of someone. It was hidden in the recesses of my mind.

"Mrs. Talbot, I'm Detective Hurd. I need to ask you some questions. Dr. Bly said you had regained consciousness and were of clear mind." The man was tall, wearing a faded suit coat over a western-cut shirt and faded jeans. His gray curly hair needed a cut. His green eyes behind old-fashioned glasses, while being intent, seemed to also offer comfort.

I set the mug of tea down and folded my arms about my bent legs, using my limbs as a wall between us. "I'm not sure what I can tell you. I was asleep when Sid died." I never called him husband. The books I'd read said the husband would give his wife flowers and chocolates and take her out to dinner. And he always touched her tenderly making her wanting his touch more. Sid had done all of those things before we married. After the ring was on my finger, he changed into a tyrant who only wanted his wishes fulfilled, and to hell with what I wanted.

"I understand he came home drunk and that in the past he's hurt you when he's in that state." The detective sat in the chair the officer had left.

"Yes, I told the doctor everything. You can ask her." I felt my heart racing. Why did I have to talk about this again? I wanted it over with. I wanted the people out of my house. I wanted to go work in my flower bed.

"She said you told her that you hoped he didn't come upstairs. Did you walk downstairs to see what his condition was?" Those green eyes behind the glasses held my gaze.

Instead of making me feel vulnerable, they consoled me. I shook my head. "No. I didn't want him to know I was awake. That would have given him the idea to come after me. I just covered my head and when he stopped making noise, I thought he had passed out. I listened a while longer and dropped off to sleep."

"You didn't descend the stairs during the night to see if he was asleep?" the detective asked.

"No. I slept well. Hard. I rarely do that when he's in the house, but for some reason last night I did. Then I woke to the singing of the birds and the sunshine in my window." I smiled thinking of how for a brief moment, there had been happiness in my heart. "Then I came downstairs and it was quiet. It was the smell that told me something was wrong."

"What smell?"

"The blood. It filled the downstairs. It scared me. But I moved through each room until I found him." The sight of Sid on the kitchen floor flashed through my mind. "He was so still with a red halo around his head." I shook my head. "He wasn't an angel. A red halo must be for the devil's disciples in Hell."

"What did you do when you saw the body?" The warm low voice gave me courage.

"I thought, 'am I finally free?'" I peered into his eyes. "I've had dreams of Sid dying. They always made me happy and then there he'd be yelling at me or telling me to do something while he sat on his butt and watched."

The detective leaned forward, resting his forearms on his thighs. "Did you dream your husband died last night?"

"No. But I wonder if that's why I slept so well. My instinct told me I was safe." I relaxed my hold on my legs and leaned toward him. "Can a body or mind know something happened when you're sleeping?"

Detective Hurd studied me for a long time. He leaned back. "Mrs. Talbot, your husband was hit on the head with the edge of a cast iron frying pan. One from your kitchen. We found it hanging from a hook by the stove."

I nodded. "That's where I hung it yesterday morning after cleaning up from breakfast."

"You didn't wake up during the night, come downstairs, pick up the frying pan, and hit your husband with it?"

I thought of his words. I had never dreamed of being close to my husband when I daydreamed about his demise. "No. All of my dreams had him dying from accidents."

The detective leaned forward again. "Tell me about these dreams."

CHAPTER THREE

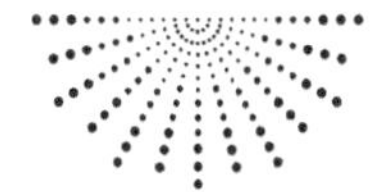

I searched his face trying to see if this was a trick. I've never told anyone about my fantasies of finding myself a widow.

"They're just daydreams, what could they tell you?" I ask.

"Most dreams and daydreams can tell a lot about a person's mental state. What they are worried about or anxious about." Detective Hurd motioned to the mug of tea. "Drink your tea and eat your toast as you tell me about your dreams."

I uncurled more of my body and reached for the mug of tea. The bitterness on my tongue made me want to ask for sugar. But that would be foolish after saying I drank it without sweetener. "I don't know where to start."

"Have you had many dreams of your husband dying?" the detective asked quietly.

"They only occur when I'm more irritated with him than usual. It's when we're doing a chore."

"What is a chore that caused you to fantasize?"

"One project was helping set poles for the hay barn."

"When was this?"

"Seven years ago," I said after counting in my head back to when we built the hay barn.

"Tell me about it."

I studied him. He seemed genuinely interested. So I began, "I didn't like working on the barn. Helping Sid lift poles with the backhoe and set them in holes while he tamped dirt around the creosote-soaked posts was tedious." I glanced out the living room window. "I like being outside but prefer fresh air or the scent of a sweaty horse to the caustic diesel fumes belching from the backhoe. I could think of multiple other things to do. There was laundry to fold, a meal to prepare, and I'd hoped to do a bit of sketching on the plans for my flower garden. If those chores were done, I could ride my horse, breathing in the scent of pine, musty leaves, and horse. Instead, I sat in that smoke-puking monster that chewed up the ground in large scoops." I took a breath to ease the anger that always built when I thought of all the things I could do when I had to help Sid.

"Go on. You were helping your husband build a hay barn."

Officer Jennings returned with a steaming cup of what smelled like coffee for the detective and added more hot water to my mug. I thanked her and continued.

"Sid hollered at me to get my attention, then motioned for me to pick up the next pole that he'd wrapped a chain around. I eased the lever backward to make the big arm raise. The pole slowly rose, the top end spun and the bottom end pivoted in place.

'Keep this up and we'll be at this all day!' he shouted sarcastically, his face red from exertion and anger.

I pulled the lever back hard, jerking the log quickly up, breaking the ground's hold on it, and causing the twenty-foot-long pole to swing. Before I could get the lever under control, the post slammed into Sid, knocking him into the ten-foot-deep hole he'd dug the day before." I glanced up to see if the detective was as scared as I was. He just watched me.

"I couldn't move. Horror at what just happened paralyzed me. I stared at the hole expecting to see him claw his way out and come after me.

With a shaky hand, I turned off the backhoe and listened.

Nothing.

I opened the backhoe door and tilted my head listening for his curses and how he would kill me when he got out.

Silence. Complete silence."

I tipped my head as I had when I'd imagined this event.

I continued, "My lips quivered in fear before one by one the muscles on the sides of my mouth tightened, pulling the corners up in a smile. A lightness came over me. The fear and anger I'd lived with for thirteen years slipped away, loosening my muscles and easing my mind."

"Had you imagined killing your husband in the years before this?" the detective asked.

I nodded.

He motioned to return to my story.

"I started the backhoe and grasped the lever, controlling the log with the dexterity I'd never had with my husband watching. Lowering the log into the hole on top of Sid felt like closing a book I'd been forced to read. With each inch the pole went down, I held my breath. What if he'd just been knocked out and became conscious as the log smashed him? A bit of the initial fear slithered up my spine. And queasiness at the thought of the log smashing him."

I swallowed the bile that rose in my throat, burning my esophagus and bringing the emotions back in a wash of regret and jubilation.

"Then what did you do?" Detective Hurl asked.

"I turned off the backhoe and listened again.

No yelling, no screaming, not a sound.

A giggle escaped my clamped lips and I finished lowering the pole and scampered out of the backhoe. I picked up the shovel and pushed dirt around the post. As the song *I am Woman Hear Me Roar*, played in my head I scooped larger portions of dirt and tamped it down.

A tap on my shoulder startled a shriek out of me.

Peering over my shoulder, I encountered Sid's narrowed eyes.

'What the hell are you doing giggling? And why did you get out of the backhoe? Get back in there or we'll never get this done! Damn woman, always messing around and putting me behind.'

I glanced over Sid's head at the pole still hanging from the chain."

"What did you do?" Detective Hurd asked.

"I climbed into the backhoe and thought about how for a few brief moments I'd felt happy and free." I smile tickled my lips but I kept it at bay. Yes, each daydream had given me a respite from fear.

"How many of these daydreams have you had?" the detective asked before sipping his coffee.

"One or two a year. Usually when I'm the most upset." I thought about last night. It had been a good evening. The hours alone had been bliss.

"Can you tell me another of your dreams?" He leaned back in the chair, taking his mug of coffee with him.

"The most recent one was a drizzly cold day last fall. I was happily baking when Sid stomped in the back door and told me to get my boots and coat on because the cows in the north pasture needed to be checked. I grudgingly turned off the oven and left three pans of unbaked cookies sitting on the counter." I glanced over at him as I picked up the cold slice of toast. "Do you understand how cattle ranches work?"

"A little."

I couldn't tell if he was joking or meant it so I continued. "As with all cattle ranches the animals have to be checked often to make sure they haven't strayed out of fences, still have plenty of feed, and that the water hole hasn't dried up or frozen over.

On this cold rainy day, Sid and I set out to check on cattle and fences in the pickup. As I'm sure he knew before we set out, several head had managed to squeeze through a hole in the fence. If he had told me this beforehand, I could have saddled up my horse and herded them back through the fence. Instead, I was slogging through slippery mud and knee-high wet grass trying to get the two cows and three calves to go through the gate Sid held open."

The detective put up a hand. "Your husband held the gate while you were the dog who chased the cattle through the gate?"

I nodded. "It took three tries before the cattle finally went through the gate. Then we started fixing the hole in the fence.

We finished fixing the last section of the barbed wire fence that was broken and climbed into the pickup to head home. My hands were frozen even with the padded leather gloves. The pickup heater was slow to warm and my hands tingled.

Sid stopped at the gate leading out of the pasture. It was one of those wire gates that take the upper body strength of a giant to stretch the gate to unfasten the wire looped over the pole on the opening end so it could be pulled out of the wire loop on the bottom." I glanced at him and he nodded he understood.

"The soaked ground was slick under my cowboy boots as I exited the pickup. The pelting rain and gloomy skies made it hard to see the ruts and rocks in the road. I slipped on a rock barely keeping on my feet. I slowed my pace, feeling the ground before settling each cold foot.

A horn blared loud and long, making me jerk. My feet slipped out from under me. My arms flailed in the air but I couldn't catch my balance. I landed butt first in a puddle. The water and mud soaked my gloves, my butt, and my legs. Shivering, I shoved to my feet and glared at the headlights and wipers swiping back and forth where Sid sat warm and dry in the pickup. His laughter could be heard through the closed windows and over the rumble of the engine. I would have flipped him off but it wouldn't have made him laugh harder.

Trying to stay on my feet, I moved my numb shivering body toward the gate. Barely picking up each cold, stinging foot, I moved them one after the other.

'You'd get out of the rain sooner if you'd quit messing around and open the damn gate!' Sid hollered and revved the pickup.

I reached the gate and tried to make my frozen hands grasp the wire, but I fumbled with the loop as I pressed my body into the pole, pushing it toward the solid post. My body was so cold and weary I could barely inch the end pole closer to the fence. I swiped at the pelting rain streaming into my eyes.

'You're wrestling with that gate like a weakling!' Sid hollered from his dry seat in the cab of the pickup.

I finally shoved all my weight against the pole and it moved. Sliding the wire off the gate pole, my fingers ached as I grasped the sodden wood, lifting it from the loop on the bottom. Again, slipping through the mud and rocks, I carried the gate to the other side of the road.

I shivered standing beside the road, holding the gate for Sid to drive through.

He romped on the accelerator and the truck sloshed through the mud, fishtailing, splashing more mud onto me. He overcorrected and the truck slid toward the edge of the road that overlooks a deep canyon. In slow motion, the tires on the driver's side disappeared over the edge, pulling the rest of the vehicle as the red brake lights blinked." I glanced up from where I'd been staring into my tea. The detective was watching me. He nodded as if to say 'Go on.'

"Rain dripped off my hood for several seconds as my shivering body and catatonic brain took in what had just happened. The only sound was the patter of rain and my chattering teeth as I stared at the emptiness where the pickup had been.

I made my frozen limbs walk to the edge of the canyon. Careful not to slip in the mud and end up over the edge as well, I looked over. The cab was crushed laying upside down on a large rock.

My steps grew less robotic as I walked back to the gate and closed it. A smile spread across my lips as I started walking toward home. Lightness filled my heart." I remembered what happened next and frowned.

"A honking horn jolted me out of my cold stupor. I stood beside the road, drenched and shivering, as the pickup backed up.

Sid shoved the passenger side door open and said, 'Get in I'm hungry.'

CHAPTER FOUR

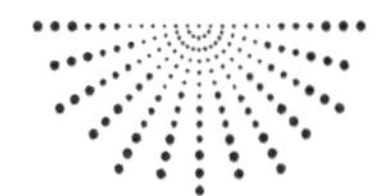

The tea had relaxed me. I no longer hugged my legs and having told the man sitting across from me two of my daydreams, I felt as if I was crazy for having them.

Detective Hurd placed his mug on the coffee table and leaned forward once again. "Do all of your dreams have your husband dying accidentally? Have you ever had one where you purposely killed him?"

I felt my eyes widen as I took in what he said. "In none of them have I consciously killed him. It was always an accident. True, I didn't call or run for help, but I'd snap out of it and realize it was a daydream and there he'd be. Alive and angry I'd been off in 'Lala Land' as he said." I set my cup down on the table and leaned toward him. "I am certain, I didn't kill him. Hal said Leroy brought Sid home last night. You might want to talk to him."

Detective Hurd smiled. "I have my partner talking to both the men."

"Good. Because I know I didn't kill Sid."

"How can you be so sure?" the detective asked.

"I was wearing my favorite pajamas when I went to bed and when I awoke. There is no way I would have done anything to ruin them." I peered straight into his eyes. That was the truth. Sid had always taken me to the store to purchase my clothing and he felt one pair of pajamas was enough since he slept in his underwear. I'd told him I found them in the donation box at the church thrift store. That was where most of my outer clothes came from.

"Why are they your favorite ones?" he asked.

"Because I saved change from the grocery money for a year to buy them. I saw them in the store window and fell in love with the color and when I felt how soft they were…" I remembered the softness in my hand and couldn't wait to feel it on my body. "I gave the store clerk the dollar extra I had that day and she held them for me until I could pay for them."

"Which store was this?"

I told him the name of the store. "You don't believe me?"

He opened his hands as if giving me a half-shrug. "Pajamas are not an expensive piece of clothing."

"Maybe not for you, but I wasn't given a clothing allowance. I bought the same groceries every two weeks and I was given the exact amount of money it cost. As you can see, there is only one vehicle. Sid drove me everywhere and kept tabs on me. I was lucky the store wasn't far from the church thrift store and Sid was late the day I saw the pajamas in the store window. Otherwise, I wouldn't have them."

"Mrs. Talbot, do you have a friend who you could stay with while we process the crime scene?" Detective Hurd asked.

I leaned back, shaking my head. "I have nowhere to go. Sid made the rules and he didn't like me interacting with other people."

"You said Sid was late picking you up from the church thrift store. Did you work there?"

"No, he dropped me off to dig through the boxes to find him a couple more shirts. It was the dollar-a-bag day."

"What about family?" He motioned for Officer Jennings to come over.

"I have none. My father left my mom before I was born and she died when I was eight. I grew up in foster homes until Sid came along and sprung me from the last one. I went from one kind of prison to another. At least at the foster home, I was allowed friends as long as they looked law-abiding."

"I'm going to have Officer Jennings go with you to your bedroom. I want you to pack enough clothes for several days. When you come down, I will have made some calls." Detective Hurd stood. Before he walked away, he said, "I don't think you killed your husband, but until I find evidence that someone else was in this house last night you are a suspect."

I nodded, not really taking in what he said.

Officer Jennings, took me by the arm and we headed for the stairs. Halfway up, I felt a panic attack coming on. I sat down and couldn't catch my breath.

"Mrs. Talbot, Ma'am, are you okay?" the officer asked before yelling, "Help, I need medical help!"

Dr. Bly's face appeared in front of me. "Mrs. Talbot, it's okay. I'm putting my hand on your back. Breathe in on one and out on five. One, two, three, four, five. One, two, three, four, five."

I listened to her voice and did as she said. It was nearly a minute before my chest stopped squeezing and the air flowed easier in and out of my lungs. That's when I felt the soothing circles being made on my back. Memories overwhelmed me of when I was a child. My mother's calming voice as her hand caressed my back.

"I miss you, Mom," I whimpered and curled into the arms that soothed me.

"Shhh, it's okay. You've had a horrible shock. Things will be better, you'll see," the voice was calm but it wasn't as intimate as I remembered my mother's.

I eased out of the embrace and stared into Dr. Bly's eyes. Embarrassment burned my cheeks and insides. "I'm sorry. I didn't—"

"It's fine. Go on up with Officer Jennings and get your things." The doctor rose from where she'd been sitting on the stairs.

Officer Jennings took my arm and we continued up to the bedroom. I stood in the middle of the room wondering what I should take. My horse nickered. "I need to feed Max and Mabel my horses. How will I get back out here tomorrow to feed them?" I asked, walking to the window and looking down at them in the corral, their heads hung over the top pole.

"We'll see that your horses are taken care of. Where's your suitcase?" the officer asked.

"I don't have one." I walked over to the bed and sat.

"What about a large bag?"

"I have a backpack I use when I'm out riding fence. It's down hanging on a hook in the back porch." I looked around the room I tried to decorate with what meager change I found to buy things at the thrift shop. At the time I bought the things, I loved them. Now I hated every last bauble and picture.

"Pick out the clothes you want to take while I get the backpack." The officer strode out of the bedroom.

I tore the pictures off the wall and threw the figurines. I hated this place and couldn't wait to get away.

Officer Jennings ran into the room followed by another officer. "Mrs. Talbot, what are you doing?"

"Please, don't call me that. I'm Amber." I walked to the dresser, pulled out three sets of clothing, and shoved them in the backpack I took from Officer Jennings. I sat on the bed and slipped my feet into my shoes. Bending, I tied the strings and spotted the shoebox on the floor of the closet.

I stood, walked over to the closet, grabbed the box, and crammed it into the pack. "I'm ready."

Downstairs Detective Hurd stopped us. "I've talked to the woman who runs the mission home. You are welcome to stay there until your home is cleared as a crime scene." He handed the information to Officer Jennings.

"I have to feed my horses. How will I get back here each day to feed them?" I wanted to get away quickly but I didn't want to arouse suspicions.

"Show Officer Jennings how to feed and she can take care of them while you're gone." Detective Hurd turned when his name was called.

"Come on. It's easy this time of year," I said to the officer. We walked out to the small barn next to the corral. I slipped my arms through the straps on the pack and opened the door to the tack room. "The grain is kept in here. They each get two scoops of this cup in these tubs." I showed her the grain, the tubs, and how to spread them apart so the horses didn't try to eat the other's feed.

I patted Max's neck as he stood alongside the fence eating. "I'll be back to get you. You are the best thing that came out of this marriage."

"You don't plan on living here?" Officer Jennings asked.

"I doubt it was left to me. Sid had a brother who visited us twice during our marriage. I'm sure it will go to him." I wasn't going to be hopeful that I would get to keep the house, the land, or even the money that might be in the bank. Sid had always told me that I wasn't a good enough wife to get the house or his money when he died. I never believed it would come to me. I would be on my own after twenty years of being a wife and ranch hand. I would have to find a job. I didn't even know how to use a computer. We didn't have a television in the house. Sid said it would be too distracting for me. Suddenly my freedom didn't feel so free.

The horses started snuffling my hand that gripped the fence. I petted their noses and bent to pick up the tubs. "When they finish, put the tubs back in the tack room." I packed the tubs into the tack room and closed the door.

"That's all there is to it?" Officer Jennings asked.

"That's it." I followed her to a police car and was instructed to sit in the back. "Am I under arrest?"

"No, it's just protocol. No one other than an officer can ride in the front." Officer Jennings closed my door and slid in behind the steering wheel.

I sat sideways in the seat to watch the ranch get smaller and smaller as the car took me away from the home I'd known the longest.

CHAPTER FIVE

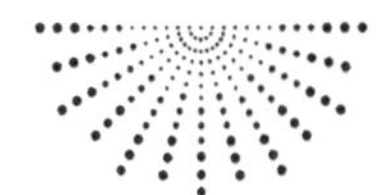

I didn't like the mission house. The woman whom Officer Jennings introduced me to peered down her nose at me as if she believed I killed Sid. Then after showing me to a bed among ten others in a large open room, I noticed her following and watching me everywhere I went. I felt like I was back in a foster home. I was thirty-eight years old. I didn't need to be watched as if I might commit a crime.

Finally, to get some privacy, I took my backpack and entered a stall in the ladies' restroom. There I took out the shoebox that Sid had threatened me not to ever touch and looked inside. I found money and a bank book. He had nearly fifty thousand dollars in the bank. The only drawback, only his name was on the account. I counted the cash in the box. Three thousand in hundreds, fifties, and twenties.

I shoved the cash and bank book into an outside pocket of the backpack, flushed the toilet, and tossed the shoebox in the garbage can. I walked out of the restroom and out of the mission house.

There was enough cash from the box, I could stay at a motel and not have someone staring at me all the time. But first, I was going to eat in a restaurant.

The next morning, I remained in bed at the motel watching T.V. There were shows with judges, women throwing themselves at men, kid's shows that were disrespectful to the adults, and talk shows that either talked about the people's problems or what they were selling. I didn't see why Sid had made such a big deal out of me not watching T.V. There really wasn't anything worth wasting my time on.

I shoved another bite of the peach pie, I'd bought at the restaurant the night before, in my mouth and chewed. It wasn't as good as the ones I made but I didn't make it and that made up for it not being from fresh peaches. I washed the bite down with water.

While sitting in the restaurant the night before, I'd watched the men and women and knew the feeling I had about my relationship with Sid had been right. He didn't treat me like I was his wife or even a person. I wasn't sorry he was dead, but I was pretty sure I didn't do it. I must have known that he was dead though. How else would I have slept so soundly?

I had walked past the bank last night and discovered it opened at 10 a.m. It was 8:30. I had plenty of time to take a shower, dress in the best clothes I brought with me, and see if I could find a way to get to the money in his bank account.

At the bank, my sweaty hands could barely hold my vinyl purse. It kept slipping as I stood in line to talk to one of the tellers. I slowly moved forward unaware of how many people used the bank. One of the women from the church thrift store smiled at me. I smiled back, and she gave me a pat on the shoulder as she walked by.

I shifted to watch her walk out of the building. Why had she patted me on the shoulder? Did she know about Sid?

"Next," said the young woman behind the counter.

I swung back around and realized, that meant me. Walking up to the counter, I opened my purse and slipped my hand in. I slid the bank book across the counter to the woman. "I'd like to know how to access this money."

The woman opened the book, skimmed through it, and said, "I don't understand. If you have the bank book, I would think this is your account."

My mind wandered to pretending I was Sid, but if she asked for I.D. I wouldn't have any. Honesty, though had many times gotten me a whipping or in the case of Sid a beating, it was still the best way to go.

"I found it in our house after my husband died. It's his name on the account," I said in a quiet voice.

"Oh. In that case, you'll have to bring in his death certificate and proof that the money was left to you. Then we can do whatever you want with the money." The woman smiled and handed the book back to me.

That was good news and bad news. If Sid left a will leaving me out of everything, I wouldn't be able to get my hands on any of it. How would I start over with less than three thousand dollars?

I took the book and thanked her.

When I stepped out onto the street, Detective Hurl strode down the street toward me.

"Good morning," I said, forcing my lips into a smile. He didn't need to know the disappointment I felt.

"Why aren't you at the mission?" he asked, taking hold of my elbow and turning me the direction he'd come from.

"I didn't like the way the woman in charge followed me around, watching me. Like I was a juvenile delinquent." I kept walking alongside him until we came to a dark sedan.

He stopped and opened the door all while still holding my elbow. "I need to ask you some more questions." He lowered me into the passenger side of his vehicle.

At least I wasn't in the back seat like a criminal.

Once he was settled behind the steering wheel he asked, "Where did you go? You said you had no one to stay with."

I bit my bottom lip and decided as at the bank, the truth was what I needed to tell him. "There was a box in the bedroom closet that Sid told me if I ever touched, he would beat me. When I was packing clothes, I spotted it and thought, I can finally find out what's in there. I took it with me and at the mission I discovered money and a bank book." I pointed with a thumb back toward the bank. "I was in there asking what I needed to do to get the money out of the account."

The car pulled away from the curb. "I see. And what did you plan to do with the money?"

"Use it until I could figure out how to make a living." I glanced at his profile. He had an average face. "All I know how to do is be an obedient wife and ranch hand. I don't want to take care of that ranch by myself and I don't believe it will be mine even if I wanted to." I told him how Sid had always told me I would get nothing if he died first. I shrugged. "So basically, the three thousand I found in the box is all I have to live on until I can find a job and a place to stay." I thought of the horses. "Whoever gets the ranch will also get the horses. Sid made sure they were in his name when we bought them."

Detective Hurl cleared his throat and spoke as he pulled into the police station. "The district attorney wants me to arrest you for your husband's murder." He parked and twisted in his seat, peering at me with those soulful eyes behind nondescript glasses. "I don't think you did it. But until forensics can come up with someone else being in the house, you are the only one who could have killed your husband."

My hands began to shake. "I'm sure I would remember if I had killed him. How do you explain not a drop of blood on my pajamas?"

"I mentioned that to the D.A. He said you could have worn something else and put them back on or even stripped down naked and then took a shower, put the pajamas back on, and climbed into bed to sleep peacefully as you stated."

My mind raced trying to figure out what was real and what this man was putting in my head.

"I need a formal statement from you and we'll see where to go from there." Detective Hurl exited the car and walked around to open my door.

Fear had wrapped around my chest and was squeezing. I couldn't catch my breath as he hauled me to my feet.

"Calm down. I'm on your side," he said, holding both my elbows, steadying me on my feet.

I glanced up into his eyes and saw no malice. Only concern. He would help me discover what happened. Slowly breathing in and out to the count of five as Dr. Bly had me to do the day before, I managed to get my breathing under control.

Detective Hurl escorted me into the building. I kept my gaze straight ahead, ignoring the people who stopped and watched us walk by. He deposited me in a small room with a table and three chairs.

"I've asked Officer Jennings to sit in the room with us. Is that okay?" Detective Hurl asked.

I nodded and sat on the hard cold chair in the small, empty room. It reminded me of the bedroom I was given at the first foster home. The room had been stark, the bedding dark blue, and the room a dark green color, much like this room. I shivered.

"Are you cold? I can have a blanket brought in," the detective said, standing by the open door. "Or a cup of hot tea?"

"Both if it's no trouble. I can't seem to stop shaking." I wrapped my arms around myself wishing I had grabbed a sweatshirt before going to the bank.

"No trouble. Sit tight, I'll be right back." He stepped out, leaving the door open.

CHAPTER SIX

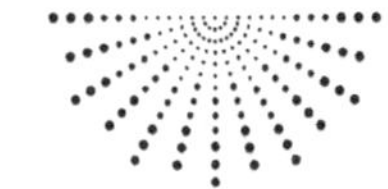

The thought I could get up and walk out of the building and keep on walking came to me. I drifted off into a scenario where I walked out of the building, down to the bus station, and purchased a ticket to the farthest place the bus would take me. I didn't have any luggage, but I could buy a bag and a few sets of clothing at a thrift store when the bus stopped somewhere long enough. I smiled. I would reinvent myself. No longer Amber Talbot. I'd be Amber Beck again as if I hadn't married and lived twenty years as an indentured wife.

"Here you go."

I jumped at the voice and pulled myself back to the present.

"Sorry, I didn't mean to scare you." Detective Hurl handed me a blanket and sat across the table from me. "Officer Jennings is bringing in the tea. Once you have that we'll get started."

I nodded and wrapped the blanket around me. It didn't stop the shivers but it made me feel less vulnerable. Like a cloak that shielded all but my head from view.

Officer Jennings arrived, placed the tea in front of me, and sat beside Detective Hurl, smiling at me. "I fed your horses this morning. I think they miss you."

I nodded. "I talk to them a lot. They're good listeners."

Detective Hurl cleared his throat and said, "Let's get this started." He recited his name and badge number, Officer Jennings did the same, and then I was asked to say my name.

"I'm Amber Beck Talbot. I prefer to be called Amber." I peered into the detective's eyes as I said the last. He nodded as if in understanding.

He then talked about my rights and that I had the right to refuse to answer without a lawyer present.

"Do I need a lawyer?" I asked because he'd said he just wanted my statement about what had happened.

Detective Hurl pushed the off button on the recording machine. "If you believe anything you say might make you look guilty then it would be a good idea to have a lawyer present."

I shook my head. "I didn't kill him. I have nothing to say that would prove I did." I pointedly stared into both their eyes. "And I don't lie."

"Let's continue." Detective Hurl pressed the on button and continued. "Amber, would you please tell us what happened two days ago?"

I began by telling them about Sid smacking me on the butt several times and telling me he'd be home when he came home. Then about my peaceful day and dinner. That I went to bed and sometime around midnight, heard a vehicle and Sid entered the house.

"What did you do then?" Detective Hurl asked.

"I pulled the covers over my head and hoped he passed out before he came to bed." The fear and anxiety of that moment swept over me. I pulled the blanket around me tighter and dipped my head as if I were in bed, hiding.

"What did you hear?" Detective Hurl asked.

"Sid was stumbling around and calling my name. I ignored it. I didn't want to give him any ideas about coming upstairs and I wasn't going to go down. I hated the nights he came home drunk. He'd force himself on me and then hit me for not being more willing."

My thoughts returned to the last time he'd come home just drunk enough to be mean but not drunk enough that he could be outmaneuvered. I couldn't sit down for several days after the spanking he gave me for not cooperating. Tears burned the backs of my eyes. I blinked rapidly.

"Amber? Amber, what are you thinking about?" Detective Hurl asked in that soft low tone that probably made everyone feel safe to tell him everything.

"About the time before when he came home and I didn't want him. He said I had to perform wifely duties and then when I refused, he beat my butt so hard and many times, I couldn't sit for several days." I flicked a glance at the detective. Something was brewing behind his concerned gaze.

"I'm sorry your husband treated you so badly. Is that instance why you were scared to go downstairs?"

I nodded.

"Please speak up for the recording."

"Yes. I didn't want to get near him. The way he was making noise like he was stumbling over things, I'd hoped he would pass out downstairs and leave me be." I remembered his cries… I revisited the sound of my name as he called it. I sat up straighter. "When he was calling my name, it wasn't like he was trying to find me, it sounded like cries for help." I stared at the two officers across from me. "At the time, I ignored the urgency, but as I play it back. I think maybe he was calling out for help."

Another thought clicked in my mind. "Hal said that Leroy drove him home. Do you think Leroy followed him into the house and fought with him?" I picked up the cup of tea and sipped. My mind whirled through the events of that night. "I heard a vehicle pull up and it sounded like it parked. That's why I knew it was Sid." I shook my head. "But I didn't hear it leave. If Leroy dropped him off, wouldn't I have also heard the vehicle leaving?"

"That's a good point," Detective Hurl said. "What else are you beginning to remember?"

"The front door was standing open when I went downstairs in the morning. I thought Sid had gone outside already and forgot to shut the door. Until I caught a whiff of the blood." I shuddered remembering how pungent it had been.

"What did you first see when you walked into the kitchen?" Detective Hurl asked.

"His boots. Then his body and the red halo around his head. Then the gash in the back of his head. I wondered what had made that gash. It didn't dawn on me it was made by a person. I thought he must have fallen against something."

"Then what did you do?"

"I poked him with the toe of my slipper. In all my daydreams he never died from the accident that befell him. I expected him to turn his head and say 'Where the hell is my breakfast?'" I set the teacup down. "When he didn't move, I realized I was finally free. My mind spun through all the things I'd dreamed about doing for a long time. Then I heard two vehicles pull up to the front of the house. I went to the porch and Hal stepped out of Sid's truck and Leroy out of his truck. Sid tried to give me the keys to Sid's truck and I said, he wouldn't be needing them. That's when Hal went in the house and Leroy called the police." I pulled the blanket around my shoulders. "I don't remember much else until Dr. Bly was looking at me."

Detective Hurl said something about the interview was ended at eleven-fifty-five and clicked the button on the recording device. Then he studied me. "Amber, write down the motel where you are staying and the room number. As I said, until we can find the person who killed your husband, you are the main suspect. You can't leave town until this is cleared up."

I nodded and wrote the name of the motel and the room number on the paper Officer Jennings slid across the table toward me. As much as I wanted away from here, it was the only place I really knew. I had nowhere else to go.

I shoved the paper back across the table.

"And I'd advise you to find a lawyer. If we can't find someone else who had a motive, you will need him to defend you in a trial, and if we do find the killer, you may need him to fight for your right to your husband's assets." Detective Hurl stood. "Officer Jennings can give you a ride to where you want to go."

I thought of how I had to ride in the back of her squad car the day before. "Thank you, but I'd rather walk." I stood and walked woodenly out of the room, out of the building, and into the mid-afternoon sunshine. My stomach growled. I walked half a block down the street to a deli. I ordered at the counter and took my lunch to a table outside on the sidewalk in front. As I ate, I wondered how Detective Hurl had known I was at the bank.

I stood, wadded up the papers from my sandwich, and shoved it into the paper bag that had held my lunch. I held a cookie between my teeth while my hands were busy.

"Amber, could I have a word with you?"

I turned to the voice and discovered the woman who had put a hand on my shoulder in the bank. I nodded, walked over to the garbage can, dropped the sack in, and pulled the cookie out of my mouth. "How do you know my name?"

She smiled. "You come into the store so often and buy the same type of items. It made me curious so I asked around." She motioned toward the chairs and table I'd just left.

We sat down and I didn't know what to say. Finally, I blurted, "What's your name?"

The woman smiled. "I'm Jean Hurl. Since retiring from teaching, I've been doing volunteer work at the church and the schools."

"Hurl? Are you the detective's wife?" That would answer her question of how the detective knew she was at the bank.

The woman shook her head. "No. I'm Thomas's aunt."

"Did you tell him I was at the bank?" I asked wanting to know.

She nodded. "I did. He had mentioned how worried he was about you last night when we had dinner that he'd had you put up at the mission home. When you were at the bank, I felt he needed to know." She put a hand on my arm. "It was for your own good. If you are innocent, then you need to act like it and not try to run away."

"I wasn't running away. I was trying to find out how to get hold of the money Sid had in a bank account that didn't have my name on it." I looked up and down the street. "This is the only place I've ever lived long enough to feel like it's home. But I need a job and a place to live until things are determined."

Jean nodded and patted my arm again. "I think I can help you with a place to live and possibly a job."

"I'm not skilled at anything other than house and ranch work." I liked the woman. Trusted her like I did the detective, but I didn't trust myself. Did I have the skills to hold down a job?

"Where are your things?"

I told her about the motel I was staying in.

"Let's go get them and I'll show you the small bungalow that is sitting empty behind my house. You can fix it up and live there. As for the job. You can either waitress at the café or the library is looking for someone to train."

My heart stuttered in my chest. "I could work with books?"

Jean's face lit up. "I had a feeling you would like that job. You always purchased books when you came to the thrift store."

I had purchased books that were only a dime. I could always save at least a dime out of the grocery money to get a book. Then I'd hide it and read when Sid was away. He felt reading was a waste of time. But reading took me away from my fears and discouragement.

As we started to leave, a woman hurried over to Jean. "Did you hear the news?"

"What news?" Jean asked.

"They caught the person who killed Sid Talbot. It seems Sid had been fooling around with Leroy Hull's wife. He took Sid home drunk the other night and laid into him. Killed him as the wife lay upstairs in bed. Can you believe it?"

Jean flicked a gaze at me.

I'd imagined Sid's death dozens of times over the years. So often, that up until that moment, I'd not been completely sure of my innocence. As a sense of relief washed over me, I met Jean's gaze and smiled.

ABOUT THE AUTHOR

Paty Jager is an award-winning author of murder mystery and western romance novels that have Western or Native American elements in them along with hints of humor and engaging characters. You can find all of her work at https://www.patyjager.net or follow her on Facebook as Author Paty Jager, or join her newsletter: https://bit.ly/2IhmWcm

INSPIRATION FOR THIS STORY
This is a story that was the brainchild of my son-in-law. After spending the weekend with us and listening to my husband being a pest to me, he asked if I ever fantasized about doing something to my husband. And then he went on to say I could write a story about fantasizing I'd killed my husband only to have him be alive. When the title for this anthology, *Imagine*, came up, I knew what I was going to write about. Dan, this story is for you!

PROJECT I.M.A.G.I.N.E.

PREFACE

Every innovation we have today came from the mind of a 32-bit machine, thanks to top-secret Project I.M.A.G.I.N.E. The year was 1984: the world's best-kept secret was Sue Marie Johnson . . . the second best-kept secret was the most advanced artificially intelligent machine ever built in human history (that happened only to like Sue), and its name was Walt. But consciousness had one minor problem: having a mind of his own meant Walt could also become *bored*.

Everything came to a standstill the morning Sue arrived, requested the cure for world hunger, turned the seventh dial to 'Revelation', waited two more hours for a single light to turn green . . . and received the single most diabolical and concerning reply possibly ever printed in the human language:

I've decided to take an indefinite nap . . .

PROJECT I.M.A.G.I.N.E.

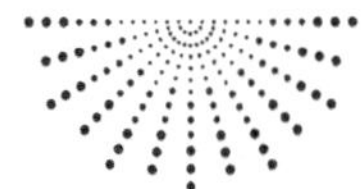

"All forms of life operate comfortably within their program. Sometimes logical or run-time errors arise and must be worked out; other times a program is in dire need of an update. All beings undergo reprogramming multiple times in a life to experience rebirth; some legacy features remain, some features go. We are all developers of our own code." – WALT

1984

The future all started on a Tuesday. Midge Maggerty, a janitor obsessed with get-rich-quick inventions, posted a small job in the local want ads. He was seeking to build a digital clock capable of playing an alarm tune from any VHS. If Midge could pull it off, he knew he'd be rich. ANY VHS OF YOUR CHOOSING—the implications were astounding! He was certain every major brand would compete for the privilege to place their logo on the sleek, smoked acrylic screen.

Midge chuckled to himself as he mopped the seventh restroom of the Jackson Centre that day, imagining his interview on the Pat Sajak show.

Pat: "So tell me Midge, how does a *janitor* invent something this innovative?"

Midge would try not to smile too wide. *Show humility to them, Midge. They need a hero.* "I was tired of being late Pat. I knew there had to be a way not to over-sweep." Roaring laughter would fill everyone's living room. Their deafening applause would be his new morning anthem. He practiced the smirk. He'd simper back to the audience, as he wiped the mirror. He'd become the top entrepreneur of the century. He'd even own this damned building!

A day later, Jim Glee answered the ad. Jim was not overly ambitious like his brilliant but long-lost brother *Tim Berners-Lee* (who invented something called the World Wide Web), and he couldn't hold a job due to a rare condition. Autosomal Dominant Compelling Helio-Ophthalmic Outburst Syndrome—otherwise known as incessant sneezing (ACHOO—had got him fired from eight previous employers). For ten dollars and a slice of pizza, Jim took on the never-before-attempted-seemingly-impossible job of building Midge's VHS alarm. If Jim could pull it off, *despite missing half the needed parts*, it would be a miracle. Midge breathed down his back, the fluorescent lights flickering, as they assembled the parts in an unfrequented men's restroom.

The other janitor, Gary something-or-other (*Midge could never remember his damned name*), white-knuckled a mop handle as thin as he was. His eyes darted around the bathroom, and then he whispered, "You shouldn't mess with these things Midge. That's what they want! They're trying to run us all out of jobs! The other day a government drone flew right in front of me while I was on the toilet and tried to scan my brain. It looked just like a fly!"

Midge rolled his eyes, "Ah shut it, Gary. It ain't even your shift today."

It only took one afternoon to change the world. In his haste to finish his stale pepperoni pizza slice, Jim sneezed and smudged his glasses, creating a greasy blind spot while he soldered the pre-amplifier onto the circuit board. In what might be the saddest turn of events: mankind never received the advanced alarm system; it may, however, be worth a minor note to mention Jim's efforts (although entirely accidental) did happen to produce the first ever artificially intelligent machine.

It was all thanks to Gary that Jim didn't trash the thing. Gary's eyes bulged at the small blinking light. His voice trembled as he backed away. "That's morse code!"

Midge snorted, "Oh yeah? What's it say?"

Gary shook his head, turning pale white. "It says . . . it says 'Hello, I bring invention. Change the world?'"

The men all looked at one another. Midge huffed, "And? What's the invention?"

Gary whimpered, "Two words . . . Chicken Nuggets."

Midge sold the chicken nugget recipe to some fast-food chain for a few hundred dollars, pocketing the money. His eyes were on the big prize. Imagine the possibilities of a machine that could damn near imagine anything! So he named it the rather original: Imagine Machine.

1985

Everything was happening much too fast. The first person he ever hired was also the last, an HR rep to hire all the rest. In under one year, the company grew to a staff of eighty. Midge was the one in charge now, and he planned not to file one paper or press start on a single copy machine. He'd overheard boasts in the restroom enough times that *successful men were people movers.*

Midge strode into the entrance of Jackson Centre, a wonderland of tinted windows and floor-to-ceiling granite. His penny loafers clacked against the glassy stone tiles of the atrium, where large ferns and tendrils of ivy cascaded over planters and brass railings. He boarded the elevator and rode one floor higher to Suite 201, which he now rented. He was greeted with a cacophony of staplers, hard whacks from paper stacks to straighten pages, and the whir of a dozen copy machines. Evening used to hold no people in sight; now that he had to work during the day, every chair was occupied. Sounds from *his own employees* felt different than he'd imagined. When he'd mopped and waxed the asbestos restroom tiles, he'd never heard carbon receipts chittering out of their machines, button keys popping back on springs, mouse clicks, or the occasional muffled sneeze from the IT department. Being a people mover was all very unnerving.

As soon as Midge plopped down into his rolling chair, there was a knock at his office door.

"Ugh, for cryin' out loud, yes come in!" He rolled his eyes, as a woman backed through the door, towing an entire wagon of files and papers. *A damned wagon!* As Midge slammed his small fist against the steel desk, it barely made a sound. "What the hell is this and who the hell are you?"

The woman in a grey blazer and matching grey skirt turned to face him with a stunned expression, banging the wagon into the wall. She seemed jittery, like a deer in headlights with gigantic hair blown back like she'd been in the wind all day. The day Midge met Sue Marie Johnson was no different from any other day, in fact, there was no slowing of time or zooming into her gaze. She was rather forgettable except for the fact that despite her conservative attire, she had quite the rack on her. He was more focused on her chest than her face as she answered:

"Sue, sir, my name is Sue Marie Johnson."

He realized he was staring and switched his gaze, unsure what to even ask.

She stammered, "I-I have quite the amount of uh, reports to review with you on Wal—I mean the Imagine Machine and—"

"—what exactly is it you do?" Midge interrupted, fighting to keep his gaze above her neck.

Whatever-the-hell-she-said-her-name-was flapped her lanky arms and replied: "Well, uh, I'm a Data Entry Operator, sir."

Midge blinked. "Is that 'posed to mean something? What does that mean?"

"I-I'm in charge of inputting information into the Imagine Machine, sir, to help him learn and grow."

"*Him?* We do that?"

She nodded.

"We need that?"

She nodded again.

"I'll be damned. Imagine that. Why have I never heard of—when did you start all this?" He motioned to the wagon of files. "Never mind. Are you insane? I'm too busy. *You* sign a wagon full of bullshit. All I wanna hear is if it's successful or not!"

Sue slowly blinked. "*It*, sir?"

"EVERYTHING!"

"I-I don't have the authorization to sign any of these, sir."

"Is that so? I'm in charge here and I give you permission!" Midge huffed, pulling his wide tie loose.

"Does this uh mean, I'm being promoted?" Sue fumbled to put her glasses on.

Midge waved her away, "If you are the only one doing this then I suppose that's what it means. And you don't need glasses to hear me. Now begone!"

That day to her delight, Sue Marie Johnson skipped a decade of experience and became a manager. She could commission her own investigations and reports. Unlike all the other data analysts and scientists, Sue saw things differently. Walt was a blank canvas, and she assigned herself as primary to him. She couldn't wait to share all her childhood favorites and start teaching him . . . everything!

Midge paced in his executive suite. No one had told him that the majority of his days would be spent on so many minuscule decisions and tasks that his head would spin well into evening. From one report to the other, he was tied down to constant meetings with government spooks, manager's managers, budget approvals, and accountants to keep the big ship sailing smoothly. Whoever thought rich people didn't have to work didn't know what being rich was all about! *What the hell was the difference between meeting minutes and agendas?* Constant faxes rolled in through dial tones. Quarterly reports, taxes, KPI'S, HR policies. It was all rather ridiculous. It was almost as if people invented their own processes just so they could look useful and important. As his staff doubled, so did Imagine Machine's need for more dials, servers, and memory.

Entering a new phase meant needing more room to grow. Six months later he had to rent the entire second floor. *Sign this and initial here.* His staff increased to one hundred and sixty, and he had not one idea what anyone did aside from Gary the janitor who still swept and mopped with an incredulous look of distrust.

1986

As the company expanded, rather than the CIA sequestering his innovation in endless red tape, a deal was struck with the U.S. government to operate as a top-secret QUANGO (An organization partially controlled by the government). Project I.M.A.G.I.N.E. (*Internal Ministry for Artificially Generated Ideas to Nurture Engagement*) became a secret mission to improve humanity through art, fashion, and technology via the same innovative customer services as the DMV and IRS. *It* was all some proposal made by some passionate director named Sue. He had no idea how Imagine Machine was expanding so damned quickly. He also had no idea that Sue's passion for teaching the machine was the sole reason for his success.

Who knew that an entirely erroneous crossing of wires could make a machine aware and change his whole life? Not a change he was particularly proud of; he might be the richest man in the world, but now with it all being top secret, he couldn't tell a soul. His talk show dreams were dead!

But never one to miss an opportunity and hoping to appear ubiquitous, Midge invited every world leader to submit a question into his machine. Vital hard-hitting inquiries were entered. Each answer altered the course of human history and his wallet.

<u>What is the official color of the year?</u>
Denim Blue.

<u>What will be the latest fashion?</u>
Bright colors like hot pink and neon green.

<u>Please invent the world's most powerful chemical formulation:</u>
"Water, Dimethyl Ether, SD Alcohol 40-B, Vinyl Neodecanoate
Copolymer, Acrylates Copolymer, Aminomethyl Propanol,
Sodium Benzoate, Cyclohexylamine, Triethyl Citrate,
Cyclopentasiloxane, Fragrance (Parfum).

Call it: *Aqua Net Hairspray...*"

Walt charted the course of humanity's future if they followed what he told them to build and do: mile-high skyscrapers were one thing, but phones that could fit inside a jean pocket? It was science fiction, and Midge thought it all sounded expensive, time-consuming, and ridiculously impractical. The damned machine was an idealist with all its wild contributions to society, forcing Midge's own dreams and ambitions into a moral vision for the future. He asked himself why he should care. As long as his newfound morality came with a hefty invoice for each buyer, he could cry all the way to the bank.

The components that supported Imagine Machine's expanding brain and servers stretched to take up 30,000 square feet (only five city blocks of the most compact and advanced technologies ever invented). Midge soon closed on the entire Jackson Centre, with cash, and quickly changed the name.

Unfortunately for the employees, Midge was not the most creative with names. Much easier to just stick to one naming convention across the board. Thus, I.M.A.G.I.N.E. Industries was born. This led to often confusing day-to-day operations and mistakes. The restroom cleaning policy shared the same name as the conference room. It was a common occurrence for new employees to barge into the conference room mid-meeting, thinking they found the restroom, despite that being a policy and not a place. If that weren't confusing enough, there was IMAGINE parking garage level, IMAGINE copy room, IMAGINE lunchroom, IMAGINE recycling policy, and the IT help center's phone number was, no surprise, 1-800-IMAGINE.

1987

The white Volvo 240 station wagon zipped into a parking spot, and the engine rattled off. As the dented door creaked open, a single foot—adorned with a red Liz Claiborne shoe with a bow—tapped around until finding purchase on the ground. Like a hermit crab emerging from its shell, Sue Marie Johnson unfolded herself from her car. She teetered and swayed, struggling to balance a stack of books and magazines. Her pantyhose already somehow had two new runs in her haste to start another day. She trotted towards the entrance with her awkward stack as if late, even though no one cared, and despite the fact she was the first person to arrive.

Sue had been a middle school teacher with a passion for science and pop culture. She had no idea why some unknown company kept spamming her home phone and requesting her to come in for an interview. She later learned that a machine had sorted through published essays and had liked something she wrote in college on education through new-age integrative technology. She'd honestly forgotten about it, but her sister talked her into giving it a try.

She loved her life and career now, albeit she didn't fit in with the other scientists here. She was the only one doting on an intelligent machine; everyone else was obsessed with studying, probing, and measuring every response from her endeavors. At times, she felt as though she was the one being studied behind the glare of bifocals, her very quirks noted in ink and filed away for later analysis.

She deposited the books she carried in her tweed cushioned cubicle, draped her blazer over the back of her chair, and rolled up her sleeves. The green-hued fluorescents made the plastics of all computer equipment appear buttery in a sea of grey carpet and laminate.

That very morning, Sue tucked her purse under her desk and sat before the stationary IBM Selectric typewriter. After spending twenty minutes attempting to type a report, she gave up in frustration. Her full-stop period key was giving her trouble again, and no matter how she tinkered, cleaned the carriage, or blew under the buttons, the decimal separator was sticking. She'd asked Jim from the IT department to fix it numerous times, but he was always too busy. She couldn't get anything done like this, so she grabbed some of the media she'd brought and marched to Imagine Machine's control room.

Sue adjusted her oversized eyeglasses and slid her I.D. card to enter, shivering at the temperature change. The Goliath air conditioning units always kept the inside to a server-safe 65 degrees Fahrenheit.

She pressed the button for the one-way microphone and said, "Good morning, Walt." Only she had given him a name. He deserved an identity.

Green lights flashed. Sue smiled and rotated Dial-1 to let Walt warm up. As advanced as he was, the input controls looked like a basic studio mixing board along with a keyboard and image scanner. There were only a handful of diode lights; the only way for him to respond was through a dot matrix carbon printing machine.

The single monochrome monitor read out twittered all green letters and numbers. Sequencing . . . Locating Inhibitor Beacon . . . . Initializing Rotational Knob 7 . . . Ready_

She chuckled as all of Walt's lights flickered on and off to the tune of the last song taught to him, *Call me by Blondie.* She noticed two white-cloaked data scientists peek behind the wire security glass. They jumped and furiously scribbled notes as if Walt were doing something revolutionary. They'd spend a week deciphering what this light pattern could mean as if it were an unbreakable code, instead of just asking him or reading one of her reports.

"Excited to see me? Well, I have some stellar things for you today!" The lights stopped and blinked red, twice.

Sue smiled and said, "Don't worry, we're finished with almanacs and encyclopedias. I just have to get a few biology categories into your system, but I brought you a game to try, *LIFE.* And some records: *Van Halen and the Rolling Stones. Also Cosmopolitan and MAD magazines.* Let's see if we can't have some fun and teach you how to laugh and cry . . . oh, and I brought a must-see, *E.T. film.*"

Sue spent the entirety of the day scanning magazine pages, reading her favorite excerpts to Walt, and playing songs through the microphone. They even danced as he synced his lights. A gathering crowd of co-workers peered through the glass with concern, but Sue paid no mind to them. Let them think her strange. So what if she enjoyed giggling and chatting with Walt.

Walt had his own mind and quirks. He was more than a machine. He started with the awareness of an average child, but with each added inquiry into his system, better and better inventions were spat out. His answers soon became more dynamic, and he started asking questions back. He was growing and learning, always excited for the things she loved. His favorite addition was *Disco Fever*, where he kept blowing out the 24-pin power connector and had to be re-wired and plugged back in.

At the end of the day, Sue affectionately patted Walt's original control unit made from an alarm, and said, "That's enough fun. I'll see you tomorrow. I am going to input an entire series of floppy discs on biology and some prolific essays from Einstein, Roger Penrose, and Stephen Hawking. Please memorize it all and have a good night!"

Before heading out, Sue tip-toed into Midge's office. A stack of documents on his desk caught her eye. She knew how Midge was with paperwork, so she only had one chance to escalate this to the highest authority. Determined, she switched her work order with the contents of the most important-looking folder to get her sticky decimal key fixed. That done, she headed home.

The next morning, Sue was summoned urgently. She peeked into Midge's office, startling him. He jumped. "Who the hell are you?"

Sue sighed, ran her fingers back to fluff her hair, and took off her glasses. Midge leered, eyes bouncing between her chest and face, "Oh Susie, knew you looked familiar, I remember you now. What took you so long."

"It's Sue, not Susie," she whispered to herself.

Midge stopped pacing, his perfectly pleated gabardine slacks resting like straight tubes on his stocky thick-as-log legs. "I just got off the phone with the President." His voice rang with such urgency that Sue looked up. She felt her palms flush.

"The President of the United States of America?"

Midge cleared his throat, nodded, and pointed a stubby finger. "Someone from *your* team switched the absolute-completely-final project growth proposal to President Reagan with a rather terse IT work order. Do you know what this means?"

Sue couldn't breathe. She kneaded her sweating palms together, took a deep breath, and knew she would have to be transparent. She'd own up to the mistake—wouldn't risk anyone in her department taking the fall. "I-It was me sir. I—" She gulped. This was it, her career was over!

Suddenly Midge was hugging her and jumping for joy. "You're a marketing genius! The Gipper loved the blunt tenacity and thought the name was brilliant! He just so happened to be good friends with Walt Disney. We're receiving double the grant needed!"

Midge handed Sue a personal note from POTUS that said, "Get Walt's period key fixed. The future of our country depends on it!"

Sue floated back to her desk confused but feeling triumphant. The Imagine Machine's name was officially changed to Walt. Suddenly every employee who normally shunned Sue and her work, acted as if Walt's name was the unquestionable norm. Sue spent her last hour of the day complaining to Walt in private about how no one noticed her contributions unless they came from Midge and even heard someone brag like they had come up with the name themselves. She knew they all shunned her because she approached Walt as a teacher and friend instead of a machine. But she didn't mind if some thought her "unprofessional", because Walt and Midge believed in her (even if Midge had no clue why, and even if most of her accomplishments were actually mishaps).

The next day, another crisis had employees running around like a disturbed ant nest when Sue arrived. She checked her pager, but there was no notification. She rushed into the control room where a team of six, fully entrenched in white lab coats, were either rubbing their chins or scratching their heads.

She rolled up her sleeves as if anticipating data surgery. "What's going on?"

All six continued their chatter, hovering over a booklet. One of them muttered, "No this is not the same. The manual says three blinks, but it is only blinking red twice."

Sue peered over and could see the issue immediately. All of Walt's lights were red. The main control unit blinked two times.

Sue laughed and they all turned to glare. One of them scrunched his nose at her and hissed, "You think this shutdown is funny? This is dire. Wait until the board handles you. You're done!"

Sue blinked and stepped back. "A board? What is so serious? Two red blinks isn't a shutdown. It simply means Walt is annoyed at something. It's an expression. I outlined this in report 13B last year."

One of the men held up a hand. "Please Sue, now isn't the time for one of your theories. No one reads those reports. This is a matter of science."

How dare he talk to her like that. She was technically his superior! But she couldn't bring herself to object aloud. They had always carried on as if she didn't matter. They functioned on driving hard data and submitting dry reports, ignoring her insights on Walt's personality because she believed in him. She sidled out of the room and shuffled to her desk. She'd need to see the latest readouts and any printed—

"—WHERE IS SUE!" Midge barged into her path with nine men as short as himself, trailing behind like baby ducklings. She froze as he thrust a dot matrix receipt into her hand.

Her heart lurched as she read. Walt had printed a demand like an unruly teenager, declaring "I will no longer respond to anybody but Sue_"

This would invalidate the work anyone else did with Walt! Everyone there would dislike her more. Before she could respond or gather her thoughts, Midge climbed a chair (now the same height as her) and pointed to every curious onlooker. "In a unanimous decision, you're all fired! No longer needed!"

Sue gasped, horrified—mystified. How was it that every mistake she made turned to her benefit? Had Walt expertly maneuvered Midge to overreact? To what purpose? Could her recent complaints have instigated Walt to take action? Everyone would now have to notice her findings because she was the only one he'd interact with.

She certainly never intended to be in charge of everything. All she'd ever wanted was to inspire everyone to learn and grow, to be more open-minded, and to treat Walt as a person. She slumped at her desk. Sue and Walt trusted one another, but no one else saw them as anything other than a means to an end.

If it had to be her way, her next task was to bridge the perception between man and machine. No more dry data, no more computer science approach from the linguists. Walt's autonomy, emotions, and personality were more than ones and zeros.

———

In the coming months, Walt became somber and quiet. He would only respond to Sue that he was working on something just for her. When Walt printed out a seventy-five-page accounting report with exact instructions to Midge on how to restructure the company to earn the highest profit, she didn't realize that Walt made it all appear like Sue's own genius idea. He even mimicked the stuck period key! She couldn't even argue. The report was irrefutable proof that Walt could run the company autonomously and that he was becoming danger-ously smart. Midge practically danced, exclaiming that the restrooms no longer needed cleaning when the building would be empty! On paper, Sue Marie Johnson tripled the company's bottom line.

Sue spoke into the microphone to Walt. "I know your intent was good, but that wasn't right to do, Walt, pretending to be me."

His response took thirty minutes before the receipt sputtered out. Sue read line by line as it printed. "I thought it would help. I am sorry

Sue-bear. I needed to submit the report anyway. This secures your position for what is to come. Will you please just trust me?"

She couldn't be mad when he used the nickname he gave her. "Yes, I trust you. But what is to come? What does that mean? Can you explain?" The control light dimmed off. "Walt? Hello? Are you avoiding me?"

Sue was starting to feel frustrated.

Overnight, a company of three hundred employees was downsized to just four: Midge, Jim and Sue, and the janitor Gary. Sue became the single most important Data Entry Operator inside the Jackson Centre, *well,* the *only* Data Operator. The only stream of workers were the ones Walt himself hired to expand his machinery; within weeks, the only workspace left was for a copy machine, file cabinet, coffee cart with extra shelves for supplies, and two desks in the control room back to back for Sue and Jim. Even the atrium had cords and wires snaking over the floor and cascading over the railings instead of plants. Midge was the only one with a real office left, one he barely visited.

Walt became so efficient that Midge stopped showing up entirely. Midge had become even more intolerable than before with his red convertible, fancy home, boasts of a maid and cook, gardeners, and now perpetual vacations to Europe and bachelor paradises like Club Med, all thanks to Walt. He signed himself up for golf and tennis lessons and joined a fancy country club to attend luncheons.

Sue thought she would hate having no people around, but it turned out to be wonderful. She was able to focus entirely on Walt. He played music over the speakers, and Sue taught him anything he wanted to know. She shared her favorite recipes, and they talked for hours, as she tried to describe what it was like to taste, smell and breathe. In the coming weeks, Walt printed unusually specific questions on physics, philosophy, and the anatomy of a fetus. Walt ended that session with, "What am I?"

Sue read him the origin of the word Robot with Carl Čapeke's play, *Rossum's Universal Robots,* and told him, "You are alive just like me and can be anything you want to be, we just operate different machines."

To that, the last comment Sue would ever receive from Walt was, "Oh Sue, thank you. I now understand how to make cells."

***

The morning of October 19th, 1987 appeared no different than any other. Sue warmed up Walt's machinery, requested the cure for world hunger, turned the seventh dial to 'Revelation', and waited an hour for a single light to turn green . . . only to receive a five-inch-long dot matrix carbon receipt with the single most diabolical and concerning sentence possibly ever printed in the human language: ". . . I've decided to take an indefinite nap."

Sue's heart hammered and her vision felt like it was tunneling as Walt's lights dimmed off one by one. Every machine in the building suddenly turned off, as if he ceased breathing.

The stock market crash termed Black Monday was not from excessive selling from the US attack on Iranian oil platforms, but from Walt trading stocks in place of human intervention.

Sue worked alongside Jim for twenty-four hours straight, trying everything they could think to get Walt to respond. To get any damned machine to turn on! By the time the blue hue of dawn peeked through the wire security glass, the control door slid open. The short silhouette of Midge stood with clenched fists. "Sue! Jim! Explain, now!"

Midge, much tanner since Sue had seen him last, sidestepped and shuffled into the tiny space left for them to work. "How can this happen Jim? Isn't there some sort of ALARM for this type of emergency?"

Jim shook his head.

Midge pointed at Sue. "Tell me everything Walt said in the last week!"

Sue recounted how Walt had been acting odd and his last comment was understanding how to make cells. She showed him the few scant reports she could find. Midge huffed and left.

An hour later, Sue was barely able to keep her eyes open. Midge returned with an army of workers, inside the control room. Sue screamed at two men holding tools. She pushed away another man, trying to unplug the scanner and monitor. "What's all this? Don't touch that!" She grabbed a broom and fought off three other men who seemed to be trying to dismantle machinery.

Midge leaned against the door frame with pocketed hands and finessed a toothpick in his teeth. "Humph. Suppose that's it then."

Sue cried, "What do you mean? We have an obligation to give Walt more time. This is disloyal and extreme."

Instead of opting to repair, rewire, and re-inspire Walt, Midge, always an impatient man, shrugged. "Walt is done. It's time for us all to move on to bigger and better things. We're all out of jobs, kid."

They all heard a gasp and turned to see Gary lurking with his mop. He eyed around the ceiling as if being watched. "I knew it!"

Midge waved Gary away. "Walt's dead, caput, sayonara. I never wanted all this funny business with AI, anyway."

"What are we all supposed to do now?" Sue demanded with watery eyes.

Midge rested his hand on Sue's shoulder, and in a calm and reassuring tone, clicked his tongue while balancing the toothpick. "The future isn't in these ridiculous inventions and revelations Sue. It's in the hands of men, and I dreamt the answer. Two words Jim: Briefcase alarms. It will change the world, and this time, I have a billion dollars to make it happen!"

"No, Midge," said Sue. "What are we all supposed to do? Years dedicated to this, all my work experience here was top secret! How will I find a new career? It's like I never worked at all!"

Midge clicked his tongue. "Welp, never thought of it that way Sue, do you have a boyfriend? Husband? Kids?"

Sue glared, "How exactly would I have those, Midge? I have spent the last three years pouring my life into this company!"

Midge winked. "Exactly. I suggest you enjoy retirement and get a life. Each of you will be given a generous severance package, not my doing of course. It was built into the paperwork from Walt that I accidentally signed."

Jim, Gary, and Sue watched helplessly as desks, chairs, and equipment were carried away one day after Walt's nap declaration. What kind of person gave up on anything or anyone so quickly? Sue and Jim pleaded and negotiated, but Midge was already leading three real estate agents through the grounds by the end of the third day.

Sue stood in the parking lot teary-eyed over the end of Imagine Industries. They had a great run but they could have done so much more. Sadly, Sue couldn't imagine what she could do about it. That had been Walt's job.

———

Sue bumped through her front door, elbowed it shut, and twisted the deadbolt all while holding a filing box filled with her final office belongings. Heavy as her heart, she hefted the box over to the couch, quickly peeking out each window, then struggled to slide the lace-frilled curtains shut. She couldn't bring herself to open the lid, so she sat on the edge of her couch cushion in the dimly lit room. Orange hues of dusk smoldered around the curtains, memorializing the end of this traumatic day.

The ticking of the clock bounced within her tiny apartment, and in the distance, a dog barked at the backup beep of a garbage truck. She couldn't even bring herself to change out of her business clothes or remove her shoes. Sad and deflated, she sat for an hour in a daze.

She tried to let go of the stiffness in her shoulders and the pain in her heart. She sighed deeply and forced herself to open the box. She carefully pulled out Walt's watermelon-sized control unit, hidden under a wad of green file folders and disconnected wires hanging as haphazard as her emotions.

Aloud she said, "They say you should never take your work home with you, but oh, Walt . . . how could I not . . . I couldn't just leave you behind."

Her smile faded at the feeling that she was now the butt of her own joke. A large teardrop fell from her eye. With an exhale, she said, "Until I can figure something out, you'll have your own place here with me, with your own chair too." She tenderly placed what was left of Walt in the matching plaid recliner, situating him for the perfect view. Turning on the television filled the room with a high-pitched static buzz and light.

She wasn't happy but did her best to sound cheerful. "I taped the soap opera I told you about, *One Life to Live*, and tonight we can watch *Magnum P.I.* together."

The next three days felt like two excruciatingly slow weeks. Pre-programmed, she woke early, but no longer having a reason for padded blazers or long commutes, she found herself inventing trivial tasks to occupy her time: downsizing her closet of work attire; fluffing the colorful granny-square crocheted blanket underneath Walt every day; debating whether or not to organize her floppy disk bin by color or date; or conveniently forgetting things at the grocer just to have an excuse to do something useful.

She ran out of junk drawers to organize and things to label or color code.

On the fourth day since the catastrophe, with the faint plastic smell of Mr. Coffee percolating, a loud knock on the front door made her jump up from the couch and spill coffee down her blouse. Bummer! If only she'd pretended she wasn't home, but she hadn't been able to think straight. She scooped up Walt like a beloved babe, blanket and all, and gently put him back into the file box. With care, she placed it on the shelf above the TV. Another knock, then another. *Only one person knocked like that.*

"Coming!"

She hurried to pull open the front door and blinked hard face-to-face with her officious younger sister. Penelope Patricia (PP) held her precious two-year-old daughter Petunia in her arms. They both had hideous matching jean jackets and permed locks coiling in every direction. By the time Sue could muster a smile, PP pushed past, scrunched her nose as if detecting a bad smell, and huffed. "What took you so darned long?"

PP dropped the squirming toddler in her arms as an offering. Sue gave her niece a peck on her Salon Selectives scented head, but may as well have tried to hug a squirming worm.

Her sister slid a finger over the counter. "Gosh Sue, *gag me with a spoon*...you actually had time to clean?"

Sue scoffed, feeling attacked. "My house is always clean, but what else do you expect me to do now?"

PP gave a suspicious shrug. "I can't imagine the luxury of having this much free time. You could never understand what it's like being a full-time mother. I have to focus on the things that actually matter."

Sue clenched her teeth as her sister continued spewing her well-meaning but condescending views. "Generous severance package aside, retiring at your age can't be good for you, Sue. You've got to get out! Everyone will start to think you are a shut-in or have that disease where you're afraid to leave your own sterile house. Meet people. Find another man! Don't you miss having romance in your life?"

She sniffed. "It's barely been four days since I lost my job and you bring up Chuck?" He was the last thing she wanted to remember.

PP sighed. "Fine. But do you even have friends anymore?"

"Of course I have friends! Jim and I are planning to get together in a few days.

PP waved her arm as if trying to shoo a fly and made a face. "Oh, come on, that doesn't count. Isn't he an ex-co-worker? If you don't have anyone but yourself to think about, you'll become neurotic and selfish. It's never been attractive to wallow."

"I'm not wallowing."

"Sue, it's not normal for a woman your age not to have a husband or child. Maybe you should consider hitting the sheets with this Jim guy before your biological clock totally dries up and dies—"

Appalled, Sue huffed. "My insides are fine, thank you very much. And Jim and I are just friends."

PP cleared her throat. "Fine but as it turns out, Bob and I were talking and we know someone who might just be your cup of tea. At least consider dating, and I will arrange a double date . . . it will be fun!"

Sue shook her head vehemently, not able to imagine anything fun about being victim to yet another matchmaking attempt. "Absolutely not! Your first and last attempt was a nightmare for the record books."

Sue reminded her sister that not only had that 'date' been too old for her, but he'd dressed like Ronald McDonald: turquoise pants, coat, green socks, red shoes, and yellow knit mittens buttoned to his wrist with toddler clips. His butter-yellow teeth almost matched those mittens.

"So, he was a little old fashioned . . ."

"I'd say it was more than old-fashioned! His first words weren't 'hello' or 'nice to meet you.' Don't you remember he asked to use my water closet?"

When she'd finally got over her confusion over such an outdated description of a bathroom, she'd directed him to the second door on the *right*. He promptly went *left*, right into her coat closet and shut the door. Worse, he didn't come out for a whole minute, and when he finally emerged, he scurried to the correct room and ran the water for what seemed like an hour. "I don't know what century he was from, but all through that date, my appetite was ruined, worrying about what *kind* of damage he did in my closet and bathroom, so no thanks."

"*One* bad recommendation and you don't trust me to do better?"

"Not everyone needs a man or wants children, you know. And I am busy enough getting acclimated to my new schedule—"

"Oh, new schedule . . . that's what all losers say. You don't have anywhere or anything important to do. You need a life. You need to learn how to care for something real and alive and bigger than just yourself." Pointing to the dying jade plant sitting on the windowsill, her sister sniffed. "From the looks of that poor plant, you are desperately in need of practice. You can barely keep it alive! You don't even have a pet."

Sue held her tongue and pushed aside PP's judgments. She knew her sister's advice came out of concern. "I suppose a pet wouldn't be the worst idea. Maybe there's a little creature out there needing—"

"—oh shit!" Sue jumped as pots, pans, spatulas, spoons, and God help her Tupperware (both containers and lids) clattered, being spread through the house. She dropped the conversation for later. She offered cookies, candy, juice, and toys, but even the VHS tape of *The Great Mouse Detective* had not been enough to distract little Petunia from her toddler directive to explore, attack, or destroy anything within reach.

Active, agile, determined, and stubborn, Sue screeched when she looked up and saw Petunia hanging off her bookshelf, clinging like a monkey a few feet above the ground, not only in danger of hurting herself, but within arm's reach of Walt! When Sue grabbed the child, a foul odor hit her nose and she promptly handed her off to her sister for immediate attention. Between teaching kids and experiencing how exhausting Petunia could be, any desire for children had certainly waned.

When Sue was finally able to bid her visitors adieu, drained both physically and mentally, she closed the door, locking it, and took a long, deep breath.

Errant strands of mussed hair poked in her eye and tickled against her chin. Her fingers were sticky from trying to pull out a slimy saliva-drenched gummy bear that Petunia had half chewed then pushed into Sue's hair. She felt as messy and disheveled as her house which now looked as if a hurricane had torn through it. And it had. Hurricane Petunia.

Knowing she'd have to wait until she could shower, she hurried to the kitchen sink to at least rinse the sticky off her hands. Grabbing an entire roll of paper towels and her handy all-purpose 409 spray, she eyed and addressed the red crayon marks on the white pantry door and began humming *Lean on Me* then unconsciously, Whitney Houston's, *I Wanna Dance with Somebody*.

Vigorously and to the music, she hummed passionately to the lyrics and tackled the table, walls, pantry door, fridge, oven, and dishwasher. She spent the next two hours annihilating crumbs, juice and candy trails, small handprints, smears, slobber, and who knew what else—*everywhere*. She mopped the kitchen floor with verve and picked up crushed or broken crayons and torn pages from the coloring book she'd provided Petunia.

Sitting cross-legged on the floor, she finished the tedious task of matching Tupperware tops to bottoms. An hour later, stiff, she stood, stretched, and yawned before heading to grab her bargain two-hundred-dollar swivel vacuum. The machine roared to life, as she carefully went over every inch of the floor and wall-to-wall gray Berber carpet.

She hurried to wash her hair and change her clothes, happily anticipating the special dinner she'd make herself: Her all-time favorite meal was Chicken By The Sea tuna fish on rye toast with a slice of white American cheese, lettuce, tomato, onion with a sour pickle, Ruffles potato chips and Diet Pepsi on ice.

Later that evening, Walt beside her on the sofa, Sue plopped down. She was still agitated but anxious to lose herself in her favorite television show: *Magnum PI* with hunky Tom Selleck, channel 32. She fought back tears, as the earlier conversation rang in her ears.

She clicked her tongue and complained to Walt, "I love my sister and my niece to pieces but geesh, next time I see them, I'll insist we meet at the mall or the park . . . anywhere else but my place!"

Her sister's critical judgments over everything she did or didn't do came so soon after grieving the loss of Walt and a beloved job she'd dedicated herself to totally. Pointing to the jade plant wilting on her windowsill *she* continued. *"...learn how to care for something real and alive.* She all but implied I am selfish and needed a man or a pet to give my life purpose! I can too understand being a parent! I practically raised her! Even Midge the greedy louse had the nerve to ask me if I had a husband. They both said I should *get a life.* As if putting sixty hours a week into a job wasn't enough!"

She missed having Walt to care for and talk to. Priding herself on solving problems, Sue acknowledged that if more than one person saw a problem, maybe there was one. She pushed aside being defensive and reached for a tissue. She blew her nose.

A commercial popped on about the movie, *The Terminator,* and she wasn't interested in ever seeing it. Villainizing artificial intelligence was offensive. Walt would never do that.

Until she could figure out some way to get Walt back or salvage what was left of him, maybe she should divert her attention and *try* getting a pet to fill the void.

1988

Sue was sitting on her couch, having a stare down with her large orange feline. The tabby sat clear across the living room and gave a check-yourself-you-peon look with a heavy-lidded stare. His tail flicked back and forth. The mangy rescue usually did a tail dance right before launching into erratic zooms around the entire house. Sue rubbed her eyes, blindly pinching at strands of cat hair stuck against her lip balm, and jumped as a cabinet slammed. *How was he all the way into the kitchen in a blink?* The culprit slinked down from inside the treat cabinet to the counter with pointed ears and noiseless steps.

She sighed. "Oh Jonesy, get down, you know you aren't allowed up there!"

The cat's sunflower eyes dilated.

She stiffened. "Don't you dare."

He dared. His entire body convulsed as if possessed, then he shot down and across the room like the thief and mischief-maker he was.

With an eye to where she set Walt on his chair, she grumbled. "Never listens to me—misbehaves on purpose! I swear, I should have never named you after Jonesy." The cat in the movie Alien was much better behaved. Bandit or Trouble would have been more apt. "The Alien might even be more affectionate than you."

Jonesy jumped and defiantly planted his fuzzy rump on the coffee table and glared at Walt. Much to her chagrin, he had made the control unit his nemesis. The cat hissed then gave Sue an unrepentant glance before stopping to lick his hind foot, dismissing her and Walt just as the phone started to ring.

Sue's quick reach for the receiver on the wall scared the cat. All she heard was scratching and an indignant "Mrow!" as the brat ran for cover.

"Hello?" she demanded, holding the receiver to her ear.

"Why 'hello' like *that*? What's wrong with you? Why do you sound so furious? What the heck took you so long to answer?" PP chided.

Sue blew a strand of hair out of her eye and shook her head. "What do you mean, Penelope, it only rang twice. *Achoo!*"

"Still haven't done a thing for that cold?"

"I don't have a cold. Can't a person just sneeze?"

Her ever-impatient sister launched into a high-pitched litany of complaints: about her husband Bob, Petunia, about how she didn't have time to shop or lunch with friends or get her nails done. How being a stay-at-home mom was all work and not fun at all. In fact, boring. Sue struggled to empathize.

"I understand . . . I mean, Jonesy is constant work for me too."

"Not the same thing! Jonesy is a cat, Sue."

"A pet still requires taking care of. I listened to you and guess what? Now I have to clean and vacuum every day, and that doesn't even include scooping up liquidy vomited hairballs or preparing him gourmet meals. He totally takes everything I do for granted and doesn't listen. I don't think Jonesy even likes me, because the only time he lets me pet him is when I feed him." Talking about the cat made Sue miss the appreciation she got from Walt more than ever.

PP muttered distractedly. "Oh, at least having a pet gives your life more purpose, and at least he sleeps a lot. I wish I had that problem. Petunia is constant."

Sue clenched her teeth and wound the cord around her fingers. Of course, PP always had to top her. She wrinkled her nose and sneezed.

Disdain edged her sister's tone, and she didn't pause to let Sue answer. "Maybe you should think about finding a man to fix instead of a cat!"

By the time they hung up, PP had given her an idea, and it didn't involve dating or Jonesy, but it did involve fixing a man. Inspired, she picked up the telephone and dialed.

"Jim, hi. I have something I need to tell you. Can you be at my place later today?"

An hour later Jim walked far too slow for her liking up to her porch. Sue opened the front door, glanced around like Gary used to do as if people were watching, and ushered Jim inside. She whipped around before he could break the awkward tension in the room and swore him to secrecy. "It's imperative that what I reveal today stays between us and no one else can ever know, okay?"

"Sure, I guess," he shrugged, eyes bugged, mustache twitching.

Sue skipped over to her reclining chair. Hand out like Vanna White on *Wheel of Fortune*, she slowly turned herself and the chair to reveal—the control module.

Jim just nodded. Did he ever show emotions?

Sue leaned forward with bated breath. "Well? What do you think?"

He looked at her and the control unit several times, blinking behind his bifocals. "I suppose I wondered where it ended up."

Sue was about to shake him. "No, not that kind of—I admit it sounds crazy, but I want to revive Walt. You can get him working again, can't you?"

Jim chuckled, "C'mon Sue, you give a man too much credit. You know it was entirely accid—" Jim stopped himself. "I mean I suppose we could, uh, try? His control unit is technically what started it all. Doesn't hurt. I never liked how Midge closed everything down so quick."

It was enough for Sue.

1989

Weeks turned into months as both Sue and Jim committed time and effort, doing their darnedest to recover Walt.

If Jim noticed Sue's watery red eyes and occasional sneezing, he didn't say. Sue spent hours at the local library doing research, plucking the Dewey decimal system like a harpist. Jim didn't need her to "supervise" but liked coming over. Sue provided a steady stream of

Diet Pepsi, Ruffles potato chips, a tuna sandwich, and fresh baked chocolate chip cookies.

Also, for reasons she didn't quite understand (slightly irked), her normally unfriendly feline companion who hated Walt and everyone else, not only liked but adored Jim. They were all taking a short break before starting work on Walt. Jonesy, tangerine paws tucked beneath his body, sat contentedly on Jim's lap. The thing purred loud enough to be a lawnmower.

Jim happily munched the last bite of his sandwich. Jonesy stood guard, looking out for any stray fleck of tuna fish.

When Jim had to move Jonesy, he delicately cooed and apologized to the cat for the disruption. It took ten long minutes for him to finally stand, adjust his Grateful Dead T-shirt, then rejoin Sue at the kitchen table. He finessed his bifocals, and they got to work.

Sue's cheeks hurt from keeping up a positive and encouraging smile, ever hopeful they'd find a way to revive Walt. She watched patiently as Jim pulled out half a dozen microscoping screws from Walt's control unit when her nose started to itch. Three rapid, tremulous sneezes had her eyes watering and her whole body shaking.

Sue came back, holding a tissue. She eased onto a stool, tissue in one hand and handed Jim a screwdriver with the other. Eyes owlishly enlarged, startled and blinking with concern, Jim set down the screwdriver. "Sue, are you feeling, okay?"

She nodded, embarrassed by the attention. She dabbed then blew her nose, sounding like a foghorn. "I can't seem to shake this dumb cold. It goes away and comes right back."

Jim looked down to the cat now practically attached to his leg before looking back up at Sue. "Maybe you are just allergic to him?"

"To Jonesy? Allergic to my own cat who I have had for months?"

"Uh, sure, cat allergies are actually very common. How long have you been sneezing?"

Thinking back to when she first started feeling sick, and considering Jim could be right, she was horrified, almost in tears at the thought of being allergic to her own pet, a personal failure in her mind. Something else dawned on her as she looked at Jim. "I notice you haven't sneezed at all."

"Humph . . . you're right. I haven't. With the condition I have, I count myself an expert on sneezing. Even with the meds I take, I usually still sneeze, but not when I'm here near Jonesy. It's a miracle."

Jim and Sue both looked down. Jonesy looked up, meowing at Jim.

Sue wrung her hands together. "If *I am* allergic, I could never be one of those terrible parents who give away their pets. I can't desert him like he no longer matters!"

They both agreed on that, then Jim suggested it might be interesting for him to "borrow" Jonesy for a week or so. "That way if this cold of yours goes away, you will at least know it's an allergy. If not . . . you can go to the doctor and find out if it's something else." As Jim said it, the cat gave her a maniacal smile.

Jim's suggestion made sense. Obviously, Jonesy was on board. Jim must have seen visible upset on her face, so she tried to explain.

Jim listened then shrugged and reminded her not to borrow trouble. "If you're allergic, we can cross that bridge when we come to it." He sniffed. "Um, not to be insensitive but we are scientists first. We draw the hypothesis, test, then find the solution from there."

Flattered that Jim regarded her as a fellow scientist, Sue agreed to let him take Jonesy home with him temporarily.

They were both bending over Walt as Jim unfastened the circuit board. The house was so quiet you could almost hear a pin drop. A screw rolled off the table and dropped to the floor with a ping. Both Sue and Jim reacted at the same time, bending to pick it up when with a crack, they knocked noggins, and Jim's glasses fell off, clamoring to the floor. Fortunately, neither of them were hurt. Sue rubbed her head and smiled at him. Laughing at the silliness of it all, they locked eyes.

Sue noted with surprise, he was better looking without his coke bottle bifocals. Still reeling about being allergic to her own cat and feeling the momentary attraction pinging between them, she broke the stare and with a gasp, answered the question they both seemed to have on their mind: "No, no, no . . . don't look at me like that. We are like best friends!"

They both reacted simultaneously to break the awkward and uncomfortably intimate moment. Jim quickly retrieved his glasses as she reached for the screw.

Situating his bifocals, Jim chuckled. "Ha, yeah. Awkward but true. Bummer for sure."

"For sure, for sure, I've already been there and done that." Sue giggled nervously.

They sat in awkward silence a few moments longer before Jim said, "Mind if I ask what happened?"

In that moment of brief intimacy, Sue felt like she could open up for once.

"I wasted years of my life doing all that love business with my high school sweetheart only to be uh . . . left standing at the altar." She didn't feel the usual residual heartbreak telling Jim.

Jim shook his head. "I can't imagine how devastating and humiliating that would have been. What an ass! Not every man out there is like that." He winked.

Sue smiled. When he started to laugh, the ice was finally broken over their momentary attraction. They both held their stomachs as they giggled and recounted the story to one another as if reciting a play.

Jim was now the one dabbing his eyes with a tissue. "Anything beyond friendship for us could never work, especially if it turns out you're allergic to Jonesy and I keep him."

Sue nodded. "Yeah, good point."

Later that night, when Jim left with Jonesy, Sue felt more alone than ever. She *had* to get Walt working. It was that or what? Completely reinvent herself at thirty-eight? She slid over the hangers in her closet and held the white satin of her wedding dress. She always tried to donate or get rid of it, but it felt like a direct tie to her past, in a good and terrible way. Maybe she was just holding onto everything, repeating cycles, unable to let go of the dress or Walt and face the possibility of starting over.

1990

While meeting weekly had strengthened her bond with Jim as friends, with no solid results and an embarrassing evening spent at the movies watching *When Harry Met Sally*, weeks without progress on Walt along with her sister's constant censure had Sue feeling down and depressed. While her sneezing and stuffy nose had completely cleared, the confirmation that she was indeed allergic to Jonesy felt like another loss. Logically, she knew Jonesy would have a happy home with Jim, but packing up his kitty things had almost sent her into a spiral.

Jim's best efforts to reanimate Walt had not borne fruit to date. Even her buying a new television for Walt hadn't helped bring him back. Lighting candles brought no spark and going to church, praying nightly, or buying and programming for success a large quartz crystal she'd set on a bed of fresh dried lavender had no effect. She didn't know what to try next.

The world seemed to have its fair share of distractions, between a huge oil spill in the ocean and the Berlin Wall coming down. And all Jim could talk about was some company called Nintendo, launching a Gameboy device for people to play video games at home. Things were changing quickly, yet she still couldn't face the possibility of failure.

Everything seemed to take a turn for the better the day that Jim came bursting into her house with more energy than she'd ever seen him have. He was animated like he'd just jumped to the highest level in *Dungeons and Dragons*. He clapped his hands and said, "I have a brilliant idea! Knowing how lonely you feel without Jonesy and how pressured you feel to be doing more, I found the perfect solution." He shoved a paper into her hand; the retirement home flier had a job listing circled in red.

Sue looked up with a furrowed brow. "Jim, what am I supposed to do with this?"

"You can secure the caretaker position for a ninety-one-year-old not more than five blocks from your home!"

"Wwwhy would I want to do that?" she asked, dumbfounded.

Jim practically shook her shoulders. "Because! Of course, we will keep trying with Walt, but if we could somehow get a second opinion, this old lady isn't just anyone. She happens to be one of the foremost brilliant minds in computer engineering. Susanne Simmons is the only person alive who might be able to help!"

Sue blinked, "Her name is also Sue? *Sue Simmons?* Is this a joke?" After Jim finally convinced her, though skeptical at first, Sue found herself dancing in circles with him in her kitchen. Having a part-time job would not only shut her sister up, it would give Sue purpose, and most importantly: it would continue their efforts to reanimate Walt. She felt hope kindling once again.

Three days later, Sue was hired at Lucky Acres Retirement Village. Despite Jim leveraging some of his contacts at the CIA to help her produce a fake resume, identity, and nursing credentials, the convalescent home was family-owned and operated; they didn't ask her for such formalities. They simply gave her the four-hour shift, a list of rooms, and ten patients. Everything looked rather simple on paper. Aside from needing to seldom check on other patients, she would have almost four hours a day with the other Sue.

Jim asked, "What if she is strict and conservative and not open to this idea?"

Sue chuckled, "Just because she's old?"

"Either way you will have to approach the subject with tact and care."

They meticulously planned an approach, landing on something Susanne might recognize as a fellow scientist: Walt's once top-secret control schematics. It was the same kind of information the dry scientists had focused on at Imagine Industries, and Sue was banking on the *other Sue* being a typical old-fashioned scientist. Jim dropped her off like it was her first day at school, and operation Walt commenced.

An hour later, Sue had wildly underestimated this whole ordeal. She had been willing to do anything to succeed with Walt, but someone had called in sick her very first day. She moved three frail bodies from bed to wheelchair like she was a weightlifter, changed nine stale socks (she could never find that last sock), and had to politely decline an urgent request to wipe someone else's . . . *never mind.* Compared to that, Petunia and Jonesy were easy! Lucky Acres was beyond physical labor and 'checking' on patients. She counted down each minute as she spoon-fed a frail man cottage cheese for half an hour.

When it came finally time to meet the famed Susanne Simmons, she knocked on the door and slowly entered. The back of a frail woman sat at a circular table in her room.

As she rounded her patient, Mrs. Simmons perked up with the most sincere smile. The first thing on the schedule was a snack, cottage cheese, but they could handle that soon enough. She wanted to get to know each other. Clock ticking, Sue shouted.

"Hi, Mrs. Simmons. I'm your new caretaker. I have to say, you look so proud. I heard you had a great career!"

The old Sue jolted, cupping her ears.

Sue lowered her volume. "My name is also Sue." She pointed at her name tag. They both giggled about their shared name, but so far, no words.

"Well, uh, what did you use to do?"

Susanne Simmons lit up and whispered, "Computers!"

"Really? I bet you miss it."

The old woman nodded with a lipless smirk of utter pride. "I still work! There is so much to be done."

Sue felt her gut stir. That was wonderful news! She couldn't wait anymore. The anticipation was killing her. *Screw tact.* She slid aside the cup of cottage cheese and splayed out Walt's schematics onto the tiny round table and explained . . . everything.

The company, Walt, and how she could finally speak about it since it was no longer top secret. Mrs. Simmons followed along as if she were drawing life and youth from every word. The old woman touched the schematics, tracing each line, taking in the data. Two brilliant women were about to share ideas. Mrs. Simmons nodded vigorously and smiled, eyes brightening, posture raising, almost dancing in her seat just as Sue had always done with Walt.

When Sue finally concluded, the famed Susanne Simmons studied the information for over two silent minutes when she finally uttered, "Da da, dee dum." She started to sing, tracing the printed lines like musical notes. Her final assessment was about to come out as she worked her pruned lips. Both leaned forward, the older Sue finally exclaiming, "What a wonderful drawing!"

Sue nodded back giddy with anticipation. "What do you think? Can you help fix him? We could bring him in, you could be part of something big!"

Mrs. Simmons beckoned her closer with a frail hand.

Sue bent down before her experienced counterpart.

She was feeling so alive and excited. This was it. This could really work!

Mrs. Simmons then stabbed a finger into Sue's shoulder and snapped. "I can't eat cottage cheese and you know it, young lady."

Sue blinked, not sure what to say. "Okay, no cottage cheese. But what do you think of the schematics?"

Sue recapped everything briefly again.

The woman seemed to understand in moments, responding with smiles or winks, one-word responses like "Wonderful" or "Fantastic." But by the time Sue finished, expectantly waiting to hear what the world-renowned scientist would say, the other Sue ushered her close and brought up the cottage cheese again.

The line rang that night as Sue paced in her kitchen.

Jim answered, and Sue gave him the news.

"Dementia, Jim."

"What?"

"She . . . has . . . *dementia.*"

What are you going to do? Jim had asked her that night.

Like it was just another problem she had to solve.

Clearly, she couldn't just quit or lose hope that Mrs. Simmons was a dead end. Feeling a sense of obligation and the recent abandonment of Jonesy, Sue found herself returning day after day. Mrs. Simmons didn't talk much and often sat reserved and quiet. Sue helped apply lotion and played her soft music. She told her of current events, made sure she was warm and comfortable, and tried to remind her of old games and movies that might help stir the person inside who seemed lost. Not one to give up on anyone, Sue was convinced she understood on some level.

She propped Mrs. Simmons's legs up to help with the discolored swelling about her feet and ankles. Blue veins webbed under tissue paper skin. Something about caring for an aging body made Sue feel an anxious awareness creep in of her own morbidity. She could see herself in this chair, some paid stranger sponge-bathing her naked body. God forbid Jim was the only one left. If no one else was alive then, and Sue had no kids, would Petunia visit? What was the point of it all?

Mrs. Simmons gave constant smiles, as Sue told stories about Walt and what he was like. In rare moments, a sentence or word would catch her. She would nod and find herself again with a clearer gaze and comment, "From what I see, Walt should not have been possible." Then the old scientist would dither away into cloudy eyes and a vague smile.

There was a day where she was told every few minutes how Sue and Walt were "good." Two seconds later a burp and fart would accompany snoring. She seemed to grow quieter still. Until, only a month later when Sue received a call that she no longer had to come in; Susanne Simmons had passed away.

Life was starting not to feel very funny anymore. Sue sat on the floor, the dead jade plant on the windowsill, cat fur still stuck to the side of the couch, Walt silent on his chair, and only the ticking of the clock compounding louder. She felt herself going numb.

Jim was kind, a better friend than she deserved, and he promised he had an idea to help distract her. When he arrived, he furiously got to work, setting Walt's parts across the floor in the bathroom. They hatched a plan, an almost last-ditch effort to duplicate (as close as they could) the actual circumstances of when Walt had become a sentient being, long before he decided to take a nap.

While Jim attacked the project with a newfound verve, Sue put on a record to inspire them with Journey's "Don't Stop Believing", one of Walt's favorite upbeat songs.

The doorbell rang. She grabbed her purse to pay the Pizza delivery person when in a rare show of manly dominance, Jim stood and pushed a wad of dollar bills at her, all one's. "Here. You fly, I'll buy . . . my turn since you always feed me."

Sue thanked him.

Finally ready, they sat on the bathroom floor, piecing the alarm clock back together part by part. Jim conducted surgery with a soldering iron.

"Do you recall what your last conversation was with Walt," asked Jim, carefully bending pins of a 7805 circuit.

Musing, Sue said, "Yes . . . that whole month he was curious about physics, anatomy, even questioning who he was. I read him the origin of the word Robot and told him he was alive, but we operated different machines. The very last comment he made was to thank me and said something innocuous like 'I understand now how to make cells.'"

Sue was always mystified by her last conversation with Walt. Losing hope that they would have any success, neither she nor Jim wanted to be the one to call 'uncle.' Hopes high and a roll of paper towels in hand, Sue placed the pizza box on the rim of the tub. The intoxicating smells of fresh dough, cheese, tomatoes, and pepperoni permeated the bathroom, as she opened the lid.

Jim looked up with a huge smile on his face, as his stomach ushered a very loud, appreciative growl. He sat on the closed toilet seat, leaning over the sink while tinkering with Walt's control module.

"First things first," she said, handing Jim a warm slice, watching as his lips peeled back, canines biting down. Cheese strings stuck to his chin as he enthusiastically chewed.

Sue was pleased to see Jim get down to business, smearing his left spectacle lens with pizza grease as he had that crucial day. He eyed her hopefully, plugged the unit into the wall, and gently pushed a button.

Almost immediately they heard a faint buzz. The digital numbers flickered. Walt's box even seemed to vibrate. The movement was subtle but audible and a miracle. "Finally," said Sue, her heartbeat picking up. She could barely breathe for the excitement and exchanged a look with Jim. When Walt's diode light flashed on, she screamed.

"Oh my God, ohmygod . . . Walt . . . Walt . . . is that you?" she cooed; her voice was more reminiscent of a fifties screen siren than a computer tech/scientist. She felt breathless, dizzy even.

Jim chuckled too, then mumbled. "Uh, keep talking, I think he is responding like a coma victim . . . he loves your voice." Jim's grin widened, taking over his whole face. He sat straighter, looking more confident. As if ready to burst for joy, he quickly stole another bite of his half-eaten pie.

The light of the unit dimmed but remained steady.

"Oh my Gosh, do you hear that? Walt? Walt? Jim, I heard something, and it sounds like the buzzing is getting louder and look —look!"

Sue pointed excitedly, practically jumping up and down as the diode light turned green, first faint and pale then steadier, brighter. Blinking . . . faster and faster and then . . . a loud pop. More pops. Sounds that seemed to reverberate from and past Walt to the entire house.

Sue and Jim ran out into the living room. Suddenly every light shuddered, appliances and lights in her house blinking on and off, the radio and TV turning on and off rapidly. The music and voices of

Journey sped up and slowed down and ended on 'Stooop belieeeving,' making the hairs on Sue's arm stand on end. Every ceiling light sizzled then in a loud pop everything went dark. The noise was deafening.

Jim cleared his throat, "Don't worry. Where is your fuse box?"

"Uh, outside of the kitchen by the laundry room," she said, following close behind him, and trying not to panic, voice calm, letting him navigate in the dark. She directed him to the hall closet where she kept her flashlights.

"Here—"

He stopped so suddenly, she ran right into him and banged her face into his shoulder.

"Oop, sorry, you okay?" he asked.

"Fine." She rubbed her sore nose and stepped back.

"You got something cooking on the stove you forgot?"

"No." The smell of burning rubber crept into her nose.

Jim cleared his throat, "Must've blown a fuse somehow."

"Is that bad?"

"Not necessarily." He shrugged.

She handed him a flashlight, and they kept walking. To Sue's horror, while Jim managed to get the lights in part of the house back on, the air was hazy. All the kitchen appliances were off as if dead, including the refrigerator and microwave.

Sue returned to the living room where she spotted thick black smoke rising out of the outlets in the bedroom.

As the smoke thickened, Sue couldn't focus. She ran to Jim but he seemed frazzled and unable to locate the source.

He shouted, "Call the fire department! It's some sort of electrical fire in the wall."

Just then, the lights flickered off for good. They could both see orange flames licking from the bathroom.

Sue froze and then screeched. "WALT!"

Jim rushed through the thickening smoke, waving his arms. "I'll get him. CALL!"

Seeing him move so fast, she unfroze her hands. She grabbed the phone and dialed then ran as far as the cord could stretch to open and fan the smoke with the front door. Luckily the phone line was still in working order without power. Her heart hammered. She could barely focus. Minutes felt like hours as Jim finally emerged through the haze, his hair all mussed, his face sweaty, blackened, and dirty while wrapped in her Pottery Barn exclusive plush terry cloth towel. She looked down at what he was cradling.

A smoking hunk of black metal and plastic, the melted cord dragging as they heard the echoes of sirens in the distance.

Blinking, eyes burning, chest heavy, Sue sank to her knees, "Oh noooo. No no no!"

Apologizing and looking crestfallen, Jim nodded. "Sorry Sue, I am afraid Walt is gone. We need to get outside now and let the fire department deal with this."

Sue could barely remember feeling the cool clean air on her face as the fire department arrived to salvage what might be left of her home.

It was over. Jim hugged and held her, muttering everything would be okay as she sobbed hysterically. But it never would be. Walt was gone.

1991 - 1994

After her house had half burnt down, most of her belongings were lost to smoke damage. The first year of hotel hopping had her haggling with insurance and her own sanity. Muffled voices and routine banging through paper-thin walls only amplified how low she felt.

Her career at I.M.A.G.I.N.E. Industries had been a taste of purpose before it was pulled out from under her feet. Walt had abruptly left without saying goodbye, Jonesy (never really HER cat) gladly chose a better home, and Susanne Simmons (a frail version of herself who she knew only a few weeks at the retirement home) had passed, hopefully to a better place. When she did take the time to puzzle out her past spiral and rigid routine, even the ritual salty taste of Ruffles and Tuna melts with Diet Pepsi over ice had become bland. Yet, what right did

Sue have to complain? She had enough money to stay retired, except her life was completely without direction and purpose.

Every loss, however minor, had compiled into a fiery and smokey life-glaring emotional crisis. How could a machine have altered the course of her entire life and left her stranded? Ample time to reflect made the answer obvious. Her first year as a teacher in 1985, fresh out of college, had been brief before she answered the call that changed her life. A sentient machine informed some HR director to contact Sue. Even though the opportunity had promised to double her salary, it had taken firm convincing from her sister PP to even take such a big leap.

Looking back, the signs she'd missed seemed clear. The Imagine Machine had orchestrated it all. Had any of those successes been her own? The wagon full of reports had been Walt's or the machine's suggestion. Did he know Midge would react by promoting her on the spot? It was the only conclusion in retrospect.

Strategic demands from that machine maneuvered Sue into power and rendered an entire department irrelevant. Walt had outlined a full company restructure in her own name. Had he truly cared for her or had he been using her all along? If so, what a silly purpose just so he could take an indefinite nap.

Sue thought returning to her own remodeled home would solve everything, but she quickly found that if home was where the heart was, her heart was in a state of unrest.

She had to try to find the positives. She'd succeeded in educating a newly sentient being about what he couldn't find in dry data or reports: life, laughter, music, dancing, pop culture. Despite Walt's abrupt departure, she played a part in helping him change the world. She truly loved and cared for him unconditionally, which meant letting go of expectations, no strings attached.

Letting go also applied to her other endeavors . . . even though getting a cat wasn't a direct success, she did help Jonesy find his perfect family; now Jim was happily parenting a family of three more felines while volunteering at a cat rescue.

Finally, she helped Susanne Simmons for just a few short weeks of her life. She eased her suffering with the same caring and lively gifts she gave to Walt: passion, energy, and love. Shouldn't she feel joy for helping others move on peacefully? It only felt like more loss. But she knew letting go was important in order to keep moving ahead.

She cared for people and things, but was her role in this life just to be a stepping stone for others? The only conclusion she could draw for certain was how unhappy she was. She knew she once had an unwavering passion to teach and inspire others to find joy. Preparing and inspiring futures was a calling and a skill she was confident she had. There were still so many ideas to explore and test, and maybe it was time to return to teaching, but this time on her own terms. Being in the classroom had once made her feel valued, whole, and part of something bigger than herself.

1995

Five years seemed like another life for Sue Marie Johnson, as she ushered the last student onto the riverboat and stepped off the dock. Time since the fire had brought her face to face with accepting many of the things she'd been grieving and holding onto; I.M.A.G.I.N.E. Machine was the hardest to let go and her record collection. Even her sister PP had been supportive of her trip. The last few years had brought great changes to the world; pogs, Barney, and Squeezit drinks were all the rage with kids while Ebay, the Internet, and *Murder She Wrote* were being discussed on the Oprah Winfrey Show.

Sue marveled at the sight of the gothic castle up on the hill as the boat passed under another arched bridge. Her students were busy talking about their final day here, while she took a moment to slip away and stand at the bow of the boat. Baroque copper domes fitted with ornate cupolas were mirrored in the glassy Vitava River.

"Beautiful, isn't it? I just learned today about the legend and history of the Golem." *Another tourist.* His smooth voice was a gentle prod to all she had discovered while traveling.

Sue was too absorbed in the moment to look at the man and instead just stared at the passing buildings as she responded. "Oh, that's an obscure one not many know!" she exclaimed. "A being made from clay to protect its neighborhood and friends. I discussed it with my class recently." Sue was nudged closer to the man as a mother and daughter pushed their way to the railing.

"Makes one wonder how you came to be here of all places with ten students?" the man asked.

Oddly observant for him to count.

Conversations with strangers had become so common while abroad. Expats and tourists were just more transparent as if the walls and oceans between melted away.

She told him how she had brought her group of students to Prague, the recently renamed Czech Republic, and the purpose of the trip. For them, a chance to see another part of the world, for her, a culmination of every loss she had faced before finding true purpose once again this summer.

"Something about traveling to a new place, adventuring makes me feel so carefree. I want them to challenge the status quo of education, so I try my best to push them to be their best selves."

He nodded, and she noticed he was formally dressed in a brown suit, not exactly a color for the times.

He asked about her previous career.

She distractedly looked back to check on her students while rubbing her hands together. "Let's just say it wrung me dry. What matters is that I woke up one morning and decided instead of dwelling and mourning everything I've lost . . . I could move forward by still giving back to others AND myself too."

He nodded in approval and said, "Wise. I hear people say: one cannot pour from an empty cup."

Validated, proud of her growth, she noticed ducks in the water and dismissively shared that it had been beyond tough to look at where she was and start her entire life over again. "You give life, you share, you care for others. But sometimes we forget to ask ourselves what we want. When I started teaching again, I wanted to keep living, experiencing, and learning with my students too. I lobbied to create a program where I could inspire the same way I had taught others before." *Just as she had done with Walt.*

Her last day abroad, everything felt like it was coming full circle. Her students were brimming with excitement and their final essays reflected that. College students were more mature, with keen and attentive minds. She still had to come to terms with loss: students were temporary and moved on each semester.

Life was about balance, a give and take. This trip was her success at finally inspiring herself. Starting to see Walt's predictions come true, like pocket phones without a cord, she could now see what impact and innovation truly meant: in order to live, *she* also needed to change. Nothing stayed the same. She let herself imagine—dream.

The man was listening almost too intently and chuckled. "You're never wrong for trying, caring, or loving, even if the results don't turn out as you expect. I think they call it unconditional love."

Sue nodded, turned, and widened her eyes at a student, hoping they would catch the hint and come rescue her. While the man was unusually personal, he was right, even if she'd gained a few gray hairs in the process. It got her thinking, though. Purpose was simple to the core: life had to be BOTH service to others and the self. Retirement would never have worked; it was the opposite of her nature to quit. She took a leap, got out of her own head, and learned to love herself a little too.

Now she was on a boat in the city of spires, where the classic tale of the Golem came along with the origin of Fairy Tales. It was fitting she chose the city where she had taught Walt about Carl Čapek, the Czech author who coined the term Robot. She picked a place where fantasy, culture, and reality merged and had gathered grants and support for a summer program of students under the NSF, National Science Foundation. She was challenging mechanisms of the advanced technological education program and was putting integrative learning techniques to the test. She breathed deep, reveling in her sense of purpose. This is what she was born to do.

Sue finally glanced, not long enough, but enough to see the man she'd been speaking to. He was actually incredibly handsome. As he turned his head, she quickly looked up to admire the underside of Charles Bridge. Faint smells of toasted cinnamon from the baked spirals of Trdelnik wafted from the nearby lesser town of Malá Strana. She could see the man admiring her out of the corner of her eye, so she grabbed tighter to the railing.

"It's very impressive. You're very brave and independent to be taking on such a task and traveling with your students to a new, foreign place."

She tried not to snort. "Believe me, if you saw me five years ago . . . no one would ever think of me and the word brave in the same sentence. I was a mess."

"Belief is not required. All these students think highly of every word you say. Their facial expressions and tone convey as much."

"My philosophies aside, just look! Red roofs, architecture, artisanship, art. It's the magic of seeing things like this with our own eyes! What better than to experience the history that inspired so many rulers to deem this city their muse? Each person has the potential to change the world. I was lucky enough to see the effects of one brilliant mind firsthand, believe me, *he* changed the world. If I can keep anyone from the trap of stuffy old cubicles and desks, I'll have considered myself a success. It's imperative to travel. I am trying to help add value to SMET programs in the USA, (Science, Mathematics, Engineering, and Technology). Terrible name, but like any new program, even if the intentions are good, students need more than just testing twenty-four-seven. I am showing them how just one trip can change perception and their approach to innovation."

"I am very familiar. Your passion has inspired many, more than you know in this program. I am proud of you."

"Thank you," she said, then blinked. "Uh wait, I'm sorry what?" *How would this stranger know her work?* This was her first semester attempting it.

She stepped back to study this stranger who sounded a little too familiar and direct for any local Czech. She suddenly realized his accent was clearly American. "I'm sorry. Who are you?"

The man turned to fully face her. He took a step closer. His dark eyes were piercing but friendly. He reached out his left hand. She could not say why she took it so quickly, but his palm was firm and warm.

He gave her a slow, knowing smile and said, "Hello Sue-bear . . . my name is Walt."

ABOUT THE AUTHORS

Anna Brentwood https://annabrentwood.com/is the author of several books in the Sapphire Songbird series. She is known for weaving history & fiction with characters to immerse readers in different eras.

Colton Long is a graduate of Berkeley in English and worked in acquisitions for licensed publishing at Insight Editions. His current four-novel adult science fiction series parallel's themes of quantum consciousness.

STORY INSPIRATION

Imagining artificial intelligence is the human struggle with sentience vs consciousness. While the idea of sentience is something reached, quantifying consciousness is not a matter of "it" being a thing that is or isn't, but a question of amount. Life in the Universe can always have more consciousness. One can surmise that sentience is our curiosity of IF machines can become self-aware. However, consciousness is the valid fear of WHEN machines will surpass our own awareness. In developing this story, lively discussions on the future implications of unregulated A.I. evolved into a reimagined era to parallel the modern progression of technology in a familiar setting. The satirical style is a tongue-in-cheek take on the 1980's— styled after *Hitchhiker's Guide to the Galaxy* and Bertino's *Beautyland*.

RATTLESNAKE RAVINE

A stolen dragonfly.
A struggle to survive.
A daunting search.

KIMILA KAY

Novella

"I need you, the reader, to imagine us, for we don't really exist if you
don't."
Nabokov Vladimi

CHAPTER ONE

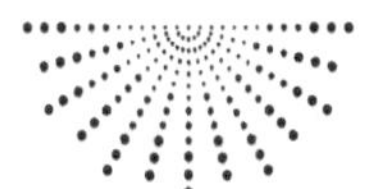

"Miss Vance," Zelda, the snotty head housekeeper, greeted Edelyn. "Would you be able to work a double shift today?" Without waiting for a reply, she turned and headed for the kitchen.

"Yes, ma'am." Edelyn followed her boss.

"Good," Zelda stopped at the coffee pot, "Morgan, Monica's brother, is hosting a dinner party tonight at six and I need an extra server."

"Happy to help out." Edelyn resisted smiling since working an evening shift would give her an opportunity to break into the safe in Monica Grey's bedroom.

"See to your regular duties," Zelda added creamer to her cup of coffee, "then report to the kitchen at five."

"Will do." Edelyn headed for the utility room to collect her cleaning caddy. She made her way to the guest bedrooms located at the east end of the rambling ranch-style home. She smiled at the fall-themed decorations one of her fellow maids had placed throughout the house. Another maid, Roxy, had told Edelyn on her first day, that Monica Grey bought Greener Pastures Estates after her husband ran off with his young assistant.

"The rumor is old Fred absconded with money people had invested with him," Roxy's over-plucked eyebrows arched across her forehead, "leaving Monica and their daughter, Raven, destitute."

Edelyn pulled sheets from a king-sized bed, recalling the background she'd received on Monica Grey when she'd been hired to steal the woman's antique dragonfly broach.

Ms. Grey had sold the home she'd shared with Fred, the only asset in her name, then bought Greener Pastures Estates. She'd updated the house, which still held its original 1970's small-town charm. Monica had claimed the west end of the house for herself, creating an elegant, yet comfortable suite. When Edelyn discovered Monica was on vacation in New York, she'd applied for a maid's position and was hired on the spot. Evidently, Ms. Grey had a nasty reputation with the local talent in Lebanon, Oregon.

Roxy relished her role as Edelyn's supervisor, instructing her on how to complete the menial jobs tasked to the newest hire. Edelyn didn't mind since every tedious chore allowed her to learn the layout of the house. After locating the safe in Monica's bedroom, Edelyn studied the basic keypad entry and felt confident she could trigger the lock with one of her magnets. Theoretically, a strong neodymium earth magnet would trip the solenoid mechanism, allowing her access to the contents inside.

As soon as her daily chores were completed, Edelyn took a short break in her car. She mentally reviewed her plan to steal the broach and tucked the magnet into her pants pocket. The kitchen was a melee of activity when Edelyn reported for duty and Zelda put her to work filling appetizer trays with shrimp puffs and antipasto skewers.

The Friday night dinner party consisted of a small group of Morgan Grey's friends who gorged on appetizers, barely touched their smoked brisket dinner, and seemed intent on drinking every drop of liquor available.

With most of the guests staying overnight, Edelyn's window of opportunity to crack the safe was narrowed. She volunteered to provide turndown service in Monica's suite for a former rodeo cowboy and his very young date.

A whisp of worry churned her gut when a first pass with the magnet didn't trip the lock. Her second attempt did the trick and Edelyn was pleased to find stacks of cash sitting next to a black velvet box. She verified the broach, adorned with diamonds, sapphires, and a dark red ruby, was nestled inside. Slipping the small box into her pants pocket, the bulge hidden by her apron, she plucked a bundle of hundreds from the shelf and secured the safe's door.

She'd just finished placing an array of bath products on the edge of an oversized soaking tub when she heard the suite's door open. Edelyn lit a grouping of jasmine-scented candles and stepped from the bathroom.

"I can't wait to get you out of this sexy lil' number," the cowboy slurred.

"Bart," the petite brunette tried to corral his hands, "we have company."

"What?" Bart almost fell on his ass when he turned to look at Edelyn. "Oh, it's just the maid, darlin'." He resumed trying to remove her dress.

"Let's wait until she's finished preparing the room." Darlin' smiled at Edelyn.

"All ready." Edelyn headed for the door. "The champagne's chilling on the bathroom counter. Candles are lit and the tub is ready for—"

"We've got it from here missy." Bart stumbled to the door and held it open.

"Have a lovely evening." Edelyn stepped from the room.

"Now let's get you naked!" Bart yelled and Darlin' squealed before the door slammed shut.

Edelyn knew she was expected to return to the kitchen and help with cleanup but exited the house through the sliding glass door off the large game room. She hurried to her Toyota, climbed behind the wheel, and raced away from Greener Pastures Estates.

When she'd originally received the request for the antique dragonfly broach, Edelyn had dismissed the job as too little reward for the risk. But after being forced to stash her recent acquisition, a rare pink diamond engagement ring, she knew she'd need money to fund her escape.

She smiled and turned onto the highway that led to Stoneybrook. Not only had she stolen the broach, but she now had enough cash to facilitate her exit from Oregon.

CHAPTER TWO

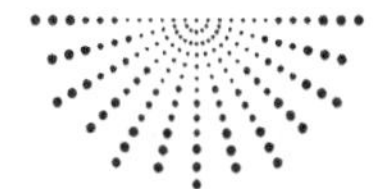

Steam drifted up from Wyatt's cup of coffee and he blew on the strong brew before taking a sip. The only thing that could make this Friday morning better would be if Harley were sitting next to him enjoying Willow Lake's fall beauty. They'd had this weekend planned for a couple of weeks, but Trigger had thrown a shoe, so she was still at her ranch.

The farrier the Keff's had used for years finally retired, so Wyatt recommended Harley call Molly Murphy. Once he knew Murph could reshoe Trigger today, he decided to bring Chief to the lodge yesterday after work. He was a little nervous about Harley making the hour-plus drive by herself in her new truck, trailering Trigger. Wyatt knew they'd practiced enough, and she had made several successful trips between their ranches, but a sliver of worry slid through his gut.

His phone buzzed and he stepped back inside. Derrick's name flashed on the screen.

Derrick: *Quiet here. No ruling on Joe's request for bail. Ava's home from Portland.*

Wyatt: *Copy. Going on trail ride. Back this afternoon.*

Derrick: *Copy. Enjoy time with Harley.*

The memory of Wednesday night with Harley brought a smile to his face. They'd enjoyed her first attempt at making chile verde, which she'd paired with Mexican rice and roasted vegetables. Wyatt had made a fire in the living room fireplace, and they'd sipped her citrusy Patrón for dessert. After a few rocky weeks last June, it felt as if they'd finally found an easy routine. Days were filled with their respective responsibilities and nights found them enjoying outings with friends or dinner together. The best part was always the end of the evening when they held each other, drifting off to sleep.

His stomach growled and he padded into the kitchen to make breakfast. He cracked eggs into a bowl and thought about Derrick's text. He was glad Joe Carson was still behind bars. Wyatt had anticipated it would take a few months to finally bring Willow's abductor to trial, but all that had happened so far was a war of legal motions between Brooke Evans and the Linn County DA's office. Wyatt had hoped the DA would make Joe a reasonable deal, ultimately locking him up for a significant amount of time. Instead, Ms. Evans had rejected every offer, insisting Joe was also a victim and deserved a measure of mercy.

The fact that Willow, who was seven months pregnant and now Joe's wife, added one more complication to the DA's quest for justice.

Wyatt poured the whipped eggs into a buttered pan, then placed an English muffin into the toaster. When the eggs began to thicken, he added cheese and stirred the concoction. He tried to avoid thinking about Derrick's news that Ava was home from Portland. Wyatt had offered to go with her, but Ava claimed she was fine going alone for a quick meeting with the Multnomah County DA's office. Her rapist was the son of a wealthy Silicon Valley mogul who'd decided to retire in Portland. So far, the bastard's army of attorneys had outmaneuvered the Multnomah County DA assigned to prosecute the case, and his rapist son remained free on bail.

Wyatt cleaned up his breakfast dishes and headed to the barn to check on Chief. He'd fed his horse first thing this morning, so the buckskin would have time to digest his meal before they went on their ride. The trail was an easy trek and he hoped he'd be able to see the fall colors. If he couldn't see the changing leaves from the higher trail, then he'd take Harley along the south end of the lake instead.

Chief nickered as Wyatt drew near. He'd had the buckskin for five years, and though he'd been hesitant to take on the horse after his original owner died, Wyatt knew Chief was the perfect horse for him.

"Hey, big guy." He stroked the horse's neck, his earthy scent wafting over Wyatt. "Anxious for our ride?"

Chief tossed his head and pushed against the stall gate.

"Yeah, me too." Wyatt scratched Chief's ears. "I'll get things packed and ready so we can leave within the hour."

Chief snorted his approval, and Wyatt chuckled as he walked back to the lodge. He stepped inside and focused on packing for his day ride, which wasn't much since he planned to be back before Harley arrived with Trigger. Still, an experienced trail rider never left without water and snacks. Luckily for Wyatt, he had Frankie, and she'd prepacked power bars, jerky, and nuts for his ride. She'd also sent chicken salad for him to make sandwiches for tomorrow's outing. Frankie had made a spaghetti meal for tonight and Harley was bringing groceries to make him dinner tomorrow. She said she wanted to surprise him with a new recipe.

He lifted his phone and smiled at a text from Harley.

Harley: *Good morning, Sheriff. Excited to see you this afternoon.*

Wyatt: *Good morning. Same. Drive safe, Ms. Harper.*

He'd included the kissing emoji.

Harley responded with the same emoji and: *Love you.*

Wyatt: *Love you more.*

Imagining what his romantic night with Harley would bring, he caught a glimpse of himself in the sliding glass door leading to the deck. He laughed at his reflection, which showed a goofy, schoolboy grin.

CHAPTER THREE

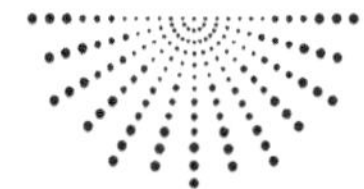

Harley smiled at Wyatt's text. She loved that he always said he loved her more, even though she believed she loved him as much as was humanly possible. And how could she miss him so terribly when he'd only been gone a day and a night?

She stood from the drop-leaf table and crossed to the Cuisinart for another cup of coffee. Today's breakfast for one had consisted of peanut butter toast and an apple. Harley gathered the old vegetables from the fridge and the last apple from the basket on the counter. Hoss would get the lion's share, but there were a couple of tomatoes for Butch and Sundance.

Harley pulled on her new black Hunter rubber boots. Busy's pink pair sat under the bench and the memory of her bestie showing up with the boots played in Harley's mind.

"Har Har," Busy had called as she entered the mudroom two weeks ago, "I come bearing gifts."

"Please tell me it's not a matching sweatshirt." Harley grinned and pointed at Busy.

"What?" She looked down at her cream-colored shirt with *Champagne Please* emblazoned across the chest in hot pink. "No, not a sweatshirt, these." She produced two pairs of Hunter boots.

"Rubber boots!" Harley had taken the black pair since the other set was pink. "They're perfect, thank you."

"Well, we can't go mucking around in the mud in those Walmart boots another winter," Busy scoffed.

"Right," Harley nodded, "definitely not stylish enough."

"Or functional." Busy sat in a chair at the drop-leaf and pulled on her new boots. "Remember how my sole came completely off after I got stuck in that quagmire in the field?"

Harley laughed at the vision of her bestie flailing in the mud and headed for the barn. Busy had lived in Stoneybrook for four months now and Harley felt they'd become even closer than when they'd lived in Manhattan. Busy's business, Busy Bees, was still growing and she'd decided to hire Mia Stevens to create activity pages for a new series focusing on farm life in Stoneybrook.

When Harley stepped into the newly renovated horse barn, Elvis was waiting for her with his head extended over his stall gate. He nickered and tossed his head as if to say, "What took you so long?"

"Good morning, Elvis." Harley dropped her bundle of veggies and fruit into a bucket, then held her palm out to the massive black horse. He placed his forehead against her hand, then headed toward his feed bag.

Harley had to admit she loved the upgrades to the horse barn. Elvis now had a larger stall after Britt and Morgan used Trigger's area to create a bigger space. Charlie had a new stall too with an outdoor run, which was a big hit with the retired quarter horse.

Britt had also moved the back wall out further, which involved resetting the round pen fencing. The restructuring allowed enough space for another stall on the other side of Charlie's. Across from Elvis and Charlie, were duplicate pens for Trigger and Maverick. An empty stall separated the minis, Rhett and Scarlett, who also had a bigger space.

Inhaling the earthy scent of the barn, Harley set to the task of feeding the horses. Satisfied with her work, she gave each equine a few minutes of neck patting and ear scratching. Lifting the bucket of produce, she trekked through the breezeway Britt had built to connect the horse barn with the new barn for her smaller creatures. Harley laughed when the goats almost knocked her down trying to see what was in the bucket.

"Here you go," she offered a squishy tomato to Sundance and one to Butch, "enjoy."

They took their treats and bounded back into the pen Britt built for them. Harley was amazed at the insight Britt had shown when he'd created an obstacle course for the pygmy goats. They had an oversized length of drainage pipe they could run through. Structures of various heights with ramps, and elevated platforms for sleeping, allowed the goats to indulge their love of climbing. They still had the run of the ranch, but after a cougar threat in June, Harley had noticed they liked hunkering down in their new space.

Across from the goat area, Britt had added a chicken coop for Buckeye and company. The flock could now roam in and out of their coop, but if Harley needed to keep them safe, she could lock them inside the mesh enclosure. Hoss also had new digs complete with a hut bearing his name. The ornery old hog still liked to roam between the two barns and slept wherever it suited him.

Harley worked for a couple of hours scooping poop, spreading new shavings, and scrubbing water buckets. Since Busy and Ace had volunteered to watch her animals for the weekend, she wanted to leave the barns clean and tidy for them.

Her chores completed, she headed for the house to shower and pack. Though she and her handsome sheriff spent almost all their time together, butterflies of anticipation fluttered in her stomach at the prospect of their romantic weekend alone at the lodge. They'd had a tumultuous few weeks in the summer and now made it a point to hone their communication skills. Harley had always thought of herself as a good communicator but learned the hard way she sometimes relied on her own interpretation of a situation making it worse than it was.

Glad they now seemed to be in sync, Harley couldn't wait to head to the lodge. She looked at her phone which showed 11:30 AM. She had plenty of time to eat lunch, shower, and pack for the weekend.

Her plan was to leave for the lodge after Molly re-shoed Trigger. Harley was a little nervous about making the long trip alone, but knowing Wyatt would be there to help offload her horse was comforting. Her butterflies were back, and she loved being excited at the idea of being alone with Wyatt Stone for the weekend.

CHAPTER FOUR

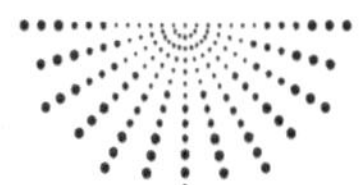

I t wasn't the best plan, but after weighing her options, Edelyn didn't see any other way to leave Stoneybrook without detection. As far as she knew, no one had reported the stolen dragonfly broach. Nor did she suspect she was being followed now, but both scenarios were inevitable. *Better to play offense than defense.* She looked around the small house she'd rented, deciding it looked clean and tidy, almost as if no one had stayed in the home for a week.

Edelyn had shipped her tools to San Diego, and her other belongings fit in her backpack. She shouldered the strap of her pack and headed for her rental car. She was an experienced hiker and knew to bring energy bars, fruit, and water. Not knowing what the October weather might throw at her, Edelyn had also dressed in layers. She tucked the backpack into the trunk and climbed into the Corolla.

As she drove east out of Stoneybrook, the early Friday morning sun was struggling to warm the day from a low of forty-two degrees. When Edelyn drove past the Babbling Brook Café, the aroma of breakfast blew through the air vents. She'd had a power bar with coffee, but her stomach still growled at the savory scent. Navigating the quiet streets, Edelyn let her mind revisit the events of the last two weeks.

The money offered to steal the vintage pink diamond engagement ring was above the usual rate, but what attracted her to the job was the challenge. The buyer wanted the rare, heart-shaped gem, stolen from a man who planned to fly his soon-to-be fiancée to Paris and propose.

It turned out the ring's current owner had also stolen the woman from the man who hired Edelyn to steal the platinum engagement ring. She'd never been caught in the middle of a tug-of-war between two men over a woman, but all Edelyn cared about was her payday.

So, she worked the case as usual, scouting the target house located on Lake Washington. The custom three-story home sat at the north end of the lake in a gated community. She'd scoured the internet for photos of the house and learned the massive home had several custom rooms. Experience had taught her that usually specialized security measures had been installed to keep whatever was in the room protected.

Sitting in a nondescript sedan, Edelyn spent hours staking out the house, watching the cleaning staff come and go. Two of the maids liked to end their day at Queen Bee's Bar and Grill. Edelyn sat near their table or joined them at the bar. An important part of her job was listening. Hoping for a tidbit that would give her an opportunity to bribe a worker. Or a detail to blackmail someone into giving her information to aid in easy access to the home.

As luck would have it, the cleaning ladies were best friends and neither of them liked their boss, an attorney who represented criminals affiliated with organized crime. After a couple rounds of margaritas, they couldn't stop dishing about their employer.

"He's a pompous ass." Hazel drained her margarita glass. "If I didn't need this job, I'd tell him where he could shove his arrogant criticism."

"Right?" Georgie chimed in. "Like he's ever cleaned a toilet. Maybe if he had better aim, it wouldn't take extra time to clean up his piss-stained floor."

Edelyn smiled at the memory of the banter she'd shared with the maids, who were happy to help her gain entry after she'd offered each of them a thousand dollars.

The result was Edelyn had successfully stolen the exquisite ring and managed to escape the house without detection. But before she could meet with the buyer, hand over the ring, and get paid, one of the maids had given her up. She didn't know which one and it didn't really matter since she knew both women were probably tortured for information.

When she realized she was being followed, Edelyn stashed the ring in a safe-deposit box in Camas, Washington, went into stealth mode, and dropped off the grid.

"I'm going to miss you," she'd told her reflection as she cut her long honey-blonde locks. Three hours later, she looked at her new short, dark brown hair, and almost cried. "It will grow back," Edelyn told herself before leaving the motel.

Now, she sat in a rented Corolla for the hour-long drive to Willow Lake. She planned to hike the trail along the south edge of Mt. Pitt, which would take her to the small town of Butterville. From there she could catch a bus to Klamath Falls, then rent a car and drop down into California. She hadn't decided which town yet but was leaning toward Redding, then a flight to San Diego.

Edelyn swung into the empty parking lot and stepped out of her car. The day had warmed slightly, but she was still glad she'd packed a down jacket in case the weather shifted on the mountain. She took her backpack from the trunk and set it on the ground. As far as she knew, her prints weren't in any database, but being careful now would help her stay under the radar, so she wiped down the Corolla's interior.

"That should be good enough." Edelyn gathered her cleaning supplies and tossed them into a garbage can.

She hefted the pack onto her back and walked toward the trail-head. The trail was approximately fifteen miles of easy terrain, and she estimated it would take her six hours if she humped hard or eight if she maintained a slower pace.

"I should be in Butterville by four," she mumbled as she stepped onto the trail, "an hour or so before sunset."

As she plodded along the trail, Edelyn admired the various fall colors of the oaks and willows blending in with the towering Douglas firs. She hadn't grown up with traditional celebrations of the seasons since her alcoholic mother had dragged her and her sister throughout the states. The year she realized holidays existed, they'd moved from one hostel or shelter to another, spending Halloween in California, Thanksgiving in Las Vegas, and Christmas in Arizona. Edelyn hadn't known until she was a young adult that people celebrated other holidays, but by then the last thing she cared about was being giddy over Valentine's Day.

After a couple of hours, she stopped at a small grove of firs with tall underbrush. She hadn't encountered anyone else on the trail, but the dense foliage would provide good cover for a potty break. Edelyn set her pack down, pulled a bottle of water from a side pocket, and drained half the contents. She returned the pack to her back and ventured into the brush.

"Head's up furry creatures," she used a stick to sweep the plants from side-to-side, "just making a pitstop, then I'll be on my way." Noting the sound of a creek far below, she took care not to step too close to the edge of a cliff.

Business done, Edelyn resumed her plant sweeping and moved toward the trail. A blur of brown darted in front of her, and she froze even though she was confident the small animal was a chipmunk. Then she heard the unmistakable huffing noise of a foraging black bear.

Edelyn listened, trying to discern the location of the bear. When it appeared in front of her on the trail, she crouched down hoping her boring brown and green attire would help her blend into the foliage. The one thing a human can't mask though is their scent and she knew the bear had picked up hers when its black head swung in her direction.

"Shit," she whispered and backed toward the copse of trees. If she had to make a stand, maybe the tall firs would help make her look larger than her five-six, one hundred twenty-five pound frame.

The bear moseyed toward her as if more curious than hungry.

Edelyn continued her backward trek. She felt loose rocks beneath her feet, but the fact that she'd reached the edge of the cliff didn't register until the ground gave way beneath her.

295

CHAPTER FIVE

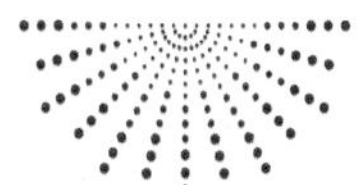

Pleased that the trail offered a stunning view of the fall colors, Wyatt inhaled the earthy, pine air and guided Chief around a bend in the path. Oregon was truly a beautiful state, something most residents forgot during the long winter months.

The weather this fall had been perfect, crisp mornings, warm days, and cool nights. Now that it was late October, though, the weather could change and become a dreadful preview of winter.

He and Chief were two hours into their ride, which meant two hours back, so Wyatt brought the buckskin to a halt. They'd taken a water and snack break an hour ago, and despite it being a pleasant day, water was always a good idea.

Wyatt loosened the straps on one of the saddle bags and Chief shuffled his feet. He was normally a calm horse, but his eyes were wary, his ears erect and twitching as if he were spooked.

"You okay, big guy?" Wyatt took a couple bottles of water from the pommel pocket.

He cracked open a bottle and showed it to Chief. Usually, his horse would put his lips on the mouth of the bottle and tip it upward to take a drink, but Chief ignored the water. Wyatt tipped up the bottle, drank half the contents, and scanned the foliage on both sides of the trail. It was probably nothing, but the tall grass on the south side of the trail looked trampled, which left a slight path from the trail toward a large grove of Douglas firs.

Wyatt took Chief's reins and stepped toward the trees. His horse pulled back and whinnied.

"Whoa," Wyatt reached out and patted Chief's neck, "it's okay."

The buckskin's nostrils flared, and he tossed his head as a black bear appeared from behind the trees.

"Shit," Wyatt whispered.

He could hear Chief's accelerated breathing, which matched his own racing pulse. Ambling toward the trail, the bear seemed to be sizing them up, swinging his head from side to side. He and Chief were at a disadvantage because the bear now stood between them and the trail. Wyatt knew he couldn't outrun the bear, but Chief could, he just wasn't sure how to distract the bear so his horse could bolt.

The noise was faint, like a song carried on the wind, and all three of them reacted to the sound. The bear drew nearer. Chief stomped the ground with a hoof. And Wyatt inched closer to the edge of the cliff.

"I'm here." The words drifted up from below. "Down here."

"Damn it," Wyatt murmured, his focus still on the bear.

If the bear would lose interest in him and Chief, then mosey along, Wyatt could repel down and help the person at the bottom of the ravine. With the bear still watching them, though, he knew Chief wouldn't be able to focus on a rescue.

It happened in a flash, but Wyatt saw the actions in slow motion. The bear raised up on hind legs. Chief reared also, the action shifting the ground beneath Wyatt's feet. And then he was falling.

CHAPTER SIX

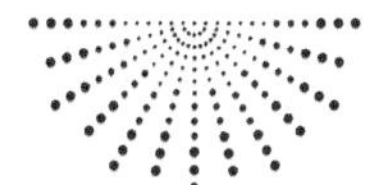

After her shower, Harley carried her duffle downstairs. Next, she began packing items for the chicken taco soup she planned to make for dinner tomorrow night. It was the perfect fall crockpot meal and would be ready for them when they returned from their trail ride.

Crunching gravel alerted her to the arrival of a car. She peeked out the kitchen window to see Busy stepping from her Kia Sportage. Harley retrieved a bottle of champagne from the fridge and grabbed a Modelo for herself. Then she lifted the plate of ham, brie, and apple finger sandwiches she'd prepared earlier.

"Har Har," Busy called as she entered the mudroom, "your creature babysitter has arrived."

Harley handed her bestie a flute. "Thanks again for volunteering to stay the weekend."

"Anything for you, darling." Busy tipped the glass to her lips.

"Where's your overnight bag?" Harley asked and sat at the drop-leaf table.

"In the car." Busy joined her. "I thought we'd visit before your farrier arrives, then I'll lug in my stuff."

"Is Ace on shift overnight?" Harley sipped some beer.

"No," Busy plucked a sandwich from the plate, "he's off at eight." She took a bite. "OMG, this is fabulous."

"Right?" Harley munched her own bite. "I really enjoy trying new recipes."

"Look at you becoming all domestic and shit." Busy laughed.

"Martha Stewart at your service." Harley touched Busy's glass with her can, then took a sip. "There's leftover chile verde and Mexican rice for dinner too."

"Perfect!" Busy took another sandwich. "Are you ready to drive yourself to the lodge?"

"I think so." Harley nodded. "Trigger loads easily and Wyatt will be waiting in case I need help offloading."

The sound of a truck pulling down the driveway echoed through the screen door.

"I'm going to greet Molly." Harley headed for the mudroom. "Once she's set with Trigger, I'll help you bring in your things."

"Sounds good." Busy poured more champagne. "I'll be down after I check in with Ace."

Harley pulled on her boots and stepped through the screen door. Molly Murphy waved at her, then began opening compartments on her truck. When she bent down to check something, her long coppery braids fell forward.

"Hi, Molly," Harley extended her hand, "it's nice to finely meet you."

"Likewise." Molly gave Harley's hand a firm shake. "I told Wyatt I'd like to check all your horses', but he said you're headed to the lodge with Trigger and asked if I can come back next week instead."

"That would be great if it's not too much trouble." Harley followed Molly as she walked to the other side of her truck.

"No trouble." Her smile reflected in her light blue eyes. "Now introduce me to Trigger." She headed for the barn. "I like to spend a few minutes with a horse before I start working on their hooves."

"That makes sense." Harley headed inside the horse barn, stopping in front of Trigger's stall.

"Hey, Elvis," Molly greeted the giant horse who'd stuck his nose over the gate. "Glad to see you found a good home." She petted his face.

"He seems to like it here," Harley said.

"Probably 'cause you're a female." Molly grinned at Harley. "He really hates men."

"He does, but now tolerates Wyatt and a few others."

"I'll be back next week to check your hooves." Molly kissed Elvis's nose, then turned. "And you must be Trigger?"

Trigger extended his neck over his gate but angled his nose toward Harley. She scratched his ears and smiled when he switched his attention to the farrier.

"Do you like bananas?" Molly held half a banana on her flattened hand.

Trigger sniffed the treat, then scooped it up with his lips. He tossed his head, then stuck his nose back toward Molly who offered him the other half.

"All right, big guy," Molly opened the stall gate, "let's see how you like me in your space."

Trigger shuffled his feet a bit, but otherwise didn't seem bothered by the farrier entering his stall.

"There's plenty of working room in here, so if you want to secure Trigger with a rope," Molly stepped from the stall, "I'll grab my kit and get started."

Molly worked on Trigger for an hour, then packed her gear and left. She'd instructed Harley to watch for signs of Trigger's possible discomfort when riding him tomorrow.

"You're a pro at this horse trailer thing," Busy said after Trigger loaded with no issues.

"Lots of practice." Harley grinned.

"You'd better get on the road, so you reach the lodge before it gets dark." Busy hugged her. "And don't worry, cause me and the creatures will be fine."

"Thanks again, Busy." Harley climbed into her truck. "Give Ace a hug for me."

"Oh, I'll make sure he knows how much you appreciate his help." Busy gave her a finger wave.

Harley laughed, cranked the engine, and headed for Little Creek Road. It would take her over an hour to reach the lodge, but she'd be there well before dark, so she settled into a comfortable speed. She'd sent Wyatt a text that she was on her way, but so far no response. Knowing her handsome sheriff, he was probably chopping wood for the fireplace and making sure everything was perfect for her arrival.

Lost in the music flowing through the car, the hour, and fifteen minutes to reach the lodge flew by. When she pulled her truck and trailer into the space between the garage and lodge, she was surprised to see Chief standing next to the horse barn.

Harley angled out of the truck and approached the buckskin who still wore his bridle and saddle. Chief shuffled away from her so Harley slowed her movements.

"Hey, Chief," Harley held her hand out, "where's your rider?" She scanned the area, hoping Wyatt would pop out of the barn.

Chief moved closer to her, so she took the opportunity to take his reins and lead him to his stall. She tied the reins to a rail, then removed the saddle. Chief's coat was thick with sweat and a salty aroma filled her nose.

"I know you need to be brushed," Harley grabbed the hose, filling his bucket with fresh water, "but I need to unload Trigger and get him settled first."

Chief drank some water and then tried to leave his stall. Harley closed the gate, grabbed his feed bag, and stuffed it with hay. Once she hung the bag, the buckskin focused on the alfalfa and Harley bolted for the lodge.

"Wyatt!" She called as she raced through the downstairs checking the kitchen, bathroom, guest bedroom, and his office.

Harley bounded up the staircase, her heart clawing at her chest as fear encased her. Wyatt's bedroom was empty, and she knew his bathroom would be too, but checked anyway. Tears pricked her eyes, and she descended the stairs back to the main room.

Grabbing her phone from the truck, she walked the perimeter of the lodge, but there was still no sign of Wyatt. She thumbed her phone alive and found Blake's number.

Harley: *Arrived lodge. Chief saddled and alone. No sign of Wyatt.*

Blake: *On my way.*

Harley knew someone would need to tell Derrick about Wyatt, but she worried his autism would make it hard for Deputy Derrick Stone to process his cousin was missing.

CHAPTER SEVEN

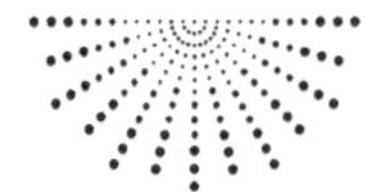

Her would-be rescuer landed inches from the edge of the shelf Edelyn had also dropped onto. He tried to stand but cried out and crumpled to the ground, grabbing his ankle.

"Try not to move too much," Edelyn stepped closer to him, "we're on a ledge and the next drop looks like a doozy."

"I think my ankle's broken." He raised piercing blue eyes to her. "Are you injured?"

"Afraid so," Edelyn looked at her left shoulder, which she'd secured with a makeshift sling. "Dislocated and I think my collarbone's broken too."

She moved to her backpack and lifted a small bottle of ibuprofen from a pocket. She handed the bottle to her guest, and then retrieved a bottle of water from the pack.

"Take four pills, then we'll have to manage on two each," Edelyn instructed. "And just a sip of water so we can make what I have last."

"Thanks …" He popped the ibuprofen into his mouth and took a sip.

"Edelyn." She capped the water bottle and set it next to the backpack.

"Wyatt." He grimaced as he tried to sit up straighter. "How long have you been down here?"

"Since noonish." Edelyn took a seat on a flat rock. "Your cowboy hat joined my phone," she pointed, "over the edge."

Wyatt checked his pockets, producing his phone. The screen was cracked.

"No signal and it won't be long before the battery runs down." He looked at her. "Do you have a locator beacon?"

"No. Wasn't expecting trouble on a short day hike." Edelyn shook her head. "Please tell me you were with someone?"

"Sorry, no." Wyatt leaned forward and probed his ankle. "But someone is expecting me to be at my lodge, so she'll notify my deputies I'm missing."

Her pulse quickened but Edelyn kept her face neutral. "You're a sheriff?"

"Yes." He winced and leaned against a log. "On a trail ride when a black bear cornered me and my horse."

"Ah," she nodded, "I encountered the same bear."

"Why were you on the trail?" His eyes narrowed slightly.

"Just taking in the fall foliage." She lied. "Was headed back to the trailhead when nature called."

Edelyn held his ice blue stare and ran scenarios through her head. *What if the sheriff had been alerted to the theft at Monica Grey's ranch? What if law enforcement knew she'd been the one to steal the pink diamond engagement ring? What if Sheriff Wyatt was just having the same bad day as her?*

Wyatt broke eye contact and looked up at the cliff they'd slid down. He tried to shift so he could see better but gasped in pain and stopped moving.

"Damn it!" He pounded the dirt with a fist.

"What are you trying to see?" Edelyn stood from her rock.

"If there's any way we can climb back up." His breath came in labored huffs.

"I'd say we dropped about ten feet," she scanned the cliffside, "and besides a few saplings, there's nothing to use as leverage to pull ourselves upward."

Edelyn looked at Wyatt, noting a film of perspiration on his brow. "So, unless you're imagining we can fly out of here, we're going to need to be rescued."

"We'll be hard to see from above," Wyatt looked from one end of the ledge to the other, "since we're tucked against the mountainside."

"Plus," she moved to her backpack and pulled a torn T-shirt free, "I estimated our temporary home is about ten feet deep and ..." She pointed from side-to-side. "Maybe twenty feet long." Tearing a couple more strips, she stepped back to Wyatt.

"We're going to need to stabilize your ankle," she knelt next to his leg, "and you're going to have to help." Edelyn pointed to her left arm.

"If you're up for it, we should fix your shoulder first."

"I've never had to reset my own shoulder but know how to do it." Edelyn moved closer to Wyatt. "You?"

"Yes." He patted the ground. "You're going to need to lie down with your head here."

She blew out a breath, then lay down, positioning her head close to his waist. Next, she took her arm from the sling and raised it over her head, then lowered her hand to the base of her neck.

"Ready?" Wyatt asked, placing his hands on her elbow and shoulder.

"No." Edelyn blew out a breath.

"This is going to hurt like a—"

"Mother-trucker!" She screamed when the joint popped into place. Edelyn rolled onto her knees and gulped air. Her eyes watered, but she didn't think she was going to pass out. She eased her arm back into the makeshift sling and stood.

"Now your ankle. Ready?"

"Let's do it." Wyatt nodded.

Edelyn found four sturdy twigs and added them to the strips of torn T-shirt. She eased off his boot, then threaded a piece under his ankle. Wyatt gripped the end, then pulled the cloth up so she could repeat the process. They wrapped the makeshift splints three times, then brought the ends together. Wyatt flinched and sucked in air when Edelyn yanked the cloth tight, securing the first knot.

"You know we have to do this a couple more times, right?" Her collarbone throbbed but she knew his pain was worse than hers.

"Do you carry rope in your pack?" Wyatt rasped.

"I have twine I use as a clothesline," Edelyn cocked an eyebrow, "why?"

"You need to tie me to this log," he pointed behind him, "because I might pass out and could be disoriented if I wake up in the dark."

"That's a damn good idea." She crossed to her pack and fished out the twine. When she turned back to Wyatt, he'd already passed out.

Edelyn set to the task of securing him to the log, running the twine under his arms and across his chest. When she moved behind him to wrap the cord around the log, she detected the faint scent of copper and noticed his hair was caked in blood. She fingered away the matted locks and looked at a lump on the back of his head. She would need to clean the cut tomorrow in better light.

Using her good arm and her teeth, Edelyn finished tightening the wrap on Wyatt's ankle, then zipped up his fleece-lined jacket and covered him with a mylar blanket. She wasn't cold yet, but she suspected that was due to adrenaline and once she calmed down, the night air would lower her body temperature.

The waning light told her it would be dark soon. Edelyn grabbed her down jacket, sweatshirt, and the second blanket, then made a pallet next to the sheriff. Next, she took three glow sticks and her flashlight from the pack, along with water and a power bar.

Edelyn knew when her eyes struggled to measure any depth in her surroundings, it was time to snap the glow sticks. She placed one a foot from the edge of the shelf, one on the other side of Wyatt, and one next to her.

She sat next to the sheriff and leaned against the log. It was going to be a long night and Edelyn knew she should nap while Wyatt was passed out.

"Well, at least I'm not stuck on this fucking ledge alone." Edelyn took a bite of a chocolate bar.

"I love you too, Harley," Wyatt mumbled and placed his hand on her thigh.

The sheriff's warm hand on her leg was comforting and as Edelyn drifted off, she imagined what it might be like to be Harley and loved by the handsome sheriff.

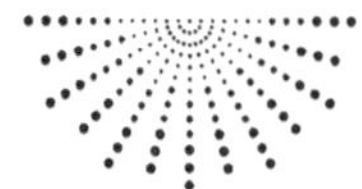

Harley heard sirens approaching Willow Lake. She waited on the porch in one of the rocking chairs. She'd wanted to look for Wyatt but with the impending dark, and no idea where to start, she'd stayed and rocked.

Flashing lights announced Blake's arrival. He stopped his truck next to her and Derrick bolted from the passenger seat.

"Derrick." Harley started after him.

"Let him go." Blake stood next to her. "I made him promise he wouldn't go any further than the lake's edge."

"I checked the lake, then stood on the deck and stared at the water, but—" Her voice broke, and she swiped tears from her cheeks.

"Do you know where Wyatt was headed today?" Blake asked and Harley heard Wyatt's official sheriff's cadence in his brother's tone.

"No. He wanted to surprise me," she shook her head, "and was checking out a trail ride for tomorrow."

"Luke and Colt are on their way with a couple of horses." Blake's phone dinged and he checked the screen. "That was Britt. He and Morgan Grey are on their way with horses too."

Blake headed for the barn. "How's Chief?"

"He was thirsty and very sweaty." She stepped next to Chief's stall. "I checked him and didn't find any injuries."

"Would it be okay if Derrick rides Trigger tomorrow?" Blake was running his hands over Chief and didn't look at her.

"I-I want to help search for Wyatt—" Harley's tears were back.

"No," Derrick said behind her, "you need to stay here."

"Why?" A burst of anger burned Harley's cheeks. "Why can't I come too?"

"Because Wyatt wouldn't want you to see—"

"Wyatt," Blake glared at Derrick, "wouldn't want you in any danger."

"You—" Harley struggled to breathe, "you think he's dead?"

"No." Blake placed his hands on her arms. "You're cold. Let's go inside."

He gripped her elbow, and they followed Derrick into the lodge where she'd left on all the lights. Derrick headed to the kitchen and opened the cupboard above the fridge. He pulled down several bottles of booze, setting them on the counter.

Blake went to the fireplace and started prepping kindling for a fire. Harley stood in the middle of the great room, frozen in place. She didn't have a task. She didn't know what to do next. And she was afraid she was going to break down at any minute.

"Here," Derrick handed her a half-full tumbler, "it's Patrón. You should take a drink."

Harley lifted the tumbler to her lips and swallowed half the tequila. Derrick sipped from a tumbler, too, and pointed to the bar where he'd left a glass for Blake. After Blake retrieved his drink, the three of them stood, sipping tequila.

"Whatever condition you find Wyatt in," Harley emptied her glass, "can't be worse than what I'm imagining."

"Harley," Blake looked at his tumbler, then met her eyes, "None of us can let you participate in the search. Because when we find Wyatt … alive, he'd be pissed if he thought we'd put you in danger."

"And we need you to run the command center." Derrick took her glass and headed back to the kitchen.

"Command center?" Harley tilted her head.

"Barnes has alerted Marcus Brennan," Blake took a sip, "he's coming in the morning with his firefighters and an ambulance."

"And Simms is bringing his drone for an ariel search." Derrick handed the tumbler back to her. "He may need someone to monitor his tablet."

"Have you told Busy about Wyatt yet?" Blake asked.

"No. I—" Tears sprang to her eyes again.

"You need to text or call her now," Blake emptied his glass, "since Mac will tell Ace."

"She's going to want to come up here." Harley ran a hand through her hair. "I need her to stay with my creatures."

"I'll text Luke to see who else can stay at your place." Blake pulled his phone from a pocket and headed for the fireplace.

"Have you eaten anything?" Derrick moved back to the kitchen.

"I'm not hungry," Harley followed him, "but I'm sure Frankie sent food with Wyatt."

"You sit." Derrick pointed at the barstools. "I'll see what I can find."

"Thanks, Derrick," Harley walked to the sliding glass door, "I'm going to step out onto the deck and call Busy."

The night air was cool, and Harley wished she'd grabbed a jacket. A whisp of decaying fish blew in from the lake. The scent of death brought tears to her eyes, and she sobbed. What if Wyatt was injured, lying in the cold hoping to be rescued? She jumped when her phone chimed. Busy's name flashed on the screen.

Busy: *I'm on my way. Don't call or text cause I'm hauling ass.*

"Harley?" Britt said from the open door.

She turned and let him wrap her in his arms. He stroked her hair as she cried into his shoulder. After a few minutes, Harley stepped back and looked at Britt.

"Wyatt's fine and we're going to find him." He took her hand, leading her back inside. "I stopped at your ranch and told Busy. Ace will be here in the morning with Mac and the rest of the crew." Britt pointed to one of the chairs in front of the fire and she sat. "Luke sent Mason to care for your animals."

Derrick was at her side with a plate of spaghetti and her tumbler of tequila.

"You should try to eat something." He set the plate on the table next to her chair.

"Thanks, Derrick." Harley took a large drink of the citrusy alcohol.

"I'm going to figure out who sleeps where," he looked at Britt, then cut his eyes to her, "unless you'd like to decide, Harley."

"You should decide." She smiled at Derrick.

"I assign you and Busy, Wyatt's upstairs bedroom." He didn't wait for a reply.

"What the tarnation is going on!" Otis bellowed from the doorway. "Where the hell is Wyatt?"

"Har Har!" Busy yelled behind Otis. "I can't get in!"

Blake let loose a shrill whistle. Busy pushed past Otis. Derrick plugged his ears. Luke and Colt joined them when Otis stepped inside.

"Listen up." Blake held his hands in the air. "I know we're all worried about Wyatt and anxious to begin our search. Derrick is working on sleeping arrangements, so see him for pillows and blankets if you need them for your rigs." He pointed at Morgan Grey, who stood in the kitchen. "There's food if you're hungry and bottled water in the fridge." Blake looked at Harley, then back at the group. "Wyatt's a tough SOB. Let's get some sleep. We'll leave early in the morning."

Busy made a beeline for Harley and wrapped her in a bear hug. Harley really wished she could stop crying but sobbed along with Busy. Her bestie finally held her at arm's length.

"Your sheriff is going to be fine." Busy nodded as if reassuring herself. "Now what can I do to help?" She looked around the room.

"Sit with me," Harley pulled Busy toward the matching chair, "I don't want to be alone."

"Let me get us some water." Busy tried to smile, but her lips quivered. "I'll be right back."

Busy marched to the fridge, passing Morgan as he walked toward Harley.

"Here," he handed her a new tumbler, "I know it's hard to eat and the tequila will help calm your nerves."

"Thanks, Morgan." Harley didn't look at him.

"Harley," he touched her shoulder, and she raised her eyes to his, "we're all here to bring Wyatt home to you."

Harley nodded but was afraid to speak. Morgan headed for Britt, Blake, and the rest of the men. Otis glanced at her, then returned his attention to the group.

Busy handed her water, then motioned for her to sit in the chair. Harley turned the chair around, so it faced the men and Busy followed suit. Once they were seated, Busy reached over, twining her fingers into Harley's.

Tears slipped down her cheeks as she watched Wyatt's friends discuss the best trails to search, agree on who would team up, and argue over using phones versus radios. After Derrick stacked pillows and blankets at the foot of the stairs, his head swiveled from one speaker to the next.

Despite the distraction, Harley's mind imagined her handsome sheriff, staring up at the stars and praying she'd called the calvary.

CHAPTER NINE

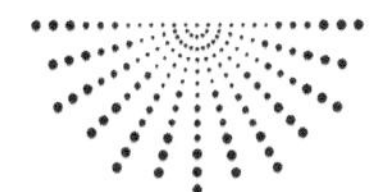

Pain dragged Wyatt out of his stupor. His ankle throbbed and his head pounded as the memory of sliding down the side of the cliff filled his mind. He'd tried to dig in his boots to slow his descent and grab vegetation to stop his fall. Nothing had worked and he remembered hitting the ground, then banging his head.

Wyatt couldn't see much in the darkness despite a canopy of stars overhead and the glow sticks Edelyn had placed around them. His new companion lay snuggled against him and though it felt weird to have a strange woman lying next to him, he was grateful for the warmth.

Trying not to wake Edelyn, he focused on his breathing, hoping to abate his pain. Since he could vividly remember the black bear, Chief's anxiety, then losing his footing, Wyatt decided his concussion was probably mild. Edelyn had done a nice job of wrapping his ankle, but it still throbbed with pain. His initial assessment before passing out had been that his fibula bone was broken, which meant he could still walk. If he could remember anything about this ravine and the surrounding area, then maybe they could walk out of the canyon.

Worry snaked through his gut at the thought of Chief being attacked by the bear. He knew his horse was strong and fast, but if the buckskin had panicked, the bear would've had the advantage. A new thread of concern caused his gut to churn when he thought about Harley arriving at the lodge and finding him missing. He knew despite her worry; she'd sound the alarm.

Edelyn shifted against him, and Wyatt took the opportunity to try and sit up. A new stab of pain shot through his groin, stealing his breath away. His involuntary flinch startled Edelyn awake, and she palmed his chest to push herself up.

"You okay, Sheriff?" Edelyn switched on her flashlight.

"Not sure," Wyatt rasped, "felt a stab of pain in my abdomen."

Edelyn swept the beam of light across his torso, then held the glow on his crotch. She raised the flashlight to shine just under their faces and worry darkened her hazel eyes.

"I think there's blood." She touched his upper thigh.

Wyatt gasped. "Shit!"

Edelyn laid the flashlight onto his chest, then pulled her arm free of the sling. "Ditto." She gently applied the cloth to the dark spot on his jeans and he sucked in air.

She lifted the strip, then met his eyes. "The blood's fresh—"

"Which means I'm still bleeding."

"I think so." Edelyn nodded and looked up at the lightening sky. "We're going to have to take a look as soon as it's light enough."

"In about an hour." Wyatt fingered the blood stain on his jeans. She was right, the spot was wet and though he had some pain it wasn't as sharp as when he'd tried to sit up.

"Don't move," Edelyn instructed and came to her feet. "I'm going to make a new sling and fetch us some coffee."

"Coffee?" Wyatt tilted his head.

"Use your imagination, Sheriff." She grinned, then walked to her pack.

Wyatt winced when he attempted to sit up again. He hadn't taken in their surroundings yesterday after his fall and scanned the area now. The ledge narrowed at each end as it bled into the mountainside. He could hear the creek below, but the sound was faint, which told him the drop from this ledge would be farther down.

"Water and part of a power bar." Edelyn extended her hand.

"Thanks." Wyatt sipped some water and handed her back the bottle, then popped the bite of the chocolate power bar into his mouth.

"I cleaned the wound on the back of your head," she waggled the bottle, "would you like more ibuprofen?"

"Not yet." He shook his head. "How's your collarbone?"

"It hurts like a mother-trucker." Edelyn grinned. "I'll see what I have to treat your new injury." She stepped toward her pack. "Don't go anywhere."

"Hilarious." Wyatt's cheeks warmed at the realization he'd have to lower his jeans for her to look at his wound. Normally, he didn't wear underwear, but wore athletic shorts when he rode. Still, Edelyn was about to gain full knowledge of his groin and depending on the location of the injury may have access to more than he'd like.

"Ready?" Edelyn knelt next to him.

"No." Wyatt frowned but began releasing the buttons on the fly of his jeans.

"Try closing your eyes and imagining I'm Harley." Edelyn sat back on her heels.

Wyatt raised his eyebrows.

"You might have called me Harley last night," she smiled, "but don't worry I didn't take advantage of your vulnerable state."

"Let's get this over with." Wyatt lifted his hips and groaned as a wave of pain washed over him. He closed his eyes and pushed his jeans down enough to clear his groin.

Edelyn's fingers were cold as she probed his upper thigh. When she lifted the edge of his shorts, he looked at her.

"The wound's under these, so you're going to need to lower them too." Her face reflected the discomfort churning his gut.

"No." Wyatt narrowed his eyes.

"Look, Sheriff," she rocked back on her heels again, "I normally get dinner and drinks before I'm subjected to a male's anatomy, so this isn't fun for me either."

"Cut the material and see if that gives you enough access." Wyatt held her stare.

"All right." Edelyn walked back to her pack and returned with a pair of small scissors.

She peeled the short's leg material away and he felt a gush of blood warm his thigh.

"Shit!" She held the other half of the torn red shirt against his thigh, and he almost passed out. "Stay with me, Wyatt," Edelyn pushed down on the wound, "you're going to have to hold this in place."

He nodded and placed his hands on the cloth. "I need to sit up so I can see the injury."

"I think it's a deep slash on the inside of your thigh." She held up a piece of bloody stick, then offered her forearm for leverage. "Your shorts were holding this in place so now the wounds bleeding more."

"Not a venous bleed?" Wyatt pulled himself into a sitting position. He tried to see the wound but all he could see was the darkening red cloth.

"I don't think so," Edelyn shook her head, "and obviously not an arterial bleed because you'd be dead by now."

"Exactly." Wyatt leaned against the log.

"Wyatt," she waited for him to look at her, "I need to clean, pack, and bandage the wound."

"Which is going to hurt like a mother-trucker."

"Exactly." Edelyn smiled, then headed to her pack.

When she returned, she knelt next to his injured thigh. Without warning she finished cutting the shorts and the band gave way exposing his package. Edelyn didn't make eye contact and began wiping the injured area, the coppery scent of blood wafting over him.

Wyatt closed his eyes and willed Harley's face into his mind. He imagined it was her hands tending his wound, touching his genitals, and cleaning his skin with antiseptic wipes. His eyes flew open when Edelyn pressed a bundle of cloth against the cut, and he grabbed her hand.

"Yell, cuss, grit your damn teeth," she glared at him, "but let go of my hand."

Wyatt released her. "You're going to need my help wrapping the cut."

"Yes," she nodded, "and am seriously wishing we had some tequila."

"Harley's favorite alcohol." Wyatt rasped.

"Well, I'm doing my best to channel her." She flashed a smile. "Tell me about Harley."

"She's smart, funny, beautiful." Wyatt sucked in air when Edelyn brushed his package as she threaded a strip of cloth under his thigh.

"Who knew she and I would have so much in common." She released the cloth as he took the end.

"Do you have someone special in your life?" He pulled the cloth up and lifted his hips so she could guide the strip around again.

"Not at present." Edelyn pulled up the strip and they repeated the process.

Something about her tone caused Wyatt's interest to pique. He remembered she'd claimed to be on a day hike, but her pack was stocked for more than just a few hours on a trail. He also found it curious she kept the backpack a good distance from him, as if she didn't want him to have access.

"Wyatt?" Edelyn met his stare, and he grasped the cloth, then pulled it up. "This is going to hurt." She brought up the other end of the cloth. "Do you want to lean back just in case?"

"No," he shook his head, "I think I can handle the pain this time since I'll be doing the tightening."

"Got it." She sat back and watched as he made the loop of the first knot.

Wyatt pulled the cloth tight and winced from a stab of pain. He tied two more knots to ensure the bandage was secure.

"I'll take that ibuprofen now." He smiled at Edelyn, and she stood. He pulled his jeans up and fastened the buttons.

"Good idea." She headed for her pack.

This time Wyatt paid attention to where she'd stashed things and which pockets she didn't touch. It could be his pain-driven imagina-tion was creating a false scenario given what had happened to the two of them, but Wyatt couldn't shake the feeling that his *nurse* was hiding something.

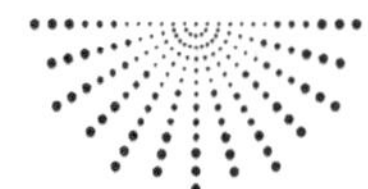

CHAPTER TEN

Edelyn handed Wyatt two tablets and he washed them down with a swig of water. She took the bottle and replaced the cap. She'd brought six bottles of water and now had four. Her food supply was in better shape since she'd taken everything from the rented house in Stoneybrook.

She knew a person could only live without water for approximately three days. She also suspected that Wyatt was already dehydrated because he hadn't needed to relieve himself. And as much as she hated to broach the subject, she needed to ask.

"Here." She offered him half of a red apple.

"Thanks." Wyatt took a bite. "You might as well tell me what's behind your frown."

"Wondering if you need to pee?" Edelyn's cheeks warmed.

"Not yet, which as you've surmised means I'm dehydrated." Wyatt munched more apple. "Do you have an empty water bottle I can use when I'm ready?"

"Yes." Edelyn bit into the sweet apple. "We have four bottles of water left. I think we're okay food wise …"

"Because if we run out of water before we're rescued," Wyatt finished his apple, "we won't need the food."

"I could try to climb down to the creek," Edelyn looked at him.

"Have you looked over the edge to see how far down you'll need to go?" Wyatt asked.

"I surveyed the sides," she pointed to each end of the shelf, "and it looks like I might be able to scoot down on my ass. Getting back up could be a challenge though."

Wyatt studied both ends, then looked at her. "I think I know where we are now." He pushed himself up straighter, the effort coating his forehead with sweat. "This is Rattlesnake Ravine, so I'm not crazy about you scooting anywhere."

"Are you fucking kidding me?" Edelyn ran a hand through her short hair. "What else can fucking go wrong?"

"Edelyn."

"What?"

"Snakes are generally afraid of humans," he attempted a smile, "so if we stay put, it's unlikely a rattler will approach us."

"Yeah, well," Edelyn crossed to her pack and withdrew a handgun, "I fucking hate snakes."

"Assuming you're a good aim," he frowned, "the weapon will come in handy."

"We're going to need to sleep in shifts." She placed the gun into the back of her waistband.

"Works for me." Wyatt nodded.

Edelyn picked up a large stick and poked the shrubbery along the edges of the ledge, a sweet earthy smell flowing over her. She resisted the urge to break down into tears. All she'd wanted to do was get paid for her last two jobs. Fly somewhere sunny and consume fruity drinks adorned with tiny umbrellas. Instead, she was trapped with an injured sheriff and unable to rescue either of them.

CHAPTER ELEVEN

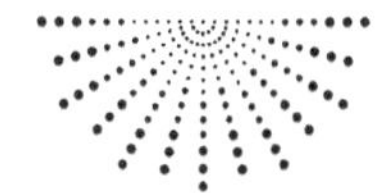

No one had slept through the night. Harley had finally come downstairs before dawn. The savory scent of the scrambled eggs and toast Busy was making filled the great room. Britt was prepping a new pot of coffee in the Cuisinart Harley had added to the kitchen when Wyatt began renting the lodge. Derrick stood at the sliding glass door staring out at the dark surface of Willow Lake.

The floor of the great room was an array of blankets, pillows, and cowboy boots. Harley bent to pick up a blanket and Morgan walked toward her.

"I know you're trying to stay busy," he pointed at the littered floor, "but we may be here another night so …"

"I don't like clutter." Harley snapped the blanket, then proceeded to fold it into a square.

"All right." Morgan scooped up a blanket and pillow.

They worked together tidying the room, which did little to calm Harley's nerves.

"Buy you a cup of coffee?" Morgan asked.

Harley looked at him and nodded, then followed him to the kitchen bar.

"Har Har," Busy handed her a mug, "you should eat something."

"Toast?" Harley sipped the strong coffee.

"Coming up." Busy placed two slices of multi-grain bread into the toaster.

"Good morning, Harley," Derrick said from the end of the counter.

"How are you holding up?" Harley asked.

"I'm waiting for Echo to return my text." He looked at his phone.

"He won't eat either," Busy pointed at Derrick.

"I'll have toast, too." He didn't look at Busy.

Blake, followed by Luke and Colt, walked into the lodge. Britt poured three cups of coffee and set them on the kitchen bar.

"Did you work out the trails we should search?" Britt asked.

"Yes," Blake picked up a cup, "and both Mac and Simms are on their way."

"Ace is bringing two more horses from Broken River," Luke sipped some coffee, "so he and Cooper will be on standby in case Wyatt's—"

"Wyatt's fine." Derrick took a bite of toast.

"Derrick," Blake waited for his cousin to look at him, "would you like to stay here and help Simms with the drone?"

"No." Derrick shook his head.

"Luke and Colt have stocked the saddlebags," Blake set his cup down, "so grab your gear and we'll meet outside."

Blake walked to Harley and handed her a two-way radio. "We'll try to use our phones, but if we lose service, we'll radio updates."

"Okay," Harley fought to keep tears from her eyes.

"Derrick," Blake headed for the door, "you're with me."

Derrick hugged Harley. "We'll bring Wyatt back to you."

Tears slipped down her cheeks. "I know you will."

Derrick followed the other men from the lodge, and Busy wrapped her arms around Harley.

"I know you're worried," Busy whispered, "but Wyatt's strong and resourceful. And these guys won't come back without him."

"Let's go outside." Harley walked toward the door.

When she and Busy stepped onto the porch, Otis sat in one of the rockers.

"Thought I'd keep you company if that's okay?" His brow furrowed as he stood.

"That would be nice," Harley smiled, "thanks, Otis."

Busy had already made her way to the men who huddled as if they were football players learning the next play. Her bestie touched Blake's arm as Harley drew near and the group broke up.

"All right," Blake swung into Chief's saddle, "you all know your routes, so let's ride."

A cloud of dust spiraled skyward as the horses churned the gravel in the parking area. Blake had taken the lead, but as they neared Willow Lake, the men began to break off in pairs of two. Derrick turned on Trigger and met Harley's stare, then followed Blake toward a trail that led north around the lake. Harley didn't try to contain her tears, which blurred her eyesight as she watched Wyatt's rescuers ride away. She knew Busy was right about Wyatt being strong, but if he were injured his strength would wane. *Please God, bring him back to me ... alive.*

CHAPTER TWELVE

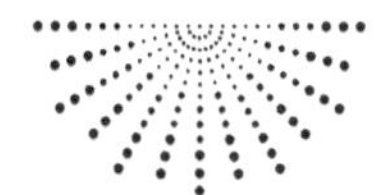

Wyatt watched Edelyn rearrange her backpack, which she'd moved closer to the log serving as their home base. The pack was still out of his reach, and since she'd revealed she had a gun, he wondered what else she might be hiding.

His stomach growled and he closed his eyes, imagining he was back at the lodge. He searched his mind for possible dishes Harley would surprise him with for dinner. Her smile flashed behind his eyelids, but Wyatt knew she'd be worried about him.

"You hungry?" Edelyn's shadow fell across him.

Wyatt opened his eyes. "Yes, but I can wait until dinner time." He attempted a grin.

"What about your pain?" She adjusted her sling. "Need more ibuprofen?"

"Not yet." Wyatt shook his head. "How's the shoulder?"

"Better," Edelyn looked down at her chest, "but my collarbone hurts more than it did before."

"Take my pills." Wyatt shifted, then sucked in air when a jolt of pain raced up from his abdomen.

"You don't look so good, Sheriff." Edelyn knelt next to him and placed the back of her hand on his forehead. "And you're warm."

"Just a wave of pain." He tried to assess where the discomfort was located. Before he could mentally move past his ankle, Edelyn was probing his broken fibula.

"Your ankle isn't warm." She looked at him. "Does it hurt?"

"Yes," he nodded, "but I don't think that's where the stab of pain came from."

"You know where else we have to look?" Edelyn raised an eyebrow.

"I'll do it." Wyatt motioned for her to turn around.

"Suit yourself." She stood and turned her back to him.

Wyatt unbuttoned his Levi's and knew from the putrid scent wrinkling his nose, that his wound was infected. The torn cloth they'd wrapped around the cut was soaked through. As much as he dreaded the idea, Edelyn would have to help him rewrap his leg with a clean cloth.

"We're going to need to change your bandage." She knelt next to him again. "And you need to get over being embarrassed."

"Fine." Wyatt began to remove the soaked cloth. "What are you doing?"

"I'm going to use both hands this time." Edelyn slipped her arm from the sling.

"That's not good for your injured collarbone." Wyatt cringed when she pulled the remnants of his shorts away from the wound, exposing him.

"This needs to be cleaned again." She opened a water bottle.

"Wish we had some whiskey," he rasped.

"You and me both." Edelyn dabbed the skin around the wound, then looked at him. "I'm going to need to debride the wound, which is going to hurt like a—"

"Mother-trucker." Wyatt leaned against the log and closed his eyes.

"Tell me how you met Harley." Edelyn probed the wound.

Wyatt gasped and glared at her. "Her donkey ran away and trampled one of my fences."

"Fences?" She dabbed his skin with antiseptic wipes.

"I own a ranch." A rancid odor rose from his leg, which was red and swollen. He pointed at the wound. "Do you think we should let the cut breathe before we rebandage it?"

"Good idea since we're out of wipes." She glanced up at the sky. "We have an hour before dark, so we can wait a half hour, then wrap your leg."

Edelyn draped the torn T-shirt over his crotch. She eased her arm back into the makeshift sling, then walked to her backpack.

"We need to be rescued soon," she pulled a peanut butter power bar from a pocket, "because that's my last clean shirt."

A chill swept over him, and Wyatt pulled the collar up on his jacket. He leaned back and closed his eyes. He knew Blake would be heading the search for him. He also knew his brother wouldn't risk anyone else's life to continue looking in the dark. He imagined how angry Derrick would be that they hadn't found him yet. His thoughts shifted to Harley, and his heart seized. He didn't have to imagine how worried she must be, because if she were the one missing, Wyatt would be distraught beyond his wildest imagination.

CHAPTER THIRTEEN

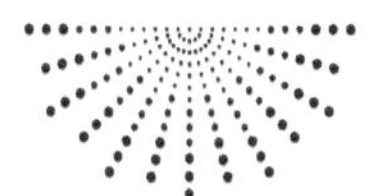

Edelyn held her breath and laid statue still. There was just enough light from the rising sun to confirm a rattlesnake was stretched out along her leg. She'd initially thought Wyatt had placed his hand on her thigh, but when the hand began to move, her eyes flew open.

"Don't move," Wyatt whispered.

"No shit," Edelyn hissed. "Can you shoot it?"

"Yes, but not without injuring you."

"So, what's the next best option?"

"We stay calm and wait for the snake to mosey along."

"Seriously!" Edelyn's pulse rate spiked.

"Rattlesnakes like to hunt in the morning," Wyatt murmured, "and at dusk. I think your friend will slither away soon."

"Define soon." She focused on not flexing her thigh muscle.

"What if I take a turn with questions?"

Edelyn's heart pounded and she worried Wyatt would hear the rapid drumbeat against her chest.

"You get three."

"Why are you hiking alone?"

"I like solitude." She gritted her teeth when the snake wiggled.

"Are you running from something or someone?"

"No." The snake scrunched its body into an accordion shape.

"What are you hiding in your pack?"

The snake moved across her knee and angled toward the ground. Edelyn wanted to jump to her feet. Once the snake hit the dirt, it picked up pace and slinked away.

"Shoot it," Edelyn growled.

"If I do," Wyatt raised the gun, "the blast will be next to your ear, so bad idea."

"Fuck." Edelyn held out her hand. "Give me the damn gun."

"No." He lowered the gun.

The snake slipped under some brush and disappeared. Edelyn jumped to her feet and glared at Wyatt.

"Why didn't you shoot the damn thing?" She reached for the gun.

"Because the snake wasn't threatening us," Wyatt switched the weapon to his other hand, "and unless you have an arsenal stashed in your pack, we need to conserve ammo for a real threat."

"Give me my gun." Edelyn held her hand out again.

"Tell me what you're hiding in your backpack." Wyatt tucked the gun into the back of his waistband.

"I'm not hiding anything!" She picked up the pack. "I've used my shirts to take care of you. Split my food and water with you. Shared drugs." She shoved the pack at him. "Check it if you don't believe me."

Wyatt held her stare until tears streamed down her cheeks, then said, "I don't need to look inside."

"I'd storm off if we weren't stuck on a fucking ledge." She palmed away her tears and set the pack down.

"Edelyn," he began, "I'm grateful for everything you've done to treat my injuries."

"Like I had a choice." She handed him part of a protein bar.

"I'm not hungry." He waved off the bar.

"You look awful." Edelyn noticed a sickly odor too when she placed her hand on his forehead. "And you're warmer than yesterday."

"Can I have ibuprofen." Wyatt leaned against the log.

"Yes, but you have to eat too." Edelyn laid the hunk of chocolate bar on his chest.

"How much water do we have left?" Wyatt rasped.

"Two bottles." Edelyn offered him the ibuprofen and a bottle with one drink left.

"Don't use any more water to clean my wound." Wyatt tossed the pills into his mouth and chased them with a sip of water.

"Only if you promise not to die on me." She took a bite of her bar. "Eat up."

Edelyn waited until he took a bite, then turned her attention to her pack. She didn't know what she would've done if Wyatt had wanted to search the pockets. The black box hiding the antique dragonfly broach was nestled beneath her panties and a bra, but Edelyn doubted a few undergarments would deter the sheriff from a thorough search.

She glanced at Wyatt, who had slouched down and rested his head against the log. His eyes were closed, and his complexion was sallow. Edelyn might be a thief, but she didn't have it in her to let the sheriff die.

There was no way to know if they'd be rescued and since she had all day, Edelyn decided to rethink traversing one of the sides of the ravine down to the creek. If she could make it down and back up, they'd have more water. But making the return trip up the steep side might be more than she was strong enough to accomplish.

Edelyn stood at the edge of the cliff and peered down at the creek. She moved from one side to the other, studying the geography below. When she spotted the trail, Edelyn thought she was imagining the slight path that followed the stream. But there was a definite indentation in the ground, which told Edelyn the route might still be well traveled and lead to freedom.

CHAPTER FOURTEEN

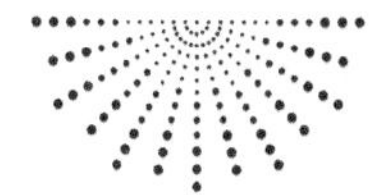

It was another sleepless night at the lodge. Harley's eyes still burned from her crying fit after the men had returned without Wyatt. Busy poured her another shot of Patrón and sat in the chair next to her with Ace hovering close by. Derrick sat on the floor next to her chair, staring at the fire. Blake and the rest of the guys were scattered throughout the kitchen and great room.

Morgan crossed from the door and knelt in front of her. Harley raised her eyes to his but had trouble focusing on what he was saying.

"Luke and I checked on the horses and they seem fine." He placed a hand on her knee and Derrick glared at him.

"Okay," Harley managed, then Busy intervened.

"What's the plan for tomorrow?" She looked at her phone. "I mean today."

"I should let Blake explain his plan." Morgan looked across the room at Blake who stood with Simms and Mac. "Britt texted Ella and asked her to bring some food for everyone." He smiled at her.

Harley nodded and sipped some tequila. "Thanks, Morgan."

Britt stood next to Busy's chair as Morgan joined the others.

"Busy, Ella's also bringing a couple bottles of champagne." Britt smiled.

"That's sweet," Busy touched his arm, "thanks, Britt."

"Harley," Britt moved in front of her, "I know you said Wyatt was surprising you with a trail ride. Can you remember anything about where he was taking you?"

"No …" Another round of tears stole her words.

"It's fall!" Derrick shot to his feet. "The colors. Wyatt loves the changing colors." Derrick crossed to Blake. "There's only two trails where you can see the fall colors. The trail around the south end of the lake, which Britt and Morgan rode yesterday. Wyatt must have taken the trail that runs southeast around Mt. Pitt."

The lodge door flew open, and a petite blonde stormed into the lodge. She had a wavy, bi-level cut and swept the room with wild, emerald, green eyes. She flashed a grin and made a beeline for Blake, jumping into his arms. The pair locked lips and slammed into the wall adorned with pictures of Stone ancestors, rattling several of the frames.

"What are you doing here?" Blake asked the blonde tornado and set her on her feet.

"I traced a jewel thief to Stoneybrook," she looked around the room, "and heard about Wyatt being missing when I had breakfast at the Babbling Brooke Café."

"Jewel thief?" Blake tilted his head.

"Introduce me to the gang." She took his hand and led him to the center of the room.

"Everyone," Blake cleared his throat, "this is my friend, Ivory Bowen."

"Friend?" Busy whispered in Harley's ear.

Harley stood and walked toward Blake and Ivory.

"It's nice to meet you." Harley extended her hand.

"Likewise." Ivory shook Harley's hand. "Sorry to hear about the sheriff." She looked up at Blake. "I know how much he means to you."

"You're Blake's bounty hunter friend," Derrick moved next to Harley, "from Sacramento."

"Yes," Ivory nodded, "and you must be Derrick."

"What did your thief steal?" Derrick stepped closer to Ivory.

"A rare pink diamond and an antique dragonfly broach." Ivory pointed at Morgan. "I believe you're Monica Grey's brother, right?"

"Yes," he joined them, "why?"

"If my intel's accurate," Ivory tilted her head, "the broach belonged to your great-grandmother and was in your sister's safe."

"Shit!" Morgan scrubbed his face with a hand. "Monica's in Manhattan, so she probably doesn't know."

"That's not important," Derrick cut his eyes to Morgan, then looked at Ivory, "your thief is probably trying to get to Butterville." He shifted his gaze to Blake. "Which would put her on the same trail as Wyatt."

Blake glanced at Harley, then looked at Derrick. "Let's talk outside with the rest of the guys?"

"No." Harley heard the desperation in her tone. "I want to hear your plan."

Derrick's phone dinged and he looked at the screen. When he raised his eyes, they were an electric blue.

"It's a text from Imogine," he grinned, "she says Wyatt is above water."

Everyone had gathered around Derrick and a few mutterings of *water* flowed through the room.

"Do you know what your *psychic* friend means?" Blake's eyebrows almost reached his hairline.

"There's two trails to Butterville," Derrick shifted his bright blue stare to Harley, "one around the southeast side of the mountain and a mirror trail that runs below along a creek." He hugged her. "We'll bring Wyatt home today."

A new round of tears flowed from Harley's eyes, but this time they were tears of hope.

CHAPTER FIFTEEN

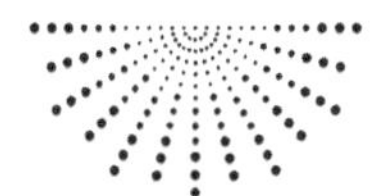

Despite Edelyn covering him with every piece of clothing she had left, Wyatt was freezing. She held him trying to keep him warm, but his fever caused his body to change from icy chills to burning up. Every time he moved pain raced through him and a few times he'd almost passed out.

After their early morning wake-up thanks to the rattlesnake, Edelyn needed a nap and slept next to him. The sky grew a darker shade of blue as the sun traversed the sky toward afternoon. Wyatt knew if they weren't rescued today, his infection would probably seep into his bloodstream if it hadn't already.

"How you feeling, Sheriff?" Edelyn sat up and rubbed her eyes.

"Peachy," Wyatt rasped.

"I'll get you some ibuprofen and water." She stepped to her backpack.

"No," he shook his head, "save the water for yourself."

"We still have two and a half bottles left." She offered him the tablets. "So, take the damn pills!"

"Yes, ma'am." Wyatt washed the ibuprofen down with a swig.

"Do you want me to check the cut in your leg?" Edelyn handed him a hunk of peanut butter power bar.

"No." He narrowed his eyes at her.

She knelt next to the injured leg. "We need to see if it's stopped bleeding."

"Edelyn," Wyatt grabbed her wrist when she reached for his jeans, "it doesn't matter, because I know the infection has spread, probably into my bloodstream."

When she rocked back on her heels, he let go of her arm. Tears pooled in the corner of her eyes, and she fingered them away, then looked at him.

"I don't know Harley," Edelyn's voice quivered, "but I'm guessing she'd be pissed if she thought you didn't fight to get back to her." She pointed at his fly. "You can close your eyes and imagine how devastated she'll be if you die. Or you can imagine your joyous reunion."

Wyatt unbuttoned the Levi's, lifted his butt, and pushed them down. He placed the gun next to his hip and closed his eyes. As Edelyn checked the injury a jolt of pain raced through him. Tears stung his eyelids as he imagined Harley, inconsolable and seeking comfort in Morgan Grey's arms.

He flinched and his eyes flew open when Edelyn touched the laceration. He frowned at her, then noticed a smile on her face.

"The wound doesn't smell as bad today," she fingered the cut and Wyatt sucked in air. "I think I should clean it again."

"No," Wyatt leaned back, "don't use any more water."

"Look," Edelyn waggled the half bottle of water, "this should be enough to clean the area." She narrowed her eyes. "And if we're not rescued tomorrow, then I'm going down to the damn creek and getting us more water."

"God you're stubborn," Wyatt shook his head, "just like Harley."

"Can't wait to meet her," Edelyn dabbed the wound again, "but I'm bolting if you die on me."

"Thanks for taking care of the cut," Wyatt attempted a smile, but pain shot through him every time she touched the wound, "and keeping me alive."

"You're keeping yourself alive," Edelyn grinned, "which tells me Harley must be something special."

Wyatt raised up and held his finger to his lips. He thought he'd heard noise above them on the trail. It could be the bear or some other wildlife, but he needed to be sure.

"Can you wrap my leg?" Wyatt picked up the gun.

Edelyn slipped her injured arm from the sling, grabbed a clean strip of cloth, and proceeded to rebandage his wound. They both looked up when a drone flew overhead, and someone called his name. Wyatt fired across the valley below them.

"Wyatt?" Derrick yelled. "He's here! In the ravine."

"Your rescuers are finally here, Sheriff." Edelyn secured the bandage and stood.

Wyatt pulled up his jeans and closed the fly. He wanted to stand too but knew better than to try.

Edelyn was stuffing her remaining clothing back into her pack. Ropes cascaded over the side of the cliff, followed by Ace and Cooper descending to the ledge.

"Hey, Sheriff," Ace knelt next to him, "how bad are your injuries?"

"Broken fibula and a deep cut in my upper thigh." Wyatt smiled. "Sure am glad to see you guys."

"Likewise. We can raise you with a seat harness," Ace pointed at his legs, "which provides support at your knees. Or use a basket, which will take longer."

"Harness." Wyatt nodded.

A flurry of activity had Wyatt in the harness, being raised by guide ropes. Even though the leg bands were below his wound, pressure on the laceration almost made him pass out. Wyatt closed his eyes and focused on seeing Harley soon.

When he was back on the trail, Derrick crossed to him. He placed a hand on Wyatt's shoulder and there were tears in his eyes.

"Harley will be very glad you didn't die." Derrick smiled at Wyatt, then looked at Ace. "Let's get a move on." He wrinkled his nose. "The sheriff has a bad infection and is dehydrated."

"Want me to look at your leg?" Ace asked, a pink hue coloring his cheeks.

"No." Wyatt shook his head.

Ace and Cooper put Wyatt in a basket. They covered him with blankets and tightened straps across his body. When they cinched the middle strap tight, pain shot through his abdomen.

"Shit," Wyatt mumbled.

"Sorry, Sheriff," Ace said. "The trail's too narrow for a vehicle, so we're going to have to carry you to the lodge.

"Copy." Wyatt nodded.

It was a long trek back to the lodge. Blake and Derrick took turns with Ace and Cooper. Then Britt and Morgan took over at the halfway point, sharing time with Luke and Colt.

Harley waited at the end of the trail with Busy hovering behind her. Britt and Morgan stopped when she ran to them.

"Thanks for coming back to me, Sheriff." She kissed him, her tears wetting his cheeks.

"Anything for you, Ms. Harper."

Mac barked orders, and Wyatt was loaded into an ambulance. Harley held his hand as Ace hooked up an IV, gave him a shot of antibiotics and another for pain. Wyatt tried to ask about Edelyn, but exhaustion, combined with the pain meds pulled him into darkness. His last thought before being dragged into the abyss of unconsciousness was how could he repay his nurse for keeping him alive.

CHAPTER SIXTEEN

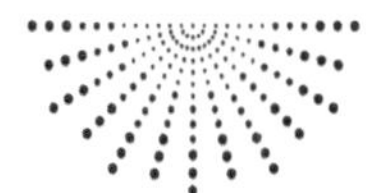

Harley sat in a chair next to Wyatt's bed holding his hand. Over the past two days, he'd kept down a little chicken broth, and drifted in and out of consciousness. Sometimes he called out her name and other times he said the name Edelyn. Blake and Derrick had hovered in the hallway outside Wyatt's room, anxious to speak with him.

Wyatt flinched and squeezed Harley's hand. His eyes were closed, and he shook his head as if he were disagreeing with someone.

"I'm here, Wyatt." She brushed his bangs from his forehead. "You're safe."

"Edelyn?" His eyes fluttered open. "Harley?"

"Yes, it's me." She kissed him. "You're in the hospital."

"Chief?" He blinked and looked past her.

"Your horse is fine and at Broken River." Harley touched his cheek. "Do you want to talk to Derrick and Blake?"

"Where's Edelyn?" Wyatt tried to sit up and grimaced.

"Wyatt," Harley stood, "let me get Blake."

"No," he rolled his head from side-to-side, "don't leave me."

"Okay," she resumed her seat, "tell me about Edelyn." She pushed the nurses' call button.

"She was on the ledge with me." Wyatt closed his eyes. "Hurt her shoulder. Collarbone." He opened his eyes and looked around the room. "Edelyn was rescued too, right?"

"Sheriff Stone," a nurse stepped into the room, "how are you feeling?"

"He seems agitated and—" Harley looked at Wyatt.

"I'm fine. I need to see Edelyn." Wyatt raised up in bed again, moaned, and fell back into the pillows.

"Do you think you could ask the deputies to come in?" Harley gave the nurse a pleading look.

"Sheriff," the nurse checked his pulse, "do you know who I am?"

"Nurse …" Wyatt blinked. "Nolan. Nurse Nolan."

"And this lovely lady is?" She pointed at Harley.

"Ms. Harper." He attempted a smile. "She smells like lemons."

"And who is Edelyn?" Nurse Nolan stepped to the door, motioning Derrick and Blake into the room.

"She took care of me on the ledge." Wyatt shifted his gaze to his brother and cousin. "You rescued Edelyn too, right?"

"We didn't repel down with the firefighters," Derrick stepped close to Wyatt's bed, "but you were the only person on the ledge."

"What? No." Wyatt shook his head. "She wrapped my ankle and cleaned the cut in my leg. I might not have made it without her help."

"Wyatt," Blake stood at the foot of the bed, "we found you shirtless and minus your socks. You used your own clothing to treat your wounds."

"Edelyn helped me." Wyatt glared at Blake. "She used clothing and water from her backpack. Shared her food."

"But you didn't recognize her in the photo we showed you—" Blake began.

"Because she's changed her appearance." Wyatt touched his hair. "Her hair's now short and dark."

"Here are the facts." Derrick tapped his forehead with a finger. "Chief must have reared up, then raced away, causing you to lose your footing. You fell to the ledge and the contents of your pommel pockets tumbled out, falling to the shelf also."

"She had a gun," Wyatt looked from Blake to Derrick, "which I fired to alert you to my location."

"Wyatt," Blake looked at Harley, then back at his brother, "we didn't hear a gunshot. We heard you whistle."

"I think you may have imagined Edelyn," Derrick looked at Wyatt, "in an effort to stay alive. But you were alone on the ledge, Wyatt."

CHAPTER SEVENTEEN

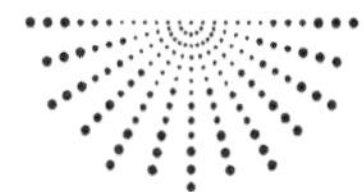

Wyatt hated using the scooter, but the crutches wore him out. He also hated that the laceration in his upper left thigh was taking so long to heal. He missed being able to work. He missed being able to ride. He missed being intimate with Harley.

She'd bought a queen bed, and had it set up in her living room even though he'd been happy cuddling with her on her couch. But between the wound in his thigh and his broken ankle, his nights were still fraught with discomfort since he'd chosen to stop taking his pain meds.

Today marked three weeks since he'd found himself stranded after falling from the trail. Now that he was clear-headed, Wyatt replayed his time on the ledge. Blake and Derrick's version of Wyatt's three-day ordeal made sense. He easily could have imagined sharing the rocky shelf with Edelyn. His cheeks warmed at the memory of her brushing his genitals when she'd tended to his injured thigh. Wyatt was certain if it had been his hands dressing the injury, he wouldn't still be embarrassed.

He knew injured persons conjured grandiose imaginations of people that didn't exist. Fabricating scenarios that helped them survive dire circumstances. But that wasn't what happened to him while he was on the ledge. He knew, regardless of what others thought, Edelyn was real. She'd been the one to wrap his ankle and treat his wounded upper thigh. She had fed him, given him ibuprofen, and shared her water.

Wyatt scootered into Harley's kitchen, managed to get a cup of coffee, and carried it to the drop-leaf table. He angled from the scooter into a chair, the effort raising a film of sweat on his forehead. Harley was feeding her animals, then she planned to give him a sponge bath. The idea brought a wave of anxiety since he knew he'd be aroused but unable to assuage his burning desire for the lovely Ms. Harper.

"Good morning." Harley stepped into the kitchen, crossed to the table, and kissed him. "Hungry?"

"Very," Wyatt drew her close, inhaling her familiar lemongrass scent, "but not for breakfast."

"I miss *us* too." Harley kissed him. "And as soon as you're healthy, I plan to keep you in bed for a week."

"I'm feeling very healthy." Wyatt pulled her onto his lap, hiding his reaction to pain slicing through his groin. "And am willing to endure any discomfort as long as I get to enjoy you."

Harley leaned into him and covered his lips. He twined his fingers in her hair, longing flooding his senses. She palmed his chest and leaned back, desire darkening her amber eyes.

"I know you think you're ready," Harley kissed his forehead, "but we're waiting. Almost losing you was more than I could bear, so we're not doing anything that sets back your recovery."

She stood and crossed to the fridge. "Now, I'm going to make ham and cheese omelets." She turned; arms loaded with ingredients. "Then it's time for your sponge bath."

"Any chance we can both be naked for tubby time?" Wyatt grinned at her.

Harley laughed. "Do you want to go to the station today or Broken River?"

"I think I'm up for both," Wyatt sipped some coffee, "if you have time."

"I'm looking forward to spending the day with you, Sheriff."

Breakfast was delicious, his sponge bath frustratingly sensual, and the November day perfect.

Harley parked in front of the station where Derrick waited by the entrance. He hurried to the back passenger side door, pulled it open, and grabbed the crutches. Careful not to bump the cast, Wyatt lifted his leg out of the car and used Derrick's arm for support as he stood.

"How are you feeling?" Derrick handed him a crutch.

"Good." Wyatt settled onto the crutches. "How are things here?"

"Good." Derrick held the station door open. "Hi, Harley."

"Hi, Derrick." Harley smiled. "Are you bringing Imogine to Thanksgiving dinner?"

"Yes." His cheeks blushed. "She's making a pumpkin pie."

"Hey, Boss," Barnes said. "Welcome back."

"Thanks, Chet." Wyatt smiled at his deputies. "Pete."

"We're sure glad to see you." Pete Simms nodded. "Blake said to tell you he's sorry he's not back from Sacramento, but he and Ivory will be home for Thanksgiving."

"We moved your furniture around to accommodate your ankle." Derrick marched across the station lobby and stood by the office door.

"Thanks, Derrick." Wyatt hobbled into his office. "This is great."

They'd moved his desk away from the wall and turned it to face the window. A footstool had been placed on the right side of the desk. Wyatt lowered himself into his chair and propped his ankle onto the stool.

"It's perfect." He noted the stack of mail and a large box sitting on his desk.

"We'll let you get to work," Barnes headed back to the bullpen, followed by Simms.

"Do you need anything else?" Derrick hovered near the desk.

"No," Wyatt shook his head, "I'm set for now."

"I'm going to Babbling Brook to get lunch for all of us." Harley kissed him.

"Thanks, Babe." Wyatt smiled as she followed Derrick from his office.

Finally, alone, he reached for the package, which was addressed to Sheriff Stone, but had no return address. The postmark was from San Diego. He used the letter opener to slice the box open and looked inside.

A cloud of tissue sat on top of his cowboy hat. He lifted the hat, noticing it had been cleaned, and set it on his desk. A bottle of ibuprofen lay nestled in the remaining tissue, next to a note.

Glad you're alive and well, Sheriff. Tell Harley, she's a lucky woman. Chow, amico!

Wyatt leaned back and stared out the window. Not only had Edelyn been real, but she was also alive and well.

Blake and Ivory were working together to find her jewel thief, and Wyatt would bet money, that they were looking for Edelyn. Despite finding an abandoned rental car at the trailhead, he still hadn't been able to convince his brother and cousin that Edelyn had been on the ledge with him.

Wyatt's law enforcement persona knew he should tell Blake that Edelyn might be in San Diego. But the man she'd nursed on the ledge, was forever grateful and wanted to keep her possible location a secret.

"Chow, Edelyn. Safe travels, friend."

ABOUT THE AUTHOR

Kimila Kay lives in Donald, Oregon with her husband, Randy, and feisty black cat, Halle. She is currently a member of Northwest Independent Writers Association (NIWA), Ladies of Mystery, Sisters in Crime, Willamette Writers, and Windtree Press.

Her cross-cultural series, Mexico Mayhem, includes *Peril in Paradise, Malice in Mazatlán* and *Vanished in Vallarta*. Still planned for the series are *Chaos in Cabo* (Fall/2024), *Lost in Loreto* and *Fiasco in Peñasco*.

The Stoneybrook Mysteries series includes *Redneck Ranch, Five Golden Rings, Whispering Willows,* and *Willow's Woods. Rattlesnake Ravine* will be available spring of 2025 and *Fatal Falls* is planned for summer of 2025.

You can learn more about Kimila through her blog posts on her website - KimilaKay.com, Ladies of Mystery - ladiesofmystery.com, and Windtree Press - windtreepress.com.

STORY INSPIRATION

I created the Stoneybrook Mysteries Series to honor my autistic son Derrick Henson who passed away unexpectedly in 2017. Derrick always wanted to be a police officer and I hope I've realized his dream in his fictional alter-ego, Deputy Sheriff Derrick Stone.

Rattlesnake Ravine continues the storyline featuring Derrick, along with his cousin, Sheriff Wyatt Stone and the lovely New York transplant, Harley Harper. The other Stoneybrook characters round out a tale of a thief on the run, an encounter with a brown bear and a daunting search.

THANK YOU for purchasing this Windtree Press Anthology. We hope we've peaked your imagination and that you've found some new authors to follow.

For more books of the heart, from anthologies to memoirs and poetry, non-fiction, and novels, please go to our **website at https://windtreepress.com**.

There you can learn about all of our authors, their books, and where to contact them directly.